THE
ADOPTION

BOOKS BY JENNA KERNAN

THE
ADOPTION

JENNA KERNAN

bookouture

Published by Bookouture in 2022

An imprint of Storyfire Ltd.
Carmelite House
50 Victoria Embankment
London EC4Y 0DZ

www.bookouture.com

ISBN: 978-1-80314-022-3
ebook ISBN: 978-1-80314-021-6

For Jim, always.

PROLOGUE

"Meanwhile, we've been trying to have a baby for more than a year!" She expelled a breath heavy with frustration. "And we're scheduled to start the fertility treatments again. The shots." She shook her head, dreading the entire thing, unsure if she had the heart to go through with it. "I'm so mad, I don't even know if I want that anymore."

"Of course you do! All you can talk about is having a baby. Being someone's mama."

"With *him*, I mean."

"You need to stop and think."

"I need..." She didn't finish because her thoughts were ugly, full of revenge and malice. She had become a wounded animal wanting only to bite and tear.

"You can still have a baby. More than one."

"I... I love him. But..." She shook her head, unable to finish.

"You need to press pause. Take a breath. You love him and you two are great together. You'll be wonderful parents. Just don't do anything stupid and you can work through this. I know it."

ONE

Dani Sutton had dreamed of the day she would be well enough to leave the psychiatric facility, and now it was here, she thought she might throw up.

"You okay with this, Dani?"

Her psychiatrist's voice snapped her attention back to her surroundings. Why did she have the feeling Dr. Allen was reluctant to let her go?

Her doctor peered at her with a concerned, steady gaze.

"Just nervous. You know. But excited, too."

"You'll do great," said Tate, full of certainty.

Her husband, Judge Tate Sutton, was two years older than her but miles more confident than she had ever been, even before the accident a little less than six months ago. Since winning his position on the circuit court, last fall, he even looked older than twenty-eight.

Tate turned to Dr. Virginia Allen. "Could I speak to you for just a minute?"

"Of course."

"Dani, why don't you have a seat?" said her husband,

motioning to the chairs opposite the masked receptionist who sat behind a wall of Plexiglas.

She wanted to say that she'd rather not. Instead, she nodded and sank to the seat in the receiving lounge in the building where she had lived since the car wreck. Her husband lowered her travel bag to the floor beside her. Anxiety crept into her chest, tightening like a constrictive band.

The accident had left her with a brain injury and a condition called acquired prosopagnosia. Face blindness. She could describe Tate's face, but she couldn't identify him or anyone else because she could no longer organize features into a useful, identifiable whole. Her neurologist had been clear. This loss was permanent. All she could do was use coping mechanisms, little tricks, to improve her chances of distinguishing a person without the innate neurological capabilities most took for granted.

Despite having lived with the condition for months, she had a terrible feeling she would never really get used to being unable to recognize people. As a result, Dani avoided situations like this one, alone in the reception area, where she would be forced to try and recognize unidentifiable faces.

"You'll be okay a few minutes," said Tate, his smile reassuring.

"Will I?"

"Of course." He chuckled and patted her hand, casting her a look of such confidence.

Meanwhile, she held doubts she was well enough to be left alone for a few minutes let alone be discharged.

Of course, she wanted to go home with Tate, but she was frightened, too.

What if it came back?

After she'd physically healed from the accident, the ensuing depression made it obvious to everyone she needed help. When she'd agreed to admission to the psychiatric hospital, she'd never expected to be here for half a year.

Strangely, over the days and weeks, this place had become a home of sorts. And it seemed safer and more familiar than the house they now owned.

Dani glanced around the grand open reception space. The wide lobby had all the characteristics of what it had once been, a boutique hotel.

She had never been to the receiving lounge before, where patients visited with guests, or the reception area where guests checked in to the private psychiatric facility. It was wholly unfamiliar and busy on this morning, with people coming and going.

She tucked farther back in her seat as the anxiety built. Behind it, the consuming darkness lurked.

Tate smiled down at her, radiating self-assurance. How she envied him that. He never felt lost or uncertain. Poise emanated from him like the glimmering magnetism of a presidential candidate. And like everyone else, she wanted to cuddle up close to that light.

But this was exactly the situation she dreaded. Hadn't she been clear?

She stared up with a pleading look, which he ignored.

"I'll be right back." He gave her another winning smile.

She studied the stripe pattern in his necktie before he turned away, committing it to memory. As always, he wore a yellow shirt and tie to help her identify him.

Tate had worn this buttery hue every day since her neurologist recommended using a color to help her identify him. He picked yellow because an internet search indicated it was least popular for both men and women's clothing, making it less likely someone else would be wearing it.

She took one last look at Tate, scrutinizing his face as he joined her doctor. His hair was light brown but coaxed toward blond by bleached highlights from both the sun and his stylist. His dark blue eyes flicked over her face.

"Just a few minutes. Okay?"

He didn't wait for a reply but followed her doctor down the hall and out of sight.

Of course, she knew his voice and his greeting. But in places like this, where there were so many people coming and going, identification was stressful and difficult.

Dani wiped the sweat from her upper lip and fidgeted, clicking her thumbnail, and resolving to stay put rather than suffer the embarrassment of following some stranger wearing yellow from the waiting area.

She perched on the edge of the chair, watching people come and go and wondered if Shelby had finished her morning rehab yet. Often, her twin sister, Shelby Durant, seemed to know when Dani was thinking of her. And when Dani's phone rang, it did not surprise her to see Shelby's image appear on her device.

Dani knew this photo.

For reasons she didn't fathom, she had better luck identifying two-dimensional images of faces, whereas three-dimensional, real ones simply flummoxed her.

This was a photo taken at the lake house. One of the properties they had sold after their parents' passing. Too many memories anchored that lake house to their mom and dad. Instead of being a comfort, they'd both been sad every time they'd visited.

But here, when Dani had snapped this image, their parents were alive. Dad likely on the boat fishing, Mom in a hammock with her eReader, and she and Shelby on the dock. Shelby's face was flushed and pink and gleaming with perspiration as she sat casually on the dock, the lake glinting all around her. She grinned at the camera, her brows arched elegantly over familiar gray eyes, rimmed in charcoal, and her blond hair was just shoulder-length, with her stubborn bangs pushed to the side and grown out to even with the tip of her narrow nose. She'd been laughing, and the image was slightly blurry, but the indentation of her chin and the straight rows of teeth were clear enough.

Dani's phone again gave the distinctive ringtone she'd set for her identical twin. "I've Got You, Babe," by Sonny and Cher, because they used to sing it at the top of their lungs at sleepaway camp.

Dani tapped the button to accept the call.

"Shelby! I was just thinking about you!"

"I know!"

The receptionist snapped her attention to Dani, eyes wide beneath her medical mask. Dani frowned and the woman returned her focus to her computer monitor.

Dani didn't like the masks because they just added to her sense of confusion. The staff had stopped wearing them for a while, but they were back at it again.

"You home yet?"

"Just leaving now. Tate wanted to speak to my doctor."

"Uh-oh."

"Maybe. We're both a little nervous."

"Well, that's natural. But you have Tate there to help you. I wish I could be there, too."

Since the accident, Shelby lived in Jacksonville in a private medical rehabilitation center that specialized in spine injuries and neurological conditions. Her days were spent with occupational and physical therapy and the progress had been slow, as her type of spine injury would never heal. All she could do was improve her upper body strength. Shelby was now paralyzed from the waist down.

Dani threaded her fists in her hair and squeezed as she remembered the day of the accident and blamed herself for the thousandth time. Why had she been driving so fast? Shelby couldn't remember even that Dani had visited her that day, and the brain injury had knocked the details from Dani's head. All that was left was the emotion.

Anger. She'd been so angry. That was all she could recall from that day. Even after the months and months of therapy.

When Dani was first recovering at Windwood, she was unclear if that jagged fury was the cause of her hitting the overpass or a result of discovering what she had done to both herself and her twin sister.

Dr. Allen suggested hypnosis to access her memories, but it had yielded nothing useful, so her doctor recommended she drop it for now, with hopes that the details would become clearer over time. But, like a splinter under the skin, the question only festered. Dani recognized obsessive thinking. It was yet another unavoidable rut in her road to recovery.

Months ago, she had asked Tate what he recalled about her reasons for going to visit Shelby only three days before Christmas. It bothered her because her sister usually came to them for the holiday.

"Shopping," he'd said. "Something about Christmas shopping and the winter carnival."

She and Shelby loved WinterFest as kids but hadn't been in years.

He had nothing illuminating. She'd gone up there to visit with Shelby, which she did often. Nothing unusual, he'd said.

"Next thing I knew, the state police were at my office telling me about the accident."

She'd seen the highway patrol report. Excessive speed. That had been Tuesday evening, December 22nd. Police arrived on the scene of the single vehicle accident at 8:05 pm. She and Shelby had been airlifted to a hospital in Jacksonville, where Dani spent the next sixteen days stabilizing from a brain injury. Shelby had been there even longer.

"Why was I driving so fast?" Dani had asked.

Tate shrugged. It was one of many unanswerable questions.

Dani sighed, recalling the burning, fiery rage.

"Did we fight?" she had asked.

"You and me?" he'd laughed. "Never."

That was right. Why would they when he gave her everything she wanted, anticipated her needs, and stood beside her during her darkest hours? Their relationship had always felt strangely perfect, so easy compared to the drama-filled antics of other people their age. The only thing missing in their marriage was children. She longed for babies and with them, the tumbling, lively chaos needed to turn their empty, silent house into a home. The yearning squeezed at her heart and the hollow feeling crept out of the darkness. She drove it back with thoughts of Tate.

He was amazing. Too good for her.

She never fought with Shelby, either.

"How's the new place?" asked Shelby.

Only a year after purchasing their first home, Tate had won the election for the vacant circuit court justice slot and insisted on moving them to Jordan Island in the gated community of Heron Shores Bayside Estates. He'd selected a grand two-story residence with all the amenities. The properties were pretentious and too closely set for Dani's taste, but if making their massive McMansion on the Intracoastal a showpiece made Tate happy, then have at it. This one sat on a canal with a boat lift. From the balcony and the dock, you could see Tampa Bay. It wasn't the direct view of the bay that Tate coveted, but that was getting closer. Their offer was accepted in September, coming up on a year ago already. They'd closed in November before their contractor took over to make changes, and they'd remained in their downtown home. Tate had made even more upgrades since she'd seen the place. Since she'd been "away," as Tate would kindly call it.

"It's not new. We closed before..." Dani didn't finish.

"Well, it's new to me," said her sister. "And I can't wait to see it."

"Me too. I guess he's made a lot of changes."

"Oh, well that's fun," said Shelby.

"Yes. I wish you could see it with me."

Since the accident, Shelby had not left the rehab center.

"Send pictures."

"I did."

"But that was when it was staged. I want to see your things there."

"Tate replaced some of them. He says the Arts and Crafts style furnishings from our first home were out of place here."

"Hmm. Have to agree with him. Wrong style. Wrong scale. You know, once he gets that home theater set up, you'll never see him."

"True." Dani smiled. "I've got a ground-floor bedroom all set for you with its own bathroom, as soon as you feel up to a visit. Do you need safety bars?"

Tate didn't like the idea of the ugly metal bars in the shower and bracketing the toilet, but as soon as Shelby could travel, Dani wanted her here in Tampa and safe when visiting their home.

"I need them," said Shelby. "Hey, any room for a horse?"

"On Jordan Island? The homeowners' association would have a fit."

They'd both gotten ponies for Christmas when they turned seven. Hers was Puddin' and Shelby's was Dumpling. Since they'd grown up on Tampa Bay, the ponies were boarded at an inland riding facility and stable. They got lessons and boarding all in one.

"Aren't they a bit young?" asked their mom.

"Never too young to learn to care for animals," said their dad.

It turned out that the ponies were gifts, but the board was not. Dani never knew how much it cost in monetary terms, but timewise it cost her and Shelby one Saturday a month where they did everything from clean tack to muck stalls.

She'd held Puddin's head when the farrier trimmed her feet and learned to curry, brush, and braid the pony's tail in that stable. The entire experience had been wonderful, and she'd loved being a horse-girl.

As they grew, they'd graduated to smaller horses and then their Morgans when they'd turned thirteen. Sugar was a white gelding and Bear was Shelby's black mare.

They'd adored horses.

Even went to a sleepaway camp with Sugar and Bear over several winter breaks. Shelby liked barrel racing and Dani preferred trail riding, but they were excellent at both. They had a natural advantage in team penning, as they could communicate so well without talking. Their poor parents must have sucked in a wheel barrel full of dust in those bleacher seats in arenas all over the state.

She wondered if Shelby still had her ribbons.

"Will you be able to ride again?"

"I don't see why not. I know people in my situation do."

"It would be heaven to be out on a trail ride with you."

"But no jumping. At least, I don't think so."

"No jumping. Check." Dani thought about what Shelby and she had enjoyed as kids. "We have a boat lift, so maybe boating?"

"Definitely! Hey, remember our jet skis?"

"Do I!"

Their childhood home on the bayfront had been a gathering point and starting place for sailing outings and bombing around in the jet skis with their school friends. Dani doubted Shelby could do that again, at least not without some modifications to the seat. And the bouncing. That had to be bad for a spine injury.

"You know," said Shelby. "Football season's comin' up. Think I could make it down there for a Bucs game?"

"Oh, Shelby! I'd love that!"

"Great. We'll figure that out."

"And make it happen."

"Absolutely!"

They always went to home games. Their dad was the Buccaneers' biggest fan. He had season tickets and all home games were full-day affairs, beginning with the tailgating from the RV. His pulled pork was legendary, and his friends needed no other excuse to gather before kickoff. She could see them now, Shelby's face painted with a white pirate skull and hers painted red. They had pirate hats and foam fingers.

After her father's passing, they let the tickets go. It just wasn't the same without him wearing his red Buccaneers jersey and Super Bowl gold-ring hat. She missed her parents so much. They'd given them the best life possible, but she was half-glad they couldn't see her like this. See Shelby like this. Would her mom and dad blame her for the accident?

"So, no horses there, but a boat," said Shelby. "What else? Do you have a garden, at least?"

"No. Backyard is right on a canal. You remember."

"Sort of."

Dani estimated the distance from the pool cage to the dock was less than ten feet. The smaller lot was to be expected. Every inch of waterside real estate was precious and expensive.

"Salt spray is hell on orchids," said Shelby.

Orchids were not all she would miss. At their first home, she could walk to the grocery and an independent bookshop. Now they were so far into the gated community, it was three miles just to drive out.

Tate said she could order whatever she needed online and have it delivered. And she could walk to the community pool and clubhouse. Somehow that did not stop her from missing browsing through new books or reading at one of her three favorite coffee shops.

But three years into their marriage, she was still madly in love with him. He was charming, supportive, and had been her rock throughout her ordeal. So, if he wanted a flashy, nouveau riche home, how could she object? She'd do anything to make him happy. Their marriage was more important to her than where they lived.

And maybe someday, if she continued to be well, they could adopt and fill this huge house with children to love and raise. Finding an adoption agency willing to overlook her hospitalization for clinical depression would prove a challenge. But still, she pictured teaching them to swim in the pool, fishing on the dock. Sailing lessons. Riding lessons, of course, and maybe a shaggy white pony? Where would they put the Christmas tree?

She could see it all. The presents piled beneath the glowing lights of the evergreen the moment before their little ones ripped into the wrapping paper. And birthday parties on the lanai, kids in bright bathing suits shouting and jumping into the water.

Yes, she wanted all that and more.

She glanced down the hall, wondering what was taking him so long and already anxious about the trip. She had to remember he was a careful driver with a perfect record. Though likely his police connections could overlook any traffic violation he might incur.

Dani thought of herself as a good driver, too. Or she had been.

So why, on that fateful night, had she been driving so fast?

Back to her circular thinking again, she realized. Whatever

the cause of the crash, she now carried that sick fury and crushing guilt with her always, an invisible backpack dragging on her shoulders. The reason for her stupid recklessness was gone with the part of her brain that recognized her husband's sweet, handsome face.

Shelby interrupted her obsessive musings, her voice ringing with excitement.

"Hey, guess what? I'm getting a van. Once I learn to drive, I can come visit you."

Except for college, six months was the longest she'd ever gone without seeing her twin. If Dani could overcome the anxiety of riding in a vehicle, and if Tate wasn't too busy with the upcoming election, he might soon bring her to Jacksonville.

With Shelby's spine injury, she'd never even considered that Shelby might be able to travel to her.

"How will you drive a van?" Dani asked.

"It's wheelchair accessible. All hand controls. Super cool, right?"

Dani let the familiar wave of guilt crash into her at the mention of Shelby's wheelchair. The depression, which had swallowed Dani whole, gurgled to life. Its stirring sent a white lightning bolt of fear lifting the hairs on her arms.

"Dani? You still there?"

"Yes, still here." Shelby had mentioned a van. Dani rallied. "That's super. What color?"

"Oh, boring white, unfortunately. Maybe I'll get a racing stripe or something. Or an airbrushed unicorn!" Shelby giggled.

Her sister's attitude was unfailingly sunny. Surprisingly, Shelby had come away from the accident in better mental shape than Dani. Physically, Dani had the better outcome because severed spinal cords didn't mend.

"I wish we lived closer," Dani said, wistful.

"Maybe Tate will get the nomination for the court up in Tallahassee. That's closer."

"Possibly."

If Tate won the party nomination, and then the election for the state supreme court, they'd be moving again.

Before their marriage, he'd accepted a position in a law firm here in Tampa. Shortly after making partner, he'd run for, and been elected to, the circuit court. But never one to rest on his laurels, he'd set his sights on Florida's highest court, which meant a campaign and fundraising, already underway. She looked forward to neither.

"How goes the campaign?"

"Fundraiser Thursday night," said Dani.

"You're going?" Shelby sounded incredulous.

"Yes. I want to." The confidence in her tone was undermined by the rising panic that filled her stomach like something thick and vile.

"Don't you think you should spend a few days getting used to being at home?"

"I can do it."

"Can you though? A sea of unfamiliar faces... I'm not sure all the tricks your doctor taught you will be much use."

"I'm going to screw it up. Aren't I?"

"I didn't say that."

Dani lowered her head, shielding her face with her palm.

"I might hurt his chances of winning the party's endorsement. Is that what you mean?"

"No. It isn't. I know you want to help him. But this might be too much too fast. I'm just worried about you."

Silence stretched.

"Dani?" Shelby's voice held concern.

She knew if she spoke, Shelby would know she was crying again, but Dani just couldn't shake the sorrow.

"Dani? Say something."

She whispered the words, trying to keep the receptionist from eavesdropping. "When I can't recognize them, they'll give me that look and try to figure out what's wrong with me. I hate that look."

The tears came then, sliding down her cheeks. Dani brushed them away.

The receptionist left her desk, hurrying down the hall.

"If you want to go, then go."

"But I might embarrass Tate."

"No chance. And you aren't the one running for office. Just tell them about the face blindness," said Shelby.

Dani sniffed again as the tears persisted, choking her attempts to reply.

Someone stood before her, a man, reaching and clasping her shoulders, guiding her to her feet. Dani struggled.

"Dani, it's Tate."

She froze instantly, recognizing his voice. Of course it was Tate. He wore his familiar gray slacks, yellow shirt, and the tie she'd studied before he'd left. His height was right as well. As long as she didn't wear high heels, he was several inches taller.

She sagged as relief pressed down on her shoulders.

"Why are you crying?"

Had the receptionist gone to fetch him? Dani's face heated in embarrassment.

She cupped her hand over the bottom of the phone and lowered her voice. "Gotta go."

"Okay," said Shelby. "Love you, little sister."

"Love you more, big sister," she whispered and lowered the phone.

Tate continued to scowl. "You're upset." It wasn't a question.

"It's nothing. I was talking to Shelby." She lifted the phone, but the screen was dark.

"She called?" He met her gaze with a troubled one. Tate didn't like her crying. Never could stand her tears.

"Yes."

Tate released her shoulders and glanced back at the receptionist, who was now returning to her desk. Dani caught her gawking, and the woman looked away.

"Why is she wearing a mask?" she whispered, looking at the administrative assistant behind the welcome desk.

"Worried about the new variant, probably, or hasn't been vaccinated yet," he replied in a conversational tone.

"What new variant?"

"It's called the Delta variant. We've gotten our vaccinations, so no worries."

The pandemic. She knew of that. For months, all the orderlies and nurses wore masks constantly. They'd even had her in one for a while. But then she'd been inoculated. Her doctor said it was safe to go out, and she trusted her psychiatrist. She knew her stuff and was up to date on all medical matters, not just mental ones.

Dr. Allen reappeared. Dani used some of the tricks her psychiatrist had taught her to make the identification, including context. This was precisely where the doctor belonged, but beyond that, she had a distinctive mop of curly red hair that defied gravity, sweeping upward away from her round face. The context of the hospital setting, along with unusual hair color, eyeglasses, and the bright lipstick, dependably red, all combined to make recognition easy.

Her doctor glanced from Dani to Tate with a critical eye. "Everything all right?"

"Dani was just talking with Shelby," said Tate.

"Ah. Well, do you have everything you need?" asked Dr. Allen. "Medication lists? Discharge papers?"

Tate took that one. "We're all set."

"Second thoughts?" she asked Dani.

"No. I'm ready for this." Did she sound confident? She'd really tried for that tone.

"Good. I'm looking forward to hearing all about your homecoming. Remember, as part of your exit plan, you'll be coming tomorrow to the outpatient side of our facility for our next appointment," said Dr. Allen.

Dani nodded her understanding.

Today, despite all her fears, she also had a sense of pride at her accomplishment. With the help of her husband and her doctors, she had beaten back depression and was managing the aftermath of a serious brain injury. Her doctor said it took time to reconcile that what preceded the accident was gone forever. She would need to live with that, and she was trying. Trying her very hardest.

"Ready?" asked Tate.

Was she?

"I am."

Dani glanced out through the big glass panels to the world beyond, uncertain despite her words.

Tate thought she was ready. Her psychiatrist agreed and Dani trusted them both. She could do this.

Returning to their new home gave her a second chance to make her life and marriage work.

Who could have predicted she'd be here so long? In six months, the world had changed, her home had changed, and she had changed. She fingered the scar that bisected her left brow. Just a small white line now. Not the gaping wound that had blinded her the night of the accident.

She'd had to grope through the cloud of white powder to the seat beside her for Shelby. Then she'd held her sister's hand until help came.

Dani shuttered and hugged herself.

"Dani? You still with us?" asked Dr. Allen, her brow creased.

She blinked herself back to the here and now. "I'm ready to go."

"Well, I look forward to seeing you tomorrow to hear all

about your homecoming, Dani." Then to Tate, she said, "Remember my suggestions. Neither confront nor encourage. Call if you have any concerns."

He nodded.

Dr. Allen spoke to Dani again. "And please call if you have any issues."

She'd just said that. Did her doctor have "concerns"?

Dr. Allen continued, "My service can find me after hours."

Dani frowned. Tate offered his elbow and she clasped hold as he steered them toward the doors.

The muscles in her forehead relaxed. With each step, she felt more confident. Tate was here to help her. Dr. Allen would see her twice a week. And she'd be home with the man she loved. A new beginning, he'd called it.

They walked in silence to the portico, where he'd parked the SUV. He stowed her bag in the back, then opened her door.

She glanced into the interior, but the empty seat... It reminded her of the accident. They'd taken her out first because Shelby's door was jammed shut.

Seeing the car made her mind roll back again to December 22nd. The day she'd left Tate and driven to Jacksonville. A police report Tate had obtained said they'd left the brewery, where Shelby worked as a marketing manager, taking the brand national. Dani had been driving when they veered across the highway and down the exit ramp, striking an overpass.

The screech of collapsing metal and percussion of the glass exploding echoed.

She pressed her free hand to her ears and wailed.

"No, no, no!" She fought against the flashback, but it came.

Before her, the airbag punched her in the face.

Smoke and dust filled the compartment as the inflated airbags to her left and before her emptied. The disorientation confused her, and her ears rang. Up, down. She didn't know.

Where was Shelby? Dani groped stupidly across the center console in the dark.

"Don't let me go."

From far away, sirens wailed. Rescue vehicles.

"Hold on. Help's coming."

Blackness and then more tearing metal as rescue workers pried the driver's-side door open. A man dragged her out of the wreck.

"My sister's in there."

Something touched her elbow and she startled.

"Dani? Do you need a hand up into the car?" Tate asked, extending his hand to her.

She blinked up at him, seeing the worry on his unrecognizable face. A glance at the yellow shirt and striped tie reassured her.

He had stood by her when she'd been shattered to pieces after causing Shelby's injuries. He'd helped her put those jagged shards back into some semblance of the woman he had married. He even helped her with strategies to assist with her acquired prosopagnosia. What other man would agree to wear yellow every day to help his wife with her face blindness?

She forced a smile and pressed a hand to her stomach to push down the panic.

"I am." With a confidence she wore like a cheap plastic mask, she slipped into the passenger seat. Tate clipped her seatbelt for her.

"I'm not a child," she said, both annoyed and flattered by his attention.

"But you hate cars. I just wanted you to know that I'll take it really slow and that you are safe with me."

The anxiety rumbled like the foreshock before a larger seismic event. She blew out a breath and then forced herself to inhale, filling her lungs, using one of many calming exercises.

She slipped the nail of her index finger under her thumbnail and clicked them again and again as Tate rounded the hood and climbed behind the wheel.

She clenched her jaw as he pulled from the curb.

"Dani, breathe," he said.

She blew out the air trapped in her lungs and sucked in another as they rolled forward.

He waited until she sat back in her seat before asking the obvious question again.

"Why did the conversation with Shelby make you upset?"

"Oh, Shelby told me she's going to get a van she can control with her hands. She said, once she learns to drive it, she'll come for a visit. Because it's modified, you know, so she can drive, and that got me thinking... it's my fault..."

This made her husband frown and clutch the wheel in a grip that whitened his knuckles.

"Stop, Dani. Don't go down that path again."

So easy to say, she thought, but she said nothing.

Tate continued to scowl.

"I should be looking forward to her visit? Right?" she asked. "Happy thoughts?"

He flexed his fingers, then wrapped them around the wheel. His mouth tightened, making the flanking lines deepen.

"Don't you want her to come?" asked Dani.

"I'd like nothing better than to see Shelby again."

She smiled and sank back into the leather interior of the pretentious luxury SUV he'd purchased for her, knowing perfectly well she would never, ever drive the thing.

"We talked about the fundraiser, too," said Dani, trying again. She turned to gauge Tate's reaction.

He exhaled sharply through his nose. "You don't need to attend. I've told you."

"But I want to."

"Dani, we aren't even home yet. Let's talk about it tomorrow."

"Are you worried I'll embarrass you?"

The blinker switched on and they glided to the wide shoulder beneath a huge ancient oak.

He placed the SUV in park and swiveled to face her. Then he took her hand, turning it so his kiss landed on the sensitive skin of her palm. The tingle of awareness and desire stirred.

"I love you, Dani. Nothing you could ever do would embarrass me."

"Really?"

"I don't want you to feel pressured to go. But I'm not trying to stop you. If that's what you want, I'll help however I can."

He leaned and she met him halfway with a kiss.

Tate was always there for her. She was so very lucky to have him.

As they settled back in their seats, he said, "I love you."

She returned his smile.

"Ready?"

"Can't wait to see the changes you've made to the house."

"I hope you like them." And he began an excited description of the alterations she had already seen in photos. Clearly, he wanted her to love the home he made for them, and she was determined to do so.

It was certainly little enough to ask.

———

Strange that her private suite at Windwood and her home on Jordan Island were less than twenty minutes apart. They seemed to each belong to a different world.

Tate drove them through the endless, curving, unfamiliar streets of the gated community of Heron Shores Bayside. They passed beautiful homes just different enough to make the carefully crafted community appear cohesive but have a modicum of individuality. She tried to spot which one was theirs, but was looking the wrong way when he finally slowed along a low hedge of hibiscus, dotted with pink blooms. They turned into the wide drive of paver stones flanked by squat columns holding wrought iron lanterns before twin towering royal palms. She saw mature matching magnolia trees framing a two-story, buff-colored home, capped with a reddish-brown Mexican tile roof. Flowering jasmine and pitch apple squatted under a row of arched windows to the right of the door. The landscaping and house were impressive, pristine, and completely unfamiliar.

It was not until they nearly reached the wide double doors beneath the archway that Tate made another turn and she saw the three-car garage, hidden from the street view. How many cars did they have?

"Remember anything?"

She had helped pick this home and authorized her trust to release the necessary funds. Because of her hazy memory, made foggier by his various improvements, Dani only vaguely recollected the walk-through in September. After the November closing, the contractor had taken over as they remained in their downtown home. As for the changes, she recalled little of that time, so close to the accident. She *had* seen some of them. She'd walked through with the contractor, but never actually lived in this grandiose, overly eager dwelling.

"Of course," she lied.

"I'll leave the car here. I want you to come in the front door."

"Like a visitor?"

He gave her a sweet, sad smile. "I want to carry my wife over the threshold."

She felt a welling of emotion and just managed to hold back tears. "Oh, sweetheart. You don't need to. We've been married for three years."

He held his smile. "Just wanted to. I did that for our first home. Remember?"

"You also hid champagne on the front porch."

"Will you indulge me?"

"Why not?"

Together, they mounted the stairs, between the lush potted ferns, and crossed under the archway. Tate used a remote to release the lock, then pushed open one of the double doors. Dani giggled as he swept her into his arms and carried her into the house.

"A tour or should I take you straight to bed?" He lowered her feet to the floor and his mouth to her neck.

"I'd like to start the tour in our suite," she said and cast him a wicked grin.

She turned, looking past the entrance to the formal dining room, pausing to lift a brow at the massive chandelier dripping with cut crystals.

Had that been there before?

Just beyond, light poured in through the arched windows that flanked the front of the home. Unfortunately, they were blocked by plantation shutters and thick, embroidered valances flanked by heavy gold-tone curtains, which she hated on sight. He took her hand and led her to the staircase of dark wood, anchored with a curving, wrought iron rail. To the right of the stairs, behind a large potted artificial banana tree, sat a baby grand piano, which neither of them could play. She did recall that feature, at least.

He narrated as they went. "We replaced the builder's grade with hurricane impact windows. Fresh paint throughout and new light fixtures in the dining room and kitchen. Added a floor over the garage for the home theater. Can't wait to show you that."

"Hmm," she said, choosing something noncommittal.

"All new window treatments. Brocade. Top-drawer stuff. Check the tassels."

They were gold, of course.

She nodded.

Leaving the main floor behind, they stepped onto the massive stairs where the ceilings soared to two stories. The staircase led to an open walkway overlooking the arching windows that fronted the home.

Tate matched her step as they reached the landing of the second floor. Why did she feel like every part of this home was trying too hard? It needed some softness to make it less like a magazine layout and more like a home. It needed children, scrambling down this long hallway in their pajamas, anxious to hear a bedtime story, shrieking as they slid down that banister with tiny toy trucks abandoned between the railings. All the things that spoke of life and living.

At the threshold of the huge unfamiliar room, Tate and Dani discarded their clothing on the cream carpeting, then explored each other's bodies while standing beside the four-poster bed bedecked with a squadron of pillows. She took the opportunity to familiarize herself with the changes in his body. He'd gained weight during her absence. Just a little.

The weight made him look older. Less like the young man she married the year she turned twenty-three and more like the judge he was becoming.

There was some premature gray, too, difficult to see amid his blond hair. And around his eyes, she noted the slight lines that she might have caused. His work, her illness, Shelby's injuries, this house, and the death of her parents all weighed on Tate. But *he* never cracked or descended into depression. He didn't use drugs or drink too much. So what if he'd gained weight? He'd had to fend for himself, likely eating at the club or pubs where single men often ate at the bar. Fast food, probably. Unhealthy food.

Tate scooped her up on the bed and soon she stopped thinking and just enjoyed his touch.

———

When they finally left the bed, it was to continue her acquaintance tour with their home.

He showed her the master bath with improvements, including a steam shower, soaking tub, and separate sinks. She paused at the balcony to glance through the sliding doors in time to see a sailboat cruise along the canal. Back in the bedroom, he pointed out the sitting area and the sliders that led to the same private upper balcony before the pool and over-looking the canal. She wondered if the screening would make it harder for the boaters to see them as they passed.

A pontoon boat rumbled by at wake speed and two of the passengers waved, answering the question.

"Isn't it great?" he asked. "You can see the bay from here." Tate pointed out past the boat lift and dock to the shimmering bay. "And the pool cage screening keeps the bugs off. I sit out here a lot watching the boaters."

"Yes, lots of boats." What he saw as a bonus she saw as an annoyance.

But he was so excited, she kept that opinion to herself.

"Plus, the stairs lead down to the pool so you can get up here without tracking through the house."

"Perfect for skinny-dips at night," she said, relaxing.

"Want to see the rest?"

"I do!"

The tour continued past three more bedrooms. They paused at the one closest to their room. It held a desk set from their old house.

He'd made this his office. The cheerful yellow paint had

been covered with an oyster-gray and he'd added crown molding. All traces of the nursery they intended had vanished.

Her throat began closing.

Dani dropped her gaze to the thick carpet, trying to hold in the pain. She'd painted those walls just before Thanksgiving. She'd put together the crib and filled it with a dozen early pregnancy test kits.

"I moved the furniture up here." His voice was just above a whisper, as if he were in a church. "Desk is a little big for the space. But it works."

Had he done this so Shelby could use the downstairs office as a bedroom when she finally came for a visit? Or because there was no point in keeping the reminder of their efforts to get pregnant?

She'd been so arrogant, as if pregnancy and children were just a given.

The accident that had torn Dani's life in two had also torn her uterus. The blood loss had nearly killed her. Emergency surgery was the only option. The complete hysterectomy saved her life, while ending her ability to have his children.

It had been the second and final assault to her reproductive system. The first had been a cyst, found just after they were married.

They'd been terrified. The scare had driven them to a specialist. The cyst was benign, but they'd removed one of her ovaries. Afterward, her doctor recommended fertility treatment, just in case her lower estrogen levels made it difficult to conceive. They'd agreed and undergone treatment last summer and seven healthy eggs were collected from the remaining ovary.

Well, the cyst and surgery *had* made it difficult to get pregnant. But they'd kept trying. Refusing to give up hope or consider surrogacy. They'd waited too long.

The letter arrived in January, just after Tate took his seat on the bench. The story broke on the news that same week. The clinic had experienced a manufacturing defect of a tank that prematurely thawed 3,500 frozen eggs, including hers. Something about liquid nitrogen levels. As a result, they now had no chance of ever having a child. Lawsuits followed, including theirs.

Tate was suing, but that could never replace what was lost.

She didn't want to spoil the mood with talk of the children they'd once planned to have, or the pain caused in seeing a dream die under a thick coat of oyster-gray paint.

"Is it okay?" He must have seen the tears in her eyes because he pulled her in for a hug. "Hey, hey," he murmured.

She clung to him, pressing her face into his neck as she sniffled.

"Oh, Tate. It's like it's all erased."

"No. It's not." He stroked her back. "I just didn't want you staring at the crib the minute you got home. I'm sorry if I made it worse."

As if he ever could. The responsibility for that rested completely on her shoulders.

"You didn't." She met his gaze, seeing only the support and love he always gave her. "It's hard. You know? Empty rooms."

"Dani, we want kids. That hasn't changed. Has it?"

She shook her head, knowing that everything had changed. And her reckless, selfish actions had taken that from them.

He next toured her through the other two bedrooms, only one of which had a bed. With both their parents gone, Tate being an only child, and Shelby still in rehab, what guests would they have? These rooms were intended for their children.

The ache began in the pit of her stomach. No, lower, in the place where her womb should have been. It stabbed, like a phantom limb.

Don't go there, she warned herself, resting a hand on her flat stomach. She knew this path. These dark thoughts led to uncontrollable, wracking sobs that would necessitate a shot, which was now unavailable.

But oh, how she wanted to fill those rooms with children. Dani hugged herself and rocked repeatedly from the heels to the balls of her feet.

Tate cast her an anxious look. "One step at a time. Okay?"

He wrapped an arm around her and dragged her in for a reassuring hug.

"I love you." He kissed her lips and then hugged her again. "I'm so glad you're finally home."

It was exactly the kind of support and affection that bolstered her confidence.

"Where next?" she asked, forcing herself to sound excited.

He led her downstairs, through the living room where he'd chosen a sage velour couch and Victorian French-style chairs upholstered with red and gold brocade. She searched in vain for one piece of mid-century modern, her preferred style, but he was right. With the formal mantel over the gas fireplace and the tray ceilings, their old things would have been as out of place as she felt right now.

The tour continued to the dining room with its sideboard and table to seat six. In the kitchen, stainless steel gleamed beside cherry cabinets and dark granite countertops. The stools at the center island were gold, as was the wallpaper. Above, ornate amber glass pendant lights spotlighted the stone island like a vaudeville stage. Beyond, set into the wall, a wine cellar the size of a large refrigerator anchored the space.

They both liked wine. Though not as much as her parents.

The Durants had an entire room devoted to wine. Or they once had. Her father, Matthew, had had a massive stroke and died a month after she graduated from college. Shelby still had a year to go, but Dani had moved back to Tampa to be near their mom and work for the city government where she renewed her acquaintance with Tate, and he'd finally asked her out. They'd met the year before, at her mother's fall gala for the city art center. Meanwhile, her sister continued her education, earning her Master of Fine Arts the following spring. Then Shelby had come home as well.

But despite both her and Shelby's best efforts, her mother, Roberta, had just withered away like a plant deprived of water. Too stubborn to see anyone for help, their mom had continued along, lost, hurting, and her mind straying for another difficult twelve months until her heart gave out a year and a day after her husband's passing. Long enough to see Shelby open her own graphic design business and Dani engaged.

After that, Shelby had dived headfirst into her new business, and Dani began wedding planning. One month after their twenty-third birthdays, her sister walked Dani down the aisle. Tate made partner later that same year.

"Do you like it?" he asked.

"Oh, the wine cooler? Yes, I do."

"Had it added. Seems a good fit. Had to lose the double ovens, though."

Dani didn't even remember the double ovens and still felt as if she were walking through someone else's house.

Beyond the kitchen was a large pantry and the entrance from the garage. Opposite was the staircase leading to the addition above the garage.

"Want to see the home theater?"

He held her hand as they ascended. Once in the huge space, he flicked on the LED lights and fiber optics that outlined the enormous screen. The room was carpeted, and several speakers nestled in the acoustic foam below the ceiling. The seating was like the reclining, motorized chairs now in the more modern movie theaters.

"Isn't it great? I even have a red curtain. It works on a

remote." He lifted the device and showed her the operation, closing them over the screen and then retracting them again.

She counted seating for twelve.

"It's... very grand."

He grinned, delighted. "Still waiting for the projector. It's backordered. Supply chain issues."

She nodded, unsure what that really meant.

The windowless room felt claustrophobic to her.

"Shall we continue?"

He led the way back through the kitchen and beyond to the adjoining family room, less formal and only partially furnished with their old couch, coffee table, and television. She smiled.

"The next room is mostly empty."

It had been his office.

"But I did move in a large table, a good light, and your scrapbooking stuff. You could use it as a craft room."

"And my sewing machine?" Dani loved to quilt.

"It's in there. With that big hoop. Hot glue guns, stickers. All of it."

She stepped into her room and turned in a circle. He'd done more than add a table. There was a dedicated sewing table, empty bookshelf and one with cubbies. He'd added a few of her quilting fabrics and specialized paper. Dani sucked in a breath.

"Oh, it's wonderful." She clapped her hands and Tate chuckled. "I love it!"

She gave him a kiss.

"You can finish setting it up." He pointed. "Boxes of fabric and art supplies are in the closet. Books too."

She reined in the urge to begin at once, instead following him into the hallway.

"Next room was intended as a mother-in-law suite."

Which neither of them had.

They moved into the open space. The guest bath and ground floor made this the obvious choice for her sister.

"This is where Shelby can stay. We won't even need a ramp. She can come in from the pool through the bathroom." She peered into the bathroom. The shower had a lip, but that could be removed. "She'll like this. Lots of natural light."

Tate nodded.

"Let me show you the pool."

They exited through the bathroom to the lanai beyond. She'd seen the two-story pool cage from the second-floor balcony. Now she admired the waterfall, hot tub, lounge chairs, seating area, and an outdoor kitchen with gas grill and a full bar.

The sparkling blue water looked inviting. But the humidity and gathering clouds warned of showers.

Tate glanced upward.

"Hmm. Let's order in." He retrieved his phone and made a call while she walked the perimeter of the caged area. The hedges gave privacy between their property and the flanking ones. When she reached the platform behind the waterfall, she froze.

There between the palms and the seawall was a playset. The yellow slide descended from the upper playhouse. Below, three swings, including one for a toddler, were molded of green plastic and hanging from sturdy chains.

Why had she blocked this detail from her mind? She remembered it perfectly. Had even slid down that slide to test it. Couldn't have it there for their children if it was not safe.

Dani pressed a hand to her mouth. Tate was beside her, hands on her shoulders, pulling her back against the solid reassurance of his body.

"Dani, it's all right."

She turned and buried her face against his unbuttoned yellow shirt.

"Oh, Tate, I wanted them."

He stroked her hair, hushing her as she fought the tears.

His words whispered over her like a prayer, a balm to her open wound.

"I know. I know. Hush now. I love you. You're home. Everything is going to be good for us from now on. I promise. I promise."

The first huge plops of rain landed. They turned and fled, reaching the cover of the lanai as the heavens opened and rain poured down.

TWO

On her first night at home, Dani had just taken her sleeping pill, and was dozing but not fully asleep

when the grating alarm roused her. The sound blared as sharp as shattering glass in the darkened bedroom.

"What? Who's there?" Dani's fuzzy mind was coming into focus. She now recognized the buzzing of a vibrating phone. But not her phone. The ringtone was wrong.

Where was she?

The momentary disorientation brought her further awake as fear overcame the drug already in her bloodstream.

She knew this place. It was the main bedroom. The one with an overabundance of pillows, area rugs atop the wall-to-wall carpeting. She lay on their huge king-sized bed beneath the tray ceiling with LED lighting and a fan so big it looked like an airplane propeller. The sound came again from somewhere across the wide stretch of mattress.

A man fumbled in the dark and something crashed from the bedside table to the floor. The water bottle. He kept it there, along with his watch and his eReader. He cursed under his breath and then lifted the phone. The strange blue light cast disturbing shadows over his face. She studied him with one eye closed, looking at the profile of a strong jaw, stubbled now, and in need of a shave. His nose was straight and his brows thick. Familiar deep lines bracketed his mouth. Surely it was a face she could remember if she just tried harder. But the disjointed pieces made no sense.

"Hello?" he said into his phone.

She closed her eyes to take comfort in the reassuring timbre of Tate's voice. There was no reason to be frightened.

Still, her heart continued its mad pumping and her skin tingled.

The voice on the other end of the call was high and upset. She could not determine the caller's gender. The note of panic was clear. She opened her eyes again and stared at Tate.

Something was very wrong. Dani's pulse pounded in her neck. She pushed herself upright, raking her hands through her fine, shoulder-length hair as she sucked in air through flaring nostrils. Dani tried to shake herself from the grip of the medication, her efforts only made her nauseous and dizzy.

Tate cast her a look of concern as he covered the bottom half of the phone and whispered to her.

"Lie down, Dani, before you fall down."

She did, pinching her eyes closed as he continued with the call.

"Yes. I understand. Yes, right now. I'm coming over. Don't do anything. Just wait for me." The blue light changed to white as he disconnected the call. He pressed a broad hand to his forehead and blew away a breath.

"I have to go." He did not wait for her reply and was already tossing aside the covers and pushing off the bed.

"Now? What time is it?"

Tate had no family. No brother or sister to fall ill and need him to rush to a sickbed. As a judge, he no longer had to deal with apprehended clients.

"Around midnight."

"Where are you going?" The thought of being alone in this strange house filled her with dread. She barely remembered it and had already once ended up in a broom closet when searching for a bathroom.

He lifted his phone again and then answered her question.

"One of Jeremy's clients is in trouble. He needs an attorney present for questioning."

"I thought you weren't handling any criminal cases. You told me that was finished."

He spoke as he headed into the bathroom. "Yes. But Jeremy's in the Caribbean and his client is in jail. I have to cover it."

"You're a judge. Isn't that something one of Jeremy's partners should do?"

"I'm still his best friend."

"Where is he?"

"Grand Cayman."

Dani groaned and pushed herself up to an elbow, glancing to the open doorway of the en suite bathroom as the light flicked on, illuminating the cool gray tiles and white cabinets. She could see him leaning over the basin, splashing water onto his face. The muscles in his back corded. He was tall, her husband, and fit with broad shoulders and just the slightest dusting of golden hair on his back and arms.

The next sound was the buzz of his electric razor and then the whir of his electric toothbrush. Tate liked his gadgets. When he strode back out of the main bath, he was already dropping his pajama bottoms and stepping into his closet. He emerged only a moment later wearing socks and gray slacks, carrying his blazer and yellow golf shirt.

He made it partway to the door, then seemed to remember her and reversed course to drop a kiss on her lips.

"Go back to sleep. Dani," he said. "I'll see you at breakfast."

"All right." But it wasn't all right, not really. He'd promised no more criminal cases. No more late-night visits to the jail or preparation for trials that stretched over weeks and months.

Stop it, Dani. You are not a child.

"Be careful. Do you have your wallet? Do you need a cell phone charger?"

Tate disappeared through the door, heading to the hall that overlooked the living room and entrance, out of sight. His voice, coming from somewhere, the stairs perhaps, already seemed far away.

"I've got everything I need. See you in the morning."

She sank back into the pillows with one arm flung across her forehead. She had her phone, the panic alarm at her bedside.

She whispered into the pillow. "Safe. You are safe, Dani."

Each door and window held an entrance alert and there were several glass-break sensors.

"You're okay," she whispered, totally alone in their home for the first time.

She stared at the ceiling fan as it spun, sending a whisper of cool air from the air-conditioning vent to the bed. The medication tugged at her clarity, slowing her mind and making her limbs heavy.

Darn Jeremy and his vacation in Grand Cayman, she thought.

The next sound was the rumble of the garage door opener as it lifted the heavy, hurricane-resistant double door. The third garage door, also reinforced, ran on a separate track.

She didn't hear him pull out. But she heard the door alarm speaking, indicating he'd armed the system again.

Dani sat up, too nervous to rest. Instead, she rose from the bed, collected her cell phone, and walked downstairs to the dining room, hoping to glimpse Tate's vehicle's taillights as he headed to the main exit for the gated community.

Instead, she saw his vehicle head in the opposite direction

and pull into the driveway across the road. She lifted the custom-made plantation shutters, an expensive form of venetian blind Tate had insisted on for the front of the house. Peering out at the dark street, she was certain that was Tate's black sedan. Had he made a wrong turn?

Doubtful.

It could be a different black sedan.

Dani frowned and peered through the gap. A dark figure shuffled heavily to the car. The cab light winked on, and she saw a man standing at the passenger door, holding it open like a driver from a car service.

Someone heading to the airport?

The smaller figure slipped into the front seat. The cab light remained on for the time it took for an athletic figure to round the hood, slip behind the wheel, and close the door. The cab light blinked off and rear lights flicked red as the sedan backed onto the road. She could not see the license plate but thought it possible another of her neighbors owned a similar car. Perhaps she had missed Tate leaving?

The car glided past their home and turned toward the main exit of the upscale gated community.

Dani frowned at the dark street.

Was that Tate picking up a neighbor or two people she didn't even know?

She wasn't even certain of the make of her husband's car, let alone know it well enough to spot on the street in the near darkness.

Car service. Definitely. But she lifted her cell phone and called Tate.

He picked up using the car's telephone system.

"Dani? What's wrong? Why are you still up?"

Tate's voice was sharp with obvious irritation.

She remained silent for a moment trying to grapple with what to ask him.

"Did you pull into a neighbor's driveway just now?"

"Dani, are you still in bed?"

"No. I'm standing in the dining room."

"I left twenty minutes ago. Almost to the ramp for the highway."

"I thought..." The sleeping pill was taking over. She needed to lie down. Dani tried again. "I'm sorry. I thought I saw your car pull in across the street."

"Nope. I'm on my way to the jail. Everything is fine. We'll talk in the morning."

She said nothing.

"Dani? Should I come home?"

Yes, she thought. "No," she said. "I'm fine. I'm heading up to bed now."

"Call me if you need me."

It occurred to her she sounded as if she didn't trust him, or worse, as if she was seeing things.

"Okay. Sorry to bother you."

"You're not."

"I'll see you later."

"I could be a while." Just before he disconnected, she thought she heard someone groan as if in terrible pain.

"Tate?" Dani pulled the phone away from her ear and glanced down at the screen. He'd disconnected.

Dani's phone woke her. She scrambled to retrieve the device from the coffee table beside the couch where she'd fallen asleep after speaking to her husband. The ringtone told her it was Tate.

"Hello?"

"Dani, did I wake you?" he asked.

"No, I was just dozing. I tried to wait up for you."

She didn't want to sleep in their enormous bed alone. The couch was narrow, more like her bed at the psych center, and she'd turned on the puck lights in the living room console to help her orient. Now, however, the sunlight cast bright bars between the plantation shutters and across the marble tile.

"Where are you?" she asked.

"I'm at the hospital."

That news caused her heart to slam into her ribs in a painful collision of muscle and tissue. Dani threw herself into an upright position.

Her voice rose an octave. "What happened?"

"I'm fine, Dani. Nothing happened to me."

She fell back to the sofa, tears leaking from her eyes, and pressed her free hand to her forehead. Dizziness assaulted her.

The scream of twisting metal and shattering glass crowded her mind. The dust from the airbag covered everything in fine white powder. Her bloody fingers groped, finding Shelby in the passenger seat.

"Dani, I'm safe. Do you understand?"

"Yes. Safe," she breathed the words, pressing her palm to the dry skin on her forehead where the gash had opened, and the blood had blinded her. She drew her hand back, reassured it was clean.

"This client of Jeremy's is a piece of work. The guy smuggled in something, a narcotic. The police missed it on search. He overdosed, then had a foaming-at-the-mouth seizure."

"Oh, my goodness." The relief came to her in a rush of air. It wasn't Tate. He was there for someone else. She pressed a hand over her heart and snatched a breath of air.

"It was a scene. I've been trying to locate his next of kin. No luck, but he's stable and back in custody. Arraignment is later today."

"So is my appointment."

"Oh, damn it."

She hated to be a bother. But seeing Dr. Allen would give her a safe place to sort out her feelings. Her internal voice was telling her she needed to go, but Tate's absence, and her unwillingness to drive or ride with anyone but Tate, was making her increasingly anxious.

"I'll make it back in time, Dani. Count on it."

Tate returned with no time to spare. He called out a greeting as he appeared through the garage entrance into the laundry room. She waited in the kitchen where she could hear his voice before seeing him.

"Dani? It's me. I'm back."

She met him as he entered the kitchen.

He dropped a kiss on her cheek and for just a moment she smelled gardenias mixing with his familiar scent. His voice assured her this was Tate, but he wore nothing yellow.

What had he been wearing when he left? She wasn't certain.

"You okay?" he asked, drawing back.

"Just worried you wouldn't make it."

He extended his arms.

"Ta-da!" he said, making her laugh.

It was so odd to have this stranger before her. His hair stood up, his blue eyes were bloodshot, and purple smudges appeared beneath them.

"Ready?" he asked.

She had been ready for over an hour and had likely paced two miles from the entrance to the dining room windows.

If they left right now, they might make the appointment on time.

"Put on something yellow," she said.

He hurried away, and she studied his powerful stride. Dr. Allen said posture and gait could help her discern identity.

"All set," he said, trotting down the stairs in a yellow shirt, green and yellow striped tie, and a blazer neatly folded over his arm.

At her SUV, she paused.

"It's okay, Dani. You're safe."

They were late.

"We won't hurry. Right?"

"I'll take it slow," he assured.

She drew a breath and plunged forward into the car. Tate buckled the seatbelt again and then got them underway.

At the end of the drive, they watched a blue motorcycle rumble past, then pulled out.

"Hope we aren't late," said Dani, pressing both hands to her stomach battling the butterflies that suddenly awoke at the movement of the vehicle.

"I'll make it."

She glanced at his determined look and clutched the handgrip.

You're fine, Dani, she told herself. *You're safe.*

Despite her eagerness to see Dr. Allen, the affirmations failed, and panic squeezed her windpipe.

The woman standing in the door to Dr. Allen's office wore a neat navy dress, floral scarf, and black pumps. The wavy red hair, glasses, and red lipstick helped Dani identify her psychiatrist. Unlike her receptionist, she wore no mask and ushered Dani in.

The psychiatric hospital was connected to this outpatient facility via a glass walkway, allowing her doctor to see all her patients. But for Dani, this meant seeing Allen in a different therapy room than the one where they had met when she was a resident. The interior was welcoming but unfamiliar and resembled a small lounge complete with two upholstered, apple-green armchairs facing a loveseat bedecked with comfortable tactile pillows. A square, maple coffee table separated the seating and held a box of tissues and several objects carefully chosen to allow a patient to fiddle. The area rug tied the room together, and if the desk, office chair, computer, and vertical blinds somewhat spoiled the illusion that they were guests in Dr. Allen's home, Dani did not mind.

Her doctor's short, curly red hair was swept up, the ringlets tight as bedsprings. She wore the familiar clear eyeglass frames, her characteristic red lipstick, and a colorful scarf coiled at her throat. Those four features grounded Dani: hair, glasses, lips, scarf. She sighed, the smile coming naturally as she felt comfortable for the first time in the twenty-four hours since she'd left Windwood.

Her doctor motioned Dani forward, and she chose the loveseat as her therapist sat in her large swivel chair and turned away from the spotless desk and monitor with a screensaver fish tank. Behind her, the digital inhabitants peacefully glided through the deep blue pixels. Above her, a philodendron plant draped the blinds in a living valance.

The session went well, almost as if she were still at Windwood.

Strange, but Dani felt more at home there than in her actual home. She said this to Dr. Allen, who believed that feeling would pass with time and was a normal reaction after her absence and the fact that she had never really lived there before.

Dani told her about the swing set that had wrecked her yesterday. That one took longer with Dr. Allen suggesting avoiding that area of the yard for now or, if the playset made her cry, asking Tate to remove it.

As for the upcoming fundraiser, Dr. Allen was generally positive.

"If you would like to attend, you should. I'm sure you will feel some anxiety, but you've been working hard on your coping techniques for the face blindness, and you are very good at self-calming."

"So I can go?"

"Dani, you don't need my permission. It's up to you."

Back in the driveway at home on Tuesday, Dani finally blew away the breath burning in her lungs and pried her stiff fingers from the armrest of the car.

Behind them, the heavy garage door rumbled closed. Tate turned off the house security system before she slipped out of her seat. As they entered the laundry room, the system announced the alarm was off. By the time she reached the kitchen, her breathing had returned to normal.

"Are you okay?" asked Tate, touching her elbow and making her jump.

"Carsick."

He headed to the massive stainless-steel refrigerator, opened one door, and retrieved a can of seltzer, neatly popping the top and pouring her a glass.

"Here."

She accepted the bubbling liquid and took a sip. The fizz burned up through her nose. She eased into a stool at the kitchen counter.

Tate grabbed a green bottle of sparkling water and twisted off the cap. Then he took a swallow, making his Adam's apple bob.

He was handsome, her husband. Everyone said so. For her, that now meant symmetrical features. His voice was the sexiest part of him now. That and his body. His face was just a jumble.

Recollections of last night floated to the surface from her hazy memory.

She thought again about his abrupt departure.

"How is Jeremy's client?"

"He's in a world of trouble. I'm still covering the arraignment. Need to head back out soon."

"Today?"

He made a humming sound of affirmation.

Dani tamped down the flash of panic. She could manage another few hours alone. After all, she wasn't a child.

"You okay with that?" he asked.

"Of course."

"If you'd like me to get you some company..."

"Unnecessary." She flashed him her most confident smile, the mask to hide the welling uncertainty. "Be a change for you, back on the other side of the bench."

He smiled and nodded. Dani drank the seltzer.

"Dani?"

She glanced to him, seeing his dark brows lifted in an expression of question. She'd missed something.

"Yes. I am feeling better."

He laughed.

"I asked if you slept all right, after I left last night, I mean."

"Oh, yes." She recalled standing in the dining room watching someone pull into the drive across the way. "After our phone call, I curled up on the couch. Honestly, those sleeping pills make me dizzy. It's really hard to wake up, you know?"

He made an affirmative sound in his throat, but her husband couldn't know, because Tate didn't even take aspirin.

"Well, I'm glad you weren't up too long. Sorry about that."

"It's fine. Like old times." Early in their marriage, he'd handled bail for more than a few clients in the wee hours.

"Want me to get your pills?"

It was nearly noon, time for her midday prescriptions.

"Oh, yes, thanks."

He disappeared and a few minutes later a man returned, carrying orange medication bottles.

It was as if a stranger was approaching holding her pills, his face completely unfamiliar. Would she ever get used to this feeling?

"Tate?"

"Yes?"

She smiled, reassured by his voice.

"Can I make you a sandwich?" she asked.

He rubbed his neck. "Arraignment. I'll grab something after."

She accepted the containers.

"Well, Dr. Allen said I should practice daily tasks. I'll start by making myself a sandwich."

He chuckled and gave her a kiss. "Just text if you need me. Really, anytime."

She spun the stool and gave him a hug, her ear on his chest, reassured by the steady, rhythmic thump. He kissed her forehead and she let him go.

Tate collected his briefcase and headed toward the garage. Pausing in the doorway, he said, "I love you, Dani."

"Love you. See you soon."

Out he went wearing the same familiar yellow shirt, but the blazer and tie were gone. Probably in the car, she decided.

Dani's bright smile faded as she faced lunch alone with zero appetite.

"Well, you have to eat," she told herself.

She made cinnamon toast for lunch because it was easy, and the butter gave her extra calories with little effort. Then she ordered fresh fish and a bag full of other items from the gourmet market, instructing them to ring the bell and leave the delivery on the bench beside the front door. Afterward, she headed to her crafting room and lost herself in cutting out fabric for a quilted table runner in red, white, and blue. When the doorbell rang, she was shocked to see two hours had passed.

The delivery van had already reached the street by the time she gathered up the groceries. She put them away and headed back to her scrapbooks. She'd fallen behind while in the psychiatric facility and soon found herself lost in the colorful borders, stickers, cutouts, and photos. Dani used her laptop to capture and print quotes.

Dani flipped through the photos she had printed of Shelby running, hiking, and skiing. All the things her sister would likely never do again. Weighed down by tremendous guilt, Dani found it impossible to lift the scissors.

Glancing at the collected photos, Dani now noted that she had printed only Shelby, blond, fit, her gray eyes flashing with mischief or sparkling with joy. The minute she recognized what she was doing, Dani stacked the photos and set them aside.

"This is bananas," she muttered.

Somehow, she'd managed to use her scrapbooking to reinforce her obsessive thinking.

"Not today."

Dani glanced at her phone for the time and realized it was too early to take her evening round of medication.

The thing about antidepressants was they didn't eradicate the sorrow. It was there, a sharp stone tucked in her pocket, the edges cushioned by soft cotton, but still impossible to ignore.

She left the photos and returned to the table runner, the project safer and unencumbered by troubling memories.

Tate found her still in the family room just before five.

He called from the kitchen, his familiar voice bringing her

out of her burrow where she had been tucking books onto the empty shelves.

"In here," she called.

He appeared in the doorway a moment later, holding an open bottle of water.

"How did it go?" she asked, accepting a hug and kiss in greeting.

"His client has recovered from the overdose. Back in jail with no bond because of that stunt in lockup. Not his first rodeo. Third actually, so he's looking at a minimum of ninety days in prison and a fine, which he can't afford."

"That's too bad."

"I suppose. But he's made some choices in life, and they bear consequences."

Spoken like a judge, she thought.

Dani had made her own share of poor choices. Driving in a rage. Fast. Too fast. The ripping sound of metal intruded, and she flinched.

"How did your afternoon go?" he asked.

"I've got all my fabric sorted. Still working on the boxes." She waved a hand at the long table. "And I've been adding to my scrapbook."

He chuckled and aimed the open water bottle at the bits of colorful paper littering the table. "So I gathered."

He didn't understand her desire to cut up and reassemble paper and fabric any better than she understood family law, and neither had any interest in learning. Predictably, he changed the subject.

"Hey, you still want to go to the fundraiser Thursday night?"

"Yes. I'm determined."

"Well, then let's get you a new dress for the occasion. We can go shopping for one tomorrow."

Shopping was something she had missed. But Dani's

affluent upbringing had included more than her share of clothing, handbags, and shoes, along with the rest. Upstairs, she had
a walk-in closet full of options and didn't need another dress.

"I have plenty."

"Dani, you've dropped a few dress sizes."

The loss of appetite did that.

"Let me get you something new."

She nodded. Clothes shopping would make her feel as if
everything were more normal.

"Why not?"

Wednesday, Dani woke to find sunlight slipping between the
open curtains casting a bright beam across the carpet. The
sound of water running and the empty place beside her in bed
told her Tate was already up. She followed him and, hoping to
take her mind off things, accepted his invitation to join him in
the walk-in shower. Together, they discovered how long the
water stayed hot.

Dressing in her walk-in closet, she looked around at the still-
unfamiliar surroundings. It even still smelled like somebody
else. The scent of gardenia was heavy in the drawers.

Finally downstairs, with pruny fingers, she made coffee and
he made eggs and toast. They sat in the formal dining room
under the massive chandelier, just the two of them. Dani tried
and failed not to let the giant empty table get to her. But it did.

They both had a deep desire to have children and she
wanted to be a mother so sincerely it ached.

"What's wrong, Dani?"

"I was just wishing..."

He set down his tablet and coffee, giving her a critical look.
"For?"

"It's such a big house for the two of us."

"You're talking about children."

She nodded.

He took her hand and lifted it to his mouth, dropping a kiss on her palm, lingering there.

"I dream of the same thing."

"Remember when we were trying to get pregnant?" she said, grinning, hoping he didn't see the desperate yearning behind her smile.

"That was amazing. I think our names are still in the book of world records." He chuckled and let go of her hand. "Don't give up, Dani. We might fill up this house yet."

Her eyes went wide, and the breath caught in her throat.

"Really?"

He cast her that mysterious smile and wiggled his eyebrows.

"You're up to something."

"Maybe. You just focus on staying healthy." He glanced at the small dish where her medications had been. "You took them all?"

"Yes, Dr. Tate."

The happiness at his encouragement and the possibilities opened by his words buoyed her throughout the morning.

He couldn't mean adoption, could he?

She knew what would happen if they tried. She'd have to tick that box that asked if she had any mental health problems. She might just as well douse the application in lighter fluid and strike a match.

But what other choice did they have?

They arrived at the mall before noon where Tate took her for a lovely lunch at a favorite restaurant tucked in Saks Fifth Avenue. She had no anxiety on the drive; she attributed this to the preemptive antianxiety medication she'd taken, which currently gave her an unnatural level of calm.

In the women's clothing area, she began shopping for an outfit for the party fundraiser. She'd discovered Tate had been right. Most of her wardrobe was now too big. One or more of her medications at Windwood had deadened her appetite and made her two sizes smaller.

As she exited the fitting room in yet another option, Tate's eyes lit up.

"That one, Dani. You look amazing."

"It's not too low cut?"

"No. It's perfect." But his expression turned serious. "You know, you don't need to come."

"I want to."

"Please don't feel pressured. You just got home."

"I'm coming."

She returned to the fitting room and slipped back into her own clothing. After they'd checked out, Tate carried her bags as they walked through the mall.

They stopped in a candy shop and Dani selected a bag of toffee for herself and a treat to send to Shelby. Tate helped the cashier with the shipping details.

She was back in the SUV before he brought up the fundraiser again.

"If you're sure, I want to try something. I've got one of my clerks coming, too. He'll shadow us and help you with names."

He'd hired a babysitter. Dani slumped, wrapping her arms about herself.

"What is it?"

"I feel so stupid."

"It's a brain injury, Dani. You're smarter than I am, and we both know it."

"If I'm so smart, why was I going eighty-six miles an hour on an exit ramp?"

He sighed. "I don't know, Dani. We may never know. I'm just grateful you survived."

"Yes. We were lucky." She'd seen the car or what was left of it. "A miracle we survived."

The silence stretched and Tate fiddled with the radio, pulling up something calm and jazzy.

She opened the console for some hand sanitizer and a large legal-sized envelope slipped from between her seat and the center divider.

"What's this?" she asked.

"The trust documents. Hewitt sent me a copy."

Her parents' trust had paid all the medical bills for both her and Shelby, which had been enormous. She was thankful every day for her father's business acumen.

After her parents' passing, Dani and Shelby had tried and failed to have Tate added as a trustee. Her parents had been specific in creating the twenty-three-million-dollar trust entity. No relation, by blood or marriage, could serve as a trustee and only a senior partner at the law firm used by her parents could oversee distributions of funds at the request of the Durants' daughters.

If the accident had gone another way, the entire thing would have gone to the art museum, since neither of the Durants' daughters had produced heirs.

Dani lifted the envelope.

"I'm sorry Mr. Hewitt couldn't authorize you to make distributions," she said.

"That was a long time ago, Dani. Water under the bridge."

"Okay." She let the matter go.

Tate was an attorney and understood the law and estate planning, thank God. After they were married, they had set up their legal documents. They each had the other's medical proxy, power of attorney, and notarized wills. Tate had unfortunately already had to use the medical proxy. If he had not been so thorough, he could not have made the medical decisions that had saved her life after the accident. And he'd exercised the proxy again to request her release.

He said if it were up to her doctors, she'd never get out.

They'll keep you as long as the insurance and trust keep paying your bills.

"Could we take the long way home?"

"You don't like the highways," he said. It wasn't a question.

Really, she didn't like the exit ramps, but you couldn't have one without the other. He changed lanes and took them along the industrial complexes, new building developments, and finally down the tree-lined streets near their community. This time, she recognized the route and that pleased her.

They cleared the gate closest to their home, this one unmanned and operated by a control tucked behind the rearview mirror causing the gate to operate automatically.

"I'm still lost in this development," she said.

He commentated the route, taking her past the community clubhouse, tennis courts, soccer fields, and pool. The result was, she was even more lost by the time they turned onto their street.

Across from their property, on the landlocked side of their road, the houses were pristine, but much more modest. As always, the money got the water views and other touches. For instance, the sidewalk had been placed across the street so as not to disturb the majestic impression of the waterfront homes. Beyond the walkway sat a low wall and a uniform row of trimmed jasmine bushes.

Tate put on his blinker and Dani noticed a woman standing beyond the wall and bushes across the road from their property. She wore a large straw hat and waved a hand tucked in a clean garden glove.

"Someone is waving at us."

"That's Enid," said Tate, sounding surprised. "What's she doing out in this heat?" Now he sounded aggravated.

He did this so naturally, recognizing a face. His eyes took in the bits and pieces, the slopes and angles, hair color, shape of the mouth and brow, providing the details for both temporal lobes of his brain to assemble the parts into a recognizable form. From there, the identity shot along neurons to the amygdala within the limbic system, deep in the middle of the brain, where the collected knowledge blended with emotional responses associated with this face. Next, down a different pathway, the brain added memories of this person. Did he like them, hate them? Were they friend or foe, relative or rival, coworker or boss, lover or stranger? With the name and known details then accumulated, the neural impulse headed along another pathway where the brain added the emotions evoked by this person's face.

Tate's brain did all this in the blink of an eye. Dani's never would.

When confronted with a new face, all she had was the rudimentary lizard brain grappling with the decision to freeze, fight, or flee.

He turned to Dani. "Do you remember Enid Langford?"

"Enid? Paul Langford's wife?"

"That's right." His attention swung back to Enid, and he scowled.

She knew *both* Paul and Enid, of course.

Paul, a fellow attorney in her husband's old law office, was a good friend of Tate's. And Enid, Paul's wife, was the firm's administrative assistant. She remembered that, at least.

Paul had worked with Tate until Tate ran for and won appointment to the court. Dani had first met Enid at the firm. And they had been out with Enid and her husband, Paul, on several social occasions. Her recollection was that Enid was approachable, kind, generous, and very bright.

"I didn't know they were our neighbors," said Dani.

He swerved, parking on the wrong side of the road at the house diagonally opposite theirs.

The woman in the hat grinned and moved closer to the thick greenery of the hedge. Dani noted she held clippers in her hand.

"Doesn't the HOA cover landscaping?" Dani asked.

"No, everyone arranges their own," he said, lowering his sunglasses to stare. "Didn't expect to see her out."

"Why not?"

He glanced at her. "She's going through a thing."

"What kind of thing?"

He had his hand on the button to lower the window.

"Separation."

"Oh, no!"

Tate nodded, his expression grave. "According to her, the split is contentious. Maybe apocalyptic is a better word."

"To her? What does Paul say?"

"Nothing to me. He made me pick sides and isn't happy with my choice."

"Oh." She sat back, surprised at this. He'd known Paul since Stetson University.

"When did this happen?"

"Been a while. Several months, anyway. You were at Windwood."

"Poor Enid. What happened?"

"I'll tell you about it in a minute." He was lowering the window now. "Hey, neighbor."

"Hello, Tate." Her smile was broad. Beneath her hat, Dani saw that Enid's thick brown hair was pulled back. A ponytail draped over her shoulder.

Because of the hedge, all she could see of their neighbor was from the shoulders up. Still, Dani went to work noting the kind of details that might help her recognize Enid in the future. The hat and large designer sunglasses might work, if she kept those on. Enid slipped her sunglasses down her nose to reveal deep brown eyes, rimmed with thick lashes. Her skin was flawless, if flushed, with not a freckle, blemish, or scar to make identification easier.

"Is that Dani?"

"It is!" said Tate.

"I thought I saw her. That's just wonderful." She smiled and Dani noted dimples, adding it to her list for Enid. Long hair the color of a mink, designer shades, eyes so dark she could not see her pupils and dimples. It might be enough to make an identification if she met her in the neighborhood.

Dani had to hunch to see past Tate, and Enid stooped to get a glimpse of her.

"Hey, Dani! So glad you're home. You settling in okay?"

"Yes. Thanks. How are you, Enid?"

"Oh, you know, keeping busy. Did Tate tell you I got canned from the firm?"

Dani lifted a hand to her chest at this bombshell. According to Tate, that office only ran because of Enid. She was smart, competent, and organized as hell.

"Oh, Enid. No, he didn't. But he did tell me about Paul. I'm so sorry."

"Paul's an ass. He thinks he'll be in a better bargaining position if I don't have a job. But I'm going to find something better. Oh, excuse me for not coming to the car. Social distancing now, you know."

"That's really terrible. I am sorry." Anytime a marriage broke into pieces, it was a sad day. At least, that was how Dani felt.

"He's a piece of shit. I could tell you stories."

"You need anything, Enid?" asked Tate, moving the conversation on.

"I need a job," she said, half laughing.

"I'll put some feelers out. Legal?" he asked.

"Any office job will work."

"Weren't you a teacher?" asked Tate.

"Yes, I worked a few years in the public schools before I met Paul. Early childhood, but since the pandemic, I'd rather work at home. Safer. You know?"

"Everybody is doing that," said Tate.

Were they?

"Our president said masks off by the Fourth of July," said Enid.

"Yeah. Maybe," said Tate.

"I got my second shot yesterday," said their neighbor. "I'm sore all over."

"Should you get out of the sun?" asked Tate.

Enid said nothing to this, just gave them a long silent stare.

"Gotta go, Enid. Groceries in the car."

"See you both soon, I hope. I'll bake something to welcome Dani home."

"Sounds great." Tate eased them away from the curb and managed a neat three-point turn before rolling into their drive between the squatty pillars holding twin, wrought iron carriage lights with the flame effect.

They reached the double garage door. The single section was empty, since Tate sold his sport car and Dani could see only the shelving and the side door leading out to the yard. The sedan came next and the open place closest to the stairs was for "her" SUV. The one she knew she'd never drive.

"So, what happened with Paul?" Dani asked.

"He's filed the papers. Beat her to the punch, is what I heard. They're separated now. He lives in a townhouse closer to the office."

Downtown. Dani smiled recalling their old neighborhood. Tate had walked to work back then.

"It's getting nasty. Paul closed their line of credit and stopped paying the mortgage."

"Can he do that?"

Tate killed the engine. "He can. Did. She's going to lose the house."

"This is awful. I can't believe Paul would do that."

"Well, she's holding his watch collection as ransom."

"Rolexes." Now, why could she remember that Paul collected watches but couldn't recall what took her to Jacksonville before the accident?

"That's right," said Tate. "Threatened to pawn his precious watch collection if he doesn't pay the mortgage."

"And she really lost her job at your old law firm?"

"Yeah. Paul was behind that. A jerk move. But they were fighting at work. Can't have that."

They sat in the darkened garage, still in the vehicle as the door rumbled closed behind them.

"What is she doing for money?"

"Beats me. Credit cards, maybe. According to Enid, Paul shut down their joint accounts. Her money is locked up with his until they reach a settlement."

"You have to help her."

He blew away a breath. "It's a hard time for her. But she's resilient."

"She needs a job, not resilience."

Dani stepped down from the SUV and Tate stopped to retrieve the shopping bags of new clothes that suddenly made Dani feel guilty.

THREE

Her first few days back home felt more like a vacation than real life to Dani. Tate had taken the week off, so he was home, which always made it seem like a holiday. On Thursday, they'd had an early morning kayak trip and seen dolphins. Afterward, they'd gone for a swim and late lunch. He'd insisted she rest, and she'd fallen into a deep sleep that left her disoriented when he woke her in time to take her medications and get ready for the fundraiser.

Tate's legal clerk met them outside the hotel. His name was Jared, and he wore a yellow carnation pinned to his jacket and a yellow and blue striped tie.

Likely, he and Tate would be the only men not wearing political party colors at this event. Well, as a judge, he needed to be neutral, so that might actually work out.

Jared was a fresh-faced young man with short-cut dark hair, an eager expression, and intelligent green eyes.

It still confused Dani that she could read emotions, under-stand expressions, and describe a person she was looking at. But then, even moments later, she could not pick them out of a group. The doctor described it like colorblindness. You could not cheat. You either saw the color or you didn't. For her, faces had not gone into black and white, but into an assortment of undecipherable pieces.

So, she used what she could. For instance, Tate's aftershave. It was unusual, expensive, and so whenever she got close to him in a gathering, his familiar scent reassured her.

They entered the lobby together, the odd trio, and she did her best to hang at her husband's elbow as he introduced her to a dizzying variety of political operatives inside the party, along with hopeful candidates and confident incumbents.

Tate was here to charm and persuade the party to back him in his bid for the Florida Supreme Court. With their help and the money from her trust, they would have a firm base to succeed.

No one in the state had ever risen so fast or so high. Just over two years after passing the bar, he'd made partner. And recently, he'd been elected to the circuit court. Soon her husband might be a state supreme court justice.

Dani smiled, so proud of him.

She was a hundred percent behind his winning this election bid, as it would put her much closer to her sister. She might even gather the courage to take a bus from Tallahassee to Jacksonville.

The elevator whisked them up to the rooftop restaurant and bar for cocktail hour. Jared remained at her side, chatting and whispering names as various party members drew Tate away to meet with important contributors. She believed that even without her face blindness, she would have never remembered everyone in the onslaught of unfamiliar faces and names.

She sipped at her seltzer and lime served in a tumbler. Alcohol and the variety of medications she took did not mix, so Tate had the bartender create a mocktail that was a ringer for a gin and tonic.

It helped her blend in and feel more normal and she appreciated all his efforts.

Tate collected her in time for them to proceed from the rooftop to the banquet hall. The proximity of their table to the podium surprised her.

Tate's eyes sparkled, and he gave her his most winning smile as he drew out her chair. She settled, and he crouched at her side.

"It's looking very good, Dani."

"The party backing?"

"Yes! They're behind me. With their support, this can really happen."

She squeezed his hand. "I'm so happy for you."

"For us both, Dani. This will take us to a whole new level."

"Where's Jared?" Noticing his absence sent her heartbeat climbing. She craned her neck as the other guests seated themselves at their table. Did she know any of them? Did they know her?

It was likely they had already been introduced, not that this would be of any help to her.

"He's off at the back of the banquet hall. I'll be here beside you and I'll handle any introductions." His gaze flicked from her to a woman approaching the seat to Dani's right.

"Judge Sutton, it's so good to see you." The woman stared down at her expectantly, waiting. Dani's throat closed.

The new arrival had a cap of tight blond curls, sparkling blue eyes, and lips colored a brilliant red. Her dress was formfitting, accessorized with a tasteful string of white pearls. Tied on the handles of her designer handbag was a scarf of red, white, and blue. The ensemble made her seem the perfect candidate or political partner.

Dread pressed in, as Dani had not a clue to the woman's identity.

"Mrs. Newman. Lovely to see you," Tate said, clasping the

woman's hand and then motioning to Dani. "You remember my wife, Dani?"

The stranger gave her a look of surprise, further adding to Dani's unease.

"Oh, of course. Hello, dear." Her smile seemed genuine.

Tate filled the pause where Dani should have replied.

"We are both backing your husband, Bob. Not that he needs it. I understand he is way ahead in the race for state senate."

Mrs. Newman showed small, even white teeth. "Yes, it's going well. But I don't trust polls. We heard you're tossing your hat in the ring for that judicial vacancy."

"Yes, Charlotte," said Tate, giving Dani the woman's first and last name. "I have my eyes set on the state supreme court."

Dani recorded the visual information: red, white, and blue scarf, blond hair, and blue eyes. Then she added the details she knew: Charlotte Newman, wife of a candidate for the state legislature.

Tate glanced about. "Where is Bob?"

Dani noted this as well. Bob Newman, state senator.

Charlotte gave a musical laugh. "Oh, you know. Pressing the palms. Making connections. Solidifying backing." She rested a hand lightly on Dani's shoulder. Then she glided into the empty seat beside her. "My feet are killing me. I need to slip these heels off."

Dani held her smile as Charlotte Newman settled into place and out of her shoes.

"It all becomes familiar. This dance that we call politics. But I enjoy the spotlight and I couldn't be happier. Supporting Bob in his political ambitions. Who knows? First, the state senate and later a federal posting."

Dani lifted her water glass in a salute. "Well, here's wishing both of our husbands the best of luck in their upcoming campaigns."

Charlotte lifted her glass and tapped against Dani's as the two women shared a smile.

True to his word, Tate used each person's first and last name as they joined the table. Dani made careful mental notes, and the dinner went exceedingly well, despite Tate dumping the shrimp cocktail on his lap. Unfortunately, the speeches were long-winded with predictable talking points. There was dull and then there was campaign speech dull, which reached whole new levels of mind-numbing.

One of the candidates had brought his teenage son and daughter. The silent communication between them was the most interesting part of the evening. It was easy to see that it was the rising color of the current speaker that gave the pair fits of laughter because the party official had gone from a healthy shade of pink to an alarming shade of raspberry, verging on plum.

She and Shelby had laughed like that once at a fancy dinner, snorting through their noses as their mother cast them reproachful glances.

The polite applause seemed to come from far away.

But then she realized it was the close of the final speech.

The clapping ceased and the sound level in the banquet hall rose as the participants gathered their things to depart. She and Tate said their goodbyes to those at their table and swept under the arching red, white, and blue balloon bridge with the crowd, gathering in the spacious outer lobby.

Dani glanced about for the boy wearing a yellow carnation.

"Where's Jared?" she asked. The anxiety at so many unrecognizable faces made her skin prickle.

"He left when the dinner began, remember? It's all right. I'm here."

But before they reached the elevators, Tate asked her to wait as he stepped aside to speak to one of a hundred unfamiliar faces. She told him it was fine, waving him off.

Letting him do what was necessary to advance his chances was little enough help after all he did for her. At a minimum, she would not burden him by clinging like a monkey. It wasn't fine, however. *She* wasn't fine and she admitted that he'd been right. This evening was too much of a stretch for her just yet.

A woman approached her. "Phew. I thought we would never get out of there! They should give us merit badges or something just for sitting through all that. Are you headed home?"

Dani froze as the silence stretched, sweeping the woman for identity clues. She wore a flamingo-pink dress, had dark hair and her lipstick was a coral pink.

She recognized the boat collar and the shade of pink from the dress of one of the guests seated at her table.

Helen Percy who held a position in the party organization.

"I'm just waiting for Tate, and I believe we are heading home. What about you, Helen?" she asked.

"Oh, there'll be an after-party and after-after party and, unfortunately, with my responsibilities for fundraising, I'll need to attend most of them. Be here all damn night. But you and that cutie-pie husband of yours have a great evening."

She wheeled away, leaving Dani's heart racing and her palms sweating as she scanned the foyer. A sea of white men in dark suits mingled, but only one with blond highlights. That might be Tate, but she could not see the color of his shirt or tie, and he was too far away to recognize his cologne. The blond man was speaking to a solidly built older gentleman with a jowly face. She made her way to the pair.

Tentatively, she moved close enough to inhale the man's cologne and found it musky and heavy with sandalwood. The older man noticed her odd approach and cast her a curious expression.

"I'm looking for Judge Sutton," she said.

"Oh, he's speaking to the party chiefs," he said. "Over that way. I'll take you to him." He turned to the younger man. "Excuse me, Oscar."

He offered his elbow, and she latched on like an opossum as he guided her through the throng straight to a man in a dark suit with blond highlights in his golden hair.

She heard him say, "There won't be many public events. She'll be fine."

That was Tate's voice. Her shoulders relaxed until Dani realized the *"she"* he spoke of, who wouldn't have many public events, was her. Already the party saw her as a liability. Shame burned her cheeks.

"Judge Sutton," said her escort.

When Tate turned, Dani spotted the yellow shirt and tie.

"Here he is, Dani," said the man beside her.

Tate met her gaze and she blushed, recalling he'd asked her to wait where he left her. But she'd save her apologies for later.

Dani lifted her chin and smiled.

"Hi, honey," she said, transferring from her escort's elbow to Tate's.

"Judge Erie, you didn't need to do that," said Tate to her guide.

Dani failed to keep her jaw from dropping. Judge Curtis Erie was Tate's friend and advisor. Tate had clerked with him. She'd eaten out with him and his wife, Marjorie, often before the accident. Of course, he knew her, and she knew him. Only she'd not perceived a single familiar thing about him.

This condition was endlessly frustrating, and she feared she'd never get used to her limitations.

"Thank you, Curtis," said Dani, making a clumsy recovery. She was unsure what Judge Erie knew of her condition.

"My pleasure, my dear. We're so happy to have you back."

How much had Tate shared about her treatment at the psychiatric facility and with whom?

Dani swallowed and struggled to find a topic on which to make her recovery. "I didn't see Marjorie. Is she here tonight?"

He looked momentarily taken aback. "Why, no. Unfortunately, she couldn't make it tonight."

The judge's face went florid as he made a hasty departure.

Tate spoke to the men surrounding him.

"Gentlemen, this is my wife, Dani." And to her, he said, "Dani, these are the men backing my campaign."

They all stared at her with somber, cautious expressions, seemingly uncomfortable. One eyed her with a wary look as if she might suddenly burst into flames.

There were no secrets here. They knew where she had been and why. They were judging her, trying to determine if she would be an asset or liability.

"Gentlemen," she said, "I'm so proud of Tate and grateful for your support. I know he will make a fine state supreme court justice, and appreciate all you are doing on his behalf. Public service is Tate's calling and I'm certain he will be a credit to the party and an asset to the people of Florida. How lovely that he may have the opportunity to shape policy going forward."

It was as if they breathed a collective sigh. Tate wrapped an arm about her waist and grinned. She was so relieved at making a good impression, her knees nearly gave way.

"We'll be in touch," said one man.

"You get that pretty wife home safe, now," said another.

Dani held her smile. Charming party-insiders was now one of her jobs. Being objectified wasn't. But she held her tongue at the compliment she found insulting.

Tate and Dani shook everyone's hands and off they went toward the elevators.

"You did so well back there," he whispered, dropping a kiss on her temple.

"I'm sorry I didn't stay put. I was feeling anxious."

"No. That one is on me. I said I wouldn't leave you. Didn't I?"

He had.

"Then I got across the room and remembered. I'm so sorry, Dani. You seem so well, I forget that things aren't, that you're not..."

"I'm much better."

"Yes." They shared a smile.

He looped an arm around her waist, and they grabbed a crowded elevator to the lobby.

At the valet stand, they waited, and she recalled Judge Erie's odd departure.

"I didn't recognize Curtis."

"How could you?"

It wasn't her fault she couldn't identify her husband's mentor. But the interaction still embarrassed her. Actually, it *was* her fault. She'd lost control of her car and now her husband needed to hire a babysitter to help her manage this event.

Dani's spirits spiraled downward like a crashing plane as she tugged uselessly at the controls.

"Why wasn't Marjorie here tonight? I enjoy her company. She's so feisty and fun."

"His wife has breast cancer, stage four. She's been ill for some time."

"Oh, my goodness. I didn't know. I wish you'd told me."

He gave her a sad smile, one that was becoming all too familiar.

"I told you, Dani. But you were recovering, and a lot of that time isn't clear in your mind."

The pride over her accomplishment with the circle of party higher-ups was crushed beneath her clumsy questions to Judge Erie.

Sad how difficult a simple social gathering now seemed. She used to love parties, and her parents had a lot of them. Adult parties, family parties, and kids' parties. Her mother had made their birthday special with everything from a bouncy hut to an ecotour pontoon boat.

They'd been so happy. The four of them on the boat fishing or swimming in the pool. Their mom taught them a love of sailing, and their dad, who had grown up on a ranch in Central Florida, made certain his girls, born into privilege, could nonetheless ride, hunt, and bait their own hook.

Their car rolled to the curb. Tate stepped out to open the passenger door.

"Let's get you home, Dani."

On Friday, they had coffee on the upper balcony overlooking the pool and canal. She tried to ignore the swing set, but that bright yellow slide stuck out like a giant yellow hazard sign.

Tate said not to give up. As if, despite her inability to conceive, they might still have children.

"Tate, the other day, you hinted something about having children. What did you mean?"

"I meant that we should still have them. This house is too big. It's just screaming for kids."

Of course, it was, because they'd picked a five-bedroom mansion with an office, home theater, *and* a family room. Plus, that damned playhouse that seemed to be mocking her.

"Are you speaking of adoption?" She could imagine no other way for them to become parents.

"It's certainly a possibility. Yes. As soon as you're ready."

"We talked about this before. Didn't we? While I was at Windwood, I mean?"

He smiled and lifted her hand, bringing it to his lips for a gentle kiss, then setting it back on her knee with a squeeze before withdrawing.

"We did and we applied."

And every reputable agency rejected their application the minute they'd ticked that box asking about mental illness.

"Are we? I mean we already tried." *And failed*, she thought. "We don't qualify. I remember we don't." What she meant was that *she* didn't qualify. "I'm sorry."

It seemed all she was capable of now, grief and sorrow. Hollow apologies that never replaced what was lost.

"We *do* qualify."

She gaped. The shock was followed by an upwelling of joy. "But how?"

He patted her hand. "Let me worry about that."

"Really?"

Despite Tate's optimism, she felt doubtful about their chances of adopting.

"If that's what you want."

"Oh, I do!"

"All right then. Me too."

He gave her that winning smile, and everything seemed like it had once been, with nothing ahead but possibilities and dreams.

"I found a private operation. Applied again with the same details."

"When will you know?"

He nodded. "Anytime."

She popped from her chair in excitement and sat on his lap. They shared a languid kiss. He tasted of coffee and sugar.

"I love you, Dani."

"I love you, too. Thank you for sticking with me."

"Oh, Dani, I'll never let you go."

Don't let me go.

Dani shivered.

"You can't be cold," he said.

"No. I'm not." She moved back to her place and lifted her mug of coffee, taking a long swallow.

"They were all so pleased with last night's event."

He was speaking of the fundraiser. She nodded, catching up. Did he mean the higher-ups were relieved she wasn't a complete freak show?

Perhaps that was just paranoia. Everything didn't have to be about her, after all. And how could she concentrate on talk about the fundraiser when her mind was whirring with possibilities?

Adoption. A child. A family.

"It went well."

Dani held her smile, though her mind was on the playset and the image of a child on the slide.

"So well," he said.

"And you have their backing?"

He nodded, grinning. "They said I'm their candidate. I'll be on the party ticket and in all their promotional efforts. That's huge. And so is your backing from the trust. That seed money makes it possible to afford to give this a go. And I've got a few donors lined up. Need to get them to commit is all."

"You'll win. I know it."

He leaned in and they shared another kiss, the familiar scent of his cologne calming her.

Tate rose. "I have to make a few calls. Then I'm going to the market. Want to join me?"

"I think I'll stay here." She didn't want to ride in the car any more than absolutely necessary, at least for a while.

"Let me know what you want me to pick up."

Tate had taken the week off to be with her, but his job as a judge didn't stop because she'd come home. He had to get back to work and she had to find something to occupy her here without him. Like preparing for a potential adoption. She shivered with delight at even the possibility that Tate might be able to accomplish this. A miracle, *their* miracle.

Rattling around in this big, ostentatious house all day seemed doable now. She had hope and the real prospect of having a baby to love. No, she shouldn't get her hopes up. It was too early, but still, she wrapped her arms about herself, closed her eyes, and prayed that she'd soon be warming bottles and snapping tiny onesies around chubby little legs.

Tate had only just finished decorating, but perhaps a few subtle changes could be added, like painting an upstairs bedroom a soft lavender or a lovely pale yellow.

The door chime alerted Dani to Tate's late-afternoon return from the store, and she tucked away the various scissors, glue, and paper of the newest scrapbook. She'd been printing photos and adding pages all afternoon, busily capturing the memories she'd not had a chance to add, and thinking of all the new memories they might add one day with their own child. Baby's first smile. Baby's first step. Baby's first word. Oh, the very possibility made her pulse thrum as hope and longing entwined.

With the room in some semblance of order, she hurried out to help him unload.

She found Tate coming into the kitchen laden with shopping bags. Several more already sat on the kitchen island.

"I got some food for dinner from Folley's," he said, referring to the local gourmet market. "Fish okay?"

"Sounds great."

"Can you put these away?"

"Of course."

"I'll be out in a few minutes. Have to make a few calls. You have green marker on your nose."

He kissed the spot in question, then disappeared upstairs toward his new home office, once the intended nursery. He always did that, took his professional calls in private. Why he couldn't speak to a colleague in the kitchen was beyond her. It wasn't as if she made any noise. They had no dog to bark, no toddler to shriek.

Maybe it was a client privilege thing.

Dani laced her fingers together over her middle, feeling sad again. The sadness was like a sparkling lake. You waded in because the cool water seemed so inviting, thinking you were fine, that it would be easy to wade back out. Then you hit the drop-off and your feet no longer touched bottom. That was when you started wondering how deep the lake really was and how long you could tread water before going under.

The antidepressants worked. But she still sensed the weighty melancholy reaching for her. And the medication stole the high points of joy, flattening them in compensation, she felt, for filling in the valleys. A bulldozer, leveling out the road.

"Daily tasks," she said and reached into one of the bags, withdrawing a head of romaine lettuce and then tucking it in the crisper drawer of the fridge.

Dani methodically put away the groceries and washed the magic marker off her nose. Then she fixed a Caesar salad. Tate could grill the cobia and with the ciabatta bread, it would be a meal. Wine for him. Pellegrino for her because her cocktail was the delicate mixture of medications.

Next, she set the table in the dining room, adding clean linen napkins, the salt and pepper, butter, and the bread, which was tucked in a basket and wrapped in a cloth.

Tate returned as she was sprinkling spices on the fish.

"Not too much on mine," he said and then reached to select a white wine from the wine refrigerator, which held a hundred and fifty bottles.

Her parents loved travel and visiting wineries. They brought their twins along from the time they could walk. This had allowed Dani and Shelby to visit California several times, the Bordeaux area of France, Germany's Rhine, Campania, Italy, and Porto in Portugal. She remembered the lush landscape, imposing castles, and church floors bright with the kaleidoscope of colors cast by the stained glass. Of course, she recollected the tantalizing food, but most of all she recalled the hillsides, green with neat rows of grape vines, where she and Shelby played hide and seek.

"Dani. That's too much."

She glanced down at the fish, completely covered with the seasoning spices.

Tate rinsed off the fillets, then plopped them on a tray and headed to the screened lanai. She followed, carrying their drinks. What had she been doing? She'd shaken a quarter inch of spices on those fillets. That much would ruin the sweet flavor of the cobia.

She sat and watched the vessels coming and going. There were fishing boats and jet skis, cabin cruisers and sailboats, motoring through the channel, leading them back to their berths.

Dani wrinkled her nose at the odor of exhaust and the constant low rumble of the engines. Small wonder she couldn't hear the songbirds.

During dinner preparations, Tate spoke about the campaign. The seat was vacant and that meant no incumbent to defeat. There would be more dinners and fundraisers and more to do as fall proceeded, culminating with a dizzying schedule prior to the day of the election. Exhaustion pressed down on her shoulders just hearing about what was in store.

Dani felt the urge to keep working on her scrapbooks. She wasn't hungry. Maybe after supper she'd prepare another page. She'd left off their latest trip to Jamaica last November. It felt like a lifetime ago.

Tate turned the fish and then used the digital thermometer

to check the temperature again, stabbing another tiny round hole. "They're done."

She held the door as he carried their meal to the table, serving them before heading to the kitchen with the tray. He returned with the bottle of white and her sparkling water.

"Shall I serve you some salad?" she asked.

He nodded and poured himself a generous glass, then refilled hers from the green bottle that stood sweating on the pad made from a folded dishcloth.

Dani struggled through the meal, each bite less welcome than the last.

From her place, she looked out at their street, the evening quiet broken only by an occasional neighbor walking a dog. Finally, she surrendered, setting down her flatware and leaving half the fish. Tate glanced at the remains of her meal but said nothing as he carried their plates to the kitchen.

After cleaning up, they headed to the living room to the ridiculously large sectional ringing the massive coffee table like a horseshoe around a gilded stake.

Tate flicked on the ballgame on the sixty-five-inch flatscreen, and she picked up the women's fiction book she'd been reading since returning to this house.

Returning home, she corrected. *This is your home.*

"All right if I golf tomorrow?" he asked.

She knew that even well before the accident Tate had a regular Saturday tee time with the partners at his old firm.

"That's fine."

"You don't mind being alone?"

"I'm going to start another scrapbook. Everything about our life in this new house."

His smile wavered but he held on. "Great. That's super."

What was wrong with starting a new book? Was she over-doing it? She considered if she was obsessed but dismissed the idea. It was a reasonable hobby that occupied a normal amount of time.

He lifted his phone and sent a text. "Just telling the boys I'm in."

She didn't want him to miss golf, but this house still felt like it belonged to someone else. She lifted a couch pillow and inhaled. Gardenias again.

That was odd. The furniture was relatively new. Chosen by a designer for this house about the time she'd been hospitalized.

Could this be their designer's perfume?

"What's wrong?" Tate was studying her.

She lowered the pillow.

"It smells like gardenias."

"What? Let me smell."

She handed over the pillow and he pressed his nose into the fabric.

"It smells like you, Dani." He inhaled again. "Your shampoo, I think."

He handed back the pillow, and she set it on the far side of the couch as if it were an unwelcome guest.

"Any of those medications mess with your sense of smell?" he asked.

She hadn't thought of that. "I'm not sure."

His phone chimed with a text and then another. For several minutes, he was busy typing. She returned to her book as the ballgame ambled on. The third time she caught herself blindly staring at the page, she gave up. She couldn't focus and set the book aside.

"I'm going up to bed."

He flicked off the game. "Me too. Rays are stinking up the place tonight, anyway."

She climbed the grand staircase. At the landing, she turned the correct direction in the still unfamiliar house, heading for their main bedroom. In her walk-in closet, she gathered the dress she'd worn for the fundraiser and then recalled that Tate's suit also needed a trip to the dry cleaner, but despite a search of his closet, she was unable to locate it.

Perhaps the bathroom hamper?

She heard Tate shout. It was a sound of elation, but it made Dani's heart pound. She hurried out to their room.

A man held his phone up like a trophy and then did a fist pump there before the sliders to the private balcony overlooking the pool below and the canal beyond. He stood in loose gym shorts and no shirt. She froze in the hall between the two walk-in closets. This could be anyone.

It's not. It's Tate.

He turned, his smile bright.

Blond hair. That was right. Say something, she thought.

"Oh, Dani! It's amazing. I can't believe it's happening!"

FOUR

Dani exhaled her relief at the reassuring sound of Tate's voice. He stood before the dark windows, his features lit up with joy. She smiled and hurried forward, forcing down the ridiculous disquiet at being unable to identify him. After all, they were the only two people in the house.

This was Tate.

"What is it?"

He clasped both her hands and drew them to the bedroom loveseat, facing the black waters of the canal and the twinkling lights of their neighbor's homes beyond.

"Dani, something wonderful has happened."

The happiness made his voice sing. How long had it been since she'd heard that musical tone? She couldn't remember.

The worry changed to anticipation as she waited for him to speak, their hands clasped, their eyes locked.

"Everything is falling into place for us now. I finally have you back. And the campaign and my work. There's just one thing missing."

She lifted her brows, knowing what was missing, feeling it every minute, like an empty chamber in her heart.

"Remember earlier, when we were talking about starting a family?"

She nodded, biting her lower lip. "Remember? It's all I can think about. You said you applied again with a private agency."

"Yes!"

"And that somehow we qualify to adopt."

"That's right. And we're approved! They just called. We're getting a baby. We're going to be parents."

It was like the world stood still as joy flooded her body. Could this be their second chance?

A moment later, the questions pressed in, smothering the elation in doubt.

"We're approved?"

"Yes!"

"But how? We can't. I mean, I've been treated for depression. Am being treated," she corrected. "On meds, and I've only been home for..." She had to think about that because the release date was hazy.

"Five days," said Tate, there to fill in all those pesky details. "And you are doing great."

"When will we..." She could barely think, she was so excited.

"We're on the waiting list. Could be anytime."

He lifted her and spun her in a circle. Even when her feet touched down, she still felt she was floating.

"Come on. Let's open some champagne! I'll tell you all about it."

He guided her back to the bedroom loveseat facing the balcony.

"You still want a baby. Don't you?" he asked.

She did, with her whole damaged heart.

"Oh, yes. Of course."

"Then let me handle it. I've got the acceptance. We might hear any day."

He'd told her not to give up hope and he'd asked if she still wanted to adopt, but she'd never expected him to move so quickly.

"Did this just happen?"

"No. Well, not really. I mean, we spoke about adopting while you were at Windwood. And you gave me the thumbs-up. And you're right, that didn't go well. But I have some connections now, daily interactions with social workers and folks inside the system."

Inside the system, like insider trading. Alarm bells sounded in her mind.

"But the baby will be ours," she said. "Not a foster placement?"

"Yes. All ours!"

She had to ask.

"Is it legal? This adoption."

A frown flitted across his brow. He blew away a breath and kissed her hand. But he didn't offer reassurance. Instead, he said, "Dani. I'm a judge. I know the law."

That wasn't an answer. What she wanted was a simple declaration that whatever he had done, it was *within* the law.

"Do you think I would do anything that might hurt us?"

With a stab of guilt, she realized she was the one who had hurt them. Tate had done nothing but try to put the pieces back together. His wife, like Humpy Dumpty, had a great fall.

But Tate tended to cut corners. He'd done a lot of that in law school. Cheating was what she'd called it. He'd admitted to her that he had paid someone, a tutor, to do some of his assignments because he was working nights to pay for school and just could not keep up with the workload. Despite the reason, some of his choices went against Dani's moral compass. But she'd kept silent, their relationship more important to her than the ethical point.

Tate was on his feet. He trotted out the door while her mind raced.

Was this really happening?

He returned with champagne and fine, fluted glasses, a wedding gift from her college roommate. She had lost touch with that friend and others. Long hospitalization and depression could do that.

"Let's open it on the balcony."

She followed him out into the warm, moist air.

The lights of homes across the canal glistened, sending broken shafts of gold across the liquid highway and, to the left, the inviting dark waters of the bay shimmered under the rising moon.

He popped the cork expertly, sending it arching from the second story. It landed in the pool below. Tate laughed and poured two glasses, sending bubbles fizzing to the surface. He handed her one, more giddy than she had ever seen him. She clasped the stem with a trembling hand, and he touched his glass to hers, making them ring.

"To parenthood!" he toasted, before taking a huge swallow. Then he pounded one free hand on the balcony and shouted to the sky.

Dani did not drink.

He turned to her and frowned. "It's a toast, Dani."

"I know but I'm not supposed to."

"A sip for luck."

She took a sip, then set aside the glass.

Tate looked dissatisfied.

"What about your campaign? The Florida Supreme Court, I don't want anything to keep you from winning the election." Anything, she thought, like a scandal over an illegal adoption or, worse, a black-market baby.

Why was she thinking this way? Why couldn't she trust him on this most important of things?

He drew back, clearly affronted. Dani pressed her damp palms to her knees. Her racing mind made her jittery and twitchy as a lab rat.

A baby. They could have a baby. Her mind skittered all over the place. She wanted it, but the details made her anxious.

"Let me get your pills," said Tate, placing his glass on a side table.

He dashed back inside and returned carrying the tray holding her pill bottles and a glass of water. "You okay?"

"It's just a lot to take in." The anxiety gave way to excitement. She slowly shook her head in disbelief. She met Tate's gaze. "Is it really true?"

"Yes, Dani. We can be parents if that's what you want."

She did, but all she could manage was a vigorous nod and tears. They ran in rivulets down her cheeks and into the fine fabric of the designer wrap dress.

Tate gathered her up in his arms. "Oh, Dani. I love you. This will be great. You'll see. We can be a family."

Dani gazed up at him.

"My parents always wanted a grandbaby." The thought of them both gone, unable to dote on a grandchild, sent her into tears again.

Tate rubbed her back. "Dani, your parents are gone."

Did he think she didn't remember? As if she could ever forget.

"I know. I just mean, they would have loved to be grandparents."

He drew back, smiling. "Good. You had me worried there for a minute."

He helped her assemble the medications for anxiety, depression, and the sleep aid. Once that one went down, she had about thirty minutes to get into bed or fall asleep wherever she was.

The sleeping pills changed her sleep to simple unconsciousness, *the void*, she called it. No dreams, but that was the tradeoff for no nightmares.

With each sip and each pill, she tossed her head to swallow, gazing up at the silvery moon.

That task completed, he retrieved the bottle and glasses, placing them with her medication and carried them inside. She followed, continuing past him to her closet now filled with clothing from a time before her accident. A time when she worked in the family business, first answering phones, later at reception in the corporate office; then, after graduation, her father had assigned Dani her very own accounts, some of them big ones. She'd glowed under his confidence. It had been a wonderful time, Shelby working on a logo and branding update and Dani in customer service. Now she had all the professional clothes, designer bags, and rows of shoes—remnants of another life, another Dani. This one had been whole and optimistic. Brave and daring.

She missed that girl.

Mindful of the ticking clock as her medication dissolved in her stomach, she slipped into a nightshirt, cotton, like the ones at the hospital. Somehow it comforted her, the soft utilitarian fabric devoid of ties or embellishments.

Returning to their bedroom, Dani noted the flow of warm air billowing the satin curtains. She found Tate on the balcony, standing at the rail, his phone pressed to his ear.

She squinted at the ornate mantel clock on the table beside the loveseat, gilded again, wondering whom he would be speaking to at this hour. A glance confirmed it was after 10 pm.

Outside, the breeze blew moist air off the bay and the lights on the private docks sent broken blades of color shimmering across the dark water.

Before she even reached him, she could hear a woman screaming through the phone.

What on earth?

Dani stepped outside, her bare feet making a silent approach. Behind him, she lifted a hand to his shoulder. He jumped and spun. For a moment, she saw an expression of annoyance on the otherwise unfamiliar face.

The expression morphed into one of suffering and frustration.

"Who?" she mouthed.

He tapped the mute button and held the phone away from him. The female voice continued to blare, a human car alarm.

"It's Enid. Paul came back. He's drunk and threatening her."

"Oh my gosh! We need to call the police," said Dani, turning to get her phone.

"She doesn't want it in the papers."

Dani glanced at the phone. "What does she expect *you* to do?"

"We're her neighbors, Dani. She lives right across the street and she's in trouble."

"She can come here."

"I'm going there. See if I can talk some sense into Paul, then drive him home."

"That's dangerous."

"Oh, please. I outweigh Paul by fifty pounds. He's acting like an ass, always been a loud drunk, but he's not dangerous."

"Is that why they're breaking up?"

"The drinking? Yes. Part of it, I think." He lifted the phone and tapped the unmute button. "Yes. I'm here. I'm coming. Be there as fast as I can."

He ended the call. Dani clasped his hand.

"I'll go with you."

He gave her that look, the one filled with incredulity and sadness. She couldn't. They both knew it. She'd fall asleep standing if she didn't lie down. Already the medication was dulling her concentration and her body dragged, urging her to rest.

"You're going?" The sleeping pill fogged the edges of her clarity and made her words slow.

"I'll be back soon."

"What if you're in trouble? I won't know. I can't help."

"Nothing will happen, Dani."

"What if Paul—"

He cut her off. "I can handle Paul. Dani, you're slurring your words. Please go to bed. I'll be home when I can."

"How will I know it's you?"

Tate chuckled. "You won't hear me come in."

Tate was right, of course. He could lead an elephant herd into the room and have a tap-dancing competition and she'd be none the wiser.

"Let's get you into bed." He tugged on their joined hands. He was her lifeline. Her rock.

He tucked her in like a child, but the kiss he left her with was neither chaste nor innocent. The sensation of drowsiness warred with arousal as she wiggled deeper into the soft bedding.

"I'll be back soon. You rest now." His smile was wicked.

She watched him walk away, pause at the doorway, and flick the switch. The room went dark except for the blue glow of the under-cabinet lights in the main bath.

"Goodnight, sweetheart. Sleep well."

This exit echoed the night he'd had to handle Jeremy's client, her first night home. He'd been called away two evenings this week. That was so odd.

She listened for the chime indicating he'd exited the front door or the voice alerting her that the alarm was arming but heard neither. The fuzziness turned to a dragging.

The void. She'd fought this feeling in the hospital. Now she'd grown accustomed to the blackness and welcomed it like an old friend. And until she dropped into oblivion, she would imagine holding a baby, small and soft.

It was all she wanted, that warm, sleeping infant, tucked safe and close.

Dani sighed and let her mind dance with budding possibilities.

FIVE

SATURDAY MORNING, JUNE 19, 2021

Dani threw aside the coverlet and glanced to her husband's side of the bed seeing no evidence he had slept there. Had he been gone all night? In their three-year marriage, if she excluded her time recovering from her brain injury, they had never spent the night apart before the accident.

It always took her a while in the morning to wake up properly, for her brain to start functioning again, to shake off the effects of her pills. She remembered the drama with Paul. Had Tate gotten Paul home? Stayed to see him settled and prevent him from again returning to his old house? Was Enid okay?

Tate had been right to go over. A domestic dispute would not sink Paul's career, but if it escalated, he risked criminal charges and possible disbarment. Tate was a good friend to help Paul. He was always looking out for others, and he had a big heart. It was what made him such a good judge.

Still a little fuzzy-headed, she wandered to the window and peered out The rumble of an engine at wake speed preceded the appearance of an enormous motorboat trundling out to the Gulf of Mexico.

Dani preferred birdsong to boat engines and tree frogs to the slosh of the tides on the seawall. Tate had seen manatees and dolphin from the dock, but she had yet to glimpse either. All she saw was a plastic bag mired in masses of tangled, floating seagrass.

She tugged the curtain closed.

After a quick shower, she dressed in a denim skirt and cotton T-shirt, her work uniform, she liked to think of it.

She paused in the kitchen, hoping to find Tate but didn't. He could be on the lanai or in the home theater.

She called his name, tentative.

No answer.

Dani dropped a pod into the coffeemaker, and as the machine gurgled and hissed, she walked to the dining room, looking out at their empty driveway. Her attention shifted to the house across the street, to the Langfords'. The only activity was the lawn care people buzzing about in circles on the overly long grass.

Then she glanced in the opposite direction, toward the main community exit. She hadn't been here long, but knew which way was the shortest to the secure gate. There were three exits, two of which were available only to residents and functioned with a remote in the car, opening automatically upon approach.

What day was it?

Saturday.

Oh, he had a tee time! She checked the garage and found his sedan missing and Tate's clubs gone, along with the golf spikes he kept out here.

Back in the kitchen she found a note at her usual place on the counter.

Came home late. Up early. Didn't wake you.
PS Shelby dunked her phone in the whirlpool at therapy.

Lost her contacts and your number. She called the house. Has a new phone. Already added it to your contacts.
Off on the links.
19ᵗʰ hole to follow.

The 19ᵗʰ hole was a euphemism for the bar at the clubhouse where the groups gathered to drink and sometimes grab a meal. She smiled, happy he felt comfortable enough to leave her alone again, if only for a few hours.

She doubted Dr. Allen would approve but she appreciated the privacy. It was hard to relax when he treated her as if she were made of spun glass. She loved Tate, but he tended to be a little overprotective. And her psychiatrist, who had been reluctant to allow the discharge, had recommended Tate take time off to be sure Dani was adjusting. But that didn't mean being with her every second.

Her illness had been hard on Tate, the obvious crack in their perfect life. She'd left him to field all the questions about her injuries, her recovery, and then her disappearance. Back then, she couldn't seem to get herself off the floor to care about anyone or anything.

How many meals had he eaten here alone?

Luckily, he'd built a support network of friends and colleagues and she was grateful for them all, since he had no family to turn to during her illness. Her husband was an amazing man, and she was lucky and grateful.

The coffee machine completed its job with an exhausted gasp, and she returned for the mug. A glance told her it was closing on nine in the morning. From the dining room, she sipped her coffee as she watched a neighbor walk to the mailbox to drop off a letter and lift the flag to alert the mailman. A water delivery truck rolled by. Down the street another truck was delivering a pallet of mulch.

She didn't know a soul in this neighborhood except Enid

Langford. Just Enid in that big house now. She wondered if she should go over there and ask her for coffee. It would be nice to have a friend nearby. And Enid could probably use one too, after last night.

She couldn't believe Enid and Paul had split. She'd met Paul on several occasions because he and Tate attended law school together. Both had landed in the same prestigious firm, but Paul was an estate attorney. Lucrative, but boring as the dusty old widow clients, Tate said.

Paul hadn't risen as fast as Tate, but Tate had the help of her mom with school loans and securing the clerk position with the eleventh circuit court and with Judge Erie.

Tate secured the right everything: degree, wife, home, position. If he had weaknesses, they were his wife and perhaps his taste in home furnishings. She glanced about at the décor and sighed.

Tate loved shiny things.

Behind her, another large boat rumbled past the pool cage. Saturday was a big boating day. The marine traffic would be constant. Dani sipped her coffee and pictured the ornate lawn stretching down to the rows of statuesque royal palms lining the entrance road. That had been her view from her private room at Windwood. She'd never expected to miss it.

Dani drained the remains of her mug and stood, heading to the kitchen for a refill and then toward the room she considered hers. She paused in the family room beyond the kitchen. Tate had added skylights and a large sectional while she'd been in the hospital.

True, she'd preferred to fill the space with beanbag chairs, a tiny easel, plastic toys, and plush stuffed animals, but that wasn't possible.

And then the conversations on adoption hit her.

Adoption. A waiting list and a baby! Girl or a boy?

She didn't care.

The coffee cup slipped through her fingers as she let out a howl of victory.

Warm coffee ran down her legs and chards of the ceramic bounced on the tile.

A baby. Their baby.

This family room *would* be a playroom. One of the empty guest bedrooms would be the nursery. She glanced through the window to the pool, now seeing a hazard. They'd need a fence and a gate that locked.

"I have to tell Shelby!"

Dani dashed up the stairs to the charging station in the main bedroom, taking a wrong turn and ending up in one of the three additional bedrooms.

She paused. Would this be the nursery? The smile filled her entire being and she hugged herself. This was too good to be true. Instantly, the doubts crept in. Was it too good or was it that her husband had the pull to make the impossible a reality?

Dani shook her head, pushing down the doubts.

She wouldn't dwell on that now. That was the kind of thinking that dipped into an obsessive spiral. This was good news and she needed to focus on that.

Reversing course, she found her new bedroom, and retrieved her phone charging in her closet, to discover a missed call and message from Tate.

"Honey, I'm about to tee off. Wondered if you were up. Did you get my note? Shelby's got a new cell phone. Call if you need me. See you around noon."

She wanted to call him and ask what had happened last night at Enid's home, but he'd called at 8:16 am according to her phone. So Tate would be out on the links now.

She hesitated. Her questions could wait, and she wanted to tell Shelby the news. Moving to the bedroom, she sat on the loveseat facing the sliders and placed the call.

Her sister picked up on the first ring.

"Dani-o! I was about to call you," said Shelby.

"Everything all right?"

"Super. You?"

"Better than super," said Dani.

"Do tell? It's the house. It's great, right?"

"It's... different. But this is something else. You'll never believe it, Shelby. We've been approved for adoption."

"What! Oh, Dani, that's fantastic. Oh my gosh. You must be thrilled."

"I can't even believe this is happening. They told me before that my time at Windwood and the depression disqualified us."

"Well, I think you'll be a terrific mother."

"But it's odd. Isn't it?" asked Dani.

"What is?"

"Our qualifying. I mean, you know."

"You think Tate pulled some strings?"

"Yes! How did you know?"

"We're twins. Thinking alike is our thing." Shelby paused. "But, Dani, maybe he used a private agency. They have them."

"He said so. Or he influenced the process somehow."

"Tate would never break the law."

"Yes. You're right. I know you are. Oh, Shelby, I'm so happy!"

"Me too!"

"When we get the baby, you have to come."

"Of course."

"Any word on the van?"

"Yes. Ah, well, I had a driving lesson in an accessible van."

"What? That's great." Dani had a hand firmly pressed to her chest because her heart was racing and sweat popped out on her forehead. Just the thought of Shelby in a vehicle terrified her.

"Isn't it?"

"When does yours come?"

"Oh, well... It's on order. It will be a few weeks. I don't know exactly. Once I feel comfortable on highways, I'll roll on down and see the baby. Oh, gosh. Boy or girl?"

"It's just an approval. We don't have a baby yet."

"Any other details?"

"No, I forgot to ask how long a wait to expect." As Dani said it, the bottom dropped out of the world and she felt physically dizzy. What was happening? Was she really going to be a mother?

"Dani? You okay?"

"Scared."

"Of course you are. Every parent I've ever known is terrified. My friend, Erin, told me she had a recurring dream that she left the baby in the bassinet on top of the car and didn't remember until she was driving. She used to do that with iced coffee sometimes."

Dani leaned forward to send more blood to her brain.

"It's normal. Right?"

"Yes. Yes. Totally. I think you can trust Tate to be there and to give you all the help you need with the little one."

She nodded, hand still pressing tight to her chest as if trying to keep the fear inside while accepting that this would be a wonderful thing.

Wonderful, not terrible. No reason to be so scared.

"He will. I know he will." No one had ever been more supportive than her husband. She'd chosen wisely. Picked a winner. He'd been so driven. So intense. And focused on what he wanted.

"This is a dream come true," said Dani, her head now hanging between her knees.

"You better start thinking of names."

"Oh gosh," she said and pinched her eyes closed.

"What about Willow? That's a beautiful name," suggested Shelby.

"It is. If it's a girl."

"Oh, Dani, my therapist is here. Will you call me later?"

"Of course."

"I'm just so happy for you and Tate. Parents. It's fantastic. Bye now!" Shelby disconnected the call.

Dani lay on the loveseat in their bedroom for a while, trying to focus on a single blade of the spinning fan. The air conditioner flicked on, sending cool air whispering down from the ceiling.

Her watch buzzed, reminding her to take her morning round of medication.

She sat up.

She had to get the scissors and glue out of her craft room. Some of the glues and paints were toxic, and she'd left coffee and broken ceramic all over the floor.

"Bad mother," she muttered and hurried downstairs.

SIX

Dani sat at the sewing machine at noon that day, the rumble of the motor filling the air, when a man charged from the hallway into the room. She screamed and scrambled away from the intruder, striking her ironing board that tottered. She grasped for the iron, to prevent it falling and as a possible weapon.

He drew up short and raised his hands. He wore only one golf glove and a yellow golf shirt. Yellow.

"Dani, it's me!"

"Tate?"

Dani slapped her free hand on the wobbling ironing board, stopping it from toppling.

"Yes!" He was out of breath. "I just got another call from the agency. It's happened so fast! I never expected."

"Slow down."

He nodded but rushed on. "Left them on the fourteenth hole." He bounced on his toes with excitement.

"What on earth?"

"We have a baby!"

"What?" She rushed to him, and he dragged her into his arms.

"We have a baby. A girl. A newborn!"

"Really?" The fabric of his shirt, now pressed to her lips, muffled her words.

"Yes! I'm so excited. We can bring her home from the hospital tomorrow."

"Tomorrow!" Dani didn't have a crib or diapers. The anxiety made her breathing fast. She wasn't ready. Neither of them was ready.

The dizziness made her vision swim.

Tate pressed her forward, seating her before the easel and lowering her head between her knees.

"Dani, breathe. It's all right. It doesn't have to be tomorrow."

She pinched her eyes shut and willed herself not to black out. Why was getting exactly what she wanted making her tumble into panic?

When her vision returned, she eased back to an upright position. Tate was here. She could trust him. There was no need to be afraid.

Fat tears dropped to the marble tile as she waited for the dizziness to subside. Tate crouched before her and smiled. She tried to find one thing familiar about this face and settled on the gray rings on the outer limits of his blue eyes.

"Tell me about her."

"Delivered yesterday. Mother is incarcerated. A felon."

All sorts of dreadful worst-case scenarios rose like dragons in Dani's mind. "Oh, that's awful. The poor woman. Are you sure... she definitely wants to give her baby away?" Another dreadful thought occurred. "And she's not... she hasn't been on drugs or anything?"

"It's forgery. Five years and she has no family. She requested the baby be placed up for adoption."

Dani absorbed that little human tragedy. It took some of the shine off his news.

"That's so sad."

"It's not, Dani. This baby will have every advantage. She'll be our daughter, legally and in every other way." Tate gave her a long look. "Let me get you some water. You look pale."

She trailed him to the kitchen where he opened a cabinet for a glass, then used the refrigerator's reserve to fill it with cold water.

Dani spun her engagement and wedding rings around and around with nervous energy.

"A representative will bring her here sometime tomorrow. Then we sign the paperwork, and that's it." He pressed the glass into her hand.

"But don't they have to inspect our home or something first?"

He retained his smile as he shook his head. "Nope."

He offered nothing more. She knew something was wrong with this response and her desire warred with her common sense. Finally, she couldn't keep her misgivings from surfacing.

"Did you bend the rules to make this happen?"

His smile changed into a tight line. "I have connections, that's all. Remember, I worked in family court for years, made friends."

"Tate, is this legal?"

"Of course, it is. Unconventional. But completely legal." He motioned to the kitchen island, and she took a seat, sipping the water.

The icy liquid soothed her dry throat. She lowered the glass and then lifted it again to press it to her forehead.

"Hot?"

"Excited," she said.

They shared a smile.

"Me too." He leaned an elbow on the granite, grinning up at her. Tate still wore one golf glove and she recalled him saying he left before completing the round.

"Is it a problem that you didn't finish the game?"

"Naw. The guys are thrilled, about the baby and that I owe them all a beer."

She chuckled at that. Something else occurred to her.

"Hey, what happened at the Langfords' place last night?"

"Oh, that." He waved a dismissive hand. "Paul was drunk and tried to get into the house. His wife changed the locks, but she still came out on the stoop to scream at Paul. I got him out of there before the neighbors called the cops. Shouldn't have been driving but I couldn't stop him. Enid fell off the step and hurt her ankle. I got her inside and gave her some ice."

"Well, that's terrible."

"It's a big nasty battle. Hard to watch. And I'm smack in the middle."

"We should have her over."

"Maybe after we get settled with the baby."

"I need to tell Shelby."

"Yes. Absolutely. You should call her."

But just then Dani's phone played the song that she'd programmed for Shelby's ringtone.

"Perfect! That's her!"

Tate frowned, the expression deepening the lines on his wide forehead.

"Something wrong?" she asked.

He glanced from the phone back to her.

"She's calling?"

The phone repeated the song's chorus. "That's her ringtone."

He looked to her. "Then answer it, I guess."

He guessed? That was odd.

"I must have sent some twin signal to the universe." Dani grinned, scooped up the phone, and answered the call.

"Dani!"

"Shelby, guess what?"

Dani delivered the latest adoption news in a rush.

She glanced to her husband, who tugged off his golf glove with his teeth and continued to frown.

"Oh, wow. You have a baby already? That can take years."

"Well, we have one tomorrow."

"Yikes. New house. New baby."

"Same old husband," said Dani and stroked Tate's cheek. He gave her a smile. "And we've had the house for months."

"Well, I'm glad about that." Shelby laughed again. Then her voice grew serious. "Tomorrow. Dani, how will you manage? Are you off the sleeping pills?"

The terror was back, squeezing Dani's heart in a fistlike grip. She stared wide-eyed at Tate.

"No. I'm taking them. I have to take them." She whispered to Tate, "She's asking about the sleeping pills."

"But what if the baby needs you at night?" asked Shelby.

Dani pressed a hand to her forehead and sank to the white leather chair at the kitchen banquette. Tate sat beside her, watching. Could he see the panic rising within her like hot lava?

"I don't know." Her breathing was rasping like a saw.

"Dani, relax. I'm sure Tate will get you help. You can afford it."

The trust. How often had that money been a godsend?

"Thanks, Mom and Dad," said Dani.

"You can say that again. Oh my gosh, I just thought of something."

"What?"

"I'm going to be an aunt!" The sound now coming from the phone seemed like the mewing of a kitten. Shelby was crying again.

"I'll send photos tomorrow. Okay?"

"I can't wait. Do you have a name picked out?"

"Not yet." But Shelby had suggested Willow and their baby was a girl. Dani tried the name in her mind, finding it charmed.

"You better get shopping. You need a bassinet, crib, clothes, and, well, everything!"

Anxiety squeezed at her throat with sharp talons. "Yes. I'd better go."

After a pause, Shelby said, "I just got your package."

Dani smiled. Tate had helped her order the treat. "Enjoy."

Her third day out of Windwood, Dani sent Shelby a pound of her favorite gummy snack, blue sharks. They used to buy them at the candy shop down the block from their father's offices.

"Aww, Dani. Thank you! You are the best sister."

That compliment hit her middle like a tossed anchor. They both knew she was not. They both knew she was the sister who had put her twin in that wheelchair.

"Enjoy."

"Love you, little sister," said Shelby, beginning their usual farewell.

"Love you more, big sister," Dani replied and disconnected.

Tate sat in the seat next to hers, hands folded, waiting.

"Tate, we need a bassinet."

He grinned and gripped her hands, his face animated with a delight that warmed her inside and out.

"We do! Our little girl is coming home tomorrow. Can you believe it? We're going to be parents. Okay, Mommy, let's get shopping and we should go out to celebrate. Might be a while before we get a full night's sleep."

"Yes, about that." Dani squeezed his hands. "What about my medication? I need the sleeping pills and you can't be up all night and still work all day."

"I can for a while. Put in for family leave. Or we can hire help."

"So I can still stay on my routine?"

"It's working, Dani. I wouldn't do anything to jeopardize your mental health. This way, you can still see Dr. Allen. I'll handle nights for now. Then we can hire a nanny full-time before I head back from leave. If we need more help, I'll get it. Don't worry."

So easy to say.

"Any thoughts on a name?" he asked.

"I'm not sure. Shelby suggested Willow."

"I've always liked that name."

She tried it out. "Willow. Yes, that's a lovely name."

"We'll have to put something on the paperwork. Do you want to think about it?"

She smiled at him, a father-to-be all deliriously happy and anxious to please. She stroked his chin.

"I love that name."

He grinned. "Willow it is."

Dani smiled, ignoring the butterflies batting around her insides.

SEVEN

Tate did the baby shopping via the internet and telephone from the largest baby store in town and paid the manager to immediately deliver boxes and boxes of items.

Meanwhile, Dani headed upstairs to decide which of the empty bedrooms to use as a nursery. Upon her return, she found Tate standing with hands on hips before a mountain of boxes.

"Got the delivery," he said.

"Oh, my goodness, Tate! You bought the entire store!"

They unboxed the baby gear together in the living room. The whole thing seemed surreal, as if it were happening to someone else.

Dani was giddy with excitement, like a child on Christmas Eve, like she and Shelby so filled with anticipation they could hardly sleep.

Dani opened a bag and found a series of pastel-colored bibs. Rummaging in another box, she found a nubby teething mitten, an assortment of pacifiers, and several onesies.

She held the first soft, impossibly small garment to her

heart, deliriously happy. So, this was what it felt like, to be so filled with joy you closed your eyes to savor the rush.

A thought struck her. She gasped and stared wide-eyed at her husband.

"Tate, we have nothing to feed Willow."

He looked equally startled and pulled out his phone. "I'm calling Jeremy. He has two boys and I know that Sally didn't breastfeed. I'll see what they used."

He stepped away to place the call, moving to his office, as usual, while she unboxed an adorable mobile and held it aloft to watch the plush animals spin.

Then she set it aside and glanced about the chaos of their living room. Why didn't the adoption agency have to inspect their home? That was a normal step in the process. Wasn't it?

How had Tate circumvented all those standard steps? Her misgivings stirred again, and she battled them back. Tate told her the mother had given up her parental rights and they could have the baby. Either she trusted him, or she didn't.

Perhaps this was a sort of temporary placement?

But that wasn't what he'd said. He'd said adoption. An *unconventional* adoption, but completely legal. All right then.

Dani set aside her doubts and lifted the next item from the box. A baby monitor. After retrieving the batteries, she plugged the base in to charge. Tate had gotten the ones with the video and Bluetooth. She downloaded the app and began trying out the functions on her phone. It also had sound and motion notifications, audio, night vision, room temperature sensor, and a wide-angle view.

Eventually, this camera would need to be mounted above the crib and out of the reach of a toddler. She set the camera on the fireplace hearth and fiddled with the app, singing a lullaby and watching on her phone as she walked across the room and accidentally into the coffee table.

"No walking and monitoring," she said to herself as she rubbed the lump developing on her shinbone.

Tate returned, and the monitor sent her a motion alert.

She tapped at her phone, silencing the notifications for now.

"Okay. He says the cow's milk formula is best. They treat it somehow to make the protein more digestible for human babies. We can buy it in liquid concentrate because then we don't have to mess with mixing powder. Besides the pouches, they have ready-to-feed bottles. I ordered both."

"Wonderful."

She cast him a smile of relief and relaxed her shoulders. Then she stifled a yawn.

"Is it ten o'clock?" he asked. "Nuts, you need your medications. Time for bed."

"What about all this?" She waved a hand at the chaos of half-empty boxes, unopened boxes, and stacks of infant accoutrements.

Tate pressed his hands on his hips. "Looks like a baby store threw up in here. Well, we have all morning to set up the nursery. I'll get that crib together and figure out the carrier. I got two bases for your SUV, the carrier snaps into that for car rides, the other turns it into a stroller. Tomorrow we can hang the mobile."

He grinned. She thought he'd never looked so content.

She surveyed the chaos, smiling.

"Let's get some of this stuff upstairs."

They sorted out a few of the items that belonged in the nursery and up they went. In the room beside theirs, Tate stowed the changing table, yet to be assembled and a mobile, still in the box. She set the package of diapers on the floor and lay the onesies on top.

He turned in a circle, looking at the furnishings, which included a sleeper sofa, small desk holding Dani's laptop, and a two-drawer filing cabinet. Beside that sat a lounge chair and gaming gear.

"We have to get this desk out of here," he said, moving her computer to the filing cabinet and lifting the small desk. "The rest can stay for now. I'm going to bring up another load."

Dani glanced at the room, which suddenly seemed too far from the master. "Will she sleep in our room at first?"

"That's why I got the bassinet and the carrier," he said, already in the hall and heading downstairs.

She plugged in the new night-light, which also had an app to control the color, brightness, and sound, and set it beside the computer, for now.

She and Shelby would have loved this as children. And just like that, the melancholy crept forward. The nursery was upstairs, so Shelby would never see it.

"Oh, no you don't." She needed to take her antidepressant. Keeping on a schedule was key to regulating her mental state.

In the hall she found Tate, who marched up the stairs looking like a Sherpa burdened with the gear of an infant mountain climber.

"Heading to bed?" he asked and lowered the armful to the rug.

"Yes. You?"

"In a few minutes. I want to get some of this cardboard out before recycling is collected."

Dani had no idea what day was for trash or yard waste or recycling. That, too, was on Tate.

"I'm so excited," he said.

"Me too. Thank you for making this happen." She kissed him on the mouth, angling her head and feeling the rush of arousal tingling through her. She pulled away, letting him return to the boxes and following him back to the designated nursery.

Once he was unburdened, she leaned against the door-frame. "Maybe you can leave that for now. Might be the last time we have the place to ourselves for, oh say, twenty years."

He laughed. "You could be right. Let's go."

They made it to the master bedroom and spent the next hour tangled in the sheets and each other's arms.

Afterward, he brought her the night-time pills, reminding her of the orderly, discharging medication at Windwood. But here, instead of a plastic cup, the pills sat in an ornate trinket dish decorated with red geraniums. The Royal Doulton ceramic had been her mother's. Roberta Durant used this to hold whatever jewelry she had worn on an evening out. Dani knew her mother would have hated seeing the current use for her fine bone china.

"Here we are," said Tate. He'd placed a small hand towel over his forearm and held the tray like a butler.

She giggled and accepted the glass from the tray. After she'd finished downing the last, largest pill, the one that stuck in her throat, she retrieved her nightie from her closet, tunneled into the soft cotton, and crawled beneath the coverlet.

"You coming to bed?"

"In a few minutes. The boxes. Got to get them out. Maybe start the crib assembly?"

"Don't stay up all night."

"Be up soon," he promised. "Light on or off?"

"Off."

He flicked the switch.

She sighed and settled into the large bed. He kissed her lips and collected her phone. "Yikes, eighteen percent. I'll set this on the charger in your closet."

Tate had a bedside charger, but she didn't like electronics in the bedroom. He'd even conceded the point to give up the large flatscreen he wanted in here for a small one on the bureau. As consolation, he now had a huge television in the living room and an even bigger one in the home theater, along with a complicated sound system and overlarge recliners.

"Thank you. I love you," she murmured.

"I love you, too. This is going to be so great."

In the dark she knew Tate instantly, his voice always familiar.

He smoothed the coverlet over her. From the corridor his silhouette filled the doorframe. Then the door closed, shutting out the light.

She appreciated all his help getting her in a routine here, keeping track of her medication schedule, making sure she ate, driving her to appointments. She didn't know what she'd do without him.

The tears slipped from between closed lashes as she huddled into the pillow, trying to deaden her sobs.

"I'm doing better. I'm getting better," she said. But the affirmation fell flat.

Tomorrow she would have what she wanted most in the world, a husband who adored her and a baby to love.

Why was she weeping?

Sunday morning, Dani woke before eight. Orienting herself to the room and then to her last memories. They burst into her mind like fireworks. Tate unboxing a crib and the living room overflowing with baby things.

"She's coming today!" Dani threw herself into a seated position and stretched.

It was Father's Day, she realized with a jolt. How perfect that Tate would become a father on that special day.

Then she thought of her own father, Matthew. She and

Shelby always made him something. Cards and golf covers, and key chains and ceramics. Simple things.

Thoughts of her sister, learning to use her hands again after the accident, made Dani want to curl in a ball. A graphic artist needed fine motor control. The therapy was a struggle. Some of the greatest battles took place in very small arenas.

"Willow. My baby," she whispered and slipped from the bedding, now bunched at her waist.

She glanced to the rumpled sheet and blanket on Tate's side of the mattress and frowned. Clearly, he'd gotten up before her again, unless he'd been up all night unboxing.

"Be in the moment," she whispered, swinging to a seat on the edge of the bed and stretching. Today she had much for which to be in the moment.

She slipped into a robe and headed to the landing, calling down to Tate.

"Tate?"

His familiar voice came from somewhere beyond her line of vision above the living room.

"Morning!"

"Everything all right?"

"Just great. You coming down?"

"Shower?"

"Sure. You've got plenty of time."

Dani left the railing and returned to the bedroom, dropped the robe on the bed, and headed to the bathroom where she showered and dressed with care, aiming for a look that said PTA president. Competent mom.

Who was bringing the baby? She hadn't even asked.

The phone rang as she slipped into designer flats, interrupting her train of thought. The familiar song alerted her that it was her twin.

"Dani, is she there yet?"

"Not yet."

"Nuts. Hey, I was wondering, when did you buy that house?" asked Shelby.

"The offer was accepted in September, but we didn't close until November, a month before..."

"Your last visit."

"Right."

Shelby never said, "Before the accident" or "Before you went to the psychiatric hospital." It was kind of her, though they both knew what sent Dani there. Guilt. Shame. Horror at hurting the one person she loved most in the world, her twin.

The house had been the first major expenditure from the trust since the purchase of their first home. Or was it the first since financing Tate's previous campaign? And, of course, there had been the wedding. She smiled at the memories of their special day.

"Yes. A little over seven months ago, I think." She ran the dates. She and Tate did a final walkthrough together before the closing. Then they'd visited the real estate attorney to sign the paperwork. They'd been packing and moving, Dani doing most of that, as Tate went to work. In early December they'd hired a contractor and designer. Such a busy time, with the holiday gatherings, gift shopping, and preparing for the movers. So how had she found the time to visit Shelby?

And Shelby had been coming for Christmas. It made no sense.

Dani shook her head.

After the accident, both she and Shelby spent days in ICU. But only her sister needed assistance breathing. After seeing her twin, with all the tubes and the respirator, something broke inside her. She remembered signing something. A medical order? Healthcare proxy, maybe a will? They'd said they needed her signature. But after that, the curtain had fallen, and it was all gray fog and hazy memories. Then Windwood and Dr. Allen.

Shelby's voice shook her back from her reminiscence.

"What's the value now? Housing prices have skyrocketed."

"Oh, I don't pay attention to that. It's our home, not an investment."

"Are you growing into it, at least?"

"Honestly," said Dani, "it still feels like someone else's house. And I keep smelling gardenia. Isn't that weird?"

"Cleaning person using air freshener?"

"Maybe." Did they have a cleaning person? Dani would have to ask Tate. She only knew there had been no one here since her return.

"How about that potpourri stuff or scented candles?"

"I don't have any of that."

"So where is it coming from?" asked Shelby.

"I don't know. It doesn't smell like air freshener. It smells like expensive perfume."

"How could that be?" asked Shelby.

"It can't."

"Is someone else in your house?"

"Oh, don't say that!"

"Okay. Geesh, it was a joke."

Dani exhaled, then took a deep calming breath and said, "There's no one else in the house. Tate suggested that one of my medications could be affecting my sense of smell."

"Maybe. Check the house price, okay? It's worth knowing."

Dani smiled. Her sister, even though she had a creative career, had always been more practical than her. "Sure. I'll take a look now."

She flipped the call to speaker and diminished the call. She had three alerts.

"That's funny."

"What?"

"Three alerts on the baby monitor. I forgot I left it set up on the mantel last night. One at 10:51 last night. Another at 11:08 last night and the last at 6:19 this morning."

"Do you have a video doorbell?"

"Yes. But I'm not sure how to access it. Tate handles that stuff."

"Tap the monitor alert."

She did and found three recordings.

The first was a man, dressed in Tate's clothing, and strolling with Tate's gait, moving through the living room to the kitchen. The next was the same man entering from the kitchen and walking to the foyer and out the front door. The third was the man returning in daylight, in the door, through the foyer, living room, and disappearing toward the kitchen.

"This doesn't make any sense."

"What?"

She described the videos to Shelby.

"Something is wrong with your monitor. Or he was gone overnight."

Dani looked at the bed; his side looked slept in, the pillow indented, the covers rumpled. But they'd made love.

Of course, he'd slept there. She was more disturbed at the realization that the medication made her sleep so soundly, she never awakened with his coming and going.

She trusted Tate completely, and with good reason. Their marriage was forged in faith. She'd never given him cause to doubt her love and neither had he. If he had left the house overnight, it would have been for a good reason.

"You going to ask him about it?"

"There's no need."

"Curiosity is reason enough."

"I've gotta go."

"Okay. Love you, little sister."

"Love you more, big sister," said Dani, completing her part of their usual farewell.

Shelby disconnected the call.

Downstairs, she passed neatly stacked piles of baby gear and the monitor base on the hearth. Her phone vibrated, sending her another alert.

Her, she realized, captured on video.

She found a blond man sitting at the kitchen counter drinking coffee. He wore the clothing of the male she'd seen enter the house on the baby monitor. Dani stopped and placed one foot behind her, preparing to run. Her skin tingled with apprehension. She recognized the panic attack encroaching, spreading outward from her pounding heart to her numb fingers.

"Tate?"

"Good morning, sunshine."

Tate's voice. Tate's hair. Tate's elegant hands and the dusting of blond hair on his knuckles.

"Sleep well?" he asked.

"Like the dead. I didn't even hear you come up last night."

"Don't worry about it. I'm just glad to have you home." He retrieved a whisk from a drawer and pulled the eggs from the refrigerator. "I'm making raisin toast and scrambled eggs. Coffee's ready."

She accepted his offered hand and allowed him to drag her forward for a kiss.

"Big day today," he said.

In reply, she made a humming sound in her throat and pulled back.

He let her go and she settled on the stool beside him as he took another sip of coffee.

"Something is wrong with the monitor," she said.

He lowered the mug. "What monitor?"

"The baby monitor. I plugged it in last night to charge. It was on the hearth."

"What's wrong with it?"

She explained about the alerts and the video missing his return through the living room.

Tate looked confused.

He glanced in the direction of the living room, then unplugged the toaster, causing his uncooked bread to pop. Next, he unplugged the high-end barista coffeemaker.

"I blew a fuse last night. Didn't realize until a few minutes ago."

"That shut off the monitor?" she asked.

He shrugged. "Must have. Didn't figure it out until after my walk this morning. Came in. Tried the toaster." He gestured with his hands, making an accompanying sound indicating it hadn't worked. "Moved it there," he pointed to the empty spot on the counter beside the wine refrigerator. "Worked fine... so, fuse."

"You reset the fuse?"

"After the GFI reset failed. Yes. Then I moved the toaster back."

"Oh, good. I thought the monitor was broken."

"Can I see?"

She handed over her phone and he checked the videos.

"Makes sense. I put the crib together last night. Got hungry and nuked a burrito. Went out to look at the moon while it cooked. When I came in, it was ready but, you know, just barely hot."

"Because it shut off."

He nodded. "Guess so."

Dani realized then that she knew very little about what he did after her medication knocked her out. The anxiety tripped, making her palms damp. She wiped them on her skirt.

"You go out after I'm in bed?"

"Sometimes. I'm not leaving the neighborhood, Dani. I'm always close by. Call me if you don't see me. I might just be out walking. I do that quite a lot in the early morning. Before the afternoon storms roll in. Helps me relax."

There were thunderstorms nearly every afternoon in summer. Some hit them, some missed.

"Or I fish. Toss out my line from the seawall or dock at sunset. When it's cooler, I lie in the hammock and stargaze. You know, when the bugs aren't so bad."

"Hmm. Sounds nice."

"But last night I was busy putting that together." He motioned to the crib beside the dining room table, constructed with the mattress in place and still wrapped in plastic.

"Ah." Excitement bubbled at just the sight of his efforts.

"Didn't notice my burrito wasn't very hot. And I never heard the microwave beep."

"Because you were outside," she said, furnishing the reason.

"And if the fuse tripped before it finished, it likely never beeped. Only figured it out when I tried to make toast this morning."

She glanced toward the clock.

He nodded. "I reset the clock, too."

"Oh, good. I'm sorry about the monitor. I'll move it."

"Yeah. Maybe I'll move the coffeemaker, too."

"I told Shelby it was something like that."

He cocked his head, his eyes alert.

"She called again?"

Dani nodded.

"Everything okay?"

"She just wanted to know if our baby had arrived yet." She gave him a huge grin, which he returned.

Tate set aside the bowl and hugged her, lifting her right off the ground.

"This is the happiest day of my life," he said, looking into her eyes.

The gladness wrapped around her heart and squeezed the air from her lungs, the pearl of joy so warm and pure, and so long absent, she wished she could tuck it in a box and keep it with her always.

EIGHT

She turned from the dining room window and was startled to see a man beside her. She glanced at his attire, light gray slacks and a yellow button-up shirt with sleeves rolled at the forearm. His approach had been totally silent.

"They're on their way," he said, in Tate's voice, holding his phone and smiling broadly. "I just buzzed them in."

That meant they were clearing the security gate at the main entrance of the community.

Dani bounced with excitement and then brushed the nonexistent wrinkles from her skirt.

"How do I look?"

He laughed. "Like a nervous mother."

She returned his smile. "Exactly."

"They're not coming to execute a search warrant, Dani. It's just an attorney with the paperwork and the neonatal nurse."

"Are we ready for this?" Dani asked, concern lifting her brows.

"Totally." He looped an arm around her. "Let's go meet our daughter."

Tate guided her to the foyer. From the window beside the

wide double doors, she could see two vehicles. One, a white minivan, with a male driver. The other was a gray sedan. Since the accident, she'd noticed that she could only reliably identify the class of vehicle, having lost the nuances between an Audi and a Porsche. The minivan's door slid open and thumped.

Dani stood on her toes to catch the first glimpse of their daughter.

From the gray vehicle came a man dressed in a tan suit, blue shirt, and navy-blue tie. He carried the sort of extra-long brief-cases with which she was familiar. This must be the attorney handling the adoption paperwork. His shoes were brown, his sunglasses gold-rimmed, and his hair made a tight fringe around his bowling ball of a head. The dark lenses obscured much of his features, but he looked disgruntled as he spoke to the driver of the minivan.

Rounding the front bumper of the minivan came a woman with a cloth diaper bag looped over her shoulder. She carried a bassinet in one hand as easily as she might carry a tote bag. Inside was an impossibly small bundle, wrapped up so tight that it looked like a Russian nesting doll.

Too tiny to be a human being, to be their daughter.

Dani threw open the door so hard that Tate had to catch it before it banged into the stopper.

The nurse paused at the bottom step and smiled up at them, her face a geometric puzzle impossible to construct into a recognizable person. Just two amber-colored eyes, light brown skin, and dark hair styled in a neat updo wrapped in a turquoise scarf.

Tears coursed down Dani's cheeks. She wiped them away and then reached for the baby.

The nurse settled the infant into Dani's arms and then drew beside her, cooing her words to mother and child.

"This one slept all the way here. She's a good sleeper."

Dani stared at the tiny face. This face she did not need to

memorize because it would change daily, growing, shifting from newborn to infant to toddler to child. And she'd be there every day.

The feathery lashes touched the baby's pink cheeks and her mouth worked, sucking even as she slept. She watched the rosebud lips purse, a soft coral pink. Dani's heart seemed to be swelling in her chest, aching as the love there grew into every corner.

Was this what it was like—love at first sight?

Dani cradled the baby's head and pushed back the soft flannel blanket to discover dark brown hair and lush curls.

"So much hair!" Dani laughed, a sound of pure delight.

The nurse chuckled. "Sometimes they're born like that. Sometimes with no hair at all."

Dani moved into the living room, seeming to float there with Willow in her arms. She sat in the lounge chair, rested her daughter on the huge square ottoman, and began removing the swaddling.

The nurse walked straight up to her, her spongy white shoes silent on the marble tile. There she folded to sit on the floor beside the ottoman.

"They like to be wrapped up," said the nurse.

"I want to see her."

"Of course."

Behind them, Dani was aware of male voices and the pair moving to the dining room. The large briefcase went up onto the clear varnish of the massive oak dining table.

The attorney sweated in the light of the crystal chandelier, his face florid and shining as he withdrew a packet of papers, fixed on the top edge, as legal documents often were. Then she turned back to the woman now kneeling on the carpet beside the ottoman, leaning forward to help untuck the soft peach-colored blanket swaddling her baby.

Dani smiled as her heart opened wide and then melted into

a puddle. This was a new kind of love. She understood now. All her maternal instincts wove a web around her, drawing tight, building the armor necessary to protect this little one with every ounce of her being.

"Would you like to help me change her diaper?" asked the woman.

"Yes!" she said. The exhilaration buzzed through her, making her face tingle.

The nurse laughed at her excitement over the mundane task.

Dani dropped to the opposite side of the ottoman. She glanced back to see Tate, wondering why he was there with the paperwork instead of here with their precious little baby.

Together, she and the nurse removed the impossibly tiny damp diaper and Dani replaced it with a new one. At this, the baby roused enough to pinch her eyes shut tight, making her brow wrinkle as she struggled against this interruption to her sleep. The expressiveness of that tiny face made Dani suck in air in delight.

"How much does she weigh?" she asked.

"This one is a bitty thing. She's only six pounds, three ounces."

This made Dani again speculate about Willow's birth mother, wondering if she was right this minute sitting in a jail cell, regretting her decision. Then she shook her head, quashing the troubling musings.

The nurse continued. "But that will change day by day. Oh," she said, and returned to the bag she carried. "This is her bottle. I brought two extras that should go in the fridge. And some other items that you'll need. Diapers, bibs, lotion, and a couple onesies." She handed over the bag. "There you are." She glanced about the room at the stacks of infant items. "Though, looks like you already got everything you need." Her laugh was musical. "You pick out a college yet?"

Dani joined in the joke. "Well, the application isn't finished yet. But probably Stetson or FSU."

"Good choices."

The woman then showed her how to swaddle Willow. The baby's feet, now unencumbered, kicked like a tiny frog swimming across an invisible pond.

The nurse chuckled. "Those chubby legs are so adorable, I could eat her up."

Dani resisted the urge to press her nose to Willow's tiny body to breathe in the scent of her warm, fragrant skin. Nothing smelled quite so good as a clean baby.

They both paused to look at their handiwork.

"They feel better bundled up at first. Also keeps them from scratching their face with their nails."

Dani tucked in the corner of the blanket as instructed.

"That's fine. You're a natural."

"I feel so excited, but also a little sick."

"Completely normal. There's a lot to worry about. But maybe start with knowing this little gal is healthy and perfect. And the newborns aren't too much to handle. You'll get the hang of her schedule."

Willow yawned.

"See? We woke her up. She needs another hour or so. That will give you time to get her settled. You have a crib?"

Dani nodded.

"For now, she'll be best sleeping in her bassinet."

"I have one." Dani rushed to retrieve the item.

The nurse accepted it and laid Willow inside, clipping the safety strap about her and adjusting the length.

"She should sleep in the same room as you are in, but not in your bed. Let's go look at the crib." They headed to the dining room where the crib sat, the nurse carrying the baby in the bassinet with one arm looped through the handle as if she held a handbag.

"We didn't have time to get it to the nursery yet," said Dani.

"This is fine." The nurse gave it a once-over and set the bassinet on the mattress. "She can go just like this for now."

Then she easily lowered and raised the side rail.

The men paused their business to watch.

"If you want her in the crib, rest her on her back when sleeping. That's very important. The mattress should be flat and no stuffed animals inside for now. They're a smothering hazard."

Dani snatched up the pink teddy bear and set it on the buffet.

"Look, she's already sleeping again."

"Willow," Dani said. "We are calling her Willow."

"Pretty name. If you'll show me to the kitchen, I'll show you how to heat her formula."

Dani hesitated, reluctant to leave Willow even for a moment, but then she led the way and listened as the woman went over feeding, bathing, and how to prepare the bottles in the kitchen.

"They say to heat it, but really just to the temperature of your body. It should never feel warmer than you are."

All the while Willow slept, Dani felt more anxious. The responsibility now pressed down, squeezing out the elation.

What prevailed was the love. She loved this girl already and was so grateful to Tate for helping her become a mother.

"I don't know if you've got family up north, but doctors don't recommend you travel until the baby is at least a month old. And now with the pandemic, you might want to be more careful. Masks on visitors who aren't vaccinated. You know?"

Tate had told her that the CDC said masks were unnecessary for the vaccinated, but her baby was too young yet for the shot. She'd need to be careful. Another stone of worry settled with the others, making enough to build a wall.

They headed back to the dining room where Tate had some

paperwork for her to sign. Before settling at the table, she checked the baby, who lay sleeping peacefully.

Dani sat where Tate indicated. The other man passed her papers as he narrated what she was signing.

"This is your consent for a non-kinship adoption."

Dani signed.

"This is a petition for adoption, a formal request to the courts to grant you parental rights. I'll notify you of the hearing time and date."

"When will that be?"

"Hard to say. The pandemic has backlogged nonessential hearings." He retrieved another form. "You'll be able to obtain a birth certificate after the finalization. After which, you may claim the infant as your issue."

He collected the forms and began tucking them away. Then he shook Tate's hand. The woman gave Willow's cheek a gentle brush, speaking in a low whisper.

"You are one very lucky little girl." Then she turned to Dani. "Good luck, Mama. You have a blessed day."

Tate showed them out. She could see him speaking to the pair on the step, handing over something to the man with the fringe of hair and then to the woman. Another handshake and off they went, down the formal stairs and back to the minivan and sedan.

Dani turned her attention to the sleeping baby. Was there anything more beautiful than this?

Her heart squeezed as the joy overwhelmed the worry. She thought that only the ceiling kept her from floating away.

Dani wished Shelby would buy a smartphone so she could have a video call and show her this miracle breathing softly in her little bassinet.

Her phone rang, and she jumped, thinking the song she'd programmed to Shelby impossibly loud. But Willow continued sleeping peacefully.

"I was just thinking about you," said Dani as she picked up the call.

"Is she there?" The excitement in her sister's voice only increased Dani's happiness.

"Yes."

"Tell me everything!"

Dani jabbered like a magpie, telling her sister about Willow's arrival. Her excitement made her hands shake and she found herself pacing from the entrance to the dining room, her free hand pressed to her forehead. When she got to the part about the paperwork, Shelby interrupted.

"What does that mean, non-kinship adoption?" she asked.

"I think it just means we're not a blood relative of our baby."

"Did Tate sign?"

"He already did the paperwork." They'd been there at the table without her.

"Was his name on the form?"

Dani couldn't remember.

Shelby pressed on. "And why not just say adoptive? Neither one of you is related to the baby."

"It doesn't matter. What matters is that she's here."

"What does your *issue* mean?" asked Shelby.

"Legal term for a child, I think." Shelby was being a bit of a bummer.

"But shouldn't you know what it is you are signing?"

"I do know. It's the preliminary paperwork to legally adopt Willow."

"I suppose."

"Oh, Shelby, you should see her. Ten tiny fingers. She's pink and her skin is soft as a peach."

"What color hair?"

"Dark. A deep brown with a curl."

"Amazing. I can't wait to see her. Can Tate bring you here?"

"The nurse said we have to wait a month, and after that,

Tate will be back to work. And he's got the campaign and the backlog of cases because of the court shutdown."

"Shoot."

"I'm sorry."

"I understand." Shelby did not ask Dani to drive to her and Dani was grateful for that.

"Anything on the van?" asked Dani.

"It's on order. Everything is delayed now, plus this is custom, so an even longer delay. I think I'll be lucky to have it by Christmas."

Willow would be six months old. How different would she look?

"That's disappointing."

"It is, but I have some other news."

"What?"

"I put an offer in on a house here. It's wheelchair ready, wide roll-in shower. Lower cabinets that I can get my chair under. I can reach the refrigerator, and the top kitchen shelves lower, like attic stairs, so I can get to everything."

"That's amazing!"

"I'm determined to get it. I put in a bid above asking."

"I'll have my fingers crossed."

"Toes too."

"Absolutely. But, Shelby, couldn't you find a place closer to me? You're an aunt now."

"Oh my gosh! I am. That's amazing."

Dani heard a snuffling sound.

"Are you crying?" Dani realized that she was, too.

"A little. But as to the house, all my doctors are here in Jacksonville, and I still need rehab three times a week. But soon I can leave the rehab center. When I can drive, I can get myself to you. Until then, I'm stuck with the city transport's special paratransit service."

"I think we have that here."

"And I need more surgeries."

Now Dani was crying for other reasons. This was her fault.

"I'm so sorry, Shelby."

She flicked her attention to a man who stood arms akimbo, his expression grim. He wore Tate's clothing, gray slacks, yellow shirt. His voice confirmed her assumption. This was Tate.

"Who is that?" he asked.

She muted the phone. "Shelby."

"Why are you crying?"

Dani wiped at her eyes. "It's nothing. She needs more surgery."

It seemed whenever something great happened for Dani, something terrible happened for Shelby.

A glance at the phone showed the lock screen.

"She hung up."

Tate stared at her phone. "I'm sorry about her surgeries. Everything else all right?"

"Oh, she's put in an offer on a house."

"A house? That's... a surprise. In Jacksonville?"

Dani made an unhappy sound of confirmation in her throat.

Tate looked toward the crib. "Sleeping?"

Dani nodded, coming to stand beside him. He looped an arm about her waist and pulled her close. They stood there for a long time, staring at their baby. Finally, Tate broke the silence.

"You are going to be such a fantastic mother."

Then he turned her in his arms and kissed her.

She closed her eyes as their lips brushed, then he pressed his firmly to her mouth. He dragged her closer, and she wrapped her arms about him as the desire and joy sparked. She drew back. He let her go, staring down at her with a genuine smile.

"You look happy," he said.

"I'm over the moon. I can't believe this is real."

"It's what you always wanted. Big house, full of kids."

"Well, big house, but a very tiny baby."

"We'll adopt more. As many as you like."

She hugged him, pressing her ear to his chest, and listened to the steady thump of his heartbeat.

"I don't know how you made this happen, but I'm so grateful." The tears were running down her face again.

He drew her back. "Hey, now." He stooped to come to eye level, his hands on her shoulders. "You're my wife. Making you happy is my job."

Dani stared at Willow. "She's perfect. Isn't she?"

"Everything is perfect now. Except I'm starving. Can I fix you some lunch before I head to the store?"

"You're going out?"

"I don't think three diapers will last long."

"We have a huge bag of them upstairs."

"Yeah, the wrong size. She needs ones for a newborn. But now that I know the size, I can pick some up."

She turned in a circle. With all this stuff, they still needed more?

"Lunch? Or would you like to eat later on?"

"I'll make you something." She hesitated, staring at Willow. "Should I move her to the kitchen or let her sleep there?"

"Either."

She moved the baby monitor to the dining room but Tate gathered it up.

"We can hear Willow from the kitchen without this," he said, taking the device with him.

She nodded and they headed to the kitchen where she made them turkey sandwiches, adding chips and a pickle slice to each plate, as Tate downloaded the monitor app and fixed his attention between his phone and the device.

"Okay," he said. "I've erased the old recordings, downloaded the app to my phone, and set it so we both get alerts on our phones. Everything from now on will be of our baby!"

She set the plate before him. He glanced up.

"I got the night setting figured." He fiddled with his phone. "Tons of settings. This even plays music, takes photos. I've got it adjusted so we'll get alerts now on sound, too. Not just movement. Let me know if that gets to be too much." He took a bite of the sandwich and then pointed at the PDF open on his phone. "Says we should mount it well away from the crib but up on the wall, gives us an aerial view." He glanced up. "Do you want me to attach the camera over the crib in the nursery or in our bedroom over the bassinet frame?"

"In the nursery, I think. I'll be with her in our bedroom. There's nothing wrong with my hearing, at least."

He took another bite and then put the monitor aside. "I'll set it up when I get home. And that light thing, the one that plays music. One of my paralegals said she sets it so that just a tap gives her enough light to see and feed the baby. You should try it out while I'm gone."

She never thought she'd be eager to fiddle with a night-light, but everything about this day was exciting.

He rolled his shoulders, looking weary.

"Did you get any sleep last night?" she asked.

"Few hours. I've never needed more than about four a night."

She laughed. "That might come in handy over the next year or so."

He cleared his plate, and then kissed her forehead.

Tate glanced at her untouched meal. "You have to eat your lunch, Dani. The doctor said so."

"I will."

"Okay. I'll see my two best girls soon." He checked his smartphone. "Okay, diapers, milk, and drugstore for your medication. Anything else?"

"Just be careful."

"Always am."

Yes, he was a careful driver and Dani was not. The evidence of that filled most of her waking hours and more than a few nightmares.

Dani lifted the dish containing her midday medication and swallowed each one. Then she forced herself to eat. She now had another reason to stay healthy.

Tate headed out the door, leaving her alone for the first time with their baby.

NINE

Shelby called again just after Dani had bundled the infant in a soft terry blanket following Willow's bath. With her baby girl, she was contented.

"Dani! How is my favorite niece?" Shelby asked.

"Perfect. You should see her. She's amazing. Did you get the video?"

"And the photos. Yes. Tell me everything!"

"We just had a bath."

"I'll bet she smells amazing."

"She does. All the time. I wish I could bottle that scent. We'd make millions."

"We already have millions," said Shelby, deadpan.

Dani laughed. "With the cost of college, I'll need that."

"Don't fill out the application just yet. She may want to go somewhere besides FSU."

"Hey, she's going to Stetson."

"Perish the thought."

They both laughed at that.

"Any more word on the house or is it too soon?" asked Dani.

"Yes. That's why I'm calling. They accepted the offer! Waived inspection, cash."

"Is that wise?"

"It's a hot market. Everyone working remotely and scrambling for bigger homes."

Dani recalled Tate saying the same. The pandemic had forced office drones to work from home. Sounded lovely, really.

"I also offered 50K over asking."

"No wonder they took it. Are you worried about waiving the inspection?"

"I'm not."

"Well, congratulations!"

"Thanks. Hey, prices are skyrocketing. Have you checked on the value of your home yet?"

"Not since before—" She'd almost said before the accident but stopped herself.

Shelby was forgiving of both the omission and that Dani had failed to do as she'd asked in an earlier call. "Check it."

"Yes, I will." She didn't really know why her sister wanted her to, but she'd humor her.

"Let me give you my new address. It's near the hospital rehab center on Memorial Boulevard, Jacksonville. The street address is 12, 22, 15," said Shelby and then went silent.

Dani wrote the numbers of the address in the condensation of the bathroom mirror then repeated it back. "Memorial Boulevard, 1, triple 2, 1 5. Got it."

"No. It's 12, 22, 15," Shelby repeated.

Dani added a dash between the numbers in the appropriate places. City addresses could be complicated.

12-22-15

Dani waited, watching the water droplets run from the numbers she'd written and then took up the conversation.

"All right, I got it. Closing date?"

"Not yet. Hey, check the value of your place. Don't forget."

"Will do."

"Love you, little sister."

"Love you more, big sister," said Dani.

Shelby disconnected the call.

Dani rocked, uneasy. The thought of returning to Jacksonville, where everything had changed for them, made her palms sweat and the skin stipple on her arms.

She was suddenly glad that the baby couldn't travel yet. It gave her an excuse to cover the fact that she was a coward.

Dani added Shelby's new address to her phone contacts and realized she'd need to settle on a housewarming gift for when she moved in.

Willow was still fast asleep, and Dani had time to check the house value.

It only took a minute to look it up on one of the real estate sites. She scanned the photos of the staged rooms. The same ones that had attracted Tate to this place, noticing now how the lens made the rooms larger than actual size and the grass was never that green except in the rainy season. Colorized, she decided. Every television in the place had the same image, one of a gorgeous sunset as if to remind buyers that beach access went along with the property here.

She glanced at the details. *Off market.*

"That's for sure."

But then she frowned and cocked her head. "Well, that's wrong."

It said the house was seven years old, but it was a new build when they'd purchased it. The value was also a shock. They'd bought at 1.2 and the estimate was 1.8 million.

"Can that be right?"

Shelby said it was a hot market, but over a half-million-dollar increase in under a year?

She lifted her phone and dialed Shelby. Her sister picked up immediately.

"Hey, Dani-o. What's up?"

"I looked it up."

"What?"

"The house value. You just asked me to."

"Oh, yeah."

"Well, it's gone up over a half a million dollars."

"That's great."

"No, it isn't. Higher value means more property taxes, and how could it do that in less than a year?"

"You type in the wrong address?"

Dani glanced at the screen on her laptop. "No. I did it right. I mean, I heard Tate say the pandemic made the housing market go crazy, but wow! And here's the weirder part. It says the house is seven years old."

"So?"

"Unless they were lying about the new build, it's only a year old."

"Dani, those sites get things wrong all the time. Remember, they listed Mom and Dad's place for sale when it was off market?"

"I don't remember that."

"Well, they aren't updated, they get things wrong."

"Should I write them?"

"Are you selling?"

"No. Of course not."

"Then forget about it. Say how's the baby?"

Shelby didn't call her *my favorite niece* this time. And Dani had just told her how the baby was. Dani frowned, but then launched into details of Willow's first bath and first poo and first change of clothing.

"That all seems completely normal."

"Yes. Normal."

Shelby no longer sounded excited and that seemed odd.

"Did I catch you at a bad time?"

"I'm at rehab."

"Oh, I'm sorry. I'll speak to you soon."

"Okay. Love you. Bye." Shelby disconnected.

Dani frowned as she set aside the phone. Then she closed the laptop. She had a baby to rock and love and hold. She'd let Tate worry about property values and listing details. After all, he was the attorney.

Dani headed back to the kitchen with the bassinet in her hand. She had taken to carrying Willow everywhere, even the bathroom. Willow was not awake often, but when she was, her dark blue eyes were wide as if she was trying hard to focus on the face before her.

Willow woke as her carrier came to rest on the kitchen island and she began to cry.

"Are you hungry, peanut?"

Dani played with the rattle and Willow gurgled and blew a bubble.

"Who's a smart little girl? Willow! That's who. I'm your mama."

As the afternoon stretched, Dani cared for her daughter and wondered what was keeping Tate. They should be together as a family. She ordered takeout from the Peruvian steakhouse that he loved and pondered calling to check on him.

She held Willow in her arms and watched out the window for his return. Instead, she saw an unfamiliar woman walking in the street beyond the hedgerow in front of their place. The stranger paused to stare at the house.

Too early for the food delivery, and they'd have a car, anyway; the woman didn't carry a package or a clipboard, so she eliminated any kind of delivery person from the list of possibilities. A neighbor, maybe?

Then the individual stepped through the hedgerow onto the lawn just beyond the garage, barely in view. That was odd.

She and Tate had a lawn service, bug service, and pool service. She didn't know any of them but thought they all wore some sort of uniform. Might she be the cleaner for the pool?

No. Dani dismissed that notion. The pool company would come in a truck and have chemicals and things.

And as for a neighbor, a normal member of the community would never intrude on her private property this way.

The clothing she wore did not fit the neighborhood, either. No expensive walking shoes, colorful athletic attire, or smart, costly separates for strolling with the dog. This person wore shredded, cutoff jeans smeared with dirt. Her stained white T-shirt had a stretched-out collar, and her feet were bare. Everything about her was wrong.

Her attire and odd behavior put Dani on guard. The woman had moved around the back of the garage and was now out of sight. If she were walking around the house, she'd pass the family room and the former office they'd reserved for Shelby's guest room and then, behind the house, the pool cage and lanai.

Dani stopped bouncing the sleeping infant and headed through the kitchen to the family room beyond.

The woman was clearly visible through the wall of windows from Dani's crafting area. She stooped out of sight and Dani inched forward for a better look.

The intruder popped back up, holding one of the solar landscaping lights like a club. She quickly zeroed in on Dani, staring right at her.

Dani gasped and grabbed for the blinds, tugging them closed.

She stood there, panting as if she'd been running, except her breathing was more desperate.

What the hell is she doing?

She peered through the blinds.

The woman was now unsettlingly close to the window where Dani held Willow. She raised the light and threw it at the glass.

The thump caused Dani to stumble back and into one of the chairs. With Willow safe in her arms, her fall was awkward. Recovering, she moved to the far side of the room, her heart hammering in her chest.

"She's crazy," she murmured.

Was the door from the pool to the bathroom locked?

Clutching Willow to her chest, Dani ran down the hall, past the office, and into the guest bathroom as the bell on the door in the pool cage jangled.

She's inside.

Dani reached the exterior door, checking the deadbolt was engaged, just as the woman's face appeared. She had wild, dark hair and strange pale eyes, which were an unnatural icy silver. Her pupils were huge.

Dani gave a little shriek.

She'd seen eyes dilated like that before, in the psychiatric facility with the inpatients on antipsychotics. Thorazine did that, and other drugs.

She needed to call the police. She backed away, holding Willow, afraid to move and trying not to cry.

"Who are you?" she shouted through the locked door.

In answer the woman struck the sidelight with an open hand. Dani leapt back as the woman ducked away.

But silent seconds stretched.

"Where is she?"

Dani crept forward, peering through the window, cradling Willow's soft, tiny head to her shoulder.

The stranger stood on the pool deck, glaring in at them, fists balled at her sides. She moved forward, crossing out of bright sunlight and into the shadow beneath the overhang of the lanai beneath their balcony.

Dani backed up as the intruder advanced past the outdoor kitchen and the bar, past the tastefully arranged grouping of furniture. Then she turned toward Dani and rushed them again.

She lifted her fists and pounded on the glass. The vibration sent Dani into action. She yelped and ran to the kitchen, snatching up her phone and opening it with her free hand. The phone slipped to the counter as the pounding came again.

She hit the phone app and Tate's number appeared first in her favorites and she tapped his listing, placing the call. He answered on the first ring.

"Almost home," he said.

"Tate! There's a woman pounding on the windows."

"What?"

"Outside on the pool deck. She's pounding."

The sound came again.

"Did you hear that?"

"I'll be there in two minutes. Where are you?"

"Kitchen."

"Lock yourself in the pantry with the baby."

"I'm calling the police."

"Yes. And get to the pantry."

She adjusted her hold on Willow and snatched up the phone, but the device slipped from her hand. It fell to the tile with a sickening crack. Dani crouched and retrieved her phone, gasping at noting the fractured glass and screen that was now a series of blue vertical lines.

"Oh no," she whispered.

The hammering jarred her to action, and she ran, phone in one hand and Willow in the other. The pounding continued, but this time she also heard tires squealing.

TEN

"Dani!"

That was Tate's voice.

"In here!" she called from behind the pantry door, which she'd discovered only locked from the outside.

Footsteps pounded closer. The door flew open. She screamed, sheltering Willow with her arms as she hunched around the baby.

"It's me, Dani. Stay here."

He disappeared, and she listened, hearing the pool sliders rumble in their tracks.

"Don't go out there!" she called.

She stared down at Willow, who was now awake and regarding Dani with big blue eyes. This whole time she hadn't cried.

"It's fine, precious. You're safe."

Finally, Tate returned. "I walked the property—the private patio, upstairs balcony, and dock. There's no one."

"Check the security recordings."

"Yes, I will. But you can come out now."

"I broke my phone," she said, handing it to Tate.

He frowned and fiddled with the device, shaking his head. "We'll let the battery drain and see if it will boot up again."

He offered her a hand and she shifted Willow to her shoulder before accepting it, standing as the doorbell rang. Dani gave a yip of fear and cowered against the shelving.

"Wait here."

She did and heard the door open and the murmur of voices. Finally, the door shut again.

Tate returned, still in his gray slacks and yellow dress shirt, and he carried a large paper bag.

"You ordered in?"

Dani released her death grip on the shelving and nodded. Then she pressed her free hand flat to her chest as if that could slow her racing heart.

"Yes. I did that."

"All right, come out. Let me check the security system and you can set this up. I'll get the stuff from the car." He handed over the bag.

The first thing she set up was Willow, now crying as Dani warmed her bottle. She fed her as Tate checked the security system. He called to her from the foyer.

"Police are here."

Then the door shut, and he was gone. From the kitchen she watched two officers walk the property with Tate. They were in the front of the dining room window and then gone. They appeared again at the sliders, then the three of them headed back out of the pool cage.

A few moments later, Willow fussed, and Dani lifted her to her shoulder, rubbing her tiny back. What emerged was a bit more than a burp. She wiped her daughter's face and rocked her in her arms.

"We need to check that diaper."

She carried Willow to the nursery and set the baby on the newly erected changing table. There, she removed the dirty diaper as the front door chime sounded. She couldn't help it; her heart began pounding again.

"Dani?" That was Tate's voice. "The police want to speak to you."

Tate said he'd explained to the police about her condition and that she was useless for identifying the trespasser beyond what she was wearing. Despite that, she mentioned the dark hair and eyes that were silver as a mirror.

She stood in the foyer, holding the baby carrier, and giving her statement of what had happened.

"We'll check the neighborhood for anyone matching the description before leaving your gated community," said the female officer.

"Can you add a patrol? You know, drive by?" Dani asked.

"Unfortunately, no," said the male officer, who had a mole nearly central on his forehead. "These roads are private. Your homeowners' association allows us only to answer criminal calls, like intruders and burglary."

She recalled Tate saying that the police couldn't give so much as a traffic ticket to anyone here within the gates of their private community. At the time, that had seemed a perk, but with a child to protect and an intruder in their midst, that now seemed all downside to Dani.

And did that mean the intruder had come from inside their gates?

After they had gone, she and Tate had their meal, reheated via the microwave.

"Did you recognize her from the video recordings?" she asked.

"No." He glanced away.

"How did she get in past the security gate? They should

have her name and license number. And they'd have the name of the person she was visiting. Unless..." Dani gnawed on her thumbnail. "Unless she lives here." Dani said it casually, but the implications quickly prickled down her spine.

A gated community locked people out, but also locked people in.

Tate sopped up the last of the gravy on the crusty Italian bread, then paused, meeting her gaze.

Outside, thunder rumbled.

She spoke again, breathless now, feeling sick. "What if you and the police hadn't arrived in time? Or if she got in?"

"Dani, no one is going to break in. We have the security system, remember. Exterior and interior cameras, entry sensors on every window. Glass-break monitors and the panic button in the bedroom. You're safe, Dani."

"She tried to break the glass."

"We have hurricane-resistant windows. They can hold back a Category 5, including flying debris. No one is breaking in."

"If they're unbreakable," she asked, "why have glass-break sensors?"

He chuckled. "In case they break, I suppose. But I've seen them hit with a sledgehammer, so they don't break often."

Tate rested his free hand over the one fidgeting with her fork, stilling her.

She wanted to follow up and ask, if the neighborhood was so safe, why did they need entry sensors and panic alarms?

Instead, she asked, "But what if she lives here, right inside the walls of our neighborhood?"

"Dani." His voice held that tired note of aggravation. "You're safe. The baby is safe. Please. Eat something."

She glanced at the plate, surprised to see her portion nearly untouched. Hadn't she been eating all along?

His phone chimed. He glanced down, in the habit of keeping the device beside him during meals.

"Homeowners' association," he said, rising. "I have to file a report." He headed for his office to take the call, but on the way, she saw him glance toward the driveway and she followed the direction of his attention, seeing nothing.

Here in the private neighborhood, there were no street-lights. The homeowners' association required a light on each mailbox and a small lamppost with the beam directed down to prevent light pollution. Most of the residences also had land-scaping lights on the palm trees and ornamental plants.

But right now, all that meant was that it was black as a mine outside, and Dani could not see a thing. She rose and closed the blinds in the dining room, and then returned to the table to work on her meal alone. Unfortunately, her appetite had fled, so she carried her plate to the kitchen and scraped most of it into the trash, rearranging some of the garbage to hide the food.

Tate appeared as she cleared his setting.

"I have to go sign something."

"Where?"

"Doug Vanderhorn's place."

She tried to recall the name.

"Who?"

"Homeowners' association president. You've met him. Old, thin, walks a giant golden retriever."

She nodded, her recall vague.

"It's thundering out. You'll get soaked."

"Not raining yet and it's just down the street. He'll give the incident report to the homeowners' association manager tomor-row. I'd expect she'd then follow up with us."

"Can't you do it online?"

"Not yet. The forms are available at the portal, but they don't have DocuSign."

"That's too bad."

"He's shaken over this. They don't get intruder reports very often."

"I suppose that should make us feel special."

"I'll be right back."

"Tate?"

He paused between the dining room and the foyer, a question on his face.

"Could this have something to do with the baby?"

His brow furrowed. "What do you mean?"

"Could that be the birth mother?"

"What? No way."

"How do you know? Do we know anything about her?"

"Yes. I told you, the birth mother is incarcerated."

He *had* told her.

"She's in for forgery. Gave up all parental rights because of her circumstances."

The food in her stomach pitched like a boat in rough surf. "You're sure she's still in jail?"

"Of course."

"Please, Tate, can you check? I don't want to be alone here if she's not in jail."

Out came his phone, and he made a call.

"Can you check on a prisoner? Give me a status update." Tate walked back up the stairs with long strides.

Dani swore she didn't take a breath until he returned. Was it odd that Tate knew the birth mother's identity? She thought some veil of privacy separated the birth parents and the adoption parents.

That he knew her name just reinforced Dani's concern that this was not a typical adoption.

Tate reappeared as Dani finished loading the dishwasher.

"She's in lockup awaiting trial."

Dani exhaled in a long breath and let her head drop forward. Tate rested a hand on her shoulder and gave her a squeeze.

"I'll just be a minute." He kissed her temple. "Love you, Dani."

He wasn't gone a minute. He was gone ninety.

———

On Tuesday morning, Dani woke at seven to find the bassinet empty. Tate had told her he would take Willow down to breakfast with him. He was always up two hours before her to exercise. Would that change, now that he had the baby to look after?

Dani was growing more comfortable with Willow's routine. She and Tate alternated care, with her covering daytime feeds until she took her medications at around 10 pm. Then Tate handled the night feedings. Even Willow's hungry cries didn't wake her. She'd skipped her medications on Sunday night, but a phone consult with Dr. Allen on Monday convinced her that this was a bad idea.

Dr. Allen had explained that, though it was normal for most parents to lose sleep, it was not safe for her to do so. Her psychiatrist convinced her that sleep deprivation would not only affect her mental acuity, but it could also cause her to have other problems associated with managing her depression.

Tate sealed the deal by mentioning that, should the intruder return, she would have more credibility with police if she was taking her medications. She wondered, had it not been for the video footage, would anyone have believed her?

So after only skipping the medication Sunday night, she had been reassured to learn that Willow's cries woke her at one, when Tate was still awake, and then again around four.

She dressed and collected her phone before heading downstairs, finding Tate feeding Willow in the kitchen.

"Is your phone still working?" he asked, noting the device in her hand. After she'd dropped it, he'd let the battery drain and then charged it up again. On restart, everything began working and had been fine ever since.

"Yes. Seems only damage is the cracked screen. Everything else is fine."

"That's lucky," he said.

She tucked the device in her pocket. It was then she noticed that Tate was dressed for work.

Dani frowned. "Going out?"

"Have to sign some rulings. I'll be back before lunch."

Dani glanced toward the living room and the sliders where the woman had pounded on the glass.

When she looked back, Tate was watching her.

"Just two hours. Do you want me to call someone to be here with you?"

Of course, she did.

"No. We'll be fine." She spoke to Willow in Tate's arms. "Won't we be fine?"

The boop on the infant's nose caused a look of wonder that froze Dani in place as she marveled at the perfection of her daughter.

"Isn't she beautiful?" he asked.

"Yes." She tore her gaze away from Willow and smiled at Tate. "Did you two get any sleep?"

"I get up to use the toilet, anyway. I just do that and feed her while we watch the 24-hour news station."

"That will give you both nightmares."

He chuckled. Willow finished her bottle and Dani draped a cotton cloth over her shoulder.

"I'll take her."

Tate passed her over and then drained the remains of his coffee. He stood and dumped the dregs in the sink. She always felt anxious before he left but didn't want to mention it. He'd treated her as if she were made of glass when she'd first come home. But that was over a week ago and she needed to show him she was again a capable woman.

She was lucky to have a husband with an important job. Dani was proud of him. At times she even envied Tate. He was so capable of handling himself. And her illness had been a burden long enough. The last thing she wanted was to make his job more difficult.

Besides, there had been nothing further on their intruder and no more incidents. Everything seemed normal. Safe. She had to be safe here, in her own home, in her own neighborhood.

"Plans for the day?" he asked.

"Get Willow changed and dressed." Dani then spoke to Willow, still on her shoulder.

She cradled Willow's head, stroking the fine hair at her baby's crown with her thumb. Both mother and child gave a simultaneous sigh of contentment.

"We are getting dressed and then... Mommy is taking me for a walk. Isn't she?"

His brows lifted. "Really?" His surprise confirmed her conjecture that Tate expected her to hide away all day, clear of the windows and anyone or anything outside.

"Yes. I'm going to try out the new stroller."

"Not afraid?"

"You always say this is the safest neighborhood in Tampa."

Until Sunday, she'd believed that. Now she was doing what she thought Tate expected, instead of what felt safe.

Mothers went walking with their babies. They took them to the park, and they bought golden retrievers, and they played tennis. At least, that's what her mother had done.

"Well, good for you. Make sure you protect her from the sun."

"There's a wide visor."

"Early is better. Not too hot."

She nodded, cradling Willow as she walked with Tate through the laundry room to the entrance to the garage.

There he paused to kiss her. Before the accident, giving him this kind of kiss often led to him skipping his usual run to the coffee place en route to work.

"Hmm," he said, drawing back with his eyes still closed. Then they popped open, and he grinned.

"I missed you." He stroked her hair. "Can't wait to get home."

"See you soon," she said.

"Do you offer rain checks?"

"When the mood strikes me."

He took Willow's tiny hand. "Bye-bye, precious."

She gurgled happily as she squeezed Tate's index finger.

His brows rose. "Wow. Good grip."

Then he gave Dani a fast peck on the mouth and headed into the garage, which held only his vehicle and the full-sized SUV.

A moment later, he was in his seat as the heavy garage double door, reinforced to sustain hurricane winds, rumbled up on its tracks.

He gave her a wave and a toot before backing out to the drive.

The door rumbled closed behind him. Dani's smile faded as she looked to the empty spot where he'd been parked, to the champagne-colored vehicle beyond. He told her that while she had been away, that full-sized SUV sat so long that all four of the tires went flat. So long it had grown dusty.

But Tate had since driven it occasionally, and he'd taken it out and had it all cleaned before her return. Something in the rear seat caught her eye. She stepped forward, one hand cradling Willow's head and the other on her tiny bottom, as she spotted the plastic base portion of the car seat.

"When did Daddy do that?" she asked Willow.

Moving off the steps to the concrete floor, she saw he still kept the keys in the cup holder. Maybe someday she'd want a car of her own again. She'd need one if she had to drive Willow to school and playdates.

Dani bit her lower lip as the knot of fear tightened within. Willow was tiny. She didn't need to go to school or playdates, so Dani didn't need to confront this monster right now.

The first person she saw on their walk was an older man walking a stubby, fat little white dog. He stopped and introduced himself, admired the baby, and headed on his way, his dog wheezing with the effort of keeping pace. The next person was a jogger, who waved as she passed, her blond ponytail bobbing. Her final neighbor walked a friendly golden retriever. He wore an orange cap advertising a local eatery and introduced his dog as Rocket and himself as Doug Vanderhorn.

"Our association president," she said, remembering Tate having to sign papers.

"That's right." Beside him, his dog snuffled the stroller, with tail wagging.

"Sit, Rocket." The dog sat instantly, tail now thumping the pavement. "She's just curious about the baby. Loves kids, this one. We heard from Tate you adopted." He leaned over the stroller. "She's beautiful. Just a tiny thing."

Dani didn't think she could feel prouder.

As Vanderhorn admired the baby, he talked about his grandchildren up in Michigan.

"Mason plays baseball. He's good enough to play pro someday. Couldn't see them for over a year because of the pandemic."

"A year?" That wasn't right.

"Little over, actually. Missed a Christmas and two birthdays."

That was definitely wrong. Dani knew she'd been in the ICU and psychiatric facility for just under six months. And the pandemic started *after* Christmas.

Her elderly neighbor must be more confused than she'd initially thought.

Vanderhorn paused, only to draw a breath. "We're determined to get up there for a visit this fall, though. The oldest boy plays baseball. Mason's a pitcher. He's good enough to go pro."

Dani smiled politely at this repeated information, but she didn't dwell. Her condition made her more forgiving. Perhaps he had memory issues.

"I'm sorry you had trouble the other day. I want you to know that we never have that sort of thing here."

"Thank you for helping my husband with the paperwork."

He frowned and then slowly nodded, giving her an odd look.

"The manager gets all police reports from the city. Is that what you mean?"

"No, I meant the incident report."

He scratched his head. "Incident?"

"That Tate filed."

"Yes, we have a copy. At least, what they'd release. I've got the neighborhood watch on alert, too. I understand you know the resident who heads that committee, Enid Langford."

"Oh, sure. I've known Enid for years. She worked with my husband at the law firm before he was elected to the circuit court." Dani turned to look back the way she'd come. "That one. Isn't it?"

"Yes. Practically across the street from you. No water view, but she's got a peek between your property and the adjoining one. It's the one with the big yellow plumeria tree. Number 916."

"Yes. It's lovely."

"She's alone now and, if you don't mind me saying, behind on her association dues." He glanced in the direction of the Langfords'.

Dani did not know what the association dues were. Tate handled that, she supposed.

"You heard her husband left?" he asked.

Rocket panted, gradually easing to a furry side on the nearest lawn before stretching out to wait for her owner to finish his conversation.

"Yes. I did. Very sad. I know Paul as well. They seemed happy."

"No way of telling, I guess. Some folks just grow apart. She told the missus that they were trying to get pregnant. She got checked and seemed all right, but her husband refused to see a doctor. He moved out for a while, but I thought they got through that rough patch. But then we had to issue a warning because he was speeding. And there was a disturbance call. After that, she tried revoking his visitor status, but he's listed as an owner. So there's nothing we can do."

Dani nodded. The safe community was only as safe as the residents inside the gate, of course. Walls kept folks out. But they also kept folks in.

She thought again about her intruder.

Vanderhorn continued about the predicament. "I tried to explain that to her but—"

"Thank you, Mr. Vanderhorn. I'm not sure Enid would want me to have all those details."

"Oh, yeah. Right."

In Dani's opinion, this was way too much personal information and made her wonder what gossip the "missus" had shared with him about her.

"Funny, though. Haven't seen much of Mrs. Langford. Used to walk every morning, but not in months. Gosh, must be

April since I saw her walking. About the time her husband left, I guess."

"Perhaps it's still too hot. And Tate said she hurt her ankle."

"Really? That must be it. She doesn't swim at the community pool anymore. Used to be a regular. How did Enid hurt her ankle?"

Dani now regretted telling him this snippet of gossip.

"Oh, I'm afraid I don't know." The lie made her cheeks hot.

She wondered how much Vanderhorn knew about her bouts with depression and time spent in the psychiatric facility. His next question seemed to be an answer of sorts.

He gave her a concerned look. "How are *you* feeling?"

The way he said it made her suspect he knew everything. Well, she was not giving him a thing to report to the neighborhood watch.

"Oh, I'm fine. Well. Happy," she added, thinking she'd overdone it. "Heron Shores is a wonderful place to raise a family."

"Well, we think so. Raised up three boys right there. Blake's oldest son, Mason, is a whiz at baseball. A pitcher."

"I'd better get back. Willow's due for her next feeding."

"Right. You take care, Mrs. Sutton." He tipped his cap and Rocket rose and stretched. Then the pair continued on their way.

Dani hurried home, feeling suddenly exposed.

ELEVEN

Tate arrived in time to get her to her therapy appointment, but too late for lunch. Dani had changed for her session with Dr. Allen, replacing the blouse that Willow had spit up on with a clean sky-blue one. Today, Tate could take her. But when he went back to work, he planned to send a driver, which caused an entirely different set of anxieties.

She didn't know the driver. Had the driver been vetted? Would the driver have trouble clearing the gate? Would he arrive on time?

It wasn't an issue yet, but she already worried. But this was the kind of normal, reasonable situation that she needed to handle because that was what capable people did.

Tate grabbed a power drink from the refrigerator and gave Dani a quick summary of his morning and why he was late. The court system had been thrown into madness because of the pandemic and they were hopelessly behind. His leave was adding to the strain. He finished his recounting and finally drew a breath.

"I'm sorry you had to rush back," she said.

"Wouldn't miss it."

He flashed her a loving smile that warmed her insides.

Dani mentioned her morning with Willow and their walk.

"I met Mr. Vanderhorn."

"And Rocket?"

"Yes. You know it's funny. I have no problem identifying dog breeds. In fact, I used a dog on the way home to recognize the neighbor who lives on the corner. Hers is a small Lab mix, black with a white patch on its chest and tail. Her name is Kate. The dog is Oreo."

"That's a good coping technique. You should mention that to Dr. Allen."

"You know, when I thanked him for helping you with the incident report, he was confused. He said they get reports from the police, so he knew about the trespassing. But I got that right? He was the one you went to see?"

Tate sighed. "How many times did he tell you about the pitcher?"

"His grandson Mason? Several."

"He drinks. He's old. Really, he shouldn't be the association president. But if I say anything, you just know that I'll get the job."

"Oh, dear." She rubbed her neck. "He also asked how I was feeling. What's that about?"

"No idea. Maybe he thinks you're recovering from childbirth."

"You think?" She dismissed that possibility. "No. That can't be right. He said he'd heard from you that we'd adopted."

He shrugged, lifted his drink, and took a swallow, seeming to lose interest in the topic of conversation.

"What about Enid Langford?"

Tate choked. "What?"

"Are you all right?"

Tate swiped a dish towel from the counter and held it to his mouth, eyes squeezed shut, and nodded. "Went down the wrong throat," he whispered.

"Goodness."

After he'd recovered, he asked, "What about Enid?"

"She ran your old law offices. She'd be a great association president."

"Maybe." He sounded hesitant. "But she has a lot on her plate."

"With the separation, you mean? I hadn't thought of that."

"Also has to job search. At least, I assume so."

She nodded. "Mr. Vanderhorn mentioned her. He's quite the busybody. Told me she used to walk and swim at the community pool, but he hadn't seen her lately. And that's another thing. He thinks the pandemic has lasted over a year."

"Really?"

"A little over, he said."

Tate shook his head, a slow, disappointed sweep at all she'd told him. Then he glanced at his watch, a gold Rolex she didn't recognize.

"Is that new?"

He gave her that look, like she'd broken a piece of his heart. "You bought it for me for Christmas the year of the accident. I found it, wrapped, when I was packing up our bedroom."

She glanced down at the tile floor. So much of the time around the accident was covered in thick fog. "I'm sorry."

"We'd better go." He capped the empty drink and left it on the counter. "Do we have everything Willow needs?"

They'd agreed that Tate would watch Willow while Dani met with her doctor. The hour-long sessions were crucial to her recovery, and she was determined to keep her head above water.

"Yes. There's a bottle, though she likely won't need it," said Dani. "Also, a changing blanket. You can lay that down first if you need to change her."

"Got it." Tate collected the carrier and Dani grabbed the bag.

In the garage she helped Tate attach the carrier to the base, which was already fixed to the rear seat of the SUV. Seeing Willow locked in the car made Dani's mouth go dry and sweat popped out on her forehead.

"She's all right," said Tate. "We all are." When she didn't move, he added, "Come on, Dani. You next."

Getting into a roller-coaster seat would have caused less anxiety. Somehow, she climbed into the passenger side and clipped her belt, but beads of sweat rolled between her breast and her breathing came fast.

Something about having their baby in a car made Dani's skin wash cold. She shivered and wrapped her arms around herself.

"You're not cold," said Tate, glancing at her.

"No. Nervous mama." Dani blew away a breath and sucked in another.

Capable people drove their babies in cars. This was normal. Not a cause for panic. She could do this.

He nodded and put them in reverse. Dani looked back, but with the carrier facing backward, she couldn't see Willow.

"Stop," she said.

He did, and she climbed out.

"Dani. Get in the car."

"I'm riding in the back with Willow."

Tate's mouth went tight but he said, "Fine."

He'd acquiesced, letting her do what was easiest, as usual.

"Thank you."

"It's okay, Dani. But we have to go, or you'll miss the appointment."

She felt more comfortable in the rear seat. The headrest before her blocked the view of the road speeding at them, cars weaving in and out of their lanes, and much of the overpasses.

Here she could sit beside her daughter and stare at her sweet face.

———

Tate swung casually into a parking spot at the outpatient treatment center.

Dani thrust her arms out, bracing as he braked in time to avoid the cement wall before them. He gave her a concerned glance and then turned off the engine.

"I called your doctor," he said. "Told her all about Willow."

Dani now felt anxious for entirely different reasons.

"What did she say?"

"She has concerns."

Inside the medical building, they rode the elevator to the correct floor. They checked in at reception, and before they took a seat, Dr. Allen greeted them in the waiting room and fussed over Willow. Then she surprised Dani by ushering both her and Tate into her office.

Dani, her arm looped through the carrier holding Willow, paused just inside the door, waiting for Tate to pick a seat.

There were several places to choose from. The loveseat looked inviting, with nubby pillows and one of faux fur like a square teddy bear. Beyond the coffee table, two swivel lounge chairs reclined. Dr. Allen perched in her desk chair beside her workspace. Behind her, a collection of potted and hanging plants flourished.

Tate sat in a lounge chair, and Dani took the adjoining one, placing Willow's carrier on the coffee table. Dani adjusted the baby's blanket as Tate lifted the amethyst globe from the stand on the side table and spun it, glancing around.

"All that's missing is a therapy dog," he said.

Her psychiatrist settled back in her chair, her smile benign as she spoke to Tate.

"I'm glad you're here, Judge Sutton. Thank you for coming."

Dani glanced from one to the other. Had Dr. Allen arranged with Tate for him to join them?

"I wanted to talk to you both together, see how things have been going." She cleared her throat. "Dani has been home now for eight days. How are you two adjusting?"

"Wonderfully," said Dani.

"It's been challenging," said Tate.

Dani frowned as Dr. Allen looked at Tate. "Go on."

"We had a function. I didn't pressure her to come, but she insisted. It was difficult for Dani because she couldn't recognize people she knows very well. I think she found it really stressful."

"That's to be expected." She turned to Dani. "Are you using any of the strategies?"

Dani had thought Tate would say something about the woman on the lanai or the adoption and was thrown off guard that he'd raised concerns about the campaign event instead.

"Yes, but introducing myself to my husband's old mentor just makes me look foolish. Tate's wearing yellow. That helps. I'm paying more attention to the gestures people use. Individual features, like a broken nose or pierced eyebrow. And many of my neighbors have dogs. I can recognize their dogs more easily than I can their owners because their pet's breed, the leash color, and size of the dogs all help me figure out who they are."

"That's an excellent strategy. Very good. What else?" she asked Tate.

"Dani and Shelby have been speaking on the phone."

Dr. Allen nodded to Tate. "Yes. I'm aware."

"Shelby has a new number, so Dani can call her. And Shelby is still calling Dani."

Dr. Allen blinked and shifted in her seat. "I see."

She turned to Dani. "How is Shelby?"

Dani related all the news. Dr. Allen nodded and jotted some notes.

"How is the baby?"

Dani gushed about how happy she was and how lucky. She didn't mean to talk for so long, but it was amazing to speak to Dr. Allen about how happy she was for a change.

When she had finally ceased jabbering, Allen said, "Adoption is a wonderful gift all around. Any other adjustment issues?"

Dani glanced to Tate and thought about the elephant in the room.

"We had a trespasser." She explained all about the woman and how frightened she had been. How the police were called, and the homeowners' association contacted.

"Tate was away?"

"Yes. The grocery store and pharmacy."

"I see." Dr. Allen paused. "I wonder, Dani, if I could speak to Tate for a moment."

"Is everything all right?" She thought she was doing well. But was she in a position to judge?

"Everything is just as expected. To be honest, I would have advised more time adjusting back home before undertaking a huge life change such as adoption."

"But then we wouldn't have Willow." Already Dani could not imagine life without her daughter.

"True, but the mix of medications you are taking..." Her words fell off.

"Tate cares for her at night."

"But with that and your medical history... I'm surprised the adoption was possible." She glanced to Tate now and Dani closed her mouth.

She would say nothing to endanger the adoption or implicate Tate in any wrongdoing. Whatever her suspicions, Tate was her husband, and she would protect him as he protected her. And who did Dr. Allen think she was? Was it her place, as a therapist, to say these things about Willow? About them becoming parents?

"I'll call you back in, after a few minutes," said Dr. Allen.

Dani rose and brushed the wrinkles from her linen skirt. She collected the infant carrier and bag, conveying her daughter out into the empty waiting room. The receptionist, working behind Plexiglas, looked surprised to see her back but busied herself with her keyboard.

―――――

"Tell me about the intruder," said Dr. Allen to Tate.

"I was at the pharmacy picking up one of those ear thermometers and some other baby stuff when Dani called in a panic. She said there was a woman pounding on the sliders to the lanai. So, I rushed home and there wasn't anyone there."

"Do you believe there was an intruder?"

"We have pool surveillance, a video doorbell, and a camera on the garage. You can't approach our property without being picked up on one of those. I get alerts on movement. That way I know if Dani's left the house."

"I see."

"She asked me to check the video, and I did. But I had no alerts or anything in the timeline except me leaving and returning."

"What was her response to that?"

"I didn't confront her. Should I?"

"As discussed, confrontation would be unlikely to help. Police were called?"

"Yes. After calling me, Dani dropped her phone. Broke it. So I contacted a friend on the force. He and his partner came right over, along with a couple of uniforms. They arrived shortly after me. I spoke to them. Explained about Dani's condition so the report didn't mention an intruder. Just a call about a suspicious person."

"Why not mention the intruder?"

Tate threw up his hands in a gesture of frustration. "I'm running for elected office, and I don't need police logging a mentally disturbed person in their report. Plus, I'm not even certain..." His words trailed off.

"You don't believe there was an intruder?"

He broke eye contact. "I'm not sure. And that makes Dani look..." His words fell off again. "I'm worried. What do you think is happening?"

"I'm not sure. Dani's condition does not involve hallucinations. If she is seeing something that is not there, this is new and potentially dangerous, more so, since you placed a newborn in her care."

"I'm there."

"But you weren't. You were shopping. I clarified that her return necessitated you being *with* her."

"I've taken the week off."

"But you weren't there. You need to be. At least for the first few weeks."

"Yes. Okay."

"Is she taking all her medications?"

"She is. Very conscientiously."

"Any confrontations?"

"No. Her mood seems stable. She's doing well. Seems very happy."

"Wonderful. I'm so glad to hear it."

If he'd waited for Dani's doctor, his wife would still be locked up here, when she was clearly more capable and mentally ready to be home. But he didn't rub it in that her doctor had been overly cautious. Dani was fine and home where she belonged.

Since they'd both missed lunch, they stopped for a bite on the way home. Dani was glad to shorten the drive but already dreaded getting back in the SUV. Willow, fed and changed by Tate, was awake until the vehicle got underway and slept soundly as they entered the upscale gastro-diner.

Tate held the door, and the hostess showed them to a booth. The interior resembled a diner, with the stool counter seating and chrome accents, but the space was roomy and bright.

The server arrived with water and menus. Tate seemed more interested in the specials than he was in her session with Dr. Allen.

"What did you two talk about?" she asked, keeping her tone casual.

"You. Us. The baby."

"She doesn't think I can do it."

"She didn't say that. She just questioned the timing."

Dani glanced about the seating area. Most of the tables were taken with people, all of whom were unrecognizable to her. So many people, it made her anxious. The woman intruder could be right here, and she wouldn't know.

The server returned, and she ordered the blackened grouper sandwich with chips. Tate chose Korean beef barbeque tacos with beans and rice.

"Did you ask her about the medications?" Dani asked. "The sleeping pills?"

"She reiterated that skipping anything is a terrible idea. She insisted I stay on all of them. *Crucial* is the word she used."

"That settles that, then."

"But what happens when you go back to work? You can't take care of Willow all night and sit in court all day."

"No, I can't. But that little stomach can only hold so much.

She's growing. Soon she'll be sleeping through the night, and in any case, I'll hardly be the first tired dad at work."

Dani bit her lip. Babies didn't just magically sleep through the night when you wanted them to.

"How much formula is she taking at night?"

He looked confused. "I didn't know I needed to keep track."

"I'd like to know."

"Fine. I'll start measuring and keeping a log."

She gave him a smile and then checked on Willow, who slept like an angel despite the clatter of dishes and the terrible acoustics in this place.

"You doing all right, Dani? You seem anxious."

Yes, having her psychiatrist explore the possibility that she was unfit to care for their daughter certainly would do that.

"Too many strangers. It makes me nervous."

He glanced around, clearly relaxed out in public himself. Tate loved people, crowds, rallies, fundraisers. It was all exciting to his alpha type-A personality. Meanwhile, Dani had been an introvert before they met, and the need for silence, quiet, and space had only grown. But she made the stretch. Tried. Because Tate loved evenings out and needed her at his side for political events.

"Well, relax. The session today went fine. You're doing great. And so good with Willow. I'm just..."

"Relieved?"

"I was going to say thrilled. You're an excellent mother, Dani. I knew you would be." He looked on the verge of tears.

She reached across the table and clasped his hand as a weighty sadness tugged at her.

"What's wrong, Dani?"

She gave his hand a squeeze. "It's just... I wish that I could have your babies. And if I hadn't lost control of the car..."

"Dani." His voice was soft as a caress. "Don't do that. I love you. We'll have more babies."

But the tears already dribbled down her chin as regret filled her stomach like ash.

Tate, seated opposite, reached across the table to capture her other hand.

"Dani, look at me."

She did.

"I love you. I love Willow. You're doing so well. Everything is working out for us."

She nodded, wishing she could set aside the ache of regret that she dragged with her like a stone.

The server arrived with their meals and Dani realized she had no appetite. After the server left them, Dani tried again.

"Should we talk about the accident?" It would be hard, but she was determined to do everything she could to get better.

"Dr. Allen said it's not in your best interest. But that might change." He squeezed her hand. "Early days, Dani. Baby steps."

She forced a laugh. "Literally."

"Eat your food," he said, patting her hand and drawing back.

Dani liked this change in their relationship dynamic even less than she liked the look of her sandwich. It was huge and she felt defeated before the first bite.

She glanced up as the diners in the table across the aisle from their booth stood. A mother, father, and their three children. The woman ushered her ducklings expertly from the dining area as her partner collected the receipt and tucked it in his wallet. Bits of food, ice, and torn napkins littered the floor beneath their table. Dani shook her head at the mess and glanced up to notice a woman seated with a man in a booth similar to theirs on the opposite side of the large, now empty table. The woman paused and stared boldly in Dani's direction, making and holding direct eye contact.

Her heart rate jackhammered. Dani glanced to Willow, sleeping in her carrier on the table. She turned back to find the woman continuing to watch them but now the stare seemed full of menace.

Dani glared at the female diner. Most people would have glanced away by now. But not this stranger. Or was she a stranger? Did she have silver eyes?

TWELVE

Her meal was forgotten as Dani scooted closer to their daughter.

Every time she glanced up from the booth, the woman was staring back at her. She even seemed to glance to Willow's bassinet.

Dani scowled, but she did not so much as blink.

That was enough. Every maternal instinct told her that this woman posed a threat to Willow, and she was not having it.

Because of Dani's condition, she did not know if this was the same person who had tried to break into their home. What color had that woman's hair been?

She didn't know. It had happened so fast. All she recalled was those weird silver-gray eyes and the huge pupils. But this could be that woman. She had the same menacing expression.

Dani became certain that this was the trespasser and rocketed to her feet.

Tate dropped his fork, splattering salsa and hot sauce on his jacket and shirt. He glanced up at her.

"Dani, what?"

"I think that's her." She spoke out of the side of her mouth.

Tate had not been there when they had been attacked. She wasn't certain the police or Dr. Allen believed her. But she knew Tate did. He'd taken the matter seriously.

"That's who?" he asked.

"The woman. The one who tried to break in and take Willow."

Tate placed the fork back on the plate and turned to glance at the woman who now stood facing Dani.

"That one?" He pointed.

"Yes," she hissed.

"In the blue blouse and tan capri pants?" he said, verifying.

She nodded, and the woman nodded back.

"I saw her staring at Willow. Look at her, she's talking to that man!"

Tate stood, just as a second person, a big male person, rose beside her adversary.

"It's a mirror," Tate said.

"What?"

The man waved in perfect time to Tate's wave. "It's you and me, Dani. You are staring at your own reflection."

Her knees went out from under her and she bounced on the vinyl seat. Her reflection followed, sinking into her own booth.

"Oh, my God," she said and cradled her head in her hands.

Tate squatted beside her. "Take it easy, Dani."

But she was sobbing. How could she not even recognize herself in a mirror?

She was a chicken attacking her reflection. Another sob escaped her.

"Dr. Allen said that face blindness includes all faces," Tate said. "Even your own."

She spoke into her hands. "I can see all the parts, but they don't add up."

"That's because the part of your brain organizing all that geographic information is broken. Don't be so hard on yourself."

She was still sobbing.

"It's not your fault."

She lifted her head. "It is my fault! *I* drove into that overpass. Now I can't even tell if... I thought Willow was being threatened by a mirror! No, worse, by me!" She swiped at the tears. "I could see what I was wearing. I shouldn't have made that mistake."

"It's okay."

"Is it? What if I walk by a Starbucks and see my reflection staring at me?"

"Just look at the clothing, Dani. Is it what you are wearing? That will help. And give it time. You are getting better at picking up the cues that Dr. Allen suggested: beards, glasses, gait, context as to where you are and who you might expect to see."

"I know. I'm just scared. Maybe Dr. Allen is right. It is too soon." She lifted her face from her hands, but the tears continued to roll down her cheeks.

"No. She isn't. We can do this." His determination was iron. "I won't let anything happen to Willow. I'm here. She's safe."

Dani blew away a breath and lowered her elbows from the table. "Can we move her here next to me?"

"Certainly. She's yours now." He gave her a handsome smile and then moved Willow to the wide vinyl seat. She felt better having her body between her baby and anyone walking past in the aisle.

Dani sniffed. "What if I'm picking up Willow from school and someone asks me to point her out and I can't recognize my daughter?"

"That's a ways off. Let's figure out her feeding schedule before we enroll her in school." He offered a lopsided smile.

"I thought she was the woman on the lanai."

Tate's smile dropped, and he glanced away.

She might not recognize faces, but she could still perceive expressions. Tate looked decidedly uncomfortable.

"Tate? What are you not telling me?"

He rubbed the back of his neck and his face flushed.

"There was no video."

She blinked at him, trying to understand.

"What do you mean?"

"The surveillance cameras caught nothing."

"But the police told me they'd check the neighborhood," she said.

"Yes, they said that."

"You showed them the footage."

"I didn't. Because there wasn't any. I told them you have a condition, and you'd made a mistake. I know both those officers. One of them has a baby under two. They get it."

She shook her head. "No, no, no. This can't happen. My disorder is the opposite. I miss things but I've never had a hallucination."

His expression was grim. He looked around. People were staring.

"That's why Dr. Allen wanted to speak to you!"

"Dani, lower your voice."

She did, hissing now. "Why didn't you tell me before I told Dr. Allen about the break-in? What if she reports it or something?" Dani glanced to Willow and gasped. "What if they try to take her from us?"

"Dani, please. Not here."

Their server arrived.

"Everything all right?"

Tate handed over his credit card. "Ring us up, please."

"Of course." She hesitated, glancing to their meals. "Ah, wrap it?"

"No. Just the check."

"Sure thing." She scurried away.

Dani leaned in toward her husband. "This is terrible." She now understood why Tate and Dr. Allen had spoken alone. "Did you tell my psychiatrist?"

"Yes."

"Why did you do that?"

"It's important. Don't you think?"

They were going to take Willow. Dani could hardly breathe.

"What did she say?"

"She's concerned. She thinks I should have given you more time to adjust to being home. You were at the facility for a while."

"Six months," she said. That *was* a long time to be away.

"She just mentioned that the losses you've suffered, and the trauma, might cause hypervigilance. But I saw an opportunity to make us parents, and I took it. Maybe that was selfish, but I'm not sorry."

"Overprotective, I can handle. But that's not what this is. I saw a woman out there. I heard her pounding. But you're telling me none of that happened." She glanced to Willow. "I can't be alone with her."

"I'm here. We'll figure this out."

"Tate, you didn't bend any laws to get her, did you?"

"Her mother surrendered parental rights. Paperwork is signed."

"What if she's changed her mind?"

"Too late for that. Willow is legally ours."

It came spilling out then, all her worries that she'd tried to keep to herself. "I thought the adoption process took months, that there were inspections and then a court hearing."

"Traditional adoption, yes."

They both knew this adoption was anything but.

"What about the father?"

He was silent for a moment. Dani's breathing remained

unsteady. She rested a protective hand on the edge of the carrier.

"He won't be a problem," he finally said.

Dani cradled her forehead in one hand, elbow braced on the table.

"Does Dr. Allen think it's the medication?" Dani held hope that the apparition was drug-induced.

"She's not sure."

"Should I go back?"

His reply was instant. "No."

Tate grasped her hand and used his thumb to rub circles on the back of hers.

She met his troubled gaze, terrified, seeing the fear reflected back at her.

"Oh, God." She cradled her forehead in her palms.

She heard Tate speak to the server, thank her as he signed the check and collected his receipt. Then he rounded the table, guiding Dani to her feet and collecting Willow in her carrier; the baby was now wide-eyed and fussing.

Dani stood facing the mirror and shivered. Then she turned to Tate.

"We can't keep her. We have to send her back."

"What are you talking about?"

"If I'm hallucinating, it's dangerous for Willow. We have to get her somewhere safe."

Tate tried to talk her down on the ride home, but she was adamant. The pain sliced at her heart, but if she couldn't trust her eyes and ears, she couldn't see to a baby.

The grief at the thought of giving Willow up crashed against the panic at what might happen if she didn't. It pained her to admit that the greatest danger facing her baby might be her. But being a mother meant doing what was right for your child. Even if it meant sending them away.

Was this how Willow's birth mother had felt? Knowing she wasn't the right person to care for her?

Back inside the safety of their home, Tate took charge of Willow, feeding her and changing diapers and singing to her, as Dani watched from a safe distance, feeling like a waif looking in on a happy family.

"Dani, come hold your daughter." Tate presented Willow, all wrapped up in a soft towel and vocalizing her contentment with a quiet gurgling.

She shook her head and backed away.

"We have to send her back." She was not giving up on this. Why couldn't Tate understand? She loved Willow and needed to see her safe.

Tate sighed. "Why don't you call Shelby? See what she thinks about all this."

It was a good idea.

"Okay."

Tate nodded. "Do you want me to take the baby?"

She ignored the deep tug, the urge to keep Willow with her. "Yes."

Tate headed out of the nursery with Willow curled against his shoulder, wrapped up in her soft terrycloth towel and in a clean tiny diaper.

She heard him babbling to the baby as they went.

Dani retrieved her cell phone and called her sister. Shelby picked up on the first ring as if she'd been expecting Dani's call.

"Hey, Dani-o."

"Good time?" she asked. "Am I interrupting?"

"No. Just doing some reading."

"Anything good?"

"A biography. It's just okay. What's up?" Shelby preferred

fiction to nonfiction. Unusual choice, Dani thought before turning to the topic at hand.

She laid it all out.

Shelby gave a low whistle. "That must have scared you to death."

"I'm so confused. Elated to have a baby and terrified that I'm having hallucinations."

"I understand. What does your doctor say?"

"She's concerned."

"Obviously. Did she say you were unfit?"

"Not to me."

"What does Tate think?"

"He's reassuring. Downplaying it. But is that to protect me or because he's really not that worried? I *saw* a woman on our pool deck. Heard her pounding on the glass sliders. But she wasn't there. I should freak out. Shouldn't I? The incident was so real in every single way."

"Could the security system have been off? I mean, is it on when you are home alone?"

Dani's heartbeat thudded in her ears. She sank to the rocker beside the empty crib as hope beat back the terror.

"Is that possible?" she whispered.

"Of course it is. What was the system setting?"

"Setting? I'm not sure. Tate handles that. But he told me there was no footage."

Had he been covering for her before the police? Oh, God. He thought she'd imagined the entire thing.

"Well, let me explain then," said Shelby. "They have privacy shutters on cameras, you know, so it isn't recording video or audio while you are in your own house. If it's on *privacy* or *home*, there wouldn't be a recording except maybe from the doorbell. But if the system is armed or on the away setting, then all cameras, inside and out, are working. Did Tate check that?"

"He only said that there was no video."

"Maybe because the cameras were set not to record any."

"Oh, my Lord, Shelby. Do you think that's it?"

"Go ask him."

"I will."

"Dani, did they check the grounds? Look for prints on the windows?"

"I don't know."

"Ask Tate."

"I will. Thank you! Love you, big sister."

"You too."

Shelby disconnected.

Dani frowned at Shelby's abrupt goodbye, but then rushed down the hall and into the empty living room. She hurried on to find Tate in the kitchen, seated at the counter, eating some cheese and crackers beside the baby carrier.

She paused realizing that Tate had not finished his meal because of her.

Willow, fed, clean, and dry, was blowing spit bubbles and vocalizing.

"Shelby said the system might have been on home or private or something."

"What?"

She explained as best she could what Shelby had said to her.

"Yes, that's true. We don't want the alarm going off for motion if you step out on the pool deck. You were home so the security system will chime if a door or window is open, but it won't record video. Your sister is a smart cookie."

"Tell Dr. Allen. Explain to her I wasn't hallucinating about the woman."

His expression went blank.

"You knew this all along, about the system being off. Not recording her."

He glanced away.

"Tate, you believe me. Don't you? About the woman?"

He didn't answer.

"You think it was a hallucination?"

He raked a hand through his fine hair. "I know you saw something, Dani. But there's no physical evidence that it happened."

Dani's relief turned cold. "Fingerprints?"

He shook his head. "They didn't check. It wasn't even a home invasion."

In other words, there was no physical evidence and Tate chose to disregard her explanation. He didn't trust her. The realization struck like a blow.

"I'll call Dr. Allen now. Tell her the system was off." Tate drew out his phone and left the kitchen island, likely heading to his office to call Dr. Allen. He'd tell her the system was off, but that didn't mean he believed her about the intruder.

Dani sagged into the gold satin stool Tate had vacated. She was doing well, and she could keep Willow. It *wasn't* a hallucination, regardless of what Tate thought. The bubble of anguish broke. She hunched, elbows on the counter as she pressed her hands over her face and sobbed.

Shelby was an angel, figuring that out! But Tate already knew and had not told her. Had he done that to protect her?

Dani cried, draining the emotional torment with her tears. When she finally mopped her face with her sleeve, her exhaustion receded, replaced by a tender seedling of hope. Lifting her head, she saw Willow watching her with big blue eyes. At making eye contact, Willow gurgled and arched.

"Hey, there. Don't worry. Mommy's fine. We're both home now."

She pushed herself to a stand and drew a deep breath, then blew it away.

"All right then."

Dani fixed them a light antipasto salad with plenty of olives and cheese. They ate on the pool deck that now seemed welcoming and benign.

That evening, Dani took her pills and readied herself for bed. Tate was in his office catching up on some work. She thought he was not so much on family leave as working remotely. It was too much: his work, the campaign, Willow, and then all her issues with adjusting to finally being home.

She kissed them both goodnight and headed to bed alone.

Tate was doing his best for her. She knew that in her heart. But why hadn't Tate told her about the security system being off? Was it so as not to confront her about his suspicions that there was no woman? Perhaps not to scare her because if the woman had gotten in through an unlocked door, the alarm would not have been triggered. Dani could arm the system, but then opening a door would set it off.

And why didn't the police check for fingerprints? Was this too small an incident to investigate?

It was, she decided. In their eyes it was next to nothing. What she saw could have been a lawncare person at the window, the pool service heading to the back to adjust the chemicals, or the man from the bug service brushing away spiderwebs. But it was a woman. A dangerous woman. Dani had seen her.

But no one else had.

Despite all her problems, his work, his campaign, he was here, and he was caring for the baby at night so that she did not have to halt her evening doses of the medications. For that, she was grateful. After the incident with the mirror, keeping on a schedule seemed more vital. Dani needed to be able to think and reason herself out of trouble caused by her brain injury.

And she needed to convince others that what she saw was not her imagination.

In the morning, she found Tate and Willow in the kitchen. Tate was wearing a yellow T-shirt and jams. She recognized him before she even reached the doorway by his voice and the Foo Fighters song that he made sound like a lullaby.

Already dressed and showered, she felt as clean as the morning, minus the normal humidity.

"There's my two favorite people," she said.

"Look," said Tate in the cutest little voice imaginable. "There's Mommy."

He grinned and Willow waved her arms, now cocooned in sleeves that covered her hands.

"That's a cute onesie," she said, stepping forward. "I don't remember seeing that one. Are those little monkeys?"

Tate smiled and handed her a mug of coffee. "Your pills are on the table. English muffin or toast?"

She was supposed to take her morning round of medication with food.

"What kind of toast?"

"Wheat toast. Raisin muffin."

"Raisin."

He opened the packaging, then used a fork to split the muffin into two pieces before inserting them into the toaster. She noted that butter, peanut butter, and blueberry jam were already open and on the kitchen table.

"How long have you been up?" she asked.

"Oh, we were awake at four-thirty and then dozed until just before six." He turned to Willow and brushed a long finger down her tiny nose. "Weren't we, dewdrop?"

She smiled at the adorable pet name that had fallen so freely from his lips. She hadn't really been the same with Willow, not as easy. Doubts crept in and so she turned to her pile of medications, taking one and then a sip of coffee until they were all gone.

The toaster popped and Tate delivered her breakfast on a plate with a clean knife and paper napkin.

"There you go."

She mentally added short-order cook to his list of responsibilities.

"I feel you have two of us to take care of."

He leaned in and kissed her. "Which sounds like paradise to me."

"Hmm," she said as he drew back, still savoring the velvety feel of his lips on hers. "I could get used to this."

He straightened and gave her an expression of contentment.

"I'm just so glad to have you home."

Dani forced a smile and then buttered the muffin.

"What shall we do today?" he asked.

"I don't have any plans." She didn't have to see her doctor for another day. "Do you?"

"I was hoping to take a walk around the neighborhood. Show off the new baby."

The anxiety bubbled up like road tar in the summer sun.

"It's boiling."

"Only seventy-five. It's a cool front for two more days."

She thought of the stranger, the one only she had seen and that only she and Shelby believed was real. What if that woman was out there waiting to snatch Willow?

"Hey, breathe." Tate pressed a hand between her shoulder blades. "It's safe. You're safe."

"But what if she's there?"

"You went for a walk yesterday all by yourself. Everything was fine."

"Yes, but..." She thought of the woman in the mirror. How could she trust herself out there in the world? "What about the woman that only I saw?"

"You're safe, honey. It's a safe neighborhood."

"Do you believe me, about the woman?"

"Dani, I believe you. All I said was there was no evidence to back you up."

That was a start, she supposed.

"You going to spend all your life inside this house because someone bad might be out there?"

She knew he expected her to say, "No, of course not." But she wanted to scream, "Yes, certainly. Why wouldn't I want to stay where I'm safe?"

But she only really felt secure here because of Tate. But he couldn't stay with her every minute of the day. He had work. A campaign. She knew he had to go.

She took the last bite of the muffin, washing it down with orange juice. Dani hoped the anxious flutter in her belly was just the normal lull when she was at the low point of medication before her body took in the drugs and rebalanced toward optimism.

"A short walk. Okay? I don't want Willow to get overheated."

He grinned. "Sure. I'll set up the stroller."

"And the sun cover."

But he was already gone.

"Your papa certainly is keen to take a walk," she said to Willow, who now had a serious expression on her face that made her little brow furrow.

A moment later, she opened her mouth and wailed.

"Oh, precious. I'm here." She retrieved Willow from her carrier and cradled her. Was she hungry or wet?

An attempt to feed her the remains of her bottle met with resistance and a check of her diaper found her clean and dry.

Dani wondered if the trouble was her. Tate had gone, leaving the infant alone with Dani.

She knows, Dani thought. *She absolutely knows I'm an*

imposter mother. That I can't do this and that she's not safe with me.

Dani put Willow back in the carrier and offered a pacifier.

The baby continued to wail, hesitating only to fill her little lungs, before howling her outrage.

Dani used the soft bib to dry her tears and wondered if the alarming shade of red was normal.

Tate returned. "Oh, what's wrong, dewdrop?"

He lifted her from the carrier and up onto his shoulder in one smooth, natural motion. There the baby curled against Tate's body as if some tiny extension of him. The wailing stopped and Willow sighed.

"How did you do that?"

"Do what?"

"I picked her up. I tried to feed her, change her, rock her. She just kept on sobbing."

"Babies cry. That's how they get things done."

But Dani couldn't comfort her own daughter. Willow wanted Tate.

She drew a breath and blew it away with her growing anxiety.

Tate kissed the top of her head. "Don't sweat it. You'll have the hang of it soon." He started a strange bouncing walk, jostling Willow, who yawned and closed her eyes. Tate now cooed to the infant as he walked from the kitchen island to the living room. "Who needs a nap? Dewdrop, that's who."

Dani watched them go, feeling the medication dulling her emotions. Not that she didn't feel the sadness, more like the pills formed a seal around the sorrow, locking it down, smothering the flames like a campfire deprived of oxygen. But the embers still burned, emitting wisps of smoke.

Tate returned with a sleeping baby.

"Just tired." He grinned. "Ready?"

They headed out, Tate effortlessly fixing the carrier to the stroller frame and adjusting the canopy. The early morning light cut between the palm trees and houses, casting long blue shadows across the green grass. A pleasant breeze blew uncharacteristically from the north, bringing the cooler weather front Tate mentioned.

They had barely cleared the driveway when a woman approached.

Dani clenched Tate's arm.

"Look," she hissed and showed the approaching threat with a nod of her head.

THIRTEEN

"That's Enid Langford. Our neighbor," Tate whispered, then raised a hand to the approaching stranger. "Howdy, neighbor."

Dani relaxed her shoulders. This was a person both she and her husband liked and trusted.

"Hey, you two!" Enid's smile was bright as her red lipstick.

Tate's colleague was curvy and full-breasted, with wide hips sheathed in a wrap dress that emphasized both.

What in the world was Paul thinking to leave her? Enid was as voluptuous as a 1940s Hollywood bombshell.

Dani suddenly felt dowdy in her blouse, capri pants, and flats.

"Enid, what a surprise." Tate said this with a tone of irony, as if seeing her practically before her own home was really no surprise at all.

"Hello, Tate. Hello again, Dani." Enid stepped forward and offered an air kiss before moving away. "And here's little Willow." Enid bent over the carrier, now fixed to the roller frame.

Dani glanced to Tate. "She's met the baby?"

"I walk in the mornings and sometimes at night. Helps put her back to sleep."

"And I do my walking early, but for me it's beating the heat," said Enid.

It would be hot and muggy right into September. Then the drier weather would inch in, and the temperatures fall slightly. Fewer afternoon clouds would build to thunder domes and by mid-November they'd reach the end of another hurricane season. Still, they'd have to wait until well into December before they might get nights cool enough that the air conditioner finally shut off and she could open the windows.

Were early-morning walks why Mr. Vanderhorn never saw her?

"I thought you'd hurt your ankle," said Dani.

Enid's gaze shifted to Tate and then to her.

"It was nothing. Barely even swollen." She extended a shapely leg for their inspection.

Enid cooed over their daughter as Dani cleared her throat and gathered herself to broach a delicate topic.

"Enid, Tate told me about Paul. I'm so sorry," said Dani.

Enid's face reddened. "Yes. It's getting ugly."

"Oh, I'm sorry. You two seemed so happy."

"Not for a while now. And he had some medical problems he wouldn't address."

Dani wondered if she meant the fertility issues Mr. Vanderhorn had blabbed about to her. She almost asked, but it was none of her business.

"That's unfortunate."

"And he hasn't even made partner yet."

Meanwhile, Dani thought, Tate had made partner and won a seat on the circuit court bench in the same amount of time.

Enid exhaled out of her nostrils like a fire-breathing dragon. "But he gets me fired. Mr. Buckingham gave me two weeks' notice."

"Isn't that illegal?"

"It would be if he told me the reason that he fired me was Paul. But he said that business was slow because of the pandemic and they were making staff reductions."

"That's terrible." Perhaps she shouldn't have mentioned Paul because it just made Enid dwell on the hard time she was experiencing.

"You doing okay?" Enid asked Dani. "Happy to be home?"

Dani hesitated so long that both Enid and Tate exchanged a look. It was a simple question, and the answer could be as banal as this conversation.

"It's very good to be home and I'm well. Feeling well."

Her words sounded awkward and uncertain. Dani cast Tate a helpless, apologetic look. Then she glanced back to the house, struggling against the need to be away from the street where anyone in the neighborhood could watch her foundation crumble.

Who among their neighbors knew that she'd been in a psych ward? How many would question her competence to care for a baby?

"Well, that's great," said Enid, interrupting Dani's dark musings. "It's good to have you back."

Enid peered at Dani. Her smile froze as her dark eyes relayed an expression of concern.

"Yes, it's great," Dani parroted. Great, except for the possible hallucination, the fistfuls of prescriptions, and the twice-weekly appointments with a psychiatrist. Oh, and her fear of driving and unremitting guilt over causing Shelby's injuries.

"You look a little pale. You should get more sun."

Dani forced a smile.

"How's Shelby?" asked Enid.

The lump in her throat and the ripping pain across her

middle nearly toppled her. She remained standing, smiling as she grabbled with her pain.

"She's doing great. Getting a van that she'll be able to drive so she can come and see the baby."

Enid's perfect brows lifted. "Really?" She glanced at Tate. "How lovely."

The next pause in the conversation made Dani shift in discomfort. She'd forgotten how difficult small talk could be. But Tate filled the gap effortlessly.

"How goes the job hunt? You find anything yet?" he asked.

"A few irons in the fire. In the short term, I've got a part-time bookkeeping gig. Working remotely. I was thinking of starting a daycare service here, but I don't believe the HOA would allow it."

"That's right. No business of any kind," said Tate, quoting the development restrictions.

"Well, the bookkeeping isn't quite enough to replace my income, so I'm thinking of driving for Uber or Grubhub. I'm an excellent driver." She looked at Dani at this comment, and Dani's empathy for Enid wavered.

"What about substitute teaching? You're certified, aren't you?" asked Tate.

"Yes, it may come to that. Don't get me wrong, I love kids, just not twenty at a time. But by September, I may change my mind."

Dani got an idea then. Enid lived right across the street. She needed money and was an excellent driver with a degree in early-childhood education. Maybe she could help with Willow when Tate went back to court.

Tate would probably want some fancy hired nanny. But Dani didn't want a stranger in their house. At least, she knew Enid from before.

"Well, I'll let you two finish your walk." Their neighbor cast them a little wave and headed up her drive.

She and Tate strolled slowly along. Dani waited until they were well away before sharing her thoughts.

"Do you trust Enid?" she asked.

"Trust her with what?"

"Would you trust her with Willow?"

Tate stopped pushing the stroller and faced her.

"What's on your mind, Dani?"

She told him and he nodded, thinking in silence for a time.

"Well, she could certainly work her remote job around our schedule. It might be enough to hold her until the divorce finalizes, but it might not. And we could lose her to a better gig."

"Yes, but you need to get back to work. It's an election year and it looks bad for you to miss so many cases."

"You're right. It occurred to me that my opponent might use it against me. The leave time."

"Can't have that," said Dani. "And I need help. A driver and someone, you know, to be sure that everything runs smoothly."

"I don't think Enid has ever cared for a baby. I'm not sure she'd want to."

"Will you ask her?"

"You feel that comfortable with her?"

"Better than a stranger. I know Enid, at least."

They shared a smile and he headed upstairs to his office. When he reappeared, she was having a cup of tea and Willow slept in her bouncer on the table.

"She said yes. We worked out a salary and payment schedule. She'll be a private contractor, so responsible for the taxes. It all has to be done legally."

"Because of the campaign," said Dani.

"Because it's the right thing to do," he said. "She'll be over in a bit to go over details with you on Willow's care."

"Fantastic."

Enid listened and took notes as Dani and Tate went over
feeding schedules in the kitchen. Willow woke, yawned,
scrunched up her face and began to cry.

"Here, let me," said Enid.

She swooped in, expertly released the safety harness, and
lifted Willow to her chest. The baby's knees curled under
Enid's breasts as she splayed across the stranger's body.

Dani felt a tug of jealousy, which she quickly stanched.
Enid swayed back and forth, and Willow quieted. Their
neighbor moved with such confidence, it rattled Dani.

Dani refused to allow herself to feel threatened by Enid's
competence with the baby. At least, that was what she told
herself. After all, she'd invited this woman in, wanted her help.
She needed her.

"I'll take her." Dani reached out for Willow.

"Oh, of course." Enid relinquished the infant and Dani
suggested they head to the nursery.

Enid trailed behind her, stepping into the newly decorated
room.

"Oh, this is lovely. And you have all the gadgets. Is that a
light?"

"Music and light." Dani tapped the top to turn it on.

"That must be nice at night. Low light, so soothing."

"Yes." Dani realized she'd never seen the light at night. "But
Willow is in our room for now."

Enid smiled. "Certainly, easier for feeding, but then you
need to warm the formula. Such a rigmarole, and not as natural
as breast milk."

Dani drew a disposable diaper from the basket and nodded
at the observation.

"Sadly, not an option," she said.

"No. Unfortunately. Do you want me to change her?"

"I'll do this one, show you where everything is."

Dani removed the dirty diaper and cleaned her daughter as Enid watched.

Her silent observer made her so nervous she dropped the soiled diaper into the hamper and missed. She stooped to retrieve it and came up to find Enid at the changing table, a hand on Willow, whom Dani had released as she bent.

Dani sucked in a breath. She'd been right. Maybe she couldn't do this.

But Willow was too young to roll or turn over. And the mat had side bumpers. Still, her heart was hammering in her temples.

My God, Dani thought. *What if she'd fallen? Then that would be my fault, too. I'm a terrible mother.*

"Would you like me to get her dressed?" asked Enid. "My pleasure."

Dani nodded numbly as Enid snapped up the onesie, then lifted Willow and handed her to Dani.

Enid headed toward the nursery door. "I'll see you downstairs."

She sailed out of the room. Was she going to tell Tate that Dani had left the baby on the table without the safety strap?

Willow kicked her tiny legs enthusiastically. Alone with her daughter, Dani relaxed.

"This is more like it, isn't it, jellybean?" She tried out the nickname and shook her head.

Not quite right.

"Do you like Enid, gumdrop?" No, that one didn't fit, either, and was too close to dewdrop. Dani swaddled Willow, thinking she had it right, but the tucking and adjusting took longer than when the visiting nurse had done it.

Practice, she thought. And she'd have plenty.

Tate was going back to work. She knew he was an over-achiever. She loved that about him, but in this case, it added some strain. She was determined not to let him see. It was a small sacrifice to help him win the election and she could do that much after all he'd done for her.

Rather than head downstairs, she placed the baby in the crib. Staring down at the perfect little girl, she pictured what might have happened if Enid had not been there and sucked in a faltering breath.

As she wiped her sweating hands on her slacks, she drew out her cell phone and called her twin. It took three endless rings for Shelby to answer.

"Hi, Dani-o. What's up?"

"I took my hand off the baby."

"What?"

She explained, babbled really.

"I think being around someone else just made you nervous. Don't worry about it."

"She does make me nervous. I don't know why. I thought I wanted help."

"Don't beat yourself up over it."

"I feel so stupid. Incompetent."

"As all new mothers do. It's normal. Mistakes are normal, too."

Dani thought about the big mistake that had cost Shelby the ability to ever walk again. She sank to the carpet beside the crib, feeling worse.

"You think it's normal?"

"I do."

Dani wasn't sure. But now that she spoke her fears out loud, she thought she seemed to have overblown the situation.

"You're being paranoid," said Shelby.

"Hmm," said Dani. "You know what they say. Just because I'm paranoid—"

"Doesn't mean they aren't all out to get me," finished Shelby and laughed. Then she went silent for a moment as Dani gripped the phone, eyes squeezed tight against the painful thudding of her heart. Finally, Shelby asked, "My advice is to let Enid help you."

"How did you know her name?" asked Dani.

Now Shelby went silent again.

"Whose name?" she said at last.

"The neighbor. I didn't mention her name."

"Yes. You did. And you told me the only one you knew in the neighborhood was one of Tate's colleagues, Enid Langford."

"Did I?"

"Dani, are you all right?"

"No. I don't think so."

"Are you taking all the medications you are supposed to be taking?"

"Yes."

"Then my advice is to relax and let Tate and your neighbor help you. That's his job, to help you."

"Yes. All right."

"Dani, you've only been home a few days. Give yourself a break. No one expects you to be an idiot savant on child rearing."

Maybe just the idiot part, she thought.

"Okay. Yes. You're right."

"I am. So... you good?"

"I think so. Thanks, Shelby."

"My pleasure."

"Love you, big sister," said Dani.

"I love you, too."

Shelby disconnected and Dani checked on Willow, finding her asleep again. She left her there and headed out to find Tate and Enid, but found Tate alone in the living room, flipping through something on his phone.

"Everything all right?" he asked, not looking up.

She came to sit on the couch, perpendicular to his Danish leather recliner.

"Yes, fine. She's asleep."

"About time to feed her." He set his phone aside.

"Where's Enid?" asked Dani.

"Headed home. She said she'll see you tomorrow."

Dani took a deep breath. "Did she mention anything?"

"Like what?"

"Oh, nothing."

Perhaps Enid had not told him about her mistake.

"Dani?"

She flicked her attention back to Tate. "Yes?"

His brow wrinkled. "I asked if you felt all right?"

"Oh, I'm perfect."

He nodded, looking unconvinced.

That evening, Tate headed for the kitchen to grab a drink and she followed carrying the baby. As he poured her Pellegrino, he asked what kind of a bottle warmer they should get.

"I have no idea. Want me to do some research?"

"I did that. There are ones with just a quick warm and others with both a quick and steady warm feature. What do you think?"

She cast him a bewildered look.

The options yawned before her, forming unending opportunities to make mistakes. Dani placed Willow in the carrier. Willow's eyes never opened as Dani fiddled with the clip.

"Don't you have an opinion?"

She shook her head.

"I'll get the one with all the options. Better value."

It was the first time she'd heard him sound uncertain about anything.

Her gaze flashed to him. His blue eyes glittered with excess moisture.

She reacted immediately, her throat closing so she could barely speak.

"Tate? What is it?"

"I'm scared."

She sank to the kitchen stool beside him.

"You are?"

He nodded, head down.

The possibility that he felt some of the same anxiety she experienced gave her an odd sense of reassurance. "Of what?"

"That... that I made a mistake. We wanted a baby so badly, then I had a chance, and I took it. But I should have waited. Dr. Allen said so. You've only been back ten days. What if this is too much for you?"

She rested a hand on his. She'd never seen him like this before. Now it was her turn to support him. "Tate, I love Willow. She's not a mistake."

"But it's too soon."

"We'll manage. Just stop trying to handle it all. I can help."

He nodded. "Yes. Okay. I'm sorry. I just need this to work. I don't want you to get sick again."

"I'm fine, Tate. I'm better."

He squeezed her hand, drew it to his mouth, and kissed it. They sat in silence, staring at their sleeping daughter for a time, then he picked up the smartphone and ordered the bottle warmer online.

"Be here tomorrow. Can't believe I forgot to get one of these."

Before he set aside the phone, it chimed, indicating a text alert. He read the message as he spoke to her. "The doctor's office. Willow has her first check with the pediatrician tomorrow at eleven."

They had a pediatrician?

"We do? You'll drive?" asked Dani, pleased that her voice sounded calm as the needle of ice stabbed at her heart.

"Enid will."

That made her cold all over. Dani had asked for her help, thinking she was doing the right thing for everyone, and that Enid would be here in the house with her. She hadn't even considered that Enid would be chauffeuring her around. Was she brave enough to get into a car with Enid? But the thought of sending Enid alone to the appointment with Willow stiffened her spine.

"You're going back in tomorrow?"

"Unless you want me to stay."

That request seemed unreasonable, even if that was exactly what Dani wanted. Equally, she wanted him to feel comfortable going back to work, instead of worrying about her.

"That's not necessary."

"Do you want me to move the appointment?"

"No. She should have her check-up."

"All right then."

She didn't have the courage. But she'd find it.

"What about the baby seat?" Her breathing was coming fast again.

"She can drive your car. The base is already in there. You just clip in the carrier."

"Oh, right. Fine." It wasn't fine. She stanched the urge to call Shelby.

"I could stay."

"No." Her denial was sharper than intended.

Tate's ears drew back.

Dani tried again.

"No, I'm going. I can do this. I'll be fine." That time, she kept her voice level.

Tate nodded. "I asked her to wear something yellow. You know, to help you identify her because of the..." He waved his hand in front of his face, as if she needed reminding that she could not identify Enid from her own sister.

Dani nodded and looked away, fighting off the deepening sadness at her limitations. She had intended to be an equal partner to her husband, not a burden.

When Dani woke on Thursday, she found the bedroom empty and both Tate, Willow, and the baby bassinet gone. He'd gotten up before her again and she hadn't heard a thing. The stroller attachment was downstairs, so he wasn't walking.

But the carrier was missing.

She hurried to the security monitor panel but could not remember how to access video footage.

"Don't panic. Don't panic. They're out walking."

The doorbell chimed, indicating detection of motion. She hurried to the front door and peered out the window.

Tate held Willow in the carrier as he walked with a dark-headed woman in a yellow blouse and white skirt. In her hair was a yellow flower.

Enid. Dressed in yellow, as requested. Obviously, he'd walked over to pick her up.

Up the driveway they came, matching step for step, slowing as if to linger outside in the rising heat, rather than progress into the house.

They paused on the front step.

Not wishing to appear to be spying on her husband, Dani backed away from the small square bevel in one of the two clear stained-glass windows set in the massive doors.

In the kitchen, she forced herself to make a cup of coffee. When they appeared in the foyer, she sat with the brew before her, trying to look relaxed so that Tate could feel comfortable going to work.

"Good morning," Enid said to Dani.

"I feel like a lazybones. Last one up," said Dani, forcing a smile for Tate.

"Did I wake you?" he asked, stepping forward to give her a one-armed hug. He didn't kiss her, and she frowned.

Perhaps their audience made him change his usual morning greeting?

"Willow was fussing," Tate said, "so after breakfast, I took her out for some air and ran into Enid."

"I see. Some coffee?" she asked them.

"None for me." He grinned at Dani. "Did you take your pills?"

Dani flushed, both at his mention of her medication and the fact that he felt the need to check on her before their guest. She sucked in a breath at the realization that she had not taken any of them. Now her cheeks flamed.

Apparently, she did need checking on, and that shamed her.

"Just about to."

"Not on an empty stomach."

"Yes, I know." Her gaze darted to Enid and then back to the floor.

"I'll fix you some scrambled eggs and toast," said Enid.

"Oh, Enid, that's not necessary. I can do it. You're not here to look after me, after all."

This was met with silence and her smile died away. Had Tate agreed to hire her to also look after Dani? That possibility made her stomach clench.

Of course he had. Dani's doctor had counseled she not be left alone, so Enid was here for more than company and to help care for Willow.

"I'll just go change this little cutie." Enid relieved Tate of the carrier, pausing at the door and turning back. "I had to dig in my closet for this yellow blouse. Summer colors aren't my thing. I'm more winter, according to my charts. Did you see the yellow flower?" She patted it with a free hand. "Had that left over from a luau-themed party. I'll wear it here every day."

The thought of seeing Enid's bright, confident smile and that artificial flower each day further darkened Dani's mood.

Enid was gazing at Willow. "You two are so lucky. If Paul and I could have... well, he wasn't willing to try... Beginning of the end, really."

Enid headed for the stairs. Dani scooped up the monitor and flicked on the video feed.

Tate took the bread from the refrigerator and then the eggs and milk.

"She'll get you to the appointment with Dr. Lynes."

Pediatrician, thought Dani. Eleven o'clock.

"What about my appointment this afternoon?"

"I get home in time to take you. All right?"

"Yes."

Dani lowered the volume on the monitor, reducing the sound of Enid cooing and babbling to Willow as she lowered her to the changing table out of sight. The camera was set on the wall and over the crib. It didn't give a view of the opposite side of the room.

"Will you be all right until I get home?" He retrieved a bowl and cracked two eggs into the container single-handed. "I should be back by one."

"Tate, I'm not a child." Dani said this, realizing she was sitting on a stool opposite him at the kitchen island, the child she claimed not to be, as he made her breakfast.

She rose and opened the bread bag and put two slices in the toaster, then retrieved a whisk and nudged him away from the bowl.

"Dani, I want you safe and happy. This is a big adjustment for you."

Naturally shy, Dani preferred her own company to anyone else's, other than Tate or Shelby.

"Did we hire her just for the baby or is she here to look after me, too?"

Tate stilled, his expression registering shock.

"Dani, I love you. And I trust you with Willow. Everything I'm doing is to make this easier for you. You're better. Your doctor said it's safe for you to be home. We've got a baby. My work is good, and the campaign is on track. Everything is happening for us now. This is exactly what we always wanted."

"Yes. It is." So why was she so unsettled?

"I'll be back in time to take you to your afternoon appointment with Dr. Allen. All right?"

She nodded, already wishing to speak to her therapist. So much of this return home was making her edgy. She didn't want to worry Tate, but she wasn't certain she was adjusting.

Back at the facility she felt safe. Here she felt exposed and judged.

Then a more concerning thought struck. If she were honest with Dr. Allen, it might add to her doctor's concerns about the adoption. It might threaten Willow. Now her anxiety morphed into terror.

If she appeared incapable, they could take her daughter.

Tate kissed her. "See you in a few hours. You're doing just great! I'm so proud of you."

FOURTEEN

The late-morning appointment with the pediatrician had gone smoothly but took longer than Dani expected. The worst part was the drive to and from. On the way home, Dani clenched her fists in her lap and gritted her teeth against the speed Enid drove at. She pulled into Dani's drive just before one in the afternoon.

The garage door rolled upward as Enid scooted them underneath and braked, jabbing the SUV into park. Dani just managed to stifle her scream.

Enid, unaware of Dani's panic, turned to Dani, her smile bright.

"Here we are. See you tomorrow?"

She'd thought Enid was supposed to stay until Tate arrived home. She glanced at the dashboard clock just as Enid shut off the engine. It was twenty minutes to one.

Tate had assured her that Enid was not here to be her keeper. Enid's actions bore that out, but Dani discovered herself unsettled at the idea of being alone in the house.

Her husband would be home any minute. There was no problem.

When Dani didn't move, Enid frowned. "Want me to head in to get the little one settled?"

"No. That's not necessary."

"Okay. See you tomorrow."

Enid dropped the keys into the cup holder and left the SUV in the center of the garage. She gave a little wave before heading home.

Dani watched her go, noting that Enid captured the attention of several men working on the roof across the street. Only after their neighbor vanished behind the ornamental palms, did Dani realize Enid parked the vehicle in such a way that Tate would not be able to fit past her SUV and into his normal parking place.

She should be able to move it. Back it up and then back into the proper spot. Simple.

For a long time, she just stood there, beside the passenger seat, looking at the driver's side. Sweat made her hands damp. She wiped the moisture from her upper lip.

"It's just ten feet. I can do it."

She hiked her purse up on her shoulder and marched around the vehicle. But when she reached the driver's side, she found that opening the door gave her goosebumps and her hands trembled.

"We're going right out again, anyway," she whispered, justifying her cowardice.

It would not take long for the car to heat even in the open garage. Dani retrieved Willow and the stroller base in the back.

A male voice made Dani freeze with the carrier on her arm. There in the street was a man in an orange ball cap. Beside him a familiar golden retriever panted and then sat the minute his owner paused.

"Mr. Vanderhorn," she said.

He and Rocket were now heading up the drive. "Call me Doug, please."

She fixed Willow's carrier to the stroller base in one smooth movement as if she'd been doing this all her life. Satisfaction twinkled within.

"Is that the new baby?"

Did he not remember meeting Willow?

She held her smile. "Yes, it is."

He paused to bend over the carrier.

"Oh, she's beautiful."

Rocket crept closer and Vanderhorn gave a little tug on the leash.

"Sit, Rocket. You'll scare her." Then he spoke to Dani. "Rocket loves children. Tends the grandkids like they're her own." He grinned, looking back at Willow. "She's so tiny. I forget how little the newborns are." He straightened. "Lucky little girl to grow up here. You know there is a playground at the community center. Brand-new. And swim lessons offered at the community pool. She can even take boating or horseback lessons through them."

"I think we'll wait until she can sit up before swim lessons."

"They take babies. It's natural. They can already float and swim."

"Sounds dangerous."

"It's not. You check it out."

"Yes, I'll do that."

Rocket had managed to inch closer while maintaining a seated position and was working her nose overtime.

"Rocket, you rascal. Come on now." The pair retreated down the drive. "You have a lovely day, Mrs. Sutton."

Dani watched them amble down the road and out of sight. The mail truck appeared and stopped at the end of the drive, placing the mail and a padded envelope in their box.

The carrier waved and pulled away, accelerating, and then braking at the next address.

Dani looked at Willow. "Shall we go get the mail?"

Willow waved her chubby arms and made a gurgling sound. "I'm taking that as a yes."

Feeling brave and confident, Dani pushed the stroller down the drive. The midday sun beat on the top of her head. She adjusted the sun shield and continued on, thinking this was perhaps a bad idea. Newborns couldn't regulate their body temperature and it had to be over ninety out today.

"Dr. Lynes said walking outside was good for us both," she said, repeating the pediatrician's words.

But was it?

Down the street, an older man walked a familiar fat white dog. She waved, and he returned the salute before carrying both his mail and the pooch toward his front door. She could see the canine's pink tongue lolling from here.

Now she hurried along to the box. Even the metal latch scorched. Dani tucked the mail under her arm and reversed direction. Suddenly the street seemed exceedingly empty. She paused to glance about, uncertain what had caused her senses to go on alert.

The street lay devoid of cars, canines, or people. Even the roofers had vanished. Not a living person in sight. Now the breeze blew hot, and the palms rustled. Above, the white clouds climbed, billowing in preparation for the predicted afternoon showers.

"Let's get you inside," she said, but her gaze was still skyward at the monstrous cloud to the west that already had the characteristic gray underbelly.

A screech froze her in place. Dani spun in the direction of the sound. The mail, tucked under her arm, dropped to the drive. A woman with wild eyes and dark, snarled hair screeched again and shouted.

"My baby! Give her back! Give her to me."

Dani did not stop to think. She ran, pushing the stroller before her, bolting up the drive. A backward glance showed the woman charging across the yard in a path to intercept, darting through the hedge and the center garden, past the cluster of fuchsia-topped bromeliads.

Her arms reached out, white beneath the dirty pink sheath of a dress.

Dani raced beside the SUV as the woman burst through the garage's side door and into the open space before them. Why wasn't that locked?

"Give her back! Give me my baby!"

Dani disconnected Willow's carrier from the stroller in one quick jab and tug. The woman now stood before the front bumper, blocking the entrance to the house from the garage. Dani veered to the vehicle and jumped inside the rear seat and slammed the door. She fastened Willow's carrier into the infant seat base before scrambling over the console to the driver's seat. Outside the vehicle, the woman charged around the SUV. Dani jabbed at the lock button, but accidentally engaged her driver's-side window control, too. The door locked as the woman yanked at the rear door handle.

The intruder slapped her palms on the window in frustration, then cupped her hands around her eyes to peer in at Willow.

"No," Dani whispered, glancing in the rearview to check the carrier holding Willow.

Her attacker tried the locked rear door again. Failing to gain access, she moved to Dani's window, her silver-gray eyes wild as she pounded, making the partially opened window vibrate. It was going to break. Dani glanced at the door to the house just a few steps away. If she did manage to reach the entrance, she'd need to unlock it because she'd locked it before leaving. And once it was open, the woman might also get in.

House keys in your purse. Find them.

She scrambled for the key ring as the woman stopped

pounding. Dani turned to see her, noting the one-inch gap at the top of the window.

The woman's wild dark hair stuck out in all directions and the strange silver eyes flashed around dilated pupils. Her smile chilled as she thrust her fingers over the glass.

Dani could not draw a breath. She searched for escape, glancing from the door to the house, to Willow fussing in her carrier, her tiny cries of distress echoing Dani's. Her attacker now had her fingers curled to claw the window. White blood-less fingers tensed.

The fob! She dragged her purse around and hit the panic button for the house alarm. The siren screamed, along with her intruder. Her attacker jerked at the glass. Dani lifted her arms to shield her face as the window exploded and tiny cubes of glass rained outward. Dani twisted in her seat, glancing back at Willow in her carrier as their attacker reached past Dani toward the baby.

Dani screamed and hit the ignition button, jerked the SUV into reverse, and stomped the accelerator. The vehicle plowed out of the garage, dragging the woman. She dropped off before they reached the drive. Dani saw her land on all fours like a cat and then straighten.

They left the pavers and bounced over landscaping. Dani braked and then spun the wheel as she cast a glance to the empty garage.

Where had she gone?

Now the SUV hurtled down the drive, over the scattered envelopes, clipping the mailbox as she sped diagonally over the road, through the hedge and onto the lawn of Enid and Paul Langford. There she braked, one hand on the wheel and one reaching between the seats to grip Willow's carrier. The SUV narrowly missed the concrete steps. Dani leaned on the horn drowning out Willow's feeble cries.

She caught movement in her periphery and scanned the

yard to her right but saw nothing but the ornamental hedgerow of jasmine.

Her house siren continued to wail as she detached the carrier from the base and snatched it up, then dashed to the entrance to pound on Enid's front door.

A glance behind her showed the street, empty again. Her mailbox was splintered, electrical wires and the box scattered across the road with the broken post. But the woman had vanished.

"Where is she?" Her voice growled and squeaked, an unfamiliar thing. "Where's my phone?"

It was in her purse. Somewhere. Didn't the triggered house alarm call police automatically?

Dani's head was on a pivot, a periscope searching for an enemy destroyer.

"Come on!" she said, pounding again.

Finally, one of the double doors opened, and Enid stood in the same yellow blouse and skirt she had worn earlier.

"Dani! What in the world?"

———

Dani waited with Willow inside Enid's home as her neighbor went out to meet the police. She watched the woman walk confidently across the road and wave to the officer in the squad car.

Meanwhile, Dani remained where she was until a detective and her husband arrived simultaneously.

She left Willow in her carrier on the huge ottoman and rushed to Tate, throwing her arms about him as she sobbed. He gave her several minutes and then sat her on the ottoman beside Willow.

"Honey, this is Detective Jacobs. He needs to speak to you. I've already talked to them, to the alarm company, and to Enid."

What had he told them about her?

Dani sniffed and turned her attention to the man standing before her. He wore a white golf shirt with a police emblem stitched on the breast. The belt on his tan slacks held his gold shield, radio, and a black plastic gun in a plastic holster. The pocket in the front of his slacks revealed the outline of a large cell phone.

"Ma'am," he said, his voice holding a slight drawl. "Can you tell me what happened?"

His hair was so short on the sides that it was only stubble. On the top his light brown hair grew straight up. A flattop, she realized, distinctly military. As for his face, she could see the deep tan, long nose and a mole beneath his left eye. Markers to help her recognize him.

He asked what had happened. She started her retelling with the conversation with her neighbor, Mr. Vanderhorn.

He glanced to Tate. "I thought you said she couldn't identify faces?"

He nodded, and she interrupted.

"He often wears an orange ball cap and his dog, Rocket, is a large golden retriever."

The lawman nodded. "Go on."

She did, and he stopped her in places to clarify details. She tried her best to describe her attacker, the ragged dress, wild hair, and her silvery eyes.

The detective left them to speak to the patrol officers outside.

"Would you be all right if I made a phone call to the insurance company and a tow truck?" asked Tate.

"Tow truck?"

"You broke the axle either on the curb or the mailbox."

Dani lowered her head to her hands and sucked in a deep breath.

"I'm sorry."

He knelt beside her.

"Are you sure you saw someone, Dani?"

She lifted her head. "What?" Now she shivered in the air-conditioning, her skin gone to gooseflesh. "What does that mean?"

"The police told me that the glass from the broken side window was all over the garage floor. Hardly any in the cab. They said it broke outward."

"She got her hands on the top. She pulled..." Her words trailed off.

"Could you have broken it?"

"Me?" Didn't he believe her about the window being cracked open? If it were closed, the only way it could have exploded outward was... her. "The window was *open*. She grabbed it."

"You're sure?"

"Why would I break it?"

"I don't know. Maybe you saw something in the side mirror or..." His words trailed off.

"My reflection, you mean. You think I saw my image and panicked. Tate, she was there. She ran at me."

He rubbed his neck. "Dani, we checked the surveillance on the doorbell. All we see is you running up the drive and into the garage, then you flying backward in the SUV, into the land-scaping beside the entrance before disappearing out of sight."

"That doesn't make any sense. She ran at me. Followed me into the garage." Dani frowned, thinking back. "But she was in the street, behind the garage. She ran across the lawn to inter-cept me and... and through the side door. That's beyond the doorbell camera's view."

She smiled triumphantly and then saw the worry etching Tate's features. He didn't believe her.

"You think I'm hallucinating. You think it's like the woman on the lanai. I saw her, too."

"I know. I know you did."

He left the rest unsaid. He understood she saw it. But could anyone else?

Suddenly her psychiatrist's words to her husband made perfect sense.

Neither confront nor encourage.

Had she meant hallucinations? Did Dr. Allen know she was having them even before she'd left Windwood?

It explained her doctor's reluctance over the discharge. Her insistence that Dani not be left alone.

Was she hallucinating?

Dani didn't think so and she clung to her reality, for what else was there for her?

"They need to dust the knob to the door and the..." She was about to say the window, but that had broken. She remembered the sound of the glass exploding.

"The glass went outward because the window was cracked open," she repeated. Was she trying to convince him or herself? "She broke it outward."

He pressed his lips together, so they momentarily disappeared. His expression remained sympathetic. "Let's go home."

Tate collected Willow in the carrier and took hold of Dani's arm, helping her rise.

Outside, she got her first look at the chaos she'd caused. There were five police cars, a fire truck, the detective's vehicle, and a sheriff's van.

Several neighbors huddled together on the lawn with the best view, gawking and gossiping.

Dani groaned.

Her SUV sat at an odd angle across Enid's pristine lawn, which was now marred by deep gouges made by the tires across the soft earth. Beyond, her mailbox post lay splintered and in pieces, the box flattened.

She'd also managed to plow a gap in the Langfords' hedge, uprooting and flattening the jasmine.

"She was there," she said again.

Tate guided her from the entrance. He stepped away, carrying Willow, to speak to Jacobs. Dani approached her vehicle, examining the missing window.

"Don't touch that!" The command came from a female officer, who stood with hands on hips.

"No, I won't." Dani leaned forward, hands behind her, as she studied the window and that was when she saw it.

She lifted a trembling hand and pointed.

The officer stepped up beside her to look at the strands of long, dark hair caught in what remained of the glass window. Then she straightened and called over her shoulder.

"Detective Jacobs! You need to see this."

FIFTEEN

Tate left her and Willow to go speak to the neighbors—trying to control the narrative, he said. Image was important, especially during a campaign. She was certain that only the gates of the private community kept the camera crews from setting up on their lawn.

Even without video footage of her mad ride, the incident might make the news because of Tate's standing in the community and the upcoming election.

When he returned, he told her that police had arrested a dark-haired woman a mile outside the gates panhandling at the traffic light. She wore a stained blouse and held a cardboard sign.

"Silvery eyes?"

"I don't know."

Dani and Tate drove to the station in his sedan, leaving Enid with Willow, but Dani couldn't identify the suspect. She might have been Dani's attacker, or it might be any dark-haired woman in the city. All she knew for certain was that her clothing was different, and her eyes were brown.

"I'm sorry," she told the detective. "All I can say is that *could be* her."

Tate drove her home. Bone-deep weariness tugged at her shoulders.

"When did you eat?" he asked.

"I don't know. Breakfast?"

"You can't skip meals. Dr. Allen said to watch for dehydration and to keep your food intake regular."

"Yes, I'm sure she also advised against undergoing attack by strangers and crashing my car through mailboxes." Dani folded her arms, churlish despite the knowledge that Tate hated this sort of "unbecoming behavior."

He said nothing more but pressed his lips tight and adjusted his grip on the wheel.

They stopped for a bite, Tate choosing a fast-food place styled after the old-fashioned drive-ins. They parked in an empty car stall beside a huge, illuminated menu and placed their order. While waiting for their meal delivery, Tate scrolled through his mail and messages, then accepted the order at his window. She ate while Tate worked on his caramel milkshake and took several calls. One in particular grabbed her interest.

"Yes, Detective," he said, then listened, thanked the caller, and disconnected.

"That was Jacobs. They ran the prints. All they got from the car was you, me, and Enid. On the knob of the garage's exterior door only mine and Enid's."

"Enid? Why did they take her prints?"

"She drove your car. They have to eliminate her so they can check for prints that don't belong."

"Why would her prints be on the doorknob?"

"She has my permission to enter the garage. I leave that side door open so she can borrow the garden tools. She can't afford that service anymore and Paul cleared out their shed, the prick."

"I thought you liked Paul."

"Once upon a time. Divorces change people. Bring out the very worst in human nature. I see it all the time in the family law cases. I could tell you stories."

"Don't. I have enough nightmare material to last a lifetime."

They left the car stall and merged back onto the state highway. En route, she noted his gray trousers were streaked with grime.

"What happened to your pants?"

"Oh, I cleaned up what was left of the mailbox from the road. Helped Enid fill in those track marks, best I could. Must have happened then."

She hadn't thought of the damage she had done to their box or Enid's lawn.

"I need to apologize to her."

"I'll have our guy see if he can add some fill and grass seed. Fix the hedge. Apologies are fine, but making it right is better."

"Of course." She thought of the broken axle on her SUV and the probable damage to the front bumper. "I'm sorry, again."

"For protecting our baby? Don't be. You did great." He clasped her hand across the vehicle's central console and gave it a squeeze. "You're turning into a protective mama bear."

His belief meant everything. She'd been so afraid he'd tell the police she was hallucinating or that she was mentally ill. But he'd backed her up. Even with his misgivings over the doorbell footage and the car window. It kept him from accepting her accounts at face value. That was a problem for them both. But they could work through it. She knew they could because he loved her and, though he was still grappling with her conditions and new limitations, he'd taken her side.

"Instinct, I suspect."

He rubbed his neck. "I can't believe this is happening in our neighborhood."

She stared at the soiled knee of his trousers.

"We need to get that dry-cleaned." She'd have to call for a pickup because she no longer dropped off Tate's suits. That made her remember the stained suit he'd worn to the fundraiser, the one she couldn't find. She must have missed it in his closet.

For some reason that triggered a thought, and she gasped.

"I missed my appointment with Dr. Allen!"

That evening, Tate called the service and left a message for Dr. Allen but didn't explain why they had missed the appointment.

"You can explain it to her on Tuesday. Or not. That's your choice."

Why wouldn't she tell her doctor, Dani wondered. But the more she thought about it, the more she felt the episode reflected badly on her and her ability to cope.

Her psychiatrist might ask why she didn't use her cell phone to call for help or leave the garage and run to a neighbor. Why *hadn't* she done either of those things?

After Willow's evening feeding, they readied her for bed, finishing by setting the baby in her bassinet to sleep, and returned downstairs. In the living room, they had just settled before the gas fireplace when Shelby called.

She told Dani that she had had a bad feeling all afternoon. She and Shelby were like that. Their mom used to say, "Cut one and the other one bleeds."

Dani went through the horrors of the day, sparing Shelby nothing. Meanwhile, Tate watched her as he finished another generous glass of wine.

She was glad Tate left the room to open a second bottle, giving her a bit more privacy.

"Something about this doesn't sit right," said Shelby.

Dani had a similar feeling.

"She said, 'Give me my baby'?"

"Yes. Exactly. And those weird eyes. They are chilling."

"Who is she? The birth mother?"

"Can't be. The birth mother is in jail. Tate checked."

"Then why say, '*my baby*'? Plus, she had dark hair, and Willow has dark hair."

Dani rubbed her index finger absently around the rim of the water goblet, making it ring.

"What do you think happened?" Dani asked.

"Well, what if she *is* the mother and Tate has been less than honest with you?"

Dani swallowed hard, but the lump remained lodged in her throat. "You think that?"

"Yes."

"What should I do?"

Tate reappeared and offered her a glass of wine. She shook her head, and he took a seat, leaving the bottle sweating on the marble inlay side table and adding her wine to his glass. Then he directed his attention to the fire as he sipped.

"You need to confront him," said Shelby. "He's keeping something from you. I feel it."

Dani glanced to Tate to see if he overheard. If he did, he gave no sign.

"Yes. All right."

"Now, Dani. Tonight. Don't put it off."

Her nostrils flared as her breathing accelerated with her heartbeat. Already she dreaded the conversation. She didn't make accusations. But wasn't this all a part of protecting the baby?

The only times Tate had ever kept something from her was when it was in her best interest.

Or that was what she believed.

Suddenly she had doubts.

"Talk to him, now, Dani. Find out if the mother is really in prison."

"All right. But what if... what if it didn't happen? What if it's just in my head?"

"You don't hallucinate. It's real. She's real and she's a threat. Besides, you said there was physical evidence. The hairs."

"Yes. That's right."

"I'll call you in the morning. Love you, little sister."

"Love you more, big sister."

Shelby disconnected the call.

Tate glanced at her. "Your face is flushed."

"Yes. Shelby thought we should have a talk."

"Did she?" His smile was hard. "What about?"

He'd had too much to drink. Dani knew that, but instead of making her reticent, it gave her the courage she needed. Tate was a force to be reckoned with. If he didn't get his way, he'd appear to retreat, but it was only to regroup before trying again.

Tenacious, she used to think. "Pain in the ass" was how her mother had characterized her then boyfriend. She'd said Dani's father would have grouped him with the hangers-on. As if Tate were some parasite fixed to their family. She was glad the two had never met because her mother was likely right. Her daddy would have hated Tate. But would any man ever have been good enough for the daughters of the mighty Matthew Durant?

"Never can be gracious and take no for an answer. Just keeps after you. Like being pecked to death by geese," Roberta had said.

That had made her laugh at the time. Now, thinking of her father and mother both gone, it made her weary and sad. If not for Shelby, she'd have no blood family left.

Unlike her mother, Dani admired Tate. If not for his persistence, he would never have made it through law school or passed the bar or been the youngest judge ever to serve on the circuit court. Ambitious didn't cover it.

Driven was more like it. Tate got what he wanted. He knew how and he had the courage to get what he needed by recruiting necessary support and convincing others to pile on board his train.

Now she wondered what he'd been willing to do to make a family, working with only a broken, depressed, barren wife.

She drew a deep breath, bracing before saying what needed to be said. "I think you might have stolen this baby."

"What?" He sat up straight.

"I'm not her real mother, but that woman is and she wants her back. We can't keep her, Tate."

"Dani, please! Willow isn't a library book. We can't just return her."

"I'm sure you went to trouble to get her. But she isn't ours and we need to do what is right."

He gave her a long stare.

"Dani, what is it you are accusing me of?"

"I'm not stupid. I know I would never have qualified for a traditional adoption. I know you pulled some strings or cut corners." It was what he did. Impatience was one of Tate's flaws. Previously, she could afford to overlook that and indulge him.

But now she had a daughter to protect. Tate's desires came after Willow's safety.

"What do you want me to say?"

"Admit that Willow was stolen and tell me that you'll give her back to her mother."

"That's not going to happen."

She gave him a long, silent stare.

He blew away a breath and reached for the wine bottle.

"You've had enough," she said. "Now tell me what you're keeping from me and from the police. Tell me how you got Willow."

She had expected heartbreak at the thought her little girl wasn't truly hers. But she felt strangely calm. He sat back, sagging into the cushions, eyes closed as he pressed two fingers to the bridge of his nose. She knew that posture. It meant he'd done something of which she would not approve.

"Will you trust me and just let this go?"

She met his gaze and pressed her lips together in a hard line, wondering if she could. Obsessive thinking was one of her most challenging issues. This secret had all the makings of a mental forest fire. She'd never outrun it. Her only chance was knowing exactly what was really going on. She needed the truth, just as badly as she needed her medications.

"Not this time," she said.

He closed his eyes and sighed. In the silence, her mind provided a series of terrible possibilities, each worse than the last.

Dani swiped at the tears running down her face and regrouped. "I know you think you're protecting me by keeping me in the dark. But I'm not a child and I'm no longer depressed. I know you thought giving me a baby would help. We both want one. Desperately. But not like this."

"Why not like this?"

"Because I'm unfit! My God!" She used her fingers to tick off the reasons. "I just left a psych center. I'm on a half-dozen powerful medications. I confused my reflection for an attacker. I can't recognize faces. And I just crashed the car, again, with Willow inside. Can't you see this? It's all a mistake. I'm not ready to be a mother. You have to send her back. We have to keep her safe."

Finally, he met her gaze.

"All right. I'll tell you and you'll see that she belongs here with us."

She cocked her head, not sure what he'd say, but knowing she wouldn't like it.

"After the accident, you were so sick, Dani." He gave her a look that nearly broke her heart. "And for so long."

"Just over six months. It's not *that* long."

"You almost died."

A uterine tear, she'd been told. Potentially life-threatening.

"The doctor, your surgeon, was a fertility specialist. Like the one who removed your cyst."

Dani sat up straight, remembering. Her ovarian cyst had been benign, but costly just the same.

"Even before the accident, your doctor said the chance of you ever conceiving was small. We'd frozen your eggs, but the odds of them becoming viable embryos were also low. And then... then the clinic lost them."

Dani blinked away more tears. The day they'd gotten the letter saying her frozen eggs had been mistakenly destroyed had been one of the worst of both their lives. His gaze darted away and then back as if holding her stare caused him physical pain.

All her internal alarms were shrieking. What had he done? What need or whim or advantage had Tate decided he must have?

"We got a surrogate last fall."

This revelation caused a prickling apprehension to begin at her ears.

"We?"

The foreboding swarmed over her skin like bees on a hive.

His mouth went grim.

"You mean, *you*."

He met her gaze with a steady stare as he shook his head. "No, Dani. I mean *we*. Our decision. We did this together before the accident. You agreed it was time." He cast his gaze down as his shoulders sagged. "But you've forgotten that, with other things."

Suddenly Dani couldn't get enough air into her lungs. Her head swam and she swayed.

"I, we..."

His head bobbed, reminding her of her pet horse, anxious

for a sugar cube. "Yes. We signed the agreement together. Hired a surrogate."

"How could I forget that?"

"The head injury. I tried talking to you about it while you were away. But it upset you and Dr. Allen asked me to stop. But meanwhile..."

Meanwhile, their baby was growing day by day.

No wonder he wanted her home.

Dani sputtered. "But my eggs were destroyed."

"After I filed the suit, we discovered not all your eggs were in the same tank. Some—three—survived. We had the eggs transferred to a different clinic. I mean, after what happened, why would we keep them there?" He shrugged. "I gave them my sample. Paid the fee and medical bills, and they took care of the rest."

"The rest?" She blinked as she tried to process this. She had viable eggs.

"Dani, breathe."

She did, but the sound was rasping. All the time she'd been in the hospital, the psychiatric facility, there had been a baby, *her* baby, growing in a stranger's womb.

"We didn't really expect it to work."

That she recognized as a lie. Tate never did anything that he didn't expect to work.

"We did this together?"

"Yes. We wanted to be parents. We agreed to try surrogacy."

"Why tell me now?"

"Because you keep talking about sending her back, giving her away. She's your child, Dani. Yours and mine."

The realization struck like a jolt from a high-voltage line. She'd told him to cancel the adoption.

Only this wasn't an adoption. Was it?

"We can't send her back," she whispered. "Because she's mine."

"*Ours*. And when I thought you might die... that I was about to lose you forever... I was so glad that I'd, at least, have our child."

She blinked at him, trying to picture this time from his side, his wife in the ICU while their surrogate passed her first trimester.

Was this true? She didn't know. What she did know was that either he'd lied about the adoption or the surrogate. Either way, he'd deceived her.

"Why did you say it was an adoption?"

His neck was now blotchy and red. "To protect you. I was afraid if I told you, you'd get worse again." He met her gaze. "But this time, this time it's different. This time, you seem... ready to hear. And ready to be a mama. Ready to know the truth."

She knit her brow. Was she? If they'd hired a surrogate, it didn't matter if she was ready. Willow was here and she was theirs. Tate was father to a new baby and husband to a wife he had to insist be released from a psych center. She almost felt sorry for him. Almost.

Dani gasped as the revelation tingled through her bones. She was Willow's real mama. The joy came easily, warm as the pulse of blood through her veins.

The uncertainty arrived next. Did she believe him or just desperately wish to believe him?

It was a wish. She didn't know if she could or did trust Tate.

This unsettling doubt, was this what he meant when he claimed his attempts to tell her caused distress to the point that her doctor instructed him to stop?

Was any of that the truth?

This was the problem with lies in a marriage. It left you forever after not knowing what to believe.

The niggling doubts pushed forward, jabbing at her, breaking past her longing to accept his words.

"You insisted I be released. You insisted because you knew."

"I wanted you home when the baby came."

"And we never needed to qualify. That's why it all seemed unconventional."

"Yes! We only needed the surrogacy agreement—"

"But I signed adoption papers. Didn't I?"

"That was a gestational contract completing our financial obligation to the surrogate. It's standard, just part of the process. But ... there's a complication."

Obviously. *That woman.* The one who'd tried to get to Dani and Willow, twice.

She waited, bracing. What had he done?

"A complication?"

He drew in a breath that was more gasp and his lower lids filled. He blinked, sending tears in rivulets down his cheeks, casting her a practiced look of contrition. But there was no regret there.

"Yes. I'm so sorry, Dani." He gave her that apologetic look and swiped at the moisture on his cheek.

The red blood vessels in his eyes made the blue even more brilliant.

"Say something, Dani."

He gazed with that little-boy hope clear in his eyes. He expected her to forgive him before he'd even told her what he'd done. But he had lied, made up this entire adoption ruse. Was that love or just an expedient way to make her accept a baby that she had been unable to understand was theirs?

She scowled as this snake slithered through her garden.

"What did you do?"

"Me? Nothing. It's the surrogate. She's blackmailing me, us."

"You're allowed to pay a surrogate."

"Within the law and certain limitations. This was just a cash payout, outside the contract."

"Why would you do that? Why didn't you call the police?"

"Dani, she was carrying our child. I was trying to protect our baby."

"By letting her blackmail you?"

He dropped his gaze and gave a barely perceptible nod.

"You have to forgive me for not telling you, Dani. You have to understand. You were doing so well and coming home and... I'm sorry."

She stared in astonishment at this man she thought she knew. Had he made this omission to protect her or himself?

He expected her to understand because she had done so in the past. Overlooked this or that. Made allowances because of his rough childhood, his need to be successful or appear so.

Could she?

She lifted the nearly empty wine bottle, stood, and flung it at the gilded mirror above the fireplace. Glass shards rained down on the stone hearth.

"Dani!" Tate was on his feet.

Red wine dribbled down the wall like blood. Dani stared at his reflections, there in the jagged debris of the shattered mirror. A stranger inside and out.

She turned in a circle, looking at all his pretty things. They were so important to him. His status. His election and her trust fund.

She whirled, aiming a finger at him.

"You hoped that I'd never find out."

"Because you were doing so well."

He offered yet another pretty excuse. He'd done this, kept his silence, like a martyr for *her* benefit. Dani balled her hands into fists. Perhaps he even believed it.

"You told me Willow's mother was a forger. A felon."

"I... it was a mistake." Tate rarely admitted to one of those. "I thought an adoption would..."

"You thought I'd be thrilled instead of furious. Isn't that right?"

If she never knew about the blackmail, she couldn't be angry. She'd be grateful he'd managed an adoption. Lucky to have such a clever, influential husband instead of manipulated by one.

He dropped his gaze. Tate's ears turned bright pink as he hurried on.

"Dr. Allen said you were well enough to come home. That we could be a family again."

Actually, her doctor had had reservations about her discharge. Ones that Tate ignored. All that talk of how her insurance meant they'd never release her, the psychiatric facility's cash cow. How he knew what was best for them. When actually, he knew what was best for him.

"She knew about the baby?"

Whatever he was about to say, it clearly stuck in his throat.

"No. No one knows."

"You told Dr. Allen the same story? That you'd managed an adoption?" Her voice had taken a chilling edge.

Tate broke eye contact. "Yes."

"Her reaction?"

"She thought adjusting to coming home, especially to a house you were not completely familiar with, might be enough of a challenge."

And so it was.

"Dani, this is good news. The baby is ours. It's not an adoption. That's why we didn't need to qualify."

"How is this good news? You lied to your wife, made up some fantasy about a miraculous adoption."

"To keep you from regressing."

"And now someone is still trying to take Willow. And instead of telling me this, you let me think I was hallucinating."

"I never said that."

He took her hand in both of his, confirming her worst fears. He hadn't planned to tell her. Not ever.

But she'd forced him to, by asking him to cancel the adoption.

Tate clasped her hands as she resisted the urge to tug free. She knew this technique. He'd flatter, cajole, and convince. Just like he did with the luxury car, the house, and the expensive furnishings. But this was a child they were discussing. *Their* child.

Just as she'd expected, he squeezed her hands and gave her a look of longing. She tried and failed to be unmoved, but desire stirred. It always did. But with it was fury.

Why was she so angry? She wanted children. And they'd pursued that dream together. Or so he claimed. But he'd lied once and that meant that she could no longer blithely believe every word he said.

He'd lied to her. Even if she forgave him, she could never trust him again. Did he realize what he had broken between them?

She didn't think so.

If Tate did recognize what this might cost them, he seemed confident he could make things right. After all, hadn't he always done so in the past?

He'd never faced any real consequences for his actions. Rather, he'd reaped the benefits. Tate had done this, made up this story because it suited him and simplified the narrative. Not because it was best for her or for Willow. This was best for Tate.

"Why is her hair dark?"

"What?"

"Willow. Her hair is just the same color as the woman who attacked us, while you and I are both fair."

"Willow's hair is like my dad's and like your mother's."

That was true. Her mother had been a bottle blond for as long as Dani could remember; her hair's natural color was light brown.

"Then who is she? This woman who came here, attacked me, and tried to take our child?"

"She's the surrogate."

"How did she know where to find us?"

"I don't know. The surrogates aren't supposed to have contact with the birth parents unless all parties agree. I didn't."

"But you think that was her?"

"It was her." His voice echoed certainty.

"You seem positive," said Dani.

"I am, because she came to see me first."

SIXTEEN

"She showed up at the courthouse. To my office," said Tate.

Dani's stomach heaved. When she found her voice, it was a hoarse whisper. "What did she want?"

Tate snorted. "Money, what else? I didn't want to upset you. Especially when Dr. Allen said you might find the added stress of caring for our baby overwhelming."

The baby wasn't overwhelming. This, however, was a very different matter. This was a strange, dangerous extortionist who knew where they lived.

"Tate, she was at our home. Inside our house!"

"I know. I was trying to handle it."

Without telling her.

"She wants money?"

He nodded.

And, just like Tate, this surrogate and this company didn't follow rules.

Likely saw that damned gold Rolex and decided to change their arrangement.

Anyone who could afford to hire a surrogate, pay all the bills and whatever fee they'd demanded, must be rich. And rich people, ones who did things they didn't want others to know about, made easy targets.

That was if Dani could believe this latest version of events.

Then it struck her. A hard jab to the stomach.

"Is this the first time you told me this?"

He blew a breath to the ceiling and cradled his near empty glass against his stomach.

Finally, he shook his head.

"Not the first."

"Did you ever tell me this? Before today, I mean."

"Yes. We talked about it."

That did not mean he had told her. Just as likely, she had worked it out.

"You were... upset."

"When?"

But she already knew. Just before Christmas. He must have told her about the blackmail on the day she'd been so angry she had driven up to Shelby's in a rage. So angry about... this.

"The crash," she whispered and then looked up at his bloodshot blue eyes. "Oh, Tate."

"We just wanted to have a baby, Dani."

The last thing she recalled was driving like a madwoman to Jacksonville and picking up Shelby. Shelby had asked to drive, but Dani had refused.

The shiver shook her shoulders. Dani was not going back to those memories because the darkness lurked there. The pain and the loss and the guilt. Sometimes she thought it might have been easier if she had died of blood loss.

But then who would mother Willow?

Their surrogate was an extortionist, then.

Why that brought comfort was confusing. Perhaps it was the knowledge that, though a threat, she didn't want Willow and had zero claim on their baby girl.

And money was something that Dani had.

"How much?"

"I'm not paying her again."

Dani scowled. Tate was very frugal with her money unless it suited him.

"She has no legal claim. The best she can do is expose we used a surrogate. It's not strictly illegal."

The semantics of that caused Dani to narrow her eyes.

"She knows that any trouble she causes will hurt my election bid. That's why she came to me. But this time, I refused."

"So she came here."

"To scare you and to force me to pay up."

"But she didn't ask for money. She asked for *her* baby."

"To frighten you. She's read all about you, Dani. Whatever was in the paper, which wasn't much. It only said that you had suffered some mental health issues after your sister's... well, you know, your breakdown."

"It wasn't a breakdown, Tate. It was just depression. That's not an embarrassment. Is it?"

He didn't answer, and her stomach twisted.

"Tate. You're not embarrassed by me. Are you?"

"Of course not." He squeezed her hand.

Was she a liability to his career ambitions? Could this woman really jeopardize his chance to win the election and serve on the state supreme court? She did not know, but it worried her. She added this to the mental burdens she carried.

"How did she get past the guard booth and the gates?"

"I'm looking into that."

"She'll come back," Dani said.

He nodded. "If I pay her, or if I don't."

"Because you already paid her once?"

"Yes. Exactly what she asked for. But she's demanding more."

"Oh, Tate, no."

The sharp pain sliced behind Dani's breastbone, and she used her knuckles to rub it away.

Tate forged on. "Maybe she's just in debt or gambles. I don't know. But she won't be satisfied with another payment. That much is certain."

"Who is she? Where does she live?"

"I don't know."

"Call the police. You know people on the force. You know who she is."

"I don't. The surrogacy organization won't give me her name."

"They will if it's a criminal investigation."

"Dani, I know you think that's a good idea, but I'd have to explain about the blackmail and the payout. You were right, the organization and their surrogates aren't operating within the law. I'm a judge. If they catch her, she can ruin me. All she has to do is tell the police that I paid her off."

He'd broken the law. Her hand covered her mouth and the cry died in her throat. Of course, he had. He'd made the move to avoid scandal, which was another way of saying to avoid taking responsibility.

"If that information becomes public, it would be more than embarrassing. My opponent will use it to bury me. Cripple my campaign. Who wants a judge who will pay someone off? It's illegal. I broke the law."

For just a moment she hoped the story did reach the media and he lost his precious chance at the state supreme court.

"You *did* break the law. Why should you be exempt from consequences?"

"Dani, please. You don't know what you're saying."

She narrowed her eyes at him. "Don't I?"

"Sweetheart, you have to help me."

"Right now, my concern is protecting Willow. Your campaign is not as important as our child's safety."

"No. Of course not."

"So find the surrogate and have her arrested."

He said nothing to this. She was about to insist when something occurred to her. A chill prickled down her spine at the possibility that Tate had other secrets. Ones he would pay, or had paid, to keep quiet.

Shelby had been right.

Her mother had been right.

She stared at this man whom she loved. Until now, it was only his face that had been unrecognizable. Now it was more.

If he could keep the surrogacy private, even from her, and this extortion payment, what else?

Did the surrogate know something further that Tate would pay to protect, something more damaging than a wife who suffered from depression and a questionable surrogate arrangement?

The doubts spun about her like whirling dervishes and then turned into dangerous spinning sawblades as she realized that with her faulty Swiss cheese of a memory, she'd relied on Tate to fill in the blanks. Blanks that he could fill any way he wanted.

"I have to call Shelby."

Tate stood stiffly.

"It's late. Call tomorrow."

She nodded. "All right, tomorrow."

"Let's go up."

Tate flicked off the fireplace with the remote control and left the wineglasses and shattered bottle behind. Dani preceded him upstairs carrying her water glass. In their bedroom suite, they stood side by side over the bassinet, now fixed to its stand.

Willow breathed softly through her open mouth, her rosebud lips making a sucking sound.

The baby was hers, Dani realized, made of her body. It shouldn't make a bit of difference because she loved Willow with her whole heart. But the knowledge that Willow was their biological daughter did tighten the ties between them: Willow had no other mother to go back to. Dani had to protect her.

Whatever Tate had done, whatever lies he had told, he had given them Willow and no matter what happened between them, this child would connect them for now and always. Because creating a child was the one decision in a marriage that could never be annulled.

"She's perfect," Dani whispered, watching Willow draw each breath.

"She is."

"Should we feed her again?" Dani asked.

"Don't wake a sleeping baby. Take your meds. I'm going to wash up. She'll be ready for her bottle soon after that."

It was strange to speak normally after everything she'd just learned, but caring for Willow united them.

Dani checked the clock. It was after midnight, and she was late taking her medication yet again. She sat on the bed opening the pill bottles and Tate headed for the bathroom.

By the time he came out, still wearing the stained trousers, Dani could barely keep her eyes open.

Willow cried.

"I'll take her downstairs to feed her," said Tate.

She nodded, blinking wearily. "You'd better sleep down there tonight."

"Dani." His voice was coaxing.

She shook her head.

"All right. Fine. You get some rest."

He leaned over and she turned her head away. He kissed her gently on the cheek and straightened, saying nothing more.

Dani hoped she could keep back the tears until he left the room.

Then he lifted the bassinet and cooed at Willow. Dani watched them go. If nothing else, Tate was a good father.

Friday morning, Dani woke to the alarm at eight and found the bassinet gone and Tate missing. This time she did not stress, but just sent him a text. The reply came a moment later.

Be home in 10.

Dani took her morning round of medication before the bathroom mirror and then slipped into the shower, happy for a few moments alone. She needed time to gather her thoughts and make some decisions. After she dressed, she remembered Tate's grime-smeared trousers. She'd send it to the cleaners, along with the dress she wore to the fundraiser dinner—but like the stained suit, she couldn't find his pants.

Had he taken over this job, sending his things out for cleaning?

Confused, she headed for the kitchen and started her coffee. With her full mug, she wandered to the dining room, the only room facing the driveway and street.

The revelations from the night before swirled in her mind, almost unreal. Her attacker was a blackmailing surrogate, but the baby was theirs. Did the surrogate think so, too? Did she only want money or did she also want their baby? Now, because Tate had used a shady outfit, she didn't even know if the woman had a legal claim on Willow.

Well, it didn't matter what this person thought. Dani was Willow's mother. Her *real* mother.

If Willow was hers, she could shed the insecurities of being an imposter, that she had no business raising a child.

Dani was so tempted to not question any more. But Tate had lied about so much. And if she didn't have Willow checked, how would she ever know the truth?

That conundrum led directly to another. Tate had lied to

her. Her marriage had been the foundation of her life and her recovery was built on sand.

She didn't know if their relationship would survive. Should she forgive him for telling a lie with the excuse that he was only trying to protect her, when, really, he told the lie to protect himself?

And what about the incredibly ill-advised decision to raise a baby when she was recovering from a crippling depression? What if she'd never gotten over it or had had to stay in Windwood for much longer?

Then what?

A new fear rose in her mind, a fresh green weed there in her formerly perfect garden. What if he didn't care and her recovery had not entered his decision to become a father. What if he didn't need her, had planned to raise the baby with or without her? It was a good reason to not consult his wife.

But that child belonged to her as well. If she never came out of Windwood, would he have told her about Willow's birth? Or perhaps, that was why he was so anxious to have her discharged, even though her doctor had doubts. He wanted her out because of Willow and the outwardly perfect family they created for his campaign.

The fury melted into the sorrow. She needed to call her sister. The shame and embarrassment made her delay and she found herself still sitting beside her untouched coffee when the doorbell camera chimed a motion alert.

She glanced to the window and saw Tate, carrying the bassinet and dressed in a yellow golf shirt, walking shoulder to shoulder with a dark-haired woman. For just an instant, she thought it might be the surrogate.

But the woman's hair was pulled up in a tight chignon with an artificial yellow plumeria fixed there. Her flowered skirt was mostly yellow.

Enid, Dani guessed. On her way to care for Willow.

Though she appreciated the help, she missed her privacy. Enid wasn't intruding, exactly, but she was just there, chatting, offering advice, attending to everything before Dani even had a chance to think. And spying. Knowing what she knew now, it was very possible that Enid might be reporting to Tate any mistake Dani made.

Tate and Enid stopped beside the stump of a post, all that remained of the mailbox Dani had obliterated yesterday.

There they stood, gazing down, speaking together for several minutes. Tate pointed at the ground, replaying with an outstretched index finger the path Dani had cut through the hedge and across both lawns. Enid glanced toward the house and Dani stepped back, her cheeks hot.

The shame washed over her again. She'd escaped. She'd gotten help. But her ineptitude behind the wheel, the terrible bleed of terror and guilt, had made it nearly impossible even to shift the vehicle into reverse.

Willow was Dani's daughter, but was the baby safe with her?

SEVENTEEN

As Dani stood there, pressed against the wall beside the entrance like a thief in her own home, her phone played a familiar tune.

Shelby was calling, as she often did, when Dani was most upset.

Dani took the call, relieved at the distraction and the support.

"Hey, little sister. I was just thinking about you," Shelby said. "How'd it go last night? Did you two talk?"

"We did."

"Everything all right?"

"I don't think so. No. Not all right."

She relayed her conversation with Tate, leaving out nothing.

"Shelby, did I tell you about the surrogacy the day of the accident?"

"What? No, you didn't. You picked me up at work. I could tell something was wrong. But we didn't talk. We were going to my place." There was a pause. "Then the car swerved."

Her words did nothing to change Dani's suspicions. She now knew why she had been so furious. She'd found out that, after she and Tate decided to try surrogacy, he'd hired a woman from a disreputable outfit to carry their baby, and either he or this operation had not vetted the surrogate who turned around and blackmailed them. And he'd paid her! It didn't change what had happened, unfortunately.

Dani choked on sobs. "I'd just found out."

Shelby's voice cracked as she spoke.

"But Tate says you *are* her biological mother."

"Yes."

"What do you think of that?"

"Oh, Shelby, it's all I want in the world. But how can I trust what he told me?"

"You can't. But what if..."

"Then I'd be..." She drew in a breath as her heart filled with joy and possibilities. "I'd be the happiest mama in the whole world."

"And, what if you are not the biological mother?"

Dani pursed her lips, thinking. "I love her. Whether I'm her biological mother or her adoptive one, it doesn't change that. Willow is my daughter."

"So, you want to raise her?"

"If I can." She wanted this. Was that enough?

"So, get a DNA test on the baby. Then you'll know either way. The pediatrician can do it. Be sure she's a match for you."

Dani chewed her thumbnail thinking.

"Maybe," she whispered. Despite Tate's omissions, Dani had never done something like this.

"Get the test. Then you'll know if he's telling the truth or if this surrogate thing is just another lie."

"Well, if he did use a shady surrogate, she's a threat."

"You could pay her off," said Shelby.

"More like have her arrested and wreck Tate's campaign." She was good at wrecking things. Only this time she felt like doing it on purpose. Suddenly she understood some of Paul

Langford's vindictiveness. She could shut off Tate's accounts with a single phone call. See how he liked living on his own income.

"Maybe he plans to have her arrested after the election," Shelby said. "But your child's safety comes before any election. I'm ashamed of Tate to put that ahead of his wife and child. And keeping secrets. That's terrible."

It was. Dani dashed the tears from her face and sniffed as her nasal passages continued to fill.

"What are you going to do about Tate?"

"I don't know. I love him. But now…" She paused to gather the courage to say the next part aloud. "Now I don't trust him."

"I'm so sorry, Dani. Do you think you should take the baby and leave?"

"What? No! I'm not ready for that. No way."

"Okay. You're staying. For now, at least."

Dani rummaged in the buffet and located a cocktail napkin, using it to blow her nose.

"What should I do?" she asked.

"If he won't call the police, you should. Tell them everything you just told me. That Tate knows who she is, maybe where she lives, and that she threatened you and tried to take the baby."

The door opened and Enid preceded Tate into the foyer. They both paused at seeing her on the phone.

Tate cast a sideward look at Enid, as if sharing some unspoken message with her.

"Who's that, honey?" he asked.

Dani felt a sharp tug of guilt.

"It's Shelby."

Enid's nostrils flared.

"Can you call her back?" he asked.

Dani nodded, reluctant to give up the open connection between her and Shelby, tempted to put the call on speaker so her sister could also hear whatever Tate said. Instead, she spoke to her twin.

"I've got to go," Dani whispered. "Tate's here. I'll call you back. Love you, big sister."

"Okay, little sister. Love you more."

Dani ended the call. Enid checked on Willow as Tate added more packets of milk to the refrigerator.

"When did you get those?" Dani asked.

"Enid picked them up for us."

Enid headed upstairs with Willow to the nursery. The sound of their neighbor's voice came clear through the monitor. Dani started for the stairs, but Tate gently clasped her elbow and she turned back.

He picked up the white plastic device and spoke to Enid.

"Everything all right up there?" he asked.

"Fine," said Enid. "Just changing Willow. I'll bring her down in a few minutes."

"Thank you," said Tate and returned the monitor to the marble island. "Isn't that easier?"

"I should warm her formula," said Dani.

"How about you let Enid take the morning shift, as we agreed? And you," he said, booping her nose with his index finger as if she were his pet Labrador, "can walk me out."

Together, they headed through the laundry room and down the four stairs toward his sedan. He acted as if everything was fine between them, when she felt as if she were walking barefoot on broken glass.

In the garage, she saw that her SUV was missing, towed to the repair shop. Now a wave of nausea rolled in her empty stomach.

They paused as Dani grappled with the urge to beg him not to go and tell him to never come back.

"Enid is here until noon and then she's picking up your car

from the dealership. I'll be home just after that. Will that work?"

"How will Enid get there?"

"Dealership will pick her up."

"What if that woman comes back?"

"Dani, I'll deal with her before I go to the office. She won't be back."

"What does that mean? Are you calling the police?"

He looked away.

"So, you'll pay her off, or threaten her, or are you planning something else?"

"I'll tell her the truth. That she's going to jail if she pulls anything like that again. I'm bringing Gary Forde with me. He's a detective. I'm sure she'll get the point."

"I thought you didn't know who she was."

His mouth went tight, and he glanced away.

His words were hushed. "I know her."

She added another lie to the growing pile.

"Why not just arrest her? Shelby says we should. That Willow's safety comes before the campaign and that I should have her arrested if you won't."

His smile vanished. "Don't do that, Dani. The publicity will ruin any chance I have of winning."

"But—"

"I need this win, Dani." He spoke urgently. "Being a supreme court justice is only the beginning. After that, I can look at the national scene. Federal appointments. The sky's the limit. But if I lose, I'm stuck in the circuit court for another five years minimum and that's if I can convince the party to back another campaign after losing this one. I know that if word gets out about the surrogate, I'll be a local judge for the rest of my life or worse, back to the law firm after losing reelection." His charming smile returned. "Why don't you call Shelby again and see what she has to say? Ask her if she thinks I can handle this?"

She hesitated, thinking she should call the police. Finally, she nodded. "All right."

"And we'll talk more this afternoon. How does that sound?"

"Fine."

He gave her a long look and then slipped behind the wheel without trying to kiss her goodbye. It seemed Tate was still an expert at reading a room.

Dani backed away from the open door. Just the sight of him in the vehicle set her heart pounding. Cars were as dangerous as guns. Deadly, unpredictable, moving monsters, plowing down anything in their path.

"See you later," he said through the open window.

The garage door trundled up, the engine purred, and Tate rolled effortlessly down the drive past the most recent evidence of her incompetence and Tate's lies.

Enid and the baby kept her busy all morning. Willow would not take the bottle. It troubled Dani because so far she'd had a predictable appetite and a reliable schedule.

"I wouldn't worry. She'll eat when she's hungry," said Enid.

But Dani worried. It seemed all she could do with any competence was worry. At that, she was a master.

She didn't have time to call Shelby until after Enid left to pick up her car. Shelby answered on the fifth ring, just before the call headed for voice mail.

"Sorry, Dani. I was in PT. What's up?"

"I spoke to Tate about calling the police and filing charges against the surrogate. He won't do it."

"Why not?"

"The campaign. He's worried about the damn campaign."

"Well, winning the campaign will help you both and you'd be moving to Tallahassee. Closer to me!"

"And out of this place."

"What's wrong with the place?" Shelby asked.

"I told you. I don't feel at home here. It's flashy and pretentious. Even the kitchen faucet is gold tone."

"Oh. I see." Shelby seemed hurt by her admission.

"I told him the baby's safety comes before the campaign."

"He knows that, Dani. I think you can trust Tate to make decisions that will keep you both safe."

"What are you talking about? His decisions caused this! She found him and us because he went with a shady operation."

"I know you're upset."

"Upset? What if she shows up again?"

"Then call Tate."

"This morning you told me to call the police."

"And I've thought about it since. Don't wreck your marriage over this. Let Tate handle the threat. He's a judge with powerful connections with the police."

"I'm so furious with him."

"He made mistakes. But he got you both a baby. Isn't that worth any price?"

Dani sighed. "I just wish he'd gone about things differently."

"I think we'd all like the chance to do things differently."

That was as close as Shelby ever came to laying blame. But she had effectively pointed out that Dani was less than perfect. She'd caused Tate pain by her actions. And Shelby.

Her head sank and she pressed a hand to her forehead, feeling the depression kick inside her like a fetus.

"All right. But what about... do you think I'm, well, competent to raise a baby?"

"Oh, absolutely." Shelby's conviction bolstered Dani considerably.

"Really?"

"I know you can do it. You'll be a great mom. The very best."

"Thanks, big sister."

"Of course. That's why I'm here. Love you, Dani. Bye!"

And she was gone. Dani shook her head at the conflicting advice Shelby had given her.

She spent a good deal of time after the conversation pacing around the ground floor like a caged tiger. She needed to get out of this house. If only she could go back to their first place or her childhood home. The more she looked at the pretentious marble foyer and the gold fixtures, the more gauche she thought them. It wasn't her style. She preferred casual elegance, not this faux-Versailles mansion. Even the water views annoyed her because they came with neighbors squeezed so tightly on either side that she could hear them splashing in their pool when she sat on the lanai.

And the boat traffic! The constant rumble of engines at wake speed was unrelenting.

Not one spot in this entire community offered her the luxury of solitude. If she had to pace around this marble island with its clear crystal fruit in a gilded bowl once more, she thought she might just call Dr. Allen to come pick her up.

Should she call her?

She'd missed Thursday's appointment because of the intruder and accident. Maybe the doctor could see her today?

But her call went to the answering service, and they asked if it was an emergency.

"No, not an emergency. I just missed my Thursday appointment."

"I'll have the receptionist call you Monday to reschedule. Is there anything else?"

Nothing that she could verbalize, just the realization that she couldn't trust her husband, her marriage was collapsing, and both insights stirred a sense of alarm that her depression might break loose.

"Nothing. Thank you."

The call service representative disconnected.

Dani headed to the dining room and collected the sandwich Enid had made and left for her, along with a serving of fresh fruit and an unopened bottle of sparkling water beside her pills.

Having these things done for her reminded her even more of the psych ward. Had she just gone from one to another?

She twisted off the cap with more force than necessary and downed the pills in one swallow. Then she collected the plate and carried it to the trash, where she tipped the contents into the garbage.

She wasn't eating a thing Enid prepared.

Spite and malice were unbecoming, she knew. And she felt a twinge of regret looking at the perfectly good sandwich.

Dani ate a yogurt, standing at the sink, wondering why she'd done that and why she felt so much better afterward.

"I'm going out," she said to the gold-toned faucet as she rinsed the yogurt container. Not for a drive, naturally. Even if the SUV was there, she couldn't bear the thought of driving. But a walk was possible.

The gated community's amenities included a playground and pool, which she'd yet to explore, though Tate had driven her by several times. It might be good to exercise and clear her head. Prove that the surrogate wasn't waiting, lurking behind every bush, for her to emerge.

However, the thought of running into the surrogate again kept her exactly where she was, and she spent the next hour in Willow's room, reading in the rocker beside her crib. She was there when the baby stirred, to feed and burp and change her before Tate finally returned.

He found them in the nursery, with Willow awake and gurgling in Dani's arms.

"There's my girls!"

Dani accepted a kiss before Tate turned to give Willow a kiss on the forehead. Dani narrowed her eyes on him, wondering what to do about their situation.

Tate spotted her open book beside the rocker.

"Have you been up here all afternoon?" he asked.

"Change of scenery." Willow usually slept in the bassinet beside their bed, but this room felt the most normal to Dani. The pastel colors, soft plush animals, and thick area rug all added to the insular feel. And it was the only room with no gold or silver.

"Enid is gone?" he said.

Dani nodded. Enid was not a topic she enjoyed.

"Your car is back."

Dani hadn't even heard their neighbor return and for that she was grateful.

"Everything go okay?"

"She made me lunch."

"Great."

"Except I can make my lunch and take my pills without a babysitter."

His face flushed. "She's not..." He blew away a breath. "I thought she was helping."

"Intruding."

"Your doctor does not think you should be alone."

She clamped her mouth shut and stared.

Tate raked his hands through his hair. After several long moments of hard silence, he tried again.

"Want to take the boat out for dinner?"

Tate had decided for diversion over discussion. She narrowed her eyes at him once more at the suggestion. One of his favorite argument closers was diversion. In addition, putting a newborn on a boat was madness.

"I'm not putting our baby in a boat."

"It's a great boat. Perfectly safe."

"No."

He conceded the point. "I'll pick us up something then."

"By boat?"

"Why not?"

"Because you could drive or have it delivered in half the time. Because you just got home. And because taking the boat out without me is not being here."

Tate glanced toward the door. Her temper had him searching for the exits. Should she be grateful for Enid instead of insulted? No, both of them were treating her like a child. Well, she wasn't having it.

"I enjoy taking her out and we haven't been on the water for... a while."

The *her* he referenced was the cabin cruiser he named *Motion to Adjourn*. Tate had several places he loved to boat to for meals.

Dani shrugged, wanting him to stay because he *wanted* to be here with her and their baby, not because he had to. Wanting to go back to the time before she knew about the surrogate. Perhaps he was right not to tell her. Look what it was doing to her... to them.

But it wasn't the surrogate or even the attacks. It was the lie that abraded like a cheese grater on her skin.

Tate gave her shoulder a squeeze.

"Hey, how about a swim in the pool?"

Diversion, again. She nodded wearily, allowing it.

"Tate. I know you're trying to be normal. But I don't even know who you are."

He exhaled sharply, hands on hips.

"What do you want me to say? That I'm sorry? I'm not. If I hadn't gotten us a surrogate, we wouldn't have Willow."

"I'm not talking about the surrogate. I'm talking about the extortion. You should have told me."

But now she wondered if his claim that they'd made this decision together was also a lie. Otherwise, why had he said "if *I* hadn't gotten us a surrogate"? Or did he think she blamed him because the surrogate he'd hired turned out to be a crook?

He threw up his hands. "What difference does it make? You can't remember half the things I've told you. For all you know, I did tell you and you've forgotten."

That possibility hadn't occurred to her.

"Maybe I just said I hadn't told you, so you wouldn't feel so... so... broken."

"Oh, Tate." She pressed her face into her hands and wept.

He left her to cry for a few minutes, standing close but apart, then gathered her up in his arms, making hushing sounds.

"Dani, don't. I'm sorry. I screwed up. You have to forgive me. I should have told you right away. But I waited. I waited too long and... I was a coward."

She looked up. It was so rare that he admitted a mistake. And an apology was even rarer. Usually he just distracted, joked, made kind gestures. But she'd caught him in a bald-faced lie. Should she forgive him or hold his feet to the fire.

"Never do something like that again," she said.

He met her gaze. "I promise."

"Marriage is a partnership. You have to include me."

"I did. I do. But, Dani, you haven't been here."

"I'm here now."

He nodded. Perhaps he even understood.

"So... a swim?"

She puffed up her cheeks with air and blew it away, knowing he didn't understand the implications of what he'd done or how he'd hurt her. She wondered if his apology was just a different form of manipulation, instead of the display of remorse that he might not feel.

Dani gave a halfhearted nod and he scooped up the monitor, then led them out of the nursery.

In the master bathroom she washed her red, puffy face and then changed into her swimsuit. Together, they headed outside. Dani placed the monitor on the outdoor table, with the volume at max, and she and Tate floated on foam noodles in the kidney-shaped pool. Tate waved at every passing boat as if at a campaign event. Dani ducked under the water for a moment's peace. After their dip, Tate stretched out to sunbathe as she checked on, and fed, Willow.

Back outside she tried and failed to read a book in a lounge chair on the deck. The sound of motorboats cruising by at wake speed was as constant as the weekday sound of mowers and blowers. Dani sighed and lifted the monitor, watching Willow in her crib upstairs.

Tate rolled from the lounger and dipped in the pool. "I'm going to shower and then call in our order."

"Driving?" she asked.

"Yeah. I don't have time to take the boat."

Or he'd compromised. Dani nodded her approval.

"Be careful. See you soon."

He stepped through the sliders and out of sight. She wrapped up in a beach towel before seeing to Willow. Dani had just put the baby in her bouncer so she could change into a sheath dress when she heard the door chime, indicating Tate's return.

She called down the stairs and his familiar voice reassured. Dani moved Willow to the crib and met him in the living room, holding the monitor.

"Where's the baby?" he asked, setting two large bags on the kitchen island.

"Upstairs." She showed him the image of Willow on the monitor, staring up at the mobile that circled slowly overhead.

"Oh, so we have a few minutes alone to eat," he said. "Wonderful."

He stepped into the formal dining room, ignoring both the

kitchen banquette and the counter seats, and flicked on the overhead lights, sending the chandelier ablaze. Smiling now, he set out the plastic containers in the center of the dining room table.

Dani retrieved two plates, knowing Tate hated eating on or with plastic. Then she collected the gilded silverware and two bottles of water.

"I got us both steak and baked potatoes. Onion rings, too, and cheesecake." He lifted two small clear plastic containers. "Ranch or blue cheese for your salad?"

"Ranch," she said, knowing he preferred blue cheese.

"Super. I'm starving."

She sat, and he slid their meals from the containers to the plates.

"Wine?"

"No thank you."

Tate rose and retrieved a bottle of red from the wine cooler and began the process of opening it.

She glanced to the hearth, seeing no evidence of the bottle she had smashed. Had he cleaned that up or had Enid?

"Should we explain to Dr. Allen why I missed Thursday?"

"I said you can do that if you like." He popped the cork.

"Why wouldn't I?"

"Well, the accident. It might look..." His words dropped off as his silence echoed her own misgivings. "Oh, dealership called. I got the estimate on the damages. Insurance won't cover a damn thing, of course. It's over two grand."

Dani winced.

Tate poured his wine into the large goblet.

"Anyway, I'll handle it."

She changed the subject. "I was thinking of going to the park tomorrow."

"The community playground, you mean?"

She nodded.

"Take Enid with you."

"She's coming on Saturday, too?"

Tate lowered his knife and fork, giving her his full attention. "I was planning to golf, but I can stay here with you."

She didn't ask him to, but she wanted him to choose her over golfing.

"You need a break?" he asked.

"She's lovely. I just can't seem to think when she's here."

"Dani, hiring her was your idea."

"I know. I know."

"Is that why you want to go to the park?"

It was mostly why. She also wanted to escape this enormous, pretentious house, which, with all its marble, gilding, and mosaic tile, felt as homey as a mausoleum.

"Yes."

"Then we can go to the club."

It seemed Tate was determined to keep her inside. But she hated the yacht club even more than the idea of the community center and pool. If possible, she felt more uncomfortable there among all the restless members driven to display their status with things. While at the community pool, she would likely just feel exposed.

Dani sighed.

"What about golf?" she asked, referring to his regular Saturday group, which he never missed, as far as she knew.

"I can skip. They'll get a sub."

"You don't need to."

"It's fine, Dani."

"But it's not."

He set aside his wine and gave her a hard stare. "First you complain that I'm not here. When I offer to be, you try to send me away. Which is it, Dani? Do you want me to stay, or do you want privacy?"

"Both."

He rotated the remaining wine in his glass creating a red whirlpool that spun after he stilled. "Well, Dr. Allen said I need to be here, so I'm canceling."

At least tonight it was just the three of them. She'd need to ask Dr. Allen why the hospital still felt safer somehow. It made little sense.

EIGHTEEN

On Saturday, at her insistence, Tate left Dani alone with Willow to join his regular golf group. He checked in by text and phone seven times, letting her know he was uncomfortable leaving her alone, still feeling remorseful, or both.

Despite his lack of faith, she and Willow had a lovely morning. Dani delighted in her daughter's first true smile. When Willow clasped hold of her mother's finger, Dani's heart clenched with a joy so true it hurt. Everything about the baby delighted; even watching her yawn made Dani laugh. She was so tiny and precious. The time with her baby lifted her mood and she was in better spirits when Tate got home at two in the afternoon. Whatever his missteps, he'd made them parents and, while her indignation still burned, so did a deep gratitude.

He peered in from the laundry room, removing his sunglasses and spotting her at the counter, nursing a cup of tea.

"Everything good?"

Reassured at his familiar voice, she nodded. "Fine."

He visibly relaxed.

"How did you do?" she asked. She knew next to nothing

about golf and mostly just nodded as he relayed details on the morning round.

"Shot three under!"

"Good."

He gathered her up in his arms and kissed her. He smelled like beer and sweat.

"You forgiven me yet?"

"Yet, as if a foregone conclusion?"

"Of course."

"Tate, this isn't a joke."

As if sensing possible defeat, he withdrew, releasing her. She let him go.

"I need a shower."

"You do."

"Care to join me?" He wiggled his brows.

She worried that he'd misconstrue sex as absolution and she still thought they had some things to work out. Tate, however, was clearly ready to move on. Was she making too big a deal over his deceit?

No. She wasn't. And his comment about her not remembering did little to reassure. How easy was it to manipulate a wife with memory issues?

"You going to make me beg?"

He gave her an appealing grin and held his hands out offering himself to her. Despite her mixed emotions, her body did not share her mind's reluctance. She wanted him and the thought of some private time in the shower with Tate gave her stomach a little tug. Conflicted, she said nothing.

He grinned and took her hand. "Bring the monitor."

She scooped up the device. Then the two of them headed for the main bath and Willow was very patient waiting for Mommy and Daddy to finish their very long, hot shower.

Afterward, relaxed, conciliatory, and sleepy, Dani rocked

her daughter as she took her bottle. Maybe they could get past this, and things would be all right.

On Sunday, they headed to the garage and her SUV because Tate was taking them to the yacht club for brunch.

Dani tucked the diaper bag into the rear seat of the SUV beside the baby, who slumbered through being clipped in. It was a marvel to her that when Willow needed to sleep, surrounding sounds or movement did not bother her.

Tate held the door open as Dani slipped into the passenger seat. She'd taken her midday medications without food, and they now ate into the lining of her stomach, raising the acid content and making her feel nauseous. He clipped her safety belt as if she were an invalid and she scowled.

"I can do it, Tate."

"Of course you can."

Dani used the mirror in the visor to check Willow's car seat as they headed out. Tate fiddled with the radio, choosing a news station that droned on about the uptick in a new variant and the wildfires in the west.

Tate had joined the club for business reasons, justifying the cost because several of the members held real influence in local politics.

"I ate here three times a week while you were gone," he said.

Did he realize such admissions only increased her tendency for self-blame?

"Did you?"

"Yup. Easily made the monthly food minimum."

So, the club had been an important refuge during her absence.

"I'm sure it was lonely," she said.

"It's a bummer eating takeout with only the television for company." He patted her leg. "But that's over now."

She cast him a smile as her heart twisted with regret.

And guilt. Always the guilt that she wore like an invisibility cloak.

Dani tried not to let the onus of failing her husband eat at her, because Dr. Allen said it wasn't healthy.

Self-blame is useless. If you have made mistakes, you learn from them and move forward.

It was a nice sentiment, but what if your remorse stemmed from hurting someone you loved? Shouldn't you also make amends? She'd left her husband as he started a new position in the circuit court.

Now, in only six months, he had the support of the party to run for the supreme court. Had anyone in the state rocketed upward in such a spectacular trajectory?

She pressed down the resentment that he had done all that without her help or support. It almost seemed he didn't need her at all.

But he needed her money. For the campaign, his lifestyle, the house, even this club membership would be a stretch on his salary, which was more prestigious than lucrative. Public service always was.

He was doing good work. Helping the community and delivering justice.

"I wish we could take my car," said Tate. "I hate pulling up to the club in this."

Enid had picked up her vehicle from the repair shop and dropped it off at their place, and the SUV looked exactly as it had before Dani's wild ride.

Was it the class of vehicle or the make that made him self-conscious? And who would see them pull up, anyway? The valets?

"When did status become so important to you?" she asked.

"When I threw my hat in the ring."

At the club, Tate spoke to the valet as Dani retrieved Willow in her carrier. They met on the hot sidewalk, under the awning that led to the grand entrance. Inside, the air bordered on cold. Above them, the huge mobile hung, the suspended stylized boats spun languidly in the artificial breeze before the floor-to-ceiling windows. Beyond, the luxury yachts floated, moored in the private docks on the sparkling inlet.

Tate chatted with the club manager, who seemed always there to greet members. Dani wondered if he slept here. She pushed down the envy that the manager knew the names of all arrivals and could effortlessly recognize them on sight.

He turned them over to the pretty hostess with vivid green eyes, who wore a tight jade-colored dress, three-inch heels, and a face mask covered with silver sequins. Dani noticed all the servers also wore masks.

"The rest of your party is already seated, Judge Sutton."

Dani's brow wrinkled and she turned to Tate as they followed the hostess, the unspoken question on her face.

"We're meeting someone?"

Tate nodded, his voice low as they trailed behind the hostess.

"Dennis Babbet is the local party chair. His date is Sunny Malyn. We're joining them."

"Yes. So I gathered."

Was that why Tate had suggested brunch at the club, to meet this party leader? Dani tightened her grip on the carrier and reined in her irritation, rejecting the urge to turn around. He hadn't changed and he clearly wasn't willing to make amends, because this was a lie of omission.

"You should have told me," she whispered.

He said nothing to this but instead continued with his own agenda.

"Sunny is not his wife, and she's younger. He's divorced and has three boys in college. All three sail and row. She's not really important. What's important is that Dennis be charmed. He's the last hurdle for the campaign. I get his blessing and the backing will follow."

The pair sat at the table at the windows, a Bloody Mary before Babbet and a champagne flute with a mimosa before Malyn. He had a full head of silver hair and was broad and ruddy-faced. Babbet set aside his napkin and rose at their approach.

The hostess left them, and Dani glanced to the woman seated at the table. Sunny was slim and had a silver ring through her left eyebrow. She had thinning blond hair, dyed pink at the ends, and looked to be in her fifties, while Dani judged that her companion, Mr. Babbet, was closer to seventy.

Dani smiled. The pink hair would make Sunny easy to identify, even out of context.

Babbet shook Tate's hand with vigor. "Glad you could come."

Tate stepped aside and presented his wife. Dani smiled and was dragged in for a full body hug that left her flustered. The man reeked of alcohol. The clinch jostled Willow awake. She wrinkled her forehead and began to cry.

Tate gave the infant an impatient look.

Sunny stood to admire the crying baby as the men took their seats.

"I'll just go give her a bottle and be back."

Tate nodded. "Shall I order for you, or do you want the buffet?"

The buffet overflowed with an embarrassment of riches.

"Buffet is fine." She hurried away and then glanced back to make note of where in the dining room they were seated, finding them by the floor-to-ceiling windows, of course.

Willow quieted the minute she was lifted out of the carrier.

She needed a change but seemed only to want to sleep without the carrier tilting like a dinghy in rough seas.

Back at the table, Dani collected her plate and left Willow in Tate's care. Babbet and Tate seemed content to drink and talk. Sunny rose and together they walked the three stations of food, ending at the beverages where Dani chose a latte and Sunny another mimosa.

Dani cleared her throat and attempted some small talk. "Where did you two meet?"

"Oh, I work with Dennis at headquarters."

Dani nodded and wondered if the divorce was before or after Sunny had entered the picture.

Back at the table, very little was required of Dani. She picked at her food and finished her latte as Babbet switched from Bloody Marys to scotch on the rocks. She spoke highly of her husband whenever she could get a word in.

With no segue, Babbet turned to Dani and said, "So, I understand you were hospitalized for a long stretch. Psychiatric hospital, wasn't it?"

Dani didn't know what he considered a long stretch, but she held her smile despite the rude, personal inquiry. She glanced to Tate for rescue, but he only nodded slowly, encouraging her to handle the question.

She understood then—why he hadn't told her this was a brunch interview and why he insisted they come. This wasn't at all about Tate. Tate clearly had Babbet's full confidence. This was about her. Was she the liability that might torpedo Tate's chances? Tate, correctly, had not told her because she would have been so nervous, she likely would not have come.

Dani lowered her chin, cross at Tate for throwing her blind into this. But she was committed to showing Babbet that she was an asset.

"Well," she said, her smile feeling brittle and her hands moist, "that's true."

"Do you feel the pressure of the campaign might be... taxing for you?"

"I look forward to Tate winning his spot on the state supreme court. You won't find a more dedicated judge and I know he champions the party agenda."

"But what about you?"

"Mr. Babbet," she said, smiling and leaning in conspiratorially, "If you are asking how I look in party colors, you won't be disappointed. I can support my husband in this."

"*Supporting* him," he laughed. "That's exactly what I understand. Your maiden name is Durant. Correct?"

"Yes."

She knew where this was going and didn't like it. The man had money without manners. Status that he used to bully and brag. Her initial aversion grew to something like loathing.

But Dani held her smile.

At best, his words were a cruel joke at her husband's expense, and at worst, they were intended to belittle Tate. Just a sideward glance showed he recognized this. His pink face and thinning lips demonstrated clearly that he did not like the suggestion that his wife's inheritance, and not his aptitude, gave him the means to succeed. Though it was true, nonetheless.

"If you are asking if I am financially backing this campaign, the answer is yes. My husband and I believe in putting our money where our mouth is because Tate will make an exceptional state supreme court judge. I hope the party recognizes our clear commitment to Tate's success."

Babbet sat back, smiling. "Nothing wrong with *that* answer. I can see you've a quick wit." He turned to Tate. "Not easily flustered. She'll do fine with the press, and we can limit her exposure."

Tate nodded and pushed aside his plate in favor of the glass of white wine. Sunny's gaze flashed from Babbet to Tate and then to Dani.

The silence hung for a long moment.

Dani lifted her water glass. "To my husband's success."

The others followed suit, echoing the toast, then drank.

"What about dessert?" asked Sunny.

"Unfortunately not," said Tate. "We have another engagement."

"Oh, that *is* unfortunate," said Babbet.

Dani could have kissed Tate. He cast aside his napkin.

Dani rose with a dignity she did not feel.

She was the prize mare trotted out, so this close hugger could cop a feel and judge whether she'd crack on the campaign trail. He'd intentionally jabbed at Tate and at her to see if she could handle herself, the jerk.

Tate remained seated but signaled their server and asked for the check. She drew it instantly from her apron, already sheathed in the black leather holder bearing the club's logo. He offered no credit card, and she asked for none. Nothing so gauche. Just his signature was necessary to subtract this meal from the food allocation that members paid, whether they ate at the club or not.

Dani could have kissed Tate for getting them out of here. He was on his feet now, slapping the leather holder closed with more force than necessary and passing it back to their server.

Babbet rose and made a move to capture Dani again, but she stepped back and extended her hand. He grinned and lifted it to his mouth, like some ancient courtier, as she kept her brittle smile fixed. Then she collected the carrier, holding it and Willow before her like a shield.

"So nice to meet you, Dennis," she said and then to his partner, "And you as well, Sunny. You two have a lovely day."

She sailed out of the dining room before Tate. He caught her as the manager intercepted them, his brow furrowed and hands wringing in concern.

"Was everything all right?"

Tate took that one. "Babbet is drunk."

"Oh, I see." The manager visibly relaxed. This, apparently, was not news to him.

Tate took hold of Dani's elbow and out they went. As they cleared the doors, the heat blasted them, seeming all the hotter after the air-conditioning. The valet spotted them and trotted away to collect their vehicle.

"I'm sorry, Dani. The man was out of line."

"He was." And so was her husband, dragging her in there without so much as a hint of what to expect.

"He's a fool. A drunk fool," Tate added.

"But a powerful one."

"Unfortunately."

"Well, no harm done." That wasn't entirely true. Dani was so angry she was shaking, and not all her fury was directed at Babbet. "Next time, I'd appreciate some forewarning before you drop me like bait before a shark."

NINETEEN

On Monday morning, Dani called Dr. Allen first thing and was lucky enough to snag a spot because of a cancelation.

Tate took her to her appointment. He planned to bring her as far as the waiting room and then head to court. Enid would meet Dani after the appointment, bringing Willow, and take them to Dr. Lynes for Willow's one-week check.

Dani hadn't been ferried about so much since high school when her mom had transported her and Shelby to swim lessons, flute lessons, and ballet before they got their learner's permits and then licenses.

Dani smiled at that memory. They'd both passed the test on the same day. Shelby first and her second. They'd been so proud. And the freedom!

Back then, neither had realized how dangerous or tragic automobiles could be.

The doors to the elevator dinged and she and Tate rode up. He chatted with the woman who entered with them. She was small, wore a white medical mask, and was dressed in business attire, including a colorful scarf stylishly fixed about her neck.

Dani said nothing but admired how Tate could engage in a conversation with anyone.

At their floor, Dani stepped forward as Tate motioned to the woman beside him. She preceded them out.

In the vestibule between the elevators, Dani let her get ahead of them.

"How did you know this was her floor?" she asked.

He gave her that odd look, the one that she saw more and more often. It was a mix of surprise and confusion. She knew then that she should have recognized that person.

Belatedly she put the pieces together. The woman was the right height, with the right hairstyle and the scarf; surely, she should have remembered that consistent fashion accessory and noted that. If she had not been so preoccupied, she might, at the very least, have recognized her doctor's bright shock of red hair.

Likely, she would have if she wasn't so distracted with Tate's revelation about the surrogate's extortion efforts and how best to broach the topic with Dr. Allen.

She knew what he'd say. Could have said it with him but still her cheeks went hot with embarrassment.

"That was your doctor."

Dani lowered her head. "I just realized."

"Do you mind if I go in with you for a few minutes?"

She minded. Her time with Dr. Allen once belonged only to her. Tate's intrusion seemed just that, like the classmate who can't wait to tell the teacher everything you did wrong. Or in this case, to get his version of the story in first.

"Of course," she said, remembering that it was Allen herself who had invited Tate in last time.

He held the door, and they stepped up to the receptionist, still behind Plexiglas and wearing a blue medical mask, the circular opening allowing for conversation. The large blue floor stickers that assisted in social distancing last week were gone and vaccinated patients were no longer required to wear masks.

Dani had never worn one, as she'd been hospitalized during those most dangerous months, and now vaccinated, could go without the face coverings. Some people still wore them. She'd seen them on the street and at bus stops wearing all sorts of medical masks.

"Let me tell her you're here," said the masked receptionist in the pink sweater. It was that sort of pink you see in crape myrtle trees, vibrant and joyful. Dani smiled.

"I'd like to join them for a few minutes," said Tate.

"Yes, I'll let her know, Judge Sutton."

Dani's brow knit. The reply made her think Tate had already requested and received permission. She glanced to Tate, but he was already moving to a vacant seat on the opposite side of the room from the only other occupant.

Dani sat beside him in a gray plastic chair and stared at the familiar artwork. Posters of oil paintings of tropical vegetation, huge broad leaves, birds-of-paradise, and arching palm fronds.

Tate glanced about the waiting room.

"Still no magazines," said Tate and drew out his phone.

Across the room, the birdlike woman touched her thumbs to her fifth fingers, then the ring, middle, and index. There she did a double tap and repeated the sequence in reverse order.

Calming exercise. Dani almost envied her. All she could do was wonder what Tate would say.

"Dani Sutton?"

She turned to see a large woman in black scrubs standing in the open door that led to Dr. Allen's offices. Her psychiatrist was one of seven in this practice.

Dani stood and lifted a hand. The corners of the nurse's eyes crinkled as she smiled beneath her mask. Dani and Tate followed her down the corridor where Dr. Allen waited to greet them and ushered them in. Dani noted the same colorful scarf around her psychiatrist's neck and absorbed a fresh wave of embarrassment.

"Judge Sutton. Dani. Come on in." She adjusted her mask and extended a hand to the open door.

In the therapy room, Tate settled in one armchair and Dani sat on the loveseat.

Dr. Allen perched in her desk chair and casually held a tablet, with a sky-blue cover, in her hands. Her smile was welcoming, and Dani returned it.

"I didn't recognize you in the elevator," Dani said, as if confessing her sins.

"Yes. I noticed."

"I'm sorry."

"I'm sure the masks make things more difficult. And it's especially hard to place people when they pop up in locations you don't expect."

They had spoken about that. But Dani was here in her offices and she should have expected to see her outside of their therapy room.

"I'm also sorry I missed our session on Thursday."

Her doctor nodded, accepting the apology.

"Well, you're here now. Shall we get started?"

Dani felt suddenly grateful to have this woman in her corner.

"Yes. Of course."

Dani glanced to Tate. Should she tell her doctor about the break-in? Tate had hinted she might not want to discuss this because it might reflect badly on her, and Dani would have to explain, justify, and defend. She felt exhausted already but gathered a deep breath before speaking.

"Why don't we begin with your homecoming," said Dr. Allen.

Tate interrupted. "Before you get into that, I wanted to mention that Shelby is still calling Dani. They speak nearly every day."

Dr. Allen nodded, her placid expression unchanged.

Dani stared from her psychiatrist to her husband, trying to interpret this exchange.

Her psychiatrist turned to Tate.

"Would you mind stepping out in the corridor with me, Judge Sutton?"

Tate rose, and they disappeared, leaving her like the naughty child in the principal's office. Dani tried the calming exercise she'd seen the woman in the waiting room using, but then headed to the door and listened. She could hear nothing, so she pressed an ear to the door. This allowed her only to hear muffled voices. She rested a hand on the latch and considered opening the door a crack.

What was he telling her? That the woman in the garage was in her imagination? That she'd crashed the car, or that she didn't want Enid snooping on her every darn day?

The latch moved and Dani flew across the room and back into her place, hitting the coffee table on the way. The Japanese Temari ball rolled to the carpet.

Dani scooped it up and met Dr. Allen's eyes.

"Has Tate gone?"

She nodded. "Just the two of us."

Silence stretched as Dr. Allen settled in her chair.

"Dani, Tate just told me that you had an intruder."

"Yes." Why had Tate told her not to mention it and then told her doctor?

She wasn't sure what to say or how to tackle this question without implicating Tate in something.

Dani blew away a breath, sat back into the cushions, and closed her eyes.

"He told me you were attacked outside your home."

"Yes."

"Would you be willing to tell me about that?"

Dani talked about the attack, her escape, and the terror. Then Dr. Allen teased out her feelings of vulnerability, incompetence at her inability to drive, and her fury when, initially, no one believed her when she said she had been attacked.

"Until you found the hairs?" asked her doctor.

"Exactly. Then their attitudes changed, and they searched. They never found her." Dani dropped her gaze to her tightly interlaced fingers.

"Are you upset with Tate? Perhaps for not being there?"

She found Dr. Allen studying her. "My husband? Yes, I am upset with him. For that and... he did something, he lied to me. He's never done that before and I don't understand why."

Her doctor's eyebrows lifted. "Would you like to tell me about it?"

She knew Tate didn't want her to. But this was *her* therapist, *her* recovery. So she did, explaining how Tate had revealed that there was no adoption and that they had hired a surrogate before the accident.

"He says he'd tried to tell me while I was here. Well, not here. When I was at Windwood, but it upset me. He says that I couldn't remember. So he changed the narrative to an adoption, which I accepted."

"The narrative?"

"He lied to me."

Small wonder. Look what happened when she'd learned about the blackmail payout before Christmas. She'd flown up to Shelby and crashed the car, nearly killing them both.

"That's why it all happened so fast. We decided together to hire a surrogate before the accident but that I couldn't recall that part. He said that you asked him to stop bringing it up because it upset me. So he lied and said it was an adoption." Dani watched Dr. Allen's face for some indication that she knew about this surrogacy or that this, too, was untrue.

Dr. Allen's face reddened, and her mouth opened in obvious shock at Dani's gush of revelations.

"I can see why you're upset," said Allen.

"I'm furious! And confused. Wondering how much of my marriage is a lie. Can I stay married to a man I don't trust? But we have a baby now and that changes everything. And this woman is still out there."

"Yes. Also very disturbing."

"Did you know we used a surrogate?" asked Dani.

"He mentioned it to me, yes."

Yet he'd told Dani that no one knew this wasn't an adoption. She added another lie to the black marks against her husband.

"Well, if he told me, I can't remember. From where I stand, he didn't tell me until *after* the attack."

"Why *did* he decide to tell you now?"

Dani glanced away, looking everywhere but at her doctor as she wondered how much to say. One thing she was *not* saying was that she thought Willow needed to be away from her for her own safety.

"I was feeling insecure."

"Second thoughts about the adoption?"

Her doctor was so smart.

She nodded, stretching out a hand and threading her fingers in the faux fur of one of the larger pillows.

"And Tate convinced you by his revelation."

"Well, yes. If it's true she's not adopted and I'm her mother." Had she just said *if*? It revealed the depth of her mistrust. She puffed her cheeks and gathered a pillow to her chest and stomach. "He says that he tells me things, did tell me things, while I was in here that I don't remember." Dani gasped, out of breath now.

"That's true about your memory. But no longer. Your recall is perfect."

"I have gaps."

"And always will. Those memories are gone. But everything since you recovered physically is perfect."

"He's shattered me. The trust that I thought was between

us. I don't know what to do. And Tate doesn't trust me, either. He's always checking if I've taken my pills and there are surveillance cameras in the house, even on the pool deck. I think he might watch me when he's away. I feel like a zoo animal."

"Anything else?"

"Yes, actually. We hired a neighbor to help with the baby and so I wouldn't be alone when he got back to work. But I'm really... unreasonably resentful of having her there. And the ridiculous part is that this arrangement was my idea. Now that she's here, and needs the job, it's awkward. She's our neighbor. And out of work. I can't just fire her."

Her doctor's gaze drifted to the ceiling, and she fell silent.

Dani, still hugging the pillow, scratched her nails across the palm of the opposite hand as she waited to hear what Allen was thinking. Her face felt hot, and her heart was fluttering like the wings of a bumblebee.

"You *can* fire her. If you feel that is best. But I do agree that you shouldn't be alone just yet. Not all day, at least. So, if Judge Sutton can't be there, hiring someone is a reasonable option, especially in light of the attack."

"Yes. Of course, it is." Dani hunched down in her seat. Trying to smother her resentment at Enid for her help, and her doctor for her opinion. She'd asked for both. Hadn't she?

Finally, their eyes met.

"You've only been home for two weeks. Fifteen days, today. Allow yourself adjustment time."

That did make sense.

"Regardless of his questionable decisions, I believe he is trying to help you with your transition."

"He acts as if I'm made of glass."

"I believe he is eager to have you succeed. If you continue to do well, he'll be less protective of you."

"Maybe."

"And what you see as imposition may well be support.

Remember, this is a transition for him as well. Perhaps you shouldn't be so hard on him or on yourself."

"I'll try, am trying. But what about his lies?"

Her doctor, usually nonjudgmental, gave a definite shake of her head. Her mouth was tight and her brows low over her eyes like storm clouds. "The lie is a serious issue between the two of you. Forgiving his dishonesty will require time and effort from you both because trust is more easily broken than repaired. You might get past this, that is assuming that is what you both want, to remain married."

"It's so hard."

"Marriage often is. And complicated. I'm not excusing him for his decisions to lie, Dani. But he may have seen this as less hurtful to you than the truth."

Her doctor was talking about Tate protecting his wife by lying. This was a concept she rejected. Her entire marriage was built on trust. Or it had been. What was her foundation now?

"I don't like these feelings, my suspicions, and I don't like that big house."

Allen pressed her lips together and sighed. "Do you want to come back here?"

"No! Oh, no. I'd have to leave Willow."

"It's a lot, Dani. I will admit, I'm worried about you."

"Oh, but she's wonderful. I've never been happier."

"You just described the feeling of being treated like an infant and your fury at Tate's deceit. And your worry about the threat of this woman is justified."

"But nothing is wrong with Willow. She's the light of my life."

"That's good news." Her doctor made another note, then glanced up to meet Dani's gaze. "But I think you might want to seriously consider if you are ready to handle all that has been laid at your feet."

"Yes. I will."

Her doctor made a note on her tablet using the stylus, then glanced up to meet Dani's gaze.

"Tell me more about the baby. What's it like being around her? How are you getting on?"

That question filled the rest of their session. Afterward, Dr. Allen turned her over to the nurse, who walked her to the waiting room where she found Enid and Willow.

Dani collected her daughter, taking the carrier, and she and Enid headed out.

Her next appointment was for Willow with the pediatrician in the same medical building, but a different floor. Enid surprised her by having an appointment of her own.

"I figured, since I was here, I'd get my annual," she said.

The group of physicians in the practice took half the floor and included a dozen practitioners. It was a reputable organization and so it was possible her neighbor's doctor was also here, if an odd coincidence.

Enid was called in first.

"See you soon," she said and paused. "Want to meet in the coffee shop in the lobby?"

She seemed in a hurry to follow the nurse who called her. Dani knew the small café on the main floor, a quiet space tucked away from the information kiosk and elevators.

"I'll be waiting for you."

Dani nodded, though Enid didn't linger for her agreement, as she had already disappeared into the inner portion of the medical practice. Dani made careful note of her clothing.

Today she wore a floral print wrap skirt, mostly red, and a yellow blouse with three-quarter-length sleeves. Her feet were sheathed in silver flats and her purse was a periwinkle blue. Enid's hair was twisted tight into a bun.

"You can remember all that," she said aloud to herself. "She'll be easy to spot."

Dani and Willow were called shortly afterward. The

nurse asked questions as she weighed and measured Willow. The rest of the appointment went smoothly, though it bothered Dani that Willow had lost weight, nearly half a pound. Both the nurse and doctor assured her this fluctuation was normal. Even so, she wondered if she was doing everything right.

She needed to be a good mother and now missed her own mother more than ever. There were a thousand questions she wished to ask and moments she longed to share. If only her mother could be here to help her instead of Enid.

There was one more thing she had to ask but the request stuck in her throat.

"Um, how difficult is it to get a DNA test?"

The doctor cast sharp eyes on her.

"I'd need a sample from the adult in question. That requires his permission."

"It's me, actually. I'm the adult in question. It's possible that she's genetically mine."

"Oh." The pediatrician paused to glance at Willow, then back to her. "Really? It's a simple matter then."

"We used a surrogate."

"I see. Let me just get what I need. It's a cheek swab."

"When will I know?"

"One to two days after the lab receives it. So, by Thursday."

The sample collection took only a few more minutes.

Before checking out, she asked if Enid Langford had finished.

"Yes. She's gone."

Dani had hoped to wait in the safety of the small, bright waiting room. But Enid would already be downstairs, as arranged. The woman loved her coffee.

At the atrium, she waited for the elevator. When the doors opened, she saw one passenger, a man who leaned heavily on a cane and wore a black plastic boot on one foot.

She stepped into the car. He glanced at the carrier but said nothing as they descended.

On the lobby level, he motioned her to precede him, and she whisked out into the open foyer. There, couches and chairs lined the windows and colorful panels hung suspended from the ceiling to break up the enormous space. Several people waited near the information kiosk for friends and family to emerge from the elevator banks. More than one glanced up at her before returning their attention to various devices.

She made her way past the circular security counter and the second waiting area beyond the main entrance. In the corner sat the coffee shop. It was more a coffee counter with a limited menu but plenty of circular café tables and hard plastic chairs.

Dani slipped inside, surprised to find the lights off and no staff behind the counter. She held Willow's carrier before her and glanced about. Then she frowned as the first trickle of worry slithered down her spine. A second look showed that Enid was not here. No one was here.

She had meant this coffee shop and not the chain place that lay across the street. Yes, she'd said downstairs.

"They're both downstairs," Dani said to no one. Or had Enid said *in the lobby*? Dani was uncertain. "Restroom?" she said aloud.

Enid might just be using the ladies' room.

Anxious now, Dani crept to the counter to see the sign set beside the register and read:

Temporarily closed due to staffing shortages.

Dani backed away, her heart slamming into her ribs. She turned—and that's when she saw her.

The woman had wild dark hair and was wearing mirrored sunglasses. She wore tiny jean shorts, a red Wonder Woman T-shirt, and nothing on her feet. The stranger made a beeline straight for Dani.

Had Dani's legs worked or her voice, she might have run or called for help, but she seemed paralyzed. The woman stalked forward. Dani backed away, putting one of the café tables between them.

"There you are!" Her voice held a sharp edge and a definite drawl. "I knew you'd show up here eventually. Your doctor's here."

How did she know that?

Was this the same woman who had broken the window of their car? The hair was right, dark and wild, but she couldn't see her eyes.

"Who are you?" Dani spoke in an unfamiliar voice, all scratchy and thin.

"She's mine." The woman lifted her chin toward the baby.

"No. She isn't." Dani set her jaw. "You have no claim on my child. You're only the surrogate."

The woman snorted.

"I don't have any money," said Dani. If this woman didn't leave, she was going to scream.

"Surrogate? Is that what he told you? And that I want money? I don't want money, Dani. I want my child."

TWENTY

Dani pulled the carrier close to her body, preparing to run.

The woman blocked her escape and cast Dani a cruel smile. She enjoyed this game.

"He's lying to you, Dani. Your husband is lying. He's the father all right, but I'm no surrogate." She pointed a long finger at Willow. "She's mine."

"No." This was more desperate prayer than denial. "She's mine. I'm her real mother."

"How do you know? Let me guess. You were having second thoughts, rightly, about being too crazy to raise a baby. And your dear husband told you that she's really yours. Convenient timing. Isn't it?"

Her gasp caused the woman to make a sound of satisfaction in her throat.

"He did. Didn't he?"

Dani's stomach pitched.

"And look at her! Look at her hair, her face, her skin color. She isn't yours. He lied to you. Cheated on you. Been cheating and is still cheating. He made me promises. That you weren't coming back. That he'd divorce you. Now look, he's got you trying to care for my child. Did you really think they'd give a baby to a crazy person? You're nuts, but you're not stupid. Are you, Dani?"

Dani could only shake her head and grip the carrier.

"I'm not crazy."

Another snort.

"What do you want?"

Her smile was terrifying. "Everything he promised. Your house, your husband, your place."

"Go away."

"Or what? You can't stop me. I'll have Tate. I'll be Mrs. Sutton. And you'll be back there. In that loony bin."

"I'm better now."

"Nut job!"

"I'm not."

"But not well. Not well enough to support his campaign, run his household, be his wife, or raise our child."

"Stop it!" Her voice was a screech.

The woman laughed. "You know it's true. All of it. You're brain damaged. You can't even remember what happened to you. You're terrified of driving, of being in public, of strangers. Now you can deal with this. Your perfect husband married you for money, stayed married for the money, and is succeeding better than even you imagined, all while you were locked up in the nuthouse. He doesn't need you. You're an anchor. What he *needs* is for you to disappear."

Did he need her? Was it the money? Doubts swirled, flashing in her periphery like strikes of lightning.

"No. Go away."

"I'll go. And you can wonder if I was really here. Normal people don't have to ask those sorts of questions. Maybe Dr. Allen can up your medication. Make you more of a walking zombie than you already are."

How did this woman know the name of her psychiatrist?

Was she sleeping with Tate? Did she know everything about her already?

"See you around, Dani. But you won't see me, unless I want you to. Can't, right?" She waved a hand before her own face. "Just a jigsaw puzzle of pieces that don't fit. Pity." For the first time, she glanced at Willow. "I'll be back for her and to collect on all those promises Tate made me when I was sleeping in your bed."

She shoved a chair into the table and strolled out of the café.

Dani watched her go. Should she call the police or Enid or Tate?

Not Tate. Definitely not Enid.

Shelby. Call Shelby. She'll know what to do.

Dani crept out of the empty café but had already lost sight of her. She glanced into the busy lobby, searching for a woman in a red T-shirt but she was gone. Vanished.

But she had been there.

Hadn't she?

Normal people don't have to ask those sorts of questions.

A cry emerged from her throat. The stranger seated just outside the shop glanced up. She could ask this young man, dressed in business casual, if he had just seen a woman leave the café. She took one step toward him, and the jolt of terror stopped her. What if he said he hadn't? He searched her face a moment longer, then lowered his gaze to his device, his thumbs busy as he replied to some message. Dani crept to security and curled into a seat, looping an arm through the carrier as she drew out her phone. However, she didn't have a chance to call Shelby because Enid arrived carrying a white paper bag.

"I had to get a script filled." She glanced at the café. "Is it closed? Ah, shucks." Enid finally glanced at Dani. "You okay? Your color isn't good."

"I want to go home." Dani said "home" but realized that in her mind's eye she saw her room at the private facility.

"Sure. How did Willow's check-up go?"

"Everything is fine."

"Great."

They walked to the parking garage and then Enid drove them back to Heron Shores. En route, Enid babbled about something, that the fashion industry used unfair labor practices, production polluted third world countries, and how flash fashion was killing the planet.

She continued to chatter like a magpie as she fixed lunch and doled out Dani's medications. Enid chatted as Dani ate, leaving only when Willow woke and loudly demanded to be fed. Dani let Enid take the baby, just to get a moment alone to think.

Could it all be true?

Was Willow Tate's child, a result of an extramarital affair?

He'd definitely lied about the adoption. Was the story about the surrogate just that, a story told to avoid telling her there was another woman?

Tate could be using the tale of blackmail as a diversion to explain his lover's appearance. But why had she shown up looking like a crazed homeless person?

None of this made any sense.

Dani buried her face in her hands, her shoulders shaking as she wept. When she finally lifted her head, it was to a silent house.

Everything was so quiet. Too quiet.

Irrational panic gripped her. Had Enid done something to the baby?

She snatched up the monitor, but it gave only a view of the empty crib. Dani headed upstairs. She found Enid in the nursery, lifting the baby onto her shoulder where a soft white rag waited.

Enid spotted her immediately.

"Feeling better?" she asked.

Dani glared.

"I just finished feeding Willow." Her smile was bright, but her eyes seemed hawkish.

"Why is your blouse unbuttoned?" asked Dani, pointing to the top two buttons.

"Is it?" she glanced down and fastened them with her free hand. "There."

"Give her to me," Dani demanded.

Enid hesitated.

Dani stretched out her hands, determined to take her child if Enid refused. She passed the baby to Dani, and Dani swept out of the room with her, down the hall to their bedroom, pausing to lock the door.

She heard Enid's footsteps on the wood flooring. "Dani, dear? Is everything all right?"

She didn't answer, just snarled at the door and rocked her baby.

"Should I call Tate?"

Of course, Enid would call and say Dani was acting irrationally.

Was she? She'd seen Enid with her blouse open. Was there a baby bottle in the nursery? She wasn't sure.

"Dani?" The knock came again, an insistent hammering, like a determined woodpecker. "I'm getting concerned."

Dani pressed her free hand over one ear.

"Go away, Enid. Don't come back."

The knocking ceased.

Finally, Enid spoke in a voice full of hurt.

"We are only trying to help, you know?"

Dani strained to hear Enid's footsteps. But her efforts met with only silence. She did not like the way Enid had said *we*.

Dani clicked the door open to check that Enid had gone but found Enid right outside the bedroom.

Dani tried to close the door, but Enid placed her body in the opening.

"I think you should give the baby to me."

Dani backed away, holding Willow against her chest.

Enid followed. But Dani retreated to the bath, slammed the door, and locked it before Enid passed the twin walk-in closets.

"Dani, don't make me call the police."

Dani scrambled for her phone. Who would the police believe, Enid or her? Enid was in Dani's home, demanding the baby. Enid was the intruder.

But Enid hadn't been committed to a mental hospital. That truth made everything she said suspect to law enforcement.

Dani made a pad from a plush bath towel and set Willow down. Then she lifted her phone and called Tate.

The trouble was, she was no longer sure if Tate was an ally or a foe.

After speaking with Tate, Dani waited behind the locked door as Enid received a phone call. She heard her arguing with someone and believed it was Tate.

"I can't just leave her in there with the baby!" Enid said, in the sort of voice that carries.

Then she said, "It's a mistake. You can't trust her."

Another pause.

"She's acting crazy again. Seeing things. Did she tell you about the woman she thinks she saw in the medical building?"

Dani hadn't told Enid anything about that encounter.

Had she?

Now she wasn't sure.

Had it been Enid rattling on during the drive, or Dani?

She crouched, threading her hands in her hair and tugging until the roots hurt.

"What's happening to me?" she cried.

Tears fell to the black slate floor in perfect circles. Before her, Willow waved her chubby arms and kicked.

Dani lifted her daughter.

"Don't worry, sweetling. Mama's got you."

Dani gritted her teeth and waited for Enid to leave or the police to break down the door. She played with Willow until the baby yawned and closed her eyes, sending feathery lashes against perfect skin.

Then she watched the baby sleep. It was one of the few things that calmed her.

She thought of all the early mornings that Tate was out walking with Willow and wondered where he'd really gone?

Then she pondered when he left. Was he out in the morning or did he take Willow the moment Dani fell asleep? He could have been gone all night, every night. She'd never know the difference.

She needed regular sleep, but she also needed answers.

Her phone buzzed: Shelby. Dani spilled her guts to her sister, weeping as she described where she was and why.

"That woman is a monster. You should call the police."

"They already think I'm crazy."

"Call Tate."

"I just did."

She explained he had called Enid, who was giving her version of things.

"She makes me sound unfit. As if I'd ever do anything to hurt this baby."

"Dani, call your doctor or the police. You have to call somebody," insisted Shelby.

Dani repeated the poisonous accusations that the stranger had spewed. Those allegations now made her question if Tate was even in the house each night.

"He could have been with her. How would I know?"

"Dani, settle down," said Shelby, a note of alarm in her tone.

"He told Dr. Allen that you were calling me most every day."

"So? What's wrong with me calling you?" asked Shelby.

"That's what I wanted to know. It's like he's tattling on me or something."

"Did you ask him?"

"My doctor said it was just a change in my behavior, which means they're tracking my behavior. I think Tate is using the home security system, the cameras, to watch me."

"I read about this. Toxic relationships. A controlling partner. They install tracking apps on your phone. Check your odometer. Stuff like that. And control the money. Isolate you from your family. He definitely did that with Mom."

"Mom couldn't stand him. That's different."

"Do you trust your psychiatrist? You should talk to her about this."

"I do. And Dr. Allen is concerned. She's worried about my safety, because of this attacker and Tate's lies. Dr. Allen told me she knew about the surrogacy and Tate claims he didn't tell her."

"Yikes."

"I told her I was worried about my marriage."

"What did she say?"

"She didn't disagree. Oh, Shelby!"

"Go back to the woman from the coffee shop. Could that have been the same woman as in your garage?"

"I think so. Maybe. She said she's not a surrogate. That Willow is hers. That Tate cheated on me. And Willow's hair, her coloring, it's dark, like hers."

"So you believe her?"

Dani let her head sink. "I don't know what to believe."

"You have to confront Tate again. He fed you that story about adoption and now he springs on you that he hired a surrogate and that she's blackmailing him. Why not tell you that from the beginning?"

"He said he *did* tell me and it upset me. So much that I... I drove up to Jacksonville to you."

"The accident."

Dani could only make a humming sound of confirmation.

"So that explains why he didn't want to tell you... again."

Another hum as she tried to choke down the lump lodged in her throat like a peach pit. When she spoke, her voice rasped.

"And because I was having second thoughts, you know, about my competency to be her mother. Telling me that Willow is mine, well, that means it's not an adoption. Is it? But maybe..." Her mind was whirling like a propeller. "Maybe he made that up, too. He could be cheating on me and Willow is *her* baby."

"That's possible. You need to see the adoption papers or whatever that was you signed. And everything you can from the surrogacy agreement if there is one. What's her name? Where does *she* live?"

"I know I signed something. But if he is cheating on me, there won't be a surrogacy contract, unless he convinced that woman to relinquish custody to him. That's if what she said is true and he's the father."

"He wouldn't want that to get out," said Shelby.

"If that went public..." Dani imagined the headlines and shivered.

"It would ruin his reputation, his campaign, and his chance for a seat on the court."

"Oh, Shelby, do you think that's it? Does he see me as a threat?"

"More like a problem or, maybe, an obstacle."

"I only wanted to help him." She said that in the past tense, as if this had changed or was changing.

"Would you feel the same if you knew your baby resulted from an extramarital affair?"

Dani hesitated, then she gave the truthful answer instead of the one she would have preferred to give.

"No. But..."

"What?"

"I got a DNA test today. I should know on Thursday if I'm Willow's mother or if that was another lie."

"That was brave," said Shelby. "Is he taking money from the trust? You know, besides for the campaign?"

"I don't know. Probably."

"You'd have to approve it."

She thought of the brunch at the yacht club and the smarmy Dennis Babbet.

"Maybe I did approve it. I'm not sure. But I know he's still trying to get the party backing. But they know about my illness. And I don't think he has their backing yet."

"So you're financing the campaign?"

"Yes. But Tate is also trying to secure the party's backing."

"If he has you, then why is he trying so hard to secure their support?"

"I don't know. Looks better to have party backing, not run independent, I suppose."

"So why hasn't he secured the endorsement yet? What's the holdup?"

"I thought it was me. My mental illness."

"Maybe, but maybe they know about the affair. And about your illness. The combination makes him a less attractive candidate for a judicial seat."

"Or he's telling me the money is for the campaign and it's also for this woman."

"Or for the payout to a blackmailer."

"Maybe. Shelby, what do I do?"

"Confront him. He owes you the truth."

"I did. But I don't know if I can believe a word he says."

"You have to try."

Dani let the tears fall.

"Shelby? What if it's all in my head?"

"What?"

"What I saw. The woman in the garage. The one in the coffee shop."

"They found dark hairs. Real evidence."

"Did they? Or was I the only one who saw them? What if it's all been a paranoid delusion?"

"That would be... bad."

Dani glanced over at her daughter and then spoke into the phone.

"Shelby, I can't lose this baby. I love her too much."

She expected Shelby to offer reassurances. To tell her everything would be fine. That she could trust her husband.

Instead, she said, "Come here. Bring the baby."

"Now?"

"Right now."

TWENTY-ONE

The textured glass sliders in the main bath obscured the view. But they opened to the private balcony inside the screened cage, overlooking the pool and canal. A circular staircase led down to the lanai.

If Enid was still outside the bathroom door in the hall between the walk-in closets, she couldn't see the balcony. If she were in the bedroom suite, however, she'd spot Dani immediately.

Dani tucked her phone in her front pocket and lifted Willow to her shoulder, cradling her head. She unlocked and opened the slider with painful slowness, to prevent the sound of the door rolling in its tracks from alerting her captor. The door chime made her freeze.

She glanced back, expecting pounding or Enid's call. But there was only silence.

The sound had seemed impossibly loud. Could it be Enid had not heard?

Then she hurried across the open space and down the stairs. Instead of heading for the lanai and living room beyond, she crept around the side of the house along the knee-high hedge of hawthorn. When she reached the six-foot wall that shielded the garbage and recycling bins from the street, she paused.

This spot gave a clear view of the front entrance before her and, beyond the pygmy palm, the curving driveway.

At the sound of a vehicle, Dani crouched between the bins. Tate pulled into the drive and Enid charged out of the entrance and down the steps.

She looked desperate to get her side of the story to Tate first.

Dani narrowed her eyes at Enid's high, panicky voice.

Tate emerged from the climate-controlled, plush, cream leather interior and faced Enid, who threw herself into his arms.

Dani swayed, lost her balance, and collided with the wall as if she'd been slapped in the face, all the while protecting Willow with her arms. She peered from her hiding place, jaw dropping open, leaving her gaping and blinking, because what she saw clashed with what she had expected.

Tate held their neighbor in his arms, cradling her in a way that made Dani's skin flush cold and then hot. He clasped the back of her head and kissed her firmly on the mouth.

Dani gasped and crept back between the bins.

That wild-eyed female at the coffee shop had warned of another woman. Was Tate sleeping with their next-door neighbor, his former coworker? Was this why Paul left and why Enid was fired? Dani suspected it was not staff reduction, but this affair that had caused Enid's termination.

"Oh, God!" she whispered, rocking Willow against her chest.

She heard a car engine and crept forward again. An unfamiliar vehicle pulled into the drive. A silver Lexus.

Out stepped Dr. Allen. A spark of hope flared within Dani at the arrival of this ally. Then the three gathered in a circle and appearances doused hope.

Dr. Allen wasn't here to help. She had come to take Dani

back to the hospital. They'd tell her it was just for a brief stay. It would be a lie.

She'd lose the baby.

Dani glared at Enid, shaking her head, trying and failing to dispel the instinct that Tate was cheating on her with their neighbor.

How long had Tate been sleeping with Enid?

The way they touched and the fact that they did not even try to hide their embrace, even when her doctor arrived, told Dani that Dr. Allen was aware Tate had been unfaithful, was *still* unfaithful.

She tried to picture Enid in a red T-shirt and cutoff denim jeans, her meticulously coiffed hair loose and flowing wild about her shoulders.

Was this the woman in the garage and the one in the coffee shop?

The idea took hold and sprang roots.

Dani began to shake. She had no allies, no friends.

Her husband, whom she had loved and trusted, had become a stranger. Her cheeks went hot as humiliation flooded her face.

They still spoke in a huddle, old friends discussing a tiresome problem.

What should we do with Dani?

Poor, sick Dani who just can't distinguish reality from paranoid delusions.

What if that were true? What if she hadn't seen them embrace at all?

No, she still trusted her eyes. What choice did she have but to rely on the input of her senses?

And Enid smelled of gardenias. She had somehow not put two and two together until now.

Tate and Enid were colleagues. She'd worked in his law office for years, with him, for him.

Was she taking advantage of Tate? His wife was in a psychiatric facility for months and months. Poor man. And Enid had filled that void.

Was that where Tate went every morning or every night?

Dani backed away.

Had Tate been spending the nights there? Taking their child to that woman and sleeping in her bed?

Dani didn't know. Her sleeping pills ensured she wouldn't know.

"Take your pills, Dani."

She fumed. The careful attention of her loving husband now seemed self-serving.

Tate had made love to her only three times since she'd come home. That was a change. Before she had left, they'd been much more active in the bedroom. But then, Dani hadn't been drugged to keep the recurring nightmares at bay. The void seemed preferable.

But was it?

Should she confront Tate? Confront Enid and Tate? Or should she try to pretend she didn't know?

Dani was realistic about her ability to keep the shock and nausea under control. She doubted she could convince anyone that she was still blissfully in the dark.

Her buzzing astonishment morphed into fury, white hot and blinding. She sank to the concrete slab between the bins, clutching the sleeping Willow to her chest, panting like a rabid animal. Bitten by the poison of suspicion and jealousy, she became unrecognizable.

The armada of her three opponents headed inside, and the door closed behind them. It was only a matter of moments now before they realized she was gone.

She'd run. Go to Shelby like she planned.

Dani stood, playing that scenario in her mind. Dr. Allen's car blocked the drive, but she could get around it in Tate's car. But he kept the fob in his pocket and there was no infant carrier in the rear seat. She could get around both cars in her SUV, now inside the garage, if she could get through a closed garage door.

The side door, she thought. It was now locked because of the intruder. Dani's spirits fell. Time ticked. They were inside. Possibly already upstairs.

And she had no key fob. No wallet. Dani reversed course, running back the way she had come.

When she cleared the bathroom slider, the sound of pounding reached her.

She ducked inside, laying her sleeping daughter back on the folded pad she'd made from the fluffy terrycloth towel.

Dani felt the contents of her stomach heave and just made it to the toilet before vomiting.

The pounding ceased. Outside the door, Tate's voice intruded.

"Dani, open the door!"

She vomited again and then heaved, her body still trying to expel the poison that she had consumed, unable to grasp that it was not food, but lies.

She curled in a ball on the bathroom floor.

Tate rattled the door.

"Dani? Unlock this door."

His voice held the sharp edge of panic. The words were slow and measured, but the tone conflicted.

"Go away," she whispered.

He didn't, of course. Instead, he splintered the frame. He rushed to her, trying to gather her up. She fought him, slapping at his reaching arms.

"Dani, what's wrong?"

"I'm sick," she said.

He glanced about the room, spotted Willow, and then hurried to the drawer where she kept her various medications, rattling them like maracas, checking to see that she had not intentionally overdosed on something. Now her stomach tightened with rage.

Dr. Allen slipped in behind him and silently gathered Willow up from the floor, then retreated out the door.

Dani glared at Tate. He'd taken a vow. Better or worse.

The courts offered no time off because your wife had a mental breakdown. His job was to support. Not find a replacement.

And why had he stood by her at all? Was it love or the money?

Dani narrowed her eyes and pushed herself to a sitting position.

Tate's shoulders sagged as he found the medications as they should be. He turned to find her glaring at him.

"How long?" she asked.

"What?"

"How long have you been sleeping with Enid?"

"Dani." His voice was appeasing, his hands opened and outstretched.

She stood and backed away.

"Sweetheart."

He tried to gather her up, but she pushed him hard. Tate barely budged. He remained like an oak, too close and too solid to move.

"I saw you."

"Saw what?" His head swiveled as he glanced at the closed door.

"I was downstairs. I saw you in the driveway with her."

He seemed to be trying to recall what had occurred. Then he went into damage control.

"I don't know what you think you saw, but there's nothing between Enid and me beyond concern for your well-being."

He slipped into lies so effortlessly, Dani had to question all of it.

"Is that why you kissed her on the mouth?"

His voice cajoled. "Dani..."

"Did you ever love me, Tate?"

"I love you now. Always."

"You need me, my money, rather, to fund your campaign, your lifestyle, this house. But you don't really need me."

"Dani, you can't be serious. That's crazy." His eyes widened as he realized what he'd said. No doubt Dr. Allen had advised against use of terms like that.

"Actually, I've never felt less crazy. It hurts too much to be delusion. You've shattered me, Tate. How could you? I trusted you with everything and you betrayed me."

"It's not like that."

Dani lifted her fists, advancing.

"Dr. Allen!" Tate shouted over his shoulder.

Dani pounded on his chest and then moved to his face, clawing at his forearm as he lifted it to shield from attack.

She cried over and over. "How could you? How could you?"

"Dr. Allen!" Tate's voice held a note of unfamiliar panic.

Footsteps pounded and Dr. Allen appeared, her eyes wide behind the clear-framed glasses, and over her right shoulder, stood a curvy, dark-haired woman in a yellow blouse—Enid.

Dani redirected her outrage, hurling herself at Enid.

"Homewrecker! Whore!"

Tate captured Dani about the waist and held her to him as she kicked and screamed.

Her husband shouted to Enid to leave and then to Dr. Allen. Enid retreated only as far as the hall between the walk-in closets, watching Dani with a fixed fascination, her face expressionless and dark eyes bright.

Dr. Allen pushed past Enid.

"She was downstairs. Saw us through the window," Tate said. "Thinks I'm sleeping with Enid."

Dr. Allen's face went hard, and Dani felt hope at seeing the clear censure in her doctor's expression.

The psychiatrist knew and disapproved.

"Dani," she said. "You need to calm down."

"You knew!"

The accusation struck, and Dr. Allen glanced away.

"Did you know it was Enid? That he'd been cheating on me with our neighbor?"

The tears rolled down her cheeks as she stopped struggling.

"Let go," she ordered.

He did, stepping away as the three surrounded her like vultures, looking for weakness.

Dani faced Enid now.

"Was it you in the coffee shop? Did you strip off that wrap skirt and let down your hair just to plant that poison in my ear?" She repeated the stranger's words. "'He's the father... I'm no surrogate.'"

Now Tate was staring at Enid, his mouth gaping as she glanced away, refusing to make eye contact.

Dani turned to Tate.

"You said it was the surrogate. That she was blackmailing you. Was that a lie as well? Did you know it was her?"

Tate glanced to Enid, his lifted brows asking an unspoken question. The co-conspirators shared a silent exchange. Enid shook her head in denial.

Dani lifted a finger, pointing at Enid's black heart. "She's lying! She thought I'd snap. Hurry off to the center so she could have you all to herself. Move right back into my spot, raise my daughter. Is that what you want, Tate? Her instead of me?"

He shook his head. "Dani, listen. You're upset."

"You're cheating on me. Of course, I'm upset!"

"Let's go have a seat," suggested Dr. Allen, motioning toward the alcove beyond the king-sized bed. "We'll chat."

"Where is Willow?" asked Dani.

"Safe."

"Where?"

"She's fine, Dani. Please." She motioned to the bedroom.

Dani pointed a finger at Enid. "I want her out of my house."

"We can talk about that," said Dr. Allen.

"No. We aren't talking. She's leaving, and she is not coming back. Tate will not see her again."

"Dani, you don't understand," said Tate.

"I understand. Better than you, apparently. I'm not having it. You can't have her and my money. Is that plain enough?"

Tate turned to Enid. "Maybe it would be better..."

Enid's face flamed. "You are not sending me off like some dirty little secret. Not again."

"Enid, please."

Now Enid was pointing at Dani, whining to Tate like a child tattling to a parent.

"She just accused me of attacking her!"

Dani charged her. It was enough to send Enid retreating. When Dani reached their bedroom suite, Tate had a hold of his wife's arm and Enid swept out of the bedroom.

"She was trying to make me think I was crazy. That woman, the one in the garage. The one in the coffee shop. It was Enid."

"You can't be sure of that," said Tate.

"I am. I don't need to recognize her face. I know what she smells like. I know the way she walks. It was Enid."

Tate looked at the empty doorway where Enid had been.

"You know it's true."

"It's possible."

"So why did you tell me it was the surrogate?"

"Let's sit," suggested Dr. Allen.

Dani wished she'd leave. Her confidence in her doctor had shattered when she saw her with Enid and Tate in the drive. Her certainty that Dr. Allen also withheld information grew and festered as she swept past them to settle on the couch.

Dani couldn't trust any of them.

Dr. Allen spoke, but Dani wasn't listening. She could hear only the voices of doubt in her mind. Was Tate trying to help her or manage another potential problem?

She had become a liability to his ambitions and a threat to his lifestyle. And he'd been playing the dutiful, suffering husband while sneaking off to continue his affair with Enid.

God, she'd even felt sorry for him. She'd thought herself a burden. The guilt, the shame—he'd let her suffer those, while they should have been his.

She'd done nothing wrong except drive that vehicle into an overpass.

Dani sucked in a breath. Was this the real reason? Had she discovered the affair and flown up I-4 to reach Shelby? Had she driven them into that overpass because she'd discovered her husband's infidelity?

No wonder they hadn't told her. He'd never stopped seeing Enid.

"How long?" Dani said, interrupting Dr. Allen.

Tate's Adam's apple bobbed as he glanced to Dani and then back to Dr. Allen.

Dr. Allen gave a barely perceptible shake of her head.

Tate turned back to his wife.

"How long what?"

"How long have you been fucking Enid?"

As far as she knew, she'd never used that word. But all the others seemed too personal, too romantic, and too infuriating.

What if he loved her more?

"Since around the time of the accident," Tate said at last.

"It was why I went to Shelby. Wasn't it? Why I was driving. I found out."

He cast a sideward look at the doctor.

"Don't look at her. Answer me."

He did. "Yes."

Dani dropped her head into her hands and wept. Tate made the mistake of trying to touch her.

She spun her arms like an Olympic swimmer, repelling his efforts. He'd lost that right and the ability to give her anything like comfort.

"You bastard."

Dani tried to rein in the pain, but it just grew. A gaping hole, like dark matter, sucking in every ray of light. The depression she had held at arm's length saw her weakness and descended, tearing at her joints and muscles. If she didn't do something right now, it would have her again, and this time she might never climb back from that pit of sorrow.

"I think it would be wise to have you check into the hospital," said Dr. Allen.

It was the jab in the face Dani needed.

Just as expected, but still a shock.

She met Dr. Allen's gaze.

"Just overnight. Let you get some rest. You and I can talk some more."

She glanced to Tate. Predictably, he agreed with her doctor.

"It's a good idea," he said, offering a reassuring expression and a tight smile.

Dr. Allen was a physician who had withheld information from her patient: Dani's husband had cheated on her. Why in the world would she take advice from either one?

Dani was about to ask again to see the baby, but she stopped herself.

Tate was no longer an ally. Dr. Allen was not her friend. And neither would let her near Willow.

All she knew with certainty was that she didn't trust them.

"Yes. I can't stay here. Not now."

Dr. Allen nodded and cast her a sympathetic smile.

"I'd like to give you a sedative."

Dani gritted her teeth. There would be no escaping once that happened.

"Yes. Let me pack a bag first."

"All right, if you stay calm," said Dr. Allen.

"Fine." Dani stood, knowing Tate was strong enough to stop her. Better Dr. Allen than Tate, she decided. "I want him out of my sight."

Tate cast her a hurt look and Dani narrowed her eyes.

He turned and left the room.

Dani made a show of selecting a suitcase, moving from the bedroom to the closet and to the bathroom to gather up items, which she pressed into the roller bag.

Dr. Allen sat quietly on the loveseat beneath the bank of windows, observing without a word.

Dani took another trip to the bath, opened the slider, and slipped outside. From there she ran down the stairs, staying low and hoping Tate was not looking out at the water. From the lanai inside the screened living space, she slipped into the guest bathroom, which opened to the pool. She inched down the hallway toward the kitchen, pausing to crouch behind the wall as Tate paced from kitchen to dining room, on the phone as usual. Enid sat in Dani's place at the formal table, her back to Dani. There on the kitchen island sat Willow in her carrier.

From upstairs, Dr. Allen sounded the alarm.

Enid shot to her feet and she and Tate dashed out of sight.

Dani darted into the kitchen, looped her arm beneath Willow's carrier handle, and ran to the laundry room, pausing only long enough to snatch up her purse. Then she whisked her daughter out to the garage. From there, she snapped Willow's carrier into the rear seat base, opened the automatic garage door, and got behind the wheel to drive over the lawn to the road.

This time, her heart hammered for different reasons. This time, the fear of driving yielded to the need to run.

Despite the possibility that Enid had delivered Willow, Enid wasn't her mother. The woman had given the baby away, to Dani. And Dani was keeping her.

Tate could have Enid. She was taking her daughter, her money, and herself to Shelby. He had made his choice. Now he could live with it.

And as for Dr. Allen, Dani was filing a malpractice suit the minute she could reach her attorney.

Shelby had told her to come there. Meet her at her new house.

And that's what I'm doing.

Her twin was the one person in the world that she trusted, had always trusted, and the only one who could help her now.

Dr. Allen's car still blocked the driveway, so Dani left the pavement, passing through the hole she'd torn in the hedge the last time she'd been behind the wheel. When she reached the road, she cast a glance in the rearview at the gaudy showplace that Tate had chosen, thinking that Enid would fit perfectly in the space. She was just as pretentious, phony, and garish.

A cheap imitation of Dani herself.

They could enjoy their appropriated life here if they could afford it without her money.

TWENTY-TWO

Dani kept expecting to see police lights in her rearview mirror. More than once, she was passed by a sheriff or Florida Highway Patrol cruiser.

But no one stopped her.

She drew up Shelby's new address from her contacts and added it to the vehicle's navigation system.

After ninety minutes, Willow woke crying. Dani pulled off the highway and into a grocery where she bought diapers, ready-to-feed formula, and diaper wipes. Her phone app with its stored credit card allowed her to pay for what she needed. She realized Tate could access this information nearly in real time. He'd likely know where she was headed, but with her sister beside her and the law firm chosen by her family, she would feel secure. When facing a garden of snakes, it was best to bring a mongoose. She'd have two.

In the store, she spotted a woman staring at her. She wore office casual, spoiled by the service pistol on her hip.

Dani held Willow's carrier tight, choosing to drop the basket of items to be ready to fight, but the woman walked straight past her and disappeared around the aisle.

Back in the SUV, Dani fed Willow inside the running vehicle with the air conditioner blasting. Finally, she changed Willow's diaper and set her baby into the carrier for the rest of the journey.

Before leaving the lot, she called Shelby.

As the phone rang and rang, she got that familiar pressure in her ribs. The building panic. Had Shelby fallen while transferring from her chair to the shower seat?

Another ring. How many more until it flipped to voicemail?

She might just be in the bathroom. She's probably fine.

It was Dr. Allen who instructed her to counter each dark prospect with a positive possibility.

Or she left the phone in another room. She's going after it now.

Ring.

The ringing stopped. Next came her sister's familiar voice.

"Hey, Dani-o! Where are you?"

Dani exhaled her relief, the fear ebbing like a retreating wave.

"Shelby. Everything okay?"

"Yes. How's Willow?"

"Good. I'm on my way."

"Is she okay?"

"She's fine. Just fed and changed her. She's practicing her sounds. Listen." Dani held out the phone toward the rear seat so Shelby could hear Willow gurgling and squawking.

"Are you driving right now?"

Dani scowled. She would never drive and talk on the phone. Shelby should realize that. Something odd was happening. The sense of unease grew, twisting her stomach into knots.

"Are you all right, Shelby?"

"Of course. Worried about you, is all."

"I'm not driving right now. But when I do, I just won't think about it. I'm focused on seeing you."

"Should you call Tate?"

She paused. Something was wrong. She could hear it in Shelby's voice.

"Why would I do that? He's cheating on me." Dani launched into the details of all that had occurred since Shelby's command that Dani come to her.

"I think he might be worried."

"If that were true, he wouldn't be sleeping with our neighbor, plotting with my psychiatrist, or trying to put me back in that hospital."

"But what if that is what you need?"

Dani gasped. "Shelby? What are you doing? You're the one who told me to come."

"I'm worried about you driving."

"I'll be there in two hours and four minutes, according to the navigation program. I love you, big sister."

"Do you have the address?"

"12-22-15 Memorial Boulevard, Jacksonville. You told me. It's plugged into the nav system."

"Be careful. I'll see you soon."

Shelby disconnected without their usual farewell. Had they gotten to her, too?

Were they there, right now?

That was impossible. Even Tate couldn't defy the laws of physics. It took hours to drive to Jacksonville from Tampa.

But Shelby had acted so oddly, almost as if she wasn't alone.

A new urgency filled Dani as she headed out of the lot. The need to reach safety, to find the one person who always had her back, pushed her to move. Across the street, parked in a fast-food lot, facing her, was another sheriff's vehicle.

A chill lifted the hairs on her neck. She was bound to see law enforcement on the I-4 corridor. Wasn't it the deadliest road in America? This didn't necessarily have anything to do with her.

But she feared it did.

She also worried that Shelby was in trouble. That was an anxiety that gripped her heart and squeezed the blood from her.

Dani put on her turn signal before leaving the lot. The navigation program issued commands. Turn right. Left lane ahead. Take the ramp to I-4 East.

For the rest of the drive, Dani stayed in the far-right lane, behind one truck or another, to avoid the minivans and SUVs filled with families, weaving dangerously in and out of traffic, near desperate to get from the closing theme parks to their hotels.

When she arrived at her sister's address, she felt elated and exhausted. She flexed her stiff fingers and rolled her aching shoulders and smiled. She had done it. She had gotten in a car and safely driven all the way to her sister's new home.

Willow woke the instant the engine ceased. At her cry, Dani took one of the three remaining two-ounce bottles of premixed formula from the Styrofoam cooler she'd purchased, and placed it inside her bra to warm to the temperature of her skin.

Then she retrieved her daughter.

"Oh, I know. You're hungry and the streetlights are too bright." Dani expertly draped a cloth diaper over the baby's head and cradled her to a position on her shoulder. She bounced in place in the oppressive humidity, waving away the persistent mosquitoes as she locked the SUV, suddenly as starving as Willow sounded.

Her baby continued to cry.

"Let's get you inside." She turned to the house, which was a cute Spanish-style build with orange tile shingles and lush landscaping. Dani especially liked the oak that was large enough to offer shade and to accommodate a porch swing.

Dani cocked her head. Odd choice for a woman in a wheelchair, she thought. Well, it was likely a remnant from the previous owner, just like the god-awful gilded chandelier in her foyer that dripped cut crystal tear drops the way a jogger drips sweat.

Her back ached as she carried Willow to Shelby's front door.

She scowled at the entrance. The stoop was cluttered with a bench and potted succulents, but no ramp.

Now that was not just odd, it was impossible. Unless Shelby entered from the garage. Dani turned to find the single-car garage shut tight.

So far, Dani's reception had been less than stellar.

Willow continued to fuss, so Dani gave her the pacifier. It satisfied for the moment and Dani headed for the entrance.

Standing on the stoop, she got the feeling of vacancy. The curtains hung still as palm fronds on a windless day. No light escaped from the windows.

It was late, nearly midnight. But Shelby would be waiting.

The worry that Shelby had fallen squeezed her ribcage as she pressed the doorbell.

Inside, the chime echoed. As the seconds passed, her anxiety grew.

Shelby wouldn't live in a house with a step and no ramp. How would she even get through the front door?

Dani took out her phone and checked the address: 12-22-15 Memorial Boulevard, Jacksonville.

"Right house," she whispered. But something about that address gave her the creeps. This entire street disturbed her.

She glanced at the well-kept, smaller homes, mostly dark except for landscaping lights and the streetlights. Nothing obviously ominous.

So why was she trembling?

She sent Shelby a text. The reply was immediate.

There already?

Dani typed her response and the address, asking if she was at the correct street.

You're early. I'll be there in 10. Wait there.

Shelby didn't drive. That meant she'd be arriving by private van shuttle service that accommodated wheelchairs. It was expensive, but Shelby had money and no other option.

If Dani lived with Shelby, she could drive her. She sighed at the longing that image conjured. She wished to make her sister's life easier. Her fantasy was to return to the way it had been when they were girls.

Shelby understood her in a way no one, not even her parents, ever had.

And now, with the trust she'd held for her husband shattered and suspicion for her doctor seeping into her skin like poison, she had only Shelby and Willow.

Her sister she could trust.

Her daughter she would protect.

The step was sweltering. The concrete absorbed the day's heat, radiating it through the designer ballet slippers. Sweat trickled down her back and slithered between her breasts. She waved the cloth diaper to keep the mosquitoes off Willow and herself.

Willow dropped her pacifier to howl. The outrage at her current situation forced Dani into action. Willow's cries were not yet the ear-shattering volume of a toddler. Still, they relayed that all was not right in her world.

Dani retreated to the car. There she engaged the engine and waited until the rush of hot air gradually turned cool. She carried Willow back out so they both could duck into the large rear seat. The scent of leather and dirty diapers overwhelmed.

She rested Willow back in her carrier, where the baby waved her arms and cried.

But as soon as Dani offered the milk, her daughter latched on and sucked. Afterward, Dani rested her daughter over her knees, tummy down, and rubbed her back until she burped. Then she changed the soiled diaper. With the meal in her belly and a clean, dry bottom, Willow's sunny personality returned, and Dani sang a lullaby until the baby yawned and her blue eyes grew unfocused.

Dani strapped her into the carrier and sat beside the sleepy infant, feeling drowsy herself.

Where was Shelby?

Dani dozed, rousing when a large van pulled diagonally behind her vehicle, blocking the entire driveway.

"Finally," she muttered and stepped out of the running SUV, closing the door to keep the heat and bugs away from Willow.

Halfway down the drive, she realized there were more than two people in the vehicle.

The rear sliding door rolled open and came to a halt with a bang.

From within a man emerged onto the sidewalk.

"Dani. Are you okay?"

She instantly recognized the voice. What was he doing here?

"Tate?"

TWENTY-THREE

"Where's Shelby?" asked Dani, retreating with one hand gripping her throat.

Tate lifted his arms outward in the way the orderlies at the hospital did when a resident got too loud.

"Dani, take it easy."

From behind him, Dr. Allen emerged.

Panic gripped her around the chest. She gasped and then shouted, "What's happening? Where's my sister?"

Tate advanced. "We need to talk to you, Dani. Settle down."

She continued her retreat.

"Where's the baby?" asked Dr. Allen.

Dani's gaze flashed to the SUV and then to the street beyond her doctor. The oddly parked van now made perfect sense. The vehicle blocked her escape. Dani backed away, up the drive, toward the vehicle.

"What have you done with Shelby? Why isn't she here?"

Dr. Allen touched Tate's hand. He halted instantly, his expression pained. Her psychiatrist crept forward like a spider.

"Don't you know?"

"My sister lives here." Dani waved a hand back at the empty house, knowing this wasn't true, but unsure how she knew. Something was very wrong. She glanced to the entrance, but the house address had changed. It wasn't 12-22-15. Instead, three gold numbers were nailed vertically onto one of the pillars flanking the door, three wrong numbers. What was happening? "This is Shelby's home."

"Is it?" asked Dr. Allen.

Dani reached the driver's side of the vehicle and rested a hand on the latch. The door locks engaged. Dani tried the door and then glanced back to see Tate holding a key fob.

"Is the baby in the car?" he asked Dr. Allen.

She stooped and lifted her hands to glance into the rear passenger compartment. Then she straightened and nodded to Tate.

Tate rushed forward and Dani continued to retreat until she stood between the front bumper and the closed garage.

Tate released the locks, collected Willow in the carrier, and returned to the van.

"How did you find me? Where is my sister? This is her house. What did you do with her?"

"The address, Dani. Think of the address," said Allen.

"12-22-15 Memorial Boulevard, Jacksonville. Twelve. Twenty-two..." It wasn't an address. It was a date. December 22, 2015.

The date of the accident.

"Shelby," she gasped.

Dr. Allen's voice drew her back to the present.

"Dani, where is Shelby?"

The voice that Dani had once found calming now grated. Something was breaking loose inside her brain. Something sharp and dangerous.

She clutched her hands to her temples. "What's happening?"

"You're remembering. Thinking about Shelby. The accident. Can you see it?"

"No! I can't see that. Can't remember that."

"Can't or won't?"

Tate paused at the open van door, like a bystander turning at the sound of brakes squealing, not wanting to miss the collision.

"I was feeling in the smoke, trying to find her."

"And then?"

In a flash of light, Dani saw Shelby beside her, still strapped into her seat.

A road sign, sheared by the bulldozing vehicle, flew through the windshield. Glass exploded inward, peppering them with a shower of sharp cubes.

The hood collapsed like a shrieking accordion. Dani threw up her arms as the airbags exploded, hitting her with the force of wet cement.

Time warped. Powder and smoke filled the air as the bags, having fully engaged, began to deflate. Now the only sound was the rasping of someone struggling to breathe.

Was that her?

She lifted a hand to her head, feeling the splitting pain, like a metal wedge, seeming to drive deeper into her skull. But her hand flopped useless from her arm, the wrist warped like a melted candle.

Blood flowed down her face and into her mouth, choking her. It hurt. Oh, it hurt. She'd found it. That one thing that hurt more than his betrayal.

She smiled. Finally satisfied. She'd made it stop.

Then she turned to look at her silent passenger.

"Are you okay?" she asked.

Shelby's eyes blinked open, and she turned to stare, eyes wide with shock as she reached and clasped Dani's hand.

Her sister squeezed Dani's fingers and whispered, "Don't let me go."

"Never. Hold on. Help's coming."

Shelby opened her mouth and dark blood trickled out.

"Hold on, Shelby."

Dani's gaze dipped. Through the settling dust she saw the metal pole, the U-turn sign, driven like a spear through her sister's chest. Shelby held the base, in the opposite hand, directly over her heart, tugging weakly. Dani's attention flashed to her sister's pale face, the exact same as hers, like looking into a mirror—but she noted her lips already taking on an unnatural bluish tint. She wasn't breathing.

"Shelby! No!"

Her twin opened her mouth, but nothing but blood emerged.

"Don't leave me," Dani cried.

Now they were both choking, Shelby on the blood and Dani on the tears.

"This isn't happening!" Dani whispered. "I can't see this. I can't."

Dani shrieked, "Shelby!"

A voice came from somewhere far away.

"Dani? Where's Shelby now?"

Beside her in the car, Dani's sister smiled, but dark blood oozed from between her lips. Already her eyes had lost focus.

"Look at me, Shelby!"

"Shelby's not here, Dani. It's Dr. Allen."

Her sister's grip relaxed as she lost the strength to hold on. Then her hand slipped away. Her eyes remained open, but they were sightless eyes. Dull, lifeless eyes.

"No. No. No! I can't see this."

Dani lifted her face from her hands to find Dr. Allen crouching just before her. Tate stood between the bumper and the garage door, at Dani's back, a living wall between her and escape.

"She's gone," whispered Dani.

Dr. Allen and Tate exchanged a quick, meaningful glance. Dani recalled she could not trust either one.

"Who's gone, Dani?" Dr. Allen asked.

"My sister. Shelby's dead."

The psychiatrist nodded. "She is."

"Will she remember this time?" whispered Tate to Allen.

"Unsure" was the reply.

The punch of grief struck, shredding her, tearing a scream from somewhere deep inside. The sound reminded her of the shriek of the wounded rabbit she and her twin had once found beside the road. Dying, the creature had made a noise that froze them to the spot.

Dani trembled, drenched in sweat. Then, as now, she could do nothing to change what would happen. What *had* happened. Only this time she knew she was the cause of it all.

She was the reason her sister was dead.

"What are you doing to me?" she asked.

"Nothing," said Dr. Allen. "Just trying to get you to recall what happened after the accident."

Dani pushed back against this reality. She didn't want it. What she'd just remembered, or thought she'd remembered, must be a dream or some kind of hallucination.

"That wasn't real. It didn't happen because Shelby's not dead."

"No?" said Allen. Her habit of not directly challenging now irked.

"Why don't you just tell me! Where's my sister?"

"Dani, you're remembering the accident. Tell me what you remember."

She shook her head, refusing to go there again.

"I don't understand. Shelby's alive. I just spoke to her. She sent me a text not thirty minutes ago." Dani held up the phone to prove what she said. "Explain this!"

Dr. Allen drew a long breath and then blew it away.

"Call the number," she said.

"What?"

"Dial the number you use to phone Shelby."

Dani didn't know what game this was, but she didn't like it. Her ears buzzed as she turned the screen and pulled Shelby's name from her favorites. Something bad was going to happen. She knew that but couldn't understand why she knew or what was wrong.

She hesitated, then pressed the call button.

A moment later, Tate's phone rang.

She gasped and glanced down at the number Tate had programmed in for Shelby's new phone.

"Answer it," Dr. Allen said to Tate.

He tapped the answer button and held the phone to his ear. Dani did the same.

"Hello?" he said.

At the same instant, Shelby said, "Hello?"

Dani's breathing became erratic.

"Shelby. Is that you?"

"Dani, it's not Shelby," said Tate and Shelby simultaneously. Dani dropped the phone. She stood and stumbled back until she collided with the garage door.

"What's happening?" she cried, looking to her doctor for answers. "How could Tate sound like Shelby?"

"He doesn't. Didn't. Never has," said Dr. Allen. "He talks and, since you *believe* it is your sister, he sounds like Shelby."

"How is that possible?" She turned to Tate. "Why did you do this?"

In answer, he cast his gaze to the ground.

The recollection materialized like a dangerous animal emerging from the fog.

"I caused the accident." She knew it was true. Dani slid down the surface of the garage door, dropping to her seat. There, she stared up at the two of them. "Did I kill her?"

Tate sighed and squatted next to her. "It was an accident."

"Is she... she's dead. Right?"

He nodded and looked away.

"How could I not remember?"

Dr. Allen's voice penetrated the tearing grief.

"You won't let yourself. You told me that Shelby's last words were—"

Dani interrupted. "Don't let me go."

She could still hear the sirens' wail. Rescue vehicles arriving too late.

"She died right there. Right beside me in that car. There was a..." Her words trailed off as she fanned her hand at her chest, remembering the metal pole protruding from her sister's body.

"But Shelby told you not to let her go and so you haven't. Despite your experience, memories, and Shelby's absence, you have held on. Your conviction is iron. And the blank spot in your memory ensued."

"Brain injury," she murmured.

"Yes, but your denial of reality after your recovery was something else."

"None of this makes any sense."

"We explained to you what happened to your sister on several occasions."

"You got worse," said Tate. "Every time you got so much worse."

"It's called a core belief. Changing your core belief is disorienting," said Dr. Allen. "You can do it, but until now, you have been unwilling to internalize the truth. That's why you need to speak to Shelby."

"But I call Tate."

"Yes." She cast Tate a look of disapproval. "I told him not to directly challenge your core belief. I did not tell him to impersonate your sister. He only recently relayed to me that he'd been, in effect, encouraging your core belief."

"I wasn't encouraging it."

"Recommending your wife call Shelby reinforced her core belief, and possibly contributed to her certainty that Shelby is still alive."

"You don't know that," said Tate, the litigator popping up, preparing to fight.

"You were eavesdropping on our private conversations!" Dani realized as she said this that there had been no private conversations. She sucked in a breath at the revelation that followed. "Dani-o," she said.

"What?"

"Shelby never calls me that." Her thoughts seemed wrapped in cotton. Dani turned back to her doctor, growing desperate to refute what they were telling her. "But the voice sounds *just* like her."

"Because your core belief is, or rather was, that your twin is happy and living here. And although you feel responsible for the accident, Shelby holds you no grudge."

Dani shook her head, trying to again reject this entire explanation. She would have known it was Tate.

"Was Shelby ever cross? Did you ever catch her in a foul mood? Did she ever offer anything of her life unless you directly asked? Does that really sound like her?" asked Dr. Allen.

"Love you, little sister," Dani whispered. "Love you more, big sister."

"What was that?" asked her doctor.

Dani lifted her gaze to meet Tate's. "When I spoke to Shelby, we ended each call, as we always do, with our special farewell. She says, 'Love you, little sister.' And I say, 'Love you more, big sister.' If I say goodbye first, it's reversed. But when I called Shelby, she never said that. She called me Dani-o. It bothered me, but I couldn't think why." She glanced to Tate. He didn't know their special farewell, so he'd never made the correct reply.

The insight added further weight to Dr. Allen's claim about the phone calls. It wasn't Shelby. Never had been.

"But she's been calling *me*. You're telling me that's Tate, too?"

Dr. Allen pressed her lips together. Then she gave a slow shake of her head. "No. You started 'receiving' imaginary phone calls from Shelby several months ago. It was that development that made me hesitant to release you. It was a significant change."

"And now I'm calling her, too."

"Yes. That started more recently."

"When I came home." She stared at Tate as she spoke. "And you gave me her new phone number."

Allen glanced to Dani's husband. "When you call, Tate now answers, and though this may help him judge your mental state, I disapproved, as it only encourages you to avoid facing your most troubling memories."

"My... He spied on me."

"Monitored," said Tate.

Semantics, Dani thought but said, "I never lie to Shelby."

"Exactly," Dr. Allen replied.

"He's cheating on me." Dani pointed an accusing finger at him. "You know that? Right? You saw them?"

"Let's stick with Shelby for a moment," said Dr. Allen, refusing to be diverted. "Judge Sutton recently reported that you have been in contact with Shelby nearly every day. But that can't be. You know that now."

"She's reaching out from the..." Dani didn't finish. That sounded crazy, even to her. "So, when Shelby calls *me*, who am I talking to?"

"No one. Just your phone, which is off. You imagine she calls when you are under particularly intense emotional stress."

It was settling in now, the extent of her illness. This was more than a brain injury. More than depression. So much deeper and blacker. The yawning pit of despair gaped before her. The open maw threatening to gobble her up.

"When you thought of Shelby, she called you. And only when you were thinking of her. Correct?"

Dani nodded. "I'd think, 'What would Shelby say' and she'd call."

"Odd, isn't it?"

"I thought it was our twin bond." Dani struggled to control her rapid breathing. The buzzing in her ears grew worse.

She'd been walking around, talking to thin air, conversing with her own psyche.

"Core belief," she said, trying out the expression. "Why didn't you tell me? Keep telling me until I understood?" She looked from one to the other.

Dr. Allen answered. "Confronting a core delusion head-on doesn't work. This core belief wasn't dangerous. You needed Shelby, and she was there for you. Believing that she was happy and moving on allowed you to do the same. Mitigated the guilt."

"But you let me believe..."

Dr. Allen lifted a hand to stop her. "I never encouraged your core belief. Further, no amount of convincing would change your mind. Talking, arguing, persuading, even presenting you with irrefutable evidence, didn't work. You explain it all away. Rationalized. Even with all the treatment and the therapy at Windwood, the best I could manage was for you to accept that you'd hurt Shelby. For the entire course of your time with me, you've been avoiding the truth about your twin."

"You tried?"

"Repeatedly. As Judge Sutton said, you regressed. You thought we were lying to you. Deceiving you. Keeping you from your sister. No amount of evidence was too great that you could not explain it away."

"You could have shown me Shelby's grave."

"That's not my sister," said Dr. Allen, affecting Dani's manners.

"Did I say that?"

"Yes."

Dani turned to Tate, and he nodded, agreeing with her doctor. Not that she could believe anything he said.

"Before your release, you insisted on visiting Shelby. Judge Sutton decided, without consulting me, to suggest you call your sister instead. In so doing he satisfied your need to speak to Shelby. But his reinforcement of your delusion is—"

"I wasn't reinforcing it. I just wanted to keep track of her emotions."

"And I told you, when I learned about your using the phone calls to impersonate Shelby, that this might happen. I advised against it, but you went ahead."

"Because you said not to directly confront—"

The doctor interrupted. *"Or encourage."*

"I just—"

This time Dr. Allen raised her hand to Tate and then continued. "Doing so is problematic. And clearly this did not halt Dani's need to see her sister."

The pair stood, facing off, arguing.

Dani blinked up at them. Backlit by the headlights of the SUV, they looked like shadow monsters, aliens, or something devastating that just crawled from beneath a child's bed.

"How could you allow me to take care of a baby?" This accusation was aimed at them both. "If this is true, I shouldn't be allowed silverware, let alone a newborn."

"According to your husband, this was a decision you two had already made."

"And you, Dr. Allen? What do you think?"

"Well, despite your deep desire to become a mother and prevailing yearning for a baby, I expressed my concerns when he informed me, after the fact, of the surrogate."

"You disapproved?"

"The surrogacy was already underway. Entering the second trimester, I believe. My approval was beside the point."

"She's my child." Dani turned to Tate. "You said so."

"Yes," he said.

She had yet to receive the DNA results to verify Tate's claim, which she could no longer accept at face value. So the question of maternity weighed on her. But either way, Tate had lied. Dani shielded her eyes, staring up at him as she realized his affirmation meant nothing. She couldn't believe a word he said.

Seeing her, crouched against the closed garage, trapped, and confused, near blinded by the headlights, Dr. Allen moved to stand at her side, out of the glare. Tate followed.

Her doctor's expression was calm, her husband's strained. They were the perfect bookends of resignation.

But she was not done fighting.

Should she accept this version of reality over the one she believed? It wasn't so easy, to concede. Some part of her was desperate to prove them wrong. To uncover their deception and find Shelby.

Dani panted now, like the cornered animal she had become.

"Let's get you out of the heat. You look flushed."

Dr. Allen assisted Dani to a stand, and they set off down the drive, Dani still in a daze.

Suddenly they were beside the van. Within, a smiling

woman sat beside Willow, who slept in her carrier. The woman had dark skin, so not Enid. Who was this?

"Give her to me," Dani demanded.

Dr. Allen spoke in a firm voice. "No."

"Get in, Dani," ordered Tate.

"Where are you taking me?"

"Back to Tampa," he said.

"To the hospital. Just for the night," assured Dr. Allen.

It was exactly what they had said after the accident when she'd gone away for six months.

Just overnight.

Tate tried to take hold of her elbow to assist her into the van. She yanked it away.

"You don't get to touch me. Not after what you did with Enid."

"Dani, please. You don't understand. You were gone for so long."

She glared. "I'd never have done what you did, no matter how long you were away."

Tate's expression went grim.

"Six months at Windwood! You couldn't keep your dick in your pants for six months?" She hurled foul language at him in fury, hoping to hurt him with the smallest measure of what he'd done to her.

Tate was looking at Dr. Allen. She nodded, and he turned back to her. She knew that whatever her doctor had given Tate permission to say would be bad.

"Six years," he said.

"What?"

"You weren't in the psychiatric facility for six months, Dani. It's been six years."

TWENTY-FOUR

"That's impossible," Dani said.

"It's not," said Dr. Allen.

"I turned twenty-seven in May."

"You turned thirty-two in May. And I'm thirty-four," said Tate.

"I don't believe you."

"Dani," said Dr. Allen, "look at your phone. The date."

Tate handed her the smartphone, its screen now cracked. She tapped it awake and stared at the date.

1:37 am
Tuesday, June 29

That proved nothing.

She tapped the calendar app. The date read 2021.

"This is impossible." She glanced from the screen to Tate. "What did you do to my phone?"

"You see?" said Dr. Allen. "Anything that contradicts your core belief is dismissed."

"Let me see *your* phone."

Dr. Allen held out the lock screen. The date remained June 29th but now was 1:38 am. She opened her calendar and showed Dani.

"But it's 2016," Dani insisted.

Dr. Allen shook her head.

"Yours," she pointed at the woman attending Willow.

She looked startled and waited for Dr. Allen to nod before turning over her phone with the calendar app open. At the top of the screen, in orange, was 2021. Beneath, the month of June was open, with an orange box around the number twenty-nine.

Tears coursed down her cheeks as she turned to Tate.

"Six years?"

He wept but nodded.

Suddenly she recalled Shelby asking her to check her house value. The date had been wrong. But Dani had dismissed it as a mistake. Only that wasn't Shelby. It was herself, trying to bring to her consciousness what had happened.

"You're not the youngest person elected to the circuit court," she whispered.

"No," he agreed.

"Oh, Tate!" She threw herself at him and held him close, clutching his chest and burying her face in the soft fabric of his yellow shirt as she wept.

"This is an improvement," said Dr. Allen. "Your acknowledgment of the possibility that you might be wrong. It's encouraging."

No, it wasn't. Now, as well as not believing her husband and her doctor, she also couldn't trust her own mind.

She pulled back.

"Dani?" Tate said, lifting her chin so their eyes met.

"I'm scared, Tate."

He hugged her again. "I know. But I got you."

"Don't let me go again, Tate. I might not come back."

On the drive, her doctor gave Dani something to calm her so that her sobs were reduced to a steady trickle of tears. The drug also made her drowsy. Her head lolled. It occurred to her, in that hazy, semiconscious state, that she had demanded of Tate what Shelby had demanded of her.

Don't let me go.

"I tried not to," she whispered to the ethos.

Some time later (who could really say when everything was fuzzy around the edges), she realized that Willow was no longer with her and that she was in a bedroom, sitting in a chair beside a bed with rumpled linens. Had she slept there?

A small redheaded woman in a bright scarf sat before her upon a roller stool. In her hand was a familiar tablet with a sky-blue cover.

Dr. Allen, Dani realized.

She looked around the room. The rest of the furnishings, including the chair upon which Dani sat, were bolted down to prevent them from becoming projectiles. She knew this place.

"How long have I been here?"

"We arrived after five in the morning. You were admitted under my care and it's nearly three in the afternoon now."

"Psych floor?"

She didn't need an answer. The howl from outside her room was answer enough.

"Where's Willow?"

Dr. Allen's voice held reassurance, but her words bit like an icy wind.

"She's with her father."

"Tate?"

Her doctor smiled and nodded. "Yes, with Judge Sutton. They've gone home so you and I can talk."

Tate was likely at Enid's place right now.

"He goes over there at night, you know? After I take my sleeping pills."

"Is that so? How do you know that, Dani?"

"Every single time I've woken up early, he was gone. He shows up in different clothes. Once, I tried to take his suit to the dry cleaner, but I couldn't find it. Now I know why. It's in Enid's closet."

"Breathe, Dani."

She gasped, holding a hand to her mouth. "The monkey onesie! Willow is in different clothes, too!"

"Be calm," said Allen. "Did you speak to him about your suspicions?"

"Of course!"

"And what does Tate say?"

"He says he is walking the baby. Didn't want to wake me. Out for a stroll and ran into Enid. It's lies."

"I see. You don't believe him?"

Dani shook her head.

"Not so long ago you had complete faith in your husband."

And I had faith in my doctor.

Dani conceded the possibility that her husband and her doctor colluded in deceiving her.

Snakes in the garden, she thought. She needed a mongoose.

"What caused this break in your trust?"

"I saw him holding Enid Langford in our driveway. He kissed her."

"Dani, could this be a recent addition to your core delusion?"

Naturally, she'd say that. Dismiss what Dani saw and heard. With reason, she supposed. But Dani now had to reexamine everything. If she could hear Shelby speaking from the grave, she might also hallucinate Enid with her husband.

"You were standing right there. You saw them, too."

"The day I came to your house?"

Dani nodded and Dr. Allen looked away.

"Yes. I saw them," said Dr. Allen.

Dani pressed her hands to her hot face.

"Why did you run?" asked Allen.

"Shelby called. She told me to..."

But Shelby couldn't have called, because she was dead.

What good would talking do if her core belief was unshakable and her senses could not be trusted? If the doctor was right, no amount of evidence or convincing would change whatever belief Dani had adopted, whether it was true or not.

So what was the point of therapy?

She lifted her head. "This is a waste of time."

Dr. Allen's chin lowered, and her brows shot up.

"Could you elaborate?"

"You've told me I can't trust my senses and that my core delusion is fixed. So what is the point of trying to make me entertain other versions of my reality?"

"Dani, your husband and I are keen that you become your best, healthiest self."

"Because he can't do it without my money. And how much have you earned, Doctor, from my six years in a mental institution?"

"That's rather harsh."

"Is it? Your professional services, Dr. Allen, and my accommodations in one of the most expensive mental health facilities in the country, what was the cost of that? You have a dog in this fight. As long as I'm here, you've got a nice set-up."

"You needed to be in a physician's care, Dani."

"And I can afford it, can't I? Private room. Best of everything. It doesn't matter because it is just a tiny fraction of my wealth. Tate's campaign, that stupid pretentious house, the luxury cars. Even his election victory and seat on the circuit court, all financed with my parents' trust. As long as I'm my best, healthiest self, he can go on spending like there's no tomorrow. The trust pays Shelby's hospital bills and mine. But if I should die, it all crumbles. He loses my share."

Dr. Allen looked away. From the flush on her face and neck, Dani guessed that she'd worked this out years ago.

Then something else struck, a new bombshell falling from the blue sky to decimate her world.

"Whose idea was it for me to go home, Dr. Allen? Was it Tate who wanted my discharge?"

Her psychiatrist met her gaze. "For some time, I thought you were well enough to resume something like your old life, with some support. But up until a few weeks ago, Judge Sutton was resistant."

"He was against it?"

"At first, yes. Then he did a turnaround. Seemed eager to have you home."

At first, he was well situated with Enid. Likely, the woman even lived in that house with him. What had changed?

Why was he eager? Was that because Tate loved her? What advantage would he have? Better access to her money? As soon as they were married, he'd tried and failed to gain control of the trust. Even Dani did not have carte blanche. Major expenditures needed to be approved.

But as long as Dani lived, Tate's expenses were covered. The pool service, club memberships, business travel, all legitimate. But if Dani were to die, then the money went to Shelby.

No, Shelby couldn't inherit anything... because she was gone.

Dani hunched at that, curling around the pain of loss.

Her brain kept working, furrowing down the rabbit hole like a weasel. So... all the money went to the Tampa Museum of Art. Unless...

"Willow."

TWENTY-FIVE

Dani hunched in the plastic seat with the sticky vinyl padding. Tate had had her sign the adoption papers almost immediately after her return home.

The lovely, wonderful, and unexpected gift of a child now took on sinister undertones.

"Willow," she whispered, thinking of the newborn who'd appeared by magic, the entire adoption procedure subverted for them to adopt. She'd known the process had been unconventional, had even suspected Tate had cut corners.

And when she'd had second thoughts about her ability to cope with motherhood, he'd told her that he'd hired a surrogate. That had stopped her misgivings in their tracks.

Who was the woman who tried to take Willow? Was she a blackmailer, as Tate claimed, the surrogate, smelling scandal and pressing her advantage? Was that the birth mother? Was it Enid, trying to force her back to the hospital? Without the ability to recognize faces, she had no idea.

"He hurried the adoption, so I'd have legal issue," whispered Dani. This revelation dropped another bone in the coffin that had once been her marriage.

"Of what issue are you speaking?" asked Dr. Allen.

"It's a legal term. My issue is my legal offspring. Willow is my child in all ways that matter to the law and to the trust. That's why he needed me home."

Dr. Allen sat back, her hands on the tablet in her lap. She'd gone pale.

"I see," she said.

"You were against me having the baby. Right?" Dani leaned forward as the dark puzzle pieces slipped into place.

"I felt you needed more time to transition to a less structured environment before taking on the role of motherhood."

The change in his attitude about Dani returning home. The turnaround. It suddenly made sense. Was Tate using her return and this baby as a means to an end? Was Willow genetically hers, as he claimed, or was he just the father of someone else's baby, as the wild woman in the coffee shop had said?

"Enid," she whispered, sure now.

Willow and their neighbor shared the same color hair and Tate had made a point of taking Dani over to see their neighbor before Willow even arrived. Then her husband had reminded her that Enid had worked with young children, a former teacher. Hadn't their neighbor mentioned something about starting a daycare service? Enid had stayed on the other side of that wall and hedge. Gardening. But had she just delivered a baby? And had the two of them set her up—incited her idea of hiring Enid to help with the baby? As for the silver-gray eyes, she could easily have worn colored contacts.

Dr. Allen was scribbling on her tablet.

"That snake. He said he used a surrogate. That she's ours."

"That could be easily confirmed," said Dr. Allen.

"I already did a maternity test. Awaiting results now."

Dr. Allen eyed her as if she suddenly found herself in a locked room with a hungry panther.

"I think we might need to call the police."

"No. They'll take Willow away."

"Dani, you believe your husband lied to you, and had you sign legal documents to protect his access to your trust. It's criminal behavior. We have to call the police."

Dani shot to her feet. "No!" she shouted.

Her doctor glanced toward the mirror beside the door to her room and gave a slight shake of her head.

Dani stared at the observation window framed to appear to be a decorative mirror, certain someone on staff was stationed there right now for Dr. Allen's protection.

"Dani, please calm down."

"I want to go home."

Dr. Allen cocked her head. "I think you should reconsider, and at this juncture, we should call the police."

"Home!" she insisted, rising to her feet.

Dr. Allen lowered her tablet, her usually placid expression marred by the flush of pink that extended from forehead to collar.

"Where exactly are you wishing to go?"

Did Dr. Allen think she meant her childhood home or to the place she'd imagined Shelby lived? *If only.* Dani repeated the address to the home Tate had purchased and held her breath.

"I'm not sure that's advisable."

"My admission is voluntary."

"That's true, but, Dani, you've just reported a crime to me, and you had a recent break with reality."

Had she done something else she didn't remember? Something beyond stealing Willow and driving to Shelby? Just the thought of her twin caused her knees to give way and she sank back into the chair, dejected, defeated, and uncertain what to do.

"What break?"

"Your belief that your sister is phoning you. Then going to see her with Willow."

Dani nodded, acknowledging the concern. "Is the baby okay?" That question would tell her if what she recalled had even happened.

"She's safe."

"I want to see her."

Dr. Allen blew away a breath. "A moment ago, you said you wanted to go home."

"The baby first."

"I'm afraid that's not possible."

Dani suddenly hated this woman with her polite refusals and her smug, sympathetic expression.

The woman was more secret-keeper than doctor. What else was she hiding? Was she on Tate's payroll, hired to keep Dani here, locked away, while Tate raised their child and slept with anyone he liked?

She could just imagine his colleagues expressing sympathy for the Honorable Justice Tate.

Did you hear? His wife is back in the hospital. That poor man. He's been through so much. Now a single father on top of it all.

Now he could divorce her because he had their baby. Enid could step into her place, just as she'd promised she would. And Enid could mother Willow and attend campaign events. She could recognize important party members on sight.

Dani clenched her fists.

"Home. I want to be discharged this minute and be driven home."

"Dani, please be reasonable. We've all had a long twenty-four hours. You need to rest. Sleep on it and we'll talk tomorrow."

"Are you refusing to discharge me?"

Dr. Allen remained silent as she observed Dani. Finally, she said, "No. I'm not refusing."

"Then get me home."

Dr. Allen stood, collected her stool, and withdrew. Dani moved to sit on the single bed, pressing her fingers into the turquoise coverlet that had apparently been on her bed for years. She turned over one corner and studied the fabric. It wasn't new. That was certain. Next, she explored the room, looking for signs of age and proof that she'd been in this place for six full years.

She pushed the bed frame, finding it and all furniture anchored. The mini blinds in her window were set between the pains of glazed glass and controlled with a slide toggle, rather than a cord. Her desk lamp was fixed to the wall. The accompanying chair also was bolted to the floor.

"Level IV," she said. "Least restrictive."

She glanced past the seating area of the suite to the mirror beside the door, verifying her conclusion. The square glass with a gilded border appeared to hang from the wall above a narrow table, but it was no mirror. From the interior, nothing spoiled the illusion of privacy.

From the hallway, however, she knew her entire room was visible through the one-way glass. The bathroom was the only room offering any privacy, but it didn't lock. She checked and found only an indent in the wood of the pocket door, deep enough for two fingers to slide the barrier aside. But no latch or knob for residents to use to hang themselves.

How would she know the levels of patient safety if she had not run through them?

So, it was true. She was a thirty-two-year-old woman who had spent more than half a decade in this room.

The tightness in her throat forecast the raw, aching sobs. Dani lay on the bed weeping. At last, the tears slowed, and her breathing returned to normal. She dozed, waking with a start, disoriented.

Her conversation with Dr. Allen came to the forefront of her mind. She didn't know what to believe or whom to believe. But some deep inner compass told her that if she didn't leave right now, she never would.

With little effort, she located her clothing from yesterday, neatly folded and stacked inside the cubbies in her room with the rest of her apparel, the doors absent for her safety. Her things remained just where she had left them at discharge from the psychiatric center. That spoke to Dr. Allen's belief that chances were good she would fail on the outside and be returning here.

It was the push she needed. Dani changed clothing and opened the door to find a staff member rise from her chair where she had been seated to observe Dani. At Dani's appearance, her keeper greeted her politely.

"Hello, Mrs. Sutton."

She knew the voice. "Hello, Rolinda. What time is it?"

"Around six."

"At night?"

Rolinda nodded and Dani realized she had lost a day. But was it only a day?

"What day?"

"It's Tuesday."

She'd left for Shelby's in Jacksonville on Monday. That was right, then.

"Where are you heading?" asked Rolinda.

"Main reception. I'm going home."

Rolinda did not stop her, but simply fell into step, lifting her radio to relay their approach.

They walked down the familiar corridor of the private psychiatric residence facility that was once a boutique hotel. The white tile gleamed, framed with black on either side. Detailed wainscot paneling adorned the white walls. Each door was inset and painted a different bright tropical color. Hers was the orange of a bird-of-paradise, and a seated white porcelain dog guarded the entrance. These were the sorts of elegant details, grounding details, that money could bring. The illusion of grandeur in a beautiful cage, each object and color chosen to help the residents orient themselves as they moved about the facility.

A doorbell fixed to the exterior. Knockers were prohibited as a hanging hazard. Her door had a bold "7" painted on the upper right. Farther down the hall sat an artificial flower arrangement of orchids, which she knew was glued to the narrow table beneath a circular mirror.

At the vestibule, she turned and walked down another hallway. But now the doors were all painted in pastel colors, like marshmallow candy.

Dani did not glance at the observation mirrors beside each door of the various rooms as they passed but acknowledged the three employees who sat at their posts, observing various disturbed clientele.

The sight shook loose a memory.

This had been her first room in early days. They called it Level I: Direct Staff Supervision. She'd transitioned to Level II: High Observation, where she could join activities throughout the facility under supervision and be left alone for brief periods. Next came III: Periodic Observation, in another mirror room and finally to the one she left behind before going home, Level IV: Minimal Observation.

How could she know all that if she had not been here so long?

Gradually, Dani adjusted to her newest reality.

She'd made a wrong turn and reversed direction, this time reaching the elevators.

They were stopped by another attendant, of course, gaining a second escort to the main floor.

At lobby level, she waited for Dr. Allen. A glance at the desk behind Plexiglas showed several phones before the staff.

How she longed to pick up one of those phones and call Shelby.

But that was no longer possible.

Shelby couldn't hear her or help her find her daughter.

"Dani, I thought perhaps you'd changed your mind."

She faced the familiar voice of Dr. Allen, taking in her round eyeglass frames and the ever-present scarf. It was a dangerous choice in a psychiatric ward, that oh-so-tempting ligature.

"I haven't. I'm leaving. So, give me the paperwork or get out of my way."

"You'll be released against doctor's orders. That means you are responsible for all medical expenditures. Your insurance company won't pay."

Dani thought it a powerful threat to those who had little. Medical bills could bankrupt a family. But not her family.

"All right then." Dani swept past her and out into the elegant portico before the gracious building, a private zoo of the most expensive variety.

She had not walked far before the first patrol car arrived to shadow her. Clearly, the psychiatric facility had alerted the authorities that she'd left without her doctor's approval. Did they think she posed a danger to herself? She didn't. She just wanted to go home.

There was no sidewalk, of course. This was not the sort of neighborhood to encourage pedestrians to go wandering about. She kept to the shoulder, ignoring the enduring heat, conducted by the brutally hot pavement beneath her feet, and the sun, now low in the sky and blinding her as it flashed beneath the canopy of oak branches. The canal beside the road harbored mosquitoes and gnats that feasted on her as she trudged on. Sweat ran down her face and she wiped it away with her hand. After she'd left the psychiatric facility far behind, a familiar SUV, bearing the license plate she had memorized, pulled in before her.

The blond man inside reached across the space to the door release. He wore a yellow shirt. His furrowed brow and sad eyes should have been familiar.

"Dani," said Tate.

TWENTY-SIX

Dani stood in the open door. A glance in the rear seat showed the carrier turned away.

"Is Willow in there?" she asked.

"Yes. I brought her along," he said, his tone conversational, as if he had not left his wife in a psychiatric hospital and brought the one lure guaranteed to entice her into this vehicle.

"Where is Enid?"

"Dani, let's not—"

She cut him off.

"Where is she?"

"I broke it off. Told her I couldn't continue deceiving you."

"The smart choice," she said, her voice low and full of accusation.

"Dani, whatever you think, I want you to know I'm sorry. I should never have turned to her. You were right. Whether it was a day or a year, I should have been stronger."

"The smart answer," she said. "How'd you get the car back to Tampa?"

He gave her a perplexed look. "I drove it home last night."

He glanced in the side mirror. "Get in, please, before we get clipped."

She slipped into the front seat and fastened her seatbelt.

He set his jaw and pulled out. Dani unclasped her belt and ignored her feeling of incessant alarm as she crawled between the seats and settled beside Willow, who was sleeping like an angel.

Resisting the urge to scoop her up proved challenging, but Dani remained where she was, a guardian over the tiny baby, one arm draped over the top of the plastic carrier.

"I can't be trusted with her. You know that?"

Tate glanced at her in the rearview mirror, his blue eyes especially bright. She ignored the sight of the tears collecting at his bottom lid before breaching the dam and falling to his cheeks.

"I never doubted your ability to protect and raise our child."

"Really? I crashed the car with her inside. I drove her four hours north to a stranger's house. I saw the street sign when we left that house, Tate. There isn't a Memorial Boulevard in Jacksonville, is there?"

"No."

"Then how did I end up at that address?"

"Not sure. The vehicle's navigation system wasn't even on. And there is no Memorial Boulevard in Jacksonville."

She frowned, realizing that all those directions she'd heard and followed had been in her mind.

"Your doctor thinks the street was selected at random. The only obvious connection was that the street was near the overpass where you... crashed."

"Then how did you find me?"

"By tracking your phone and with the help of Florida Highway Patrol. But none of that was your fault. Dr. Allen insisted you needed that core delusion. But here we are, and clearly you don't."

"I want to move. She can't be our neighbor."

"Dani, please. I've been up for twenty-four hours. I'm exhausted."

Dani let the matter drop, veering in a different direction.

"Is she ours? All I have is your word, and that has recently taken a dip in the Dow Jones Marital Trust Index."

"What could I possibly say to convince you?"

"Nothing you can say. I'd need the DNA test results."

Another two days and she'd have them.

She thought about her core beliefs and wondered which were true and which were fantasy.

"Are you the father?"

"Yes."

"Am I the mother?"

"Yes."

"Legally, yes," she qualified, wondering if the document she'd signed was an adoption agreement or surrogacy contract. Why hadn't she paid better attention? But she knew. She'd been so thrilled to have a baby and she'd trusted Tate completely. Now she felt like a fool. "Where is the surrogate?"

"What does that matter?"

She gritted her teeth and spoke through them. "I want to speak to her."

"You don't. She's still trying to blackmail us."

"Why not have her arrested?"

"Because that would reach the papers."

"And ruin your campaign, which is more important to you than Willow's safety."

He raked a hand through his hair.

"Is it Enid?"

His gaze flashed in the mirror and then shot back to the road.

"Is this her child?" Dani pressed.

The pause stretched. Finally, he spoke.

"No."

"Then call the police."

He readjusted his grip on the steering wheel but made no reply.

"Which is more important, your bloody campaign or your daughter's safety?"

"You and Willow are the most important things in the entire world to me."

"You love us?"

"How can you ask?" He cast her a brokenhearted look, which she ignored.

"I don't want to see Enid again."

"I told you I broke things off."

"You did. But I don't want to ever see her again. We have to move," she demanded once more.

"Dani, please."

"I don't feel safe there."

"We'll talk about it tomorrow. Maybe Dr. Allen can come to the house."

"Is Enid the mother?" she asked again.

He raised his voice now. "*You* are her mother. You signed the paperwork. Willow is legally our child. The woman who bore her doesn't deserve to raise that child."

Deserve? Why hadn't he said *isn't entitled to* or *isn't her mother?*

"So I'm not her mother. She's not genetically mine. You took her from her real mother. Enid is the surrogate you keep talking about, or is she the birth mother? What did she do, get pregnant to force you to leave me? Threaten to create a scandal? Get me to create a scandal? Either way, she'd win you."

He didn't deny her allegations.

"But instead, you decided you'd hand her baby over to me and I'd raise your bastard. Pay Enid off to keep quiet. Maybe see her on the side. Well, guess what? I will raise her, but you don't get Enid."

"Is this a new core belief?"

"It's the truth you can't bear to say aloud. Might damage the campaign. Might force me to divorce your sorry ass. Can't have that. Might have to hock your Rolex."

Dani folded her arms. She was crazy. Not stupid. And this was exactly what a woman, waiting six years and collecting nothing but empty promises, would do.

And it explained Tate's turnaround and wish to have her released. Enid was due to deliver, and Dani needed to be home by then. Was this what had happened? She admitted it seemed plausible.

"Willow is Enid's daughter," she said, trying the theory aloud, watching him in the rearview mirror as his gaze flashed to hers.

"Is that what you believe?" he asked, answering with questions, just like her damned doctor.

"What I believe? I believe you tricked your way into this adoption for reasons of your own. I believe you aren't being honest with me about Willow. I believe you wanted to secure either access to my trust or this baby to prevent the trust from disappearing at my death."

He jerked the wheel, sending them careening into a lot of a combination gas-and-convenience store. Then he slammed on the brakes and turned to face her.

"Were you two going to kill me?"

"Enough!"

There he threw the SUV into park with sufficient force to send them rocking.

"Fine, Dani. You think you are ready for the truth? Here it is. I had an affair. Several over the past six years. They were all mistakes, each and every damned one of them. But I missed my wife. I was lonely, and depressed, and drinking too much. One of them got pregnant. She said she was keeping the baby."

Enid, Dani thought.

Tate continued his latest version of events. "Then you were coming home, and she was in labor, and I didn't know what to do. She's greedy. I know she did this on purpose because the minute she got pregnant, she told me she wanted me to divorce you, or she'd go to the press. Instead, I paid her off."

"With money or empty promises?"

He didn't answer.

"So both?" she asked.

"What was I supposed to do? I paid her. But she wanted more."

"Wanted you."

"Yes."

"Until you explained that you've funded your lifestyle with my trust. And that without me, that all ends."

"Yes." His chin sank to his chest. "What were my options? Willow's my daughter. We always wanted children."

"What about the eggs? The one's that weren't destroyed in the malfunction."

"I made that up. Your frozen eggs were all inadvertently destroyed years ago, before the accident. Your uterus and remaining ovary was removed after the crash."

Below the surface, the wounds of this latest deceit began to ooze and bleed. Dani said nothing, too bruised to speak.

He'd been lying to her for years.

"You were so fixated on that woman. And all that talk of sending her back. I thought if you believed she was yours..." He reached a hand back toward her. "Dani, I love you. I love Willow. Please, we can make this work. Trust me."

She batted away his hand.

"Trust you. Are you serious? You get Enid pregnant and—"

He interrupted. "It's not Enid. And I can take care of it. It's just that she's got a pimp."

Pimp?

Her theories of Enid shattered like a dropped mirror.

"You slept with a hooker?"

His chin dropped to his chest. "I slept with a lot of people while you were gone, Dani." He peeked at her through thick lashes like a naughty child, instead of a man who had crushed their relationship like an empty beer can. "When I wouldn't pay her off, he showed up. He's the one shaking me down now. Between the two of them, I've used everything I could get my hands on. But it's not enough."

Was this the truth or his latest version of the truth?

"You ask me to trust you and tell me you can handle it, then at the same time you tell me you can't. When we get home, I'm calling the police."

The silence stretched. He held out his open hands.

"Dani, I'm a judge. She's a prostitute."

"Call the police!"

He said nothing, just sat with his head bowed for several long moments. Finally, he spoke.

"All right."

They continued in silence until they reached their home and waited for the heavy hurricane-graded garage door to rumble up and out of the way.

Tate called Gary Forde, his detective associate, and explained the situation over the phone.

"Forde is going to apprehend the birth mother. Then he or someone from the Street Anti-Crime Squad is coming over."

Mollified, Dani carried Willow into the house and toward their bedroom. Tate followed. She paused on the stairs to confront him.

"I think you should take the couch," she said.

He tried and failed to gather her in his arms.

"Dani, please."

"No, Tate, I'm not having you sleep in my bed."

There was an excellent chance he had not been sleeping there. But if she believed his recent version of events about the prostitute and her pimp, they were all in danger.

She could not afford to dismiss this until she knew the truth, but neither was she going to blindly trust that this *was* the truth.

He stood there, looking friendless and bereft. Her heart twisted in sympathy, but she did not speak or move to comfort. Instead, she remained firmly rooted before him, Willow in her arms.

He might be the genetic father or this might be another lie. But he'd been right about one thing. Whether by surrogacy or adoption, Dani was Willow's mother, and she'd fight anyone who said otherwise.

Keeping Willow meant staying sane. She could not afford to take her sleeping medication or slip back into depression, except now she had something bigger than her pain. She had her child.

Satisfied, she left him downstairs, and carried Willow to the bassinet beside their bed where she covered her with a cotton blanket. The sky beyond the balcony blazed a brilliant orange as the sun finally made its retreat.

Dani lay on the bed, watching her daughter sleep, her mind whirling with thoughts and fears, questions and doubts.

"What am I going to do?"

Divorce seemed a likely option. It would remove Tate from the trust but maintain Willow as beneficiary. But if he was the father, he'd always have access through his daughter.

Where were the police? Shouldn't they be here by now?

She yawned, telling herself not to fall asleep. She needed to be there when Tate spoke to Detective Forde.

Had he really called him? Her gut gave a painful twist as she realized she had no way of knowing. She was in the habit of trusting him, even though she knew she shouldn't.

She rose to lock the bedroom door and then returned to her side of the mattress, wondering if she should call the police herself.

All she really wanted to do was call Shelby.

As she waited for Detective Forde, Dani reached for the remote and flipped on the television. At ten, the local news came on with a troubling lead.

The story had her sitting up in bed, her heart jackhammering in her chest. The video, the reporter announced, was from earlier this evening, but they expected an update shortly from their reporter at the scene.

The anchor stated that the body of a woman was recovered in a drainage ditch near the river walk in downtown Tampa. The yet-unidentified female had recently given birth. Her child had not been found.

Dani glanced at her sleeping daughter's bassinet.

Was this Willow's mother?

Had she been murdered?

The idea took hold. Dani paced until they finally went to the on-scene reporter. He appeared standing in the bright light of the camera on the shoulder of the roadside ditch. Behind him, a string of yellow police tape fluttered in the dark. He said that since his earlier report, the police had made a positive ID from a mermaid tattoo on the victim's thigh. She had multiple arrests for soliciting. Authorities were now searching for both her infant and a known associate, wanted for questioning.

The pimp, Dani thought.

This was because Detective Forde had gone to question the birth mother. That's how they discovered her missing. And now they were looking for him, the pimp.

A photo of the man in an orange prison uniform appeared in the top left of the screen. He had a record for pandering, weapons, assault, and multiple drug charges. Dani memorized every useful detail of the mug shot. He had small eyes. A bluish blob of a tattoo on his neck and the hair on his face and head were shaved to stubble. His name, Larry Rae Morgan, height, weight, sex, eye color, and complexion were detailed with his race: White/Non-Hispanic. Dani scrutinized the image, trying to pinpoint each identifiable detail.

Tattoo descriptions followed. Two skulls with flames. "Lulu" on his neck and "Peppe" on his left hand. Money sign tattoo, Superman sign on his left forearm, and a spiderweb on his neck.

Police need help locating this person, wanted for questioning in relation to the crime.

Would he come here?

Willow's cry made Dani jump before she swept away the covers and headed for the bassinet. A quick check found both Willow's diaper and sleeping sack wet.

Until this evening, Tate had taken care of the night shift, but Dani knew Willow had a meal at around one in the morning.

She changed her daughter and swaddled her in a fuzzy pink blanket, then headed with her to the kitchen to warm the ready pouch of milk.

Downstairs, Dani paused at the empty sofa, wondering where Tate might be. The house was so big, he could be in his theater, in any of the guest bedrooms or... with that woman.

Her marriage had become suspended in a strange limbo. She knew she would have to leave, and yet she was still dependent on him.

Willow began to cry, and Dani abandoned the urge to look for her husband. The baby's needs came first.

In the kitchen, Willow smacked her lips, clearly hungry and familiar with the process preceding her meals. The speed with which Willow drained the bottle pleased Dani.

She had Willow tucked against her shoulder and did her little bouncing step until Willow spit up the air she swallowed. Dani wiped the baby's face and set Willow on her back in the infant carrier on the kitchen counter, buckling her in.

Willow stretched and yawned. Dani collected the pink blanket, preparing to tuck it about her daughter, when a crash sounded from the garage, bringing Dani up short.

Something had fallen. She hurried through the laundry room and paused at the entrance to the three-car garage.

A second crash caused her to yank open the door. It sounded like Tate had overturned one of the shelving units or the ladder.

"Tate?" She clutched the wadded blanket to her heart as she crept down the steps.

"Dani!" His voice held a high note of panic.

Two running steps brought her past the front of the SUV where she found the garage door wide open, and Tate sprawled on the floor between his vehicle and a pile of kayaking paddles. The long plastic kayak lay beside him, still rocking. He clutched his chest with one hand and blood trickled from a bruise and cut on his cheek.

Had he fallen? Suffered a heart attack?

"Tate!"

She closed the distance, but he lifted a hand to halt her. The look of horror froze her blood.

"Dani! Run."

TWENTY-SEVEN

Someone stepped into the garage. He was tall with dark hair and had a spiderweb tattoo on his neck and more blue ink on his forearms. Larry Rae Morgan, she realized, the suspect in the death of his girlfriend.

Dani clutched the baby to her chest and retreated, colliding with the side of the vehicle.

"Is that her?" The man advanced, motioning with a handgun.

Dani's heart pounded in her throat, blocking her windpipe so she couldn't breathe, let alone speak.

"Is that the baby? Let me see her," he demanded, reaching with his free hand and motioning her forward.

The handle of the car door jabbed into her back. She reached behind and wrapped sweaty fingers around the latch. One yank and the door flew open. He lunged, and she jumped backward into the compartment, gripping Willow, swaddled in the pink fleece.

He reached her now, grasping, gripping her ankle as she kicked, trying to free herself and protect the baby.

"No!" she cried.

But he was dragging her from the safety of the SUV, back out into the garage, and she could only struggle and kick because she still held tight to her baby.

Where was her phone?

In the house.

Two pale hands gripped her attacker by the shoulders and yanked. Both the intruder and Tate fell to the floor. Her husband glanced at her.

"Dani, go!"

Instead, she darted into the vehicle, tugged the car door shut, and locked the door. She pressed Willow into her carrier and clipped the harness, ignoring Willow's cries, as Dani crawled into the front seat. From there she could lock all the doors. From there she could call the police if Tate's phone was anywhere near the vehicle. The Bluetooth would pair with the car's computer system.

Dani jabbed the lock button engaging them all.

Wait. The key fob was in the cup holder. She could start the car. Drive the car.

Outside, her attacker pounded the heel of his hand against the window.

She screamed, stabbed her foot down on the brake, and pushed the ignition button.

The engine engaged and the lights all flashed as the systems came online.

Dani fumbled with the gearshift.

Tate tugged her attacker off again, and this time, the man turned, abandoning her in favor of Tate.

She stepped on the gas and the vehicle lurched forward. More fumbling and the rear camera appeared. Dani flew backward from the garage.

She stabbed the talk button, and the system aroused as she stared out the windshield at the nightmare unfolding in her garage.

Tate and his attacker gripped each other by the throat as they spun in a sickening mockery of a dance.

"What would you like to do?" The calm female voice of the system's computer filled the cab. "You can say things like 'call home,' 'start a new route' or..."

"Call the police!"

"I'm sorry. I didn't get that." The automated voice remained universally calm as Dani felt the bile rising in her throat. Before her, the men grappled.

Tate and the attacker crashed into the bicycles, toppling with them to the floor.

"Call 911!" Dani shouted.

"Calling nine-one-one, emergency services."

Tate rose first, gaining his feet and punching the man before him in the face. His head snapped back, and he fell hard to his seat. Where were the tattoos?

Tate advanced as Dani gripped the wheel and tugged herself forward for a better view.

The attacker spun and rose, lifting the pistol. Aiming it at Tate.

"No!" Dani howled. She seized the shift, engaging the gears, and stamped the accelerator as if it were a cockroach in her kitchen. The car lurched forward.

Too late.

She saw the barrel flash and Tate jerk simultaneously. Blood covered his pale face, illuminated by the running lights as she sped at his attacker. Tate crumpled to the ground, lifeless from the shot to the head.

Dani gave an animal scream.

His attacker spun, swinging the pistol in her direction as she collided with him. His body crashed up onto the hood. Dani stomped the brake, and he rolled like a rag doll and then thumped to the floor.

She didn't wait for him to rise or try again to take the baby.

He'd killed Tate. She'd seen his face and jaw explode from the shot. In reverse now, she had a clear view of their attacker on hands and knees beside Tate, who lay still as blood continued to pump from his facial wound to the thirsty concrete floor.

The puddle seeped toward her, his life force ebbing away as his daughter lay behind her in her car seat.

Dani had to get Willow away.

Somehow, she reached the street, still in reverse. A quick shift and she sped away.

Where? Where should she go?

Finally, the call connected.

"911. What is your emergency?"

She sobbed and shouted, relaying the attack, and giving the operator the name of the shooter.

The EMS operator asked for her address, and she gave it to him.

"He killed my husband. He killed Tate. Shot him in the head."

Dani neared the interstate, driving without a destination.

Just away. Get away.

Glancing in her rearview mirror for signs of pursuit, she recognized that she might be heading to Jacksonville. But why? Shelby wasn't there. Hadn't been there for six years.

Was she buried with their parents?

They'd killed Tate. They'd shot him.

Where should she go? Where was it safe?

There was only one answer. Back to Windwood. Back to Dr. Allen, who would know what to do.

The baby's howls made it nearly impossible to think. She

pulled the SUV into the portico, gathered up Willow in the fuzzy blanket, and hurried to the reception desk.

"I need Dr. Allen."

"I'll have to page her."

She spotted a security guard and told him what had happened, about Tate and the shooter, and she held out Willow to show that her daughter was unhurt.

"She's just crying because she's scared. I think he killed Tate. Did the police get there? And call my doctor. Dr. Virginia Allen."

"Yes. I know the doctor. We're getting ahold of her now. If you'll just have a seat right there," he said, showing a row of plastic chairs fixed one to the other beneath a bank of dark glass.

He began speaking into his radio. Something about the way he whispered, and the way he and the receptionist exchanged a certain look, made her nervous. So, she headed back out of the entrance.

Two men in white scrubs appeared.

"Mrs. Sutton. Welcome back."

Of course, she could not recognize the man speaking to her. He had his thick hair in dreadlocks and beamed a wide toothy smile, bright and welcoming against his dark skin. A small gold hoop earring glinted.

"A pirate," she said.

He chuckled at that.

"I'm Valentine. You know me." The Caribbean accent was very familiar.

She did. Her shoulders drooped. She knew this orderly, liked him, and even trusted him.

"Can you get Dr. Allen?"

"We're getting her." He did not try to grab her but just motioned back to the waiting area. "I'll sit with you 'til she come."

"Thank you."

Dani was relieved Willow had stopped crying. Now all she heard was the pounding of blood in her ears.

Shock. That's what it was. She was likely in shock.

She lifted Willow from her shoulder and glanced down at the tiny face. The baby's brow scrunched as if she were trying to understand what was happening. Her daughter's expression was so earnest it made Dani laugh, relieving the tension.

Why was Willow wrapped in both her blanket and the silver fleece jacket? Dani kept the pullover in the backseat to wear when the air-conditioning was too aggressive because Tate liked it colder than she could stand.

Had she scooped it up when she'd retrieved Willow from her car seat?

Tate.

Her husband had been shot in the head. Even if he'd been alive, she'd seen the amount of blood flooding the garage floor. His spotless garage floor. He'd been so proud of the three-car garage and his fancy luxury vehicle.

"Did they call the police?" she asked Valentine.

He glanced at reception where the other orderly stood. The two spoke in what she thought was a Jamaican dialect.

"Robert say they called the police. They at your place now. That what you wanted?"

"Yes. My husband has been shot."

His face crumpled in sympathy. "Oh, that's very bad."

Another exchange between the two men, and Valentine added, "Melissa called 911 when you come in. They got everybody goin' there. Did you shoot him, Mrs. Sutton?"

"Me?" What did they think of her? "No. It was a man. He was on the news. Wanted for questioning."

"Okay. You safe now. What you got here?" he asked, looking to the bundle she held.

"This is Willow. My daughter. I must have grabbed the fleece when I scooped her up from the car."

"Oh. Your daughter, is it? That's nice."

"I checked her over. She's unharmed. Just shaken up."

"Ah."

"I *was* going to Shelby. But I can't. My sister is dead."

"Oh, I'm sorry to hear that."

"I killed her."

It felt good to say that and to let the hot poker of guilt burn deep into her. She'd killed Shelby. In stupid blind rage. She'd tried to make the pain stop and all she had done was gain a temporary reprieve from pain that seemed endless.

"My husband cheated on me and I was angry and..." She pressed Willow to her face and sobbed.

Valentine rubbed her back.

"Ah, Mrs. Sutton. I got you. Doctor's comin'. Be here soon."

Dani held the scalding pain close and hoped it kept her from slipping back into her delusions. They tugged at her mind, beckoning and offering relief.

The temptation throbbed behind her eyelids and her cell phone began to ring.

"No. It's not Shelby."

TWENTY-EIGHT

Dani ignored the ringing phone but that didn't stop Shelby.

Her sister beckoned, just below consciousness. Begging her to let her back.

Dani glanced to the reception area where Shelby emerged from the solid surface of the desk, vaporous and semi-transparent.

"She's not there." Dani squelched the surge of joy as Shelby drifted forward. Her delusion now manifested her twin as a ghost, as if Dani had accepted her sister was dead but refused to let that stop them from meeting.

"Call me back," Shelby whispered.

Dani shook her head. "You're not here."

She held her daughter tighter, so she squawked in protest.

"Let me see the baby," said Shelby.

Dani held Willow up for Shelby to see. But still she shook her head knowing this was wrong. That Shelby could not be here.

"You're dead, Shelby."

"Who you talking to, Mrs. Sutton?" asked Valentine.

She looked away from the spectral ghost of her sister.

"No one."

When she glanced up again, her delusion had vanished. The twisting sense of loss bored into her chest, seeking her heart.

She turned to Valentine, clutching Willow, who was now wailing. How perfectly her daughter picked up on her mother's panic, thought Dani.

"What's happening?"

"We're waiting for the police and Dr. Allen."

"Good."

The police arrived first. Dani was escorted from reception to an examination room by the orderlies, Valentine and Robert, and the police.

The windowless room had a stool, a counter with a sink, and an exam table. Dani sat on the white paper that made a crinkling sound whenever she shifted her weight. The officer stood by the door with Robert. Valentine settled on the stool usually reserved for the doctor.

Willow had quieted, which surprised her. She'd missed her first night feeding and it must be getting time for her second, though Dani was unfamiliar with her daughter's night schedule, as she had not cared for her after dark. Tate had done that.

Oh, Tate!

He'd died defending her and the baby. Dani's heart ached as she realized, whatever mistakes he had made, whatever betrayal she'd experienced, she forgave him because in the end he had given his life for theirs.

Tate was a hero.

Some time later, a freckled, balding man, who identified himself as a detective, joined them. She described to him the series of events of this tragic evening while he scribbled on his pad. The investigator went over several details more than once and asked her to move backward through the night, starting with coming to this examination room.

He learned, from Valentine, she was under the care of Dr. Allen, her psychiatrist, who was en route.

"Could you call Detective Gary Forde?"

"You know Detective Forde?"

"He's a friend of my husband, Judge Sutton. We called him earlier this evening about the blackmail. We were expecting him when all this happened."

"I see. We'll bring him in."

"Thank you." Dani adjusted Willow in her arms. "Did you catch him?"

"Who, Mrs. Sutton?"

"The man who attacked Tate."

"Not to my knowledge."

Meaning she could not go home. Likely, her house was crawling with CSI and crime technicians.

Who would clean up the blood?

Being trapped in this room with the sweating detective and two orderlies made her anxious. And any minute now, Willow would need to be fed.

"Can I go?" she asked. She did not know where she might go, but out of this room would be a start.

"No," said the detective.

Dani knew her rights. She had given a statement. They were done here.

"Am I being charged with a crime?"

"Not at this time."

"Then I'm free to go."

"No. You aren't."

"If I'm not a suspect or being charged..." Her words fell off and she looked to her interrogator.

"Mrs. Sutton, you struck a man with your vehicle tonight."

"And I called the police and reported that."

"Yes, you've said. Are you familiar with the Baker Act?"

She shook her head. But somehow, she knew before he even spoke.

"It allows doctors and health professionals to commit a person for mental treatment for up to seventy-two hours."

"It's never only seventy-two hours."

"Your doctor has signed the paperwork for the hold."

Dani was on her feet now. "You're trying to take Willow."

"Mrs. Sutton, please sit down."

"I won't let you take her. They won't take Willow!"

The detective spoke in measured tones. "No one is taking Willow."

Dani sat, cradling her daughter, the injustice of this detention burned. She set her jaw to keep from shouting at her captor.

They hadn't even caught Tate's attacker.

But the woman who'd given birth to Willow was dead, murdered by her boyfriend, who was now at large. But they'd catch him, and he would be convicted for her husband's murder.

Her husband was dead.

Instead of feeling the deep grinding sorrow she expected, she felt... free.

TWENTY-NINE

FOUR MONTHS LATER

Dani waited in her suite for Dr. Allen. She'd be here any minute and her doctor was very punctual. To prepare for the encounter, Dani reminded herself she was safe.

She still saw Dr. Allen and had reestablished the trust that had been broken. Her doctor wanted what was best and had even helped her move. This community did not judge. And here at Windwood, when she left her room, she recognized most individuals, if not on sight, after they'd exchanged a few words or by the name tags.

"They can't hurt you here," she told herself.

Several deep breaths also helped to bring a sense of calm.

She lifted the bundle. When the knock came, she swayed and hummed a lullaby.

Finally, out of the public eye after the police investigation, and free of her husband's campaign and of her husband, she had nothing more to fear.

She was wealthy enough to buy any home anywhere in the world, more than one if she wished. Instead, she stayed here, at least for the time being, in the place she felt safest.

The knock on her front door came again. She lifted her

head, as if just now noticing. This sort of intrusion would have sent the old Dani into a panic. But here, she was protected from Tate's attacker, who was now in custody.

Dani set the bundle in the bouncer on the coffee table, then answered the knock.

Dr. Allen stood on the steps with a dark-haired woman, who held in her arms a chubby-cheeked baby with the same dark hair as Dr. Allen's companion.

"Oh, you're a little early today," said Dani.

Since the shooting, Dr. Allen had made daily trips to see Dani. Dani didn't worry about the cost. She could afford the luxury of peace of mind that came from having a concierge psychiatrist.

"I'm sorry, but I wanted to introduce you to someone."

Dani looked into the expressive brown eyes and perfectly applied makeup, already knowing before her visitor's arrival whom to expect.

The woman beside her doctor wore a white pleated blouse and pink pencil skirt. She had no distinguishing features.

She cast Dani a brittle smile and then glanced to the infant she carried. Her baby brought its fist to its mouth and sucked.

Dani was now eye to eye with the mother and child. The baby had features like the woman, the thick dark hair, dark eyes, and thin arching brows. Even the ear shape was identical, though the woman's were pierced and held both studs and gold hoops.

It was hard not to reach for the baby. Dani loved children.

"This is Enid and her daughter, Willow."

Dani paused, then smiled vaguely.

"I once knew an Enid," said Dani.

"Yes, Dani. I'm *that* Enid." She held her daughter for Dani to get a better look. "And this is Willow."

Dani wrinkled her brow as she studied the baby.

"Could we come in?" asked Dr. Allen.

She stiffened at the request. Enid was the woman who had slept with her husband. Dr. Allen said this affair, and her husband's betrayal, was one reason Dani felt so little sadness after the shooting. He had used her for her money, cheated on her for years, and expected her to forgive him.

Then he had stepped before a bullet to protect her life. That deserved some forgiveness, didn't it?

Dani blocked the door with her body.

"Let her in, Dani."

She turned toward the seating area and spoke. "I don't want to." Then she paused and listened, before speaking once more. "All right then."

Dani stepped aside, speaking to her guests now. "Please come in."

Enid gave her a cautious look, then swept into the room.

"You're doing great," Dr. Allen said.

The trust between them was fragile, but she nodded her assent.

"Won't you have a seat, Enid?" She was surprised at her own calm demeanor. A short time ago, she'd have happily clawed this woman's eyes out. But there was more than one way to gain reparation.

Enid settled on the loveseat and arranged the blanket on the ottoman, laying her daughter on the fleece. Willow got her elbows beneath her and pushed up. Lifting her head. Enid smiled.

Dani noted the object of Willow's attention from the collection of several plush toys before the baby. She lifted a blue dog with a furry white underbelly and set it before Willow, who fell forward and reached.

"What a smart little girl." Dani handed over the toy and it went immediately into Willow's mouth.

"No, no, sweetie. That isn't yours," said Enid.

The infant made a sound of frustration and Dani waved a

hand. "It's fine. Willow is too young to even notice." Then she turned to the bouncer, lifted a rattle, and pressed it beside the swaddling. "Our daughters have the same name. Isn't that funny?"

Dani looked to Enid, who had a frozen smile on her face. Her guest glanced to Dr. Allen, then back to the infant rocker, and then back to the doctor, as if she didn't know what to say.

Dani motioned to the infant seat. "This is my daughter, Willow."

At last, Enid said, "She looks well."

"Thriving." Dani grinned. "Would either of you like coffee? Shelby is in the kitchen; I'll ask her to bring some out."

Enid lifted a hand. "Oh, no thank you." Then she threaded her fingers together, twisting them back and forth. "I've just had mine for the day."

The silence stretched. Dr. Allen looked from Dani to Enid. Dani waited for the reason for this visit.

"Dani," Enid said. "I want to apologize to you personally. I know Tate was still married to you when we were together."

Now the old anger flared. It rattled Dani, the emotions bubbling up with memories.

Tate and Enid, heads together, whispering outside Dani's home. Kissing in the drive. She wanted to ask if Tate had spent each night Dani lived in their terrible house over at Enid's place.

Instead, she remained mute.

"It was wrong, and I hope someday you will forgive me."

Dani lowered her chin because today was not that day.

"In time, perhaps."

Dani collected the pacifier from the ottoman. "I'll have to clean this before she wakes up."

Enid said nothing.

"Do you think she remembers you?" Dani said, motioning to the rocker.

"Oh, I don't know. But she's certainly a beauty." Another glance to Dr. Allen. "Be crawling in no time."

Dani chuckled at that. "Willow is only two weeks old. She can't even roll over yet. Be some time before she'd be crawling."

"Of course."

Dr. Allen stood. "Well, Dani, thank you for seeing us. I hope this helps you move forward. Please thank Enid for taking the trouble to visit."

Dani narrowed her eyes on the woman. "I don't think so."

Enid lifted her daughter and the blanket in one smooth motion.

Dani stood, too. Enid plucked the plush toy from her daughter's grasp. The tiny forehead wrinkled, and the baby began to cry.

"I'll wash this and get it back to you," said Enid.

"Oh, she can keep it. Willow won't know the difference."

Enid returned the gift to her daughter. "Well, thank you. That's very generous."

Dani walked them to the door and held it open. Both women swept out and then turned, standing side by side before her.

"Lovely to see you, Dani. I'm glad you are happy here."

"Thank you, Enid. I appreciate that."

Dani noted Enid wore no wedding band.

"How's Paul?" she asked.

"Oh. I haven't seen him." Her gaze darted to Dr. Allen, then back to Dani. "So... I'm not sure."

Both women stared at Dani in silence.

Dani glanced beyond them. Across the familiar black-and-white corridor of the psychiatric hospital, beyond her orange door, stood a tall man with blond hair. He wore loafers, dress slacks, and a yellow shirt and tie. He carried a familiar diaper bag on his shoulder. His face was terribly scarred with a misshapen jaw and angry red suture lines tugging at his mouth.

He stared at her with an expression of such pain.

"Hello, Dani."

Dani slammed the door. She pressed her back to the reassuring solid surface and stared up at the ceiling, counting to ten. Then she glanced at herself in the mirror flanking the door. Her face was flushed, but everything else was normal.

Dani looked over her shoulder as she spoke to thin air.

"I don't know who it was, Shelby. I thought I saw... someone."

Dani rocked from toe to heel, clasping her arms about herself, her head lowered.

"There's no one there," she said, repeating this again and again, waiting for whatever came next.

THIRTY

"She didn't know me," said Tate, staring at the closing door to Dani's room here at the psychiatric facility.

Beside him, Enid stood, holding Willow in her arms. He never glanced at her, but kept his eyes on his wife, visible through the observation window as she rocked in some internal wind.

The longing to go to her made his heart ache.

Enid stomped her foot, like a toddler. He ignored her, speaking to Dr. Allen.

"I want to go in there," said Tate, unable to take his eyes off Dani, her peaceful smile drawing him with a visceral allure. She was still so beautiful, like an enchanted fairy princess.

Dr. Allen shook her head, her face grave.

"That would be too much for today. She's self-calming now. As you can see." She motioned to the observation mirror behind which Dani continued to sway. "She now has another core belief that you are dead, Mr. Sutton. Confronting you will just panic her. I had hoped visiting with Enid, seeing Willow so grown, and then glimpsing you might cause a shift in her thinking."

"I could just go in there. Even with her face blindness, she'd recognize my voice. We could try again."

Enid's voice was sharp. "Tate, she's already said no."

Allen inclined her head. "Mrs. Langford is correct. We've tried that. She couldn't internalize that you'd survived the gunshot to the head."

He didn't need reminding. He'd been told the night he was rushed into surgery with a gunshot wound, Dani had come here, carrying a blanket and her polar fleece jacket like a baby, seeking help. And her call to 911 had saved his life.

Meanwhile, Willow had been safely secured in the kitchen in her carrier the entire time.

After his release, Dani had called him an imposter. Her hysterical scream would ring in his nightmares forever.

The doctor was still speaking. "... still unaccepting of challenges to her core belief. She's clever enough to explain it all away, finding it preferable to paint you as a hero instead of..." Her words trailed off, but Dr. Allen regrouped quickly. "It's taken considerable effort to get her to this place. We need to go slow."

"It's been months."

"Every attempt to confront her new core beliefs has brought a setback. Unfortunately, she doesn't want or need you or the stress presented by her marriage, the unfamiliar home, and your political ambitions. I warned you, you were expecting too much before releasing her to your custody."

"If I left it up to you, she'd never leave here." As he said it, he conceded to himself that her doctor had been right, a slower transitional release would have been smarter.

"For the time being, this is the safest place for Dani. She requires predictable routine, and she desperately wants Shelby to be here with her."

"Shelby is dead," said Tate. "She died years ago in that crash."

Allen said nothing. Just leveled her judgmental gaze on him.

Did she blame him? They both knew that it was Dani's discovery of his affair with Enid that caused Dani to race off to Shelby all those years ago.

Unfortunately, Shelby could not keep Dani from losing control of the vehicle. The crash had killed Shelby instantly and broken Dani. She could not cope with her sister's death or the added burden of being the cause. It had broken her in some fundamental way. Dani's mind had gone into protective mode, walling off those memories and creating an alternative reality where Shelby survived.

"We know her sister is dead and buried," said Allen. "But for Dani, Shelby is very much alive."

"And that baby doll?" asked Enid. "She really thinks that thing is a real infant?"

"She does."

It disturbed Tate to have seen his once bright and loving wife treating a plastic doll like a living, breathing baby.

"She's still my wife," he said, challenging the doctor.

"She is." Allen stretched the words. "But, according to her attorneys, not for much longer. You are both here only because of their permission."

"They have her conservatorship," said Tate to Enid.

"The money?" she asked.

"All gone. The bastards moved like lightning. I was still in the ICU when they took it before a judge."

Enid staggered, a little moan issuing from her lips. She'd forsaken her marriage for a chance to have him. Clearly, she'd hoped to keep it all. Dani's trust fund, the house, the cars, and Tate. Enid hadn't known about Tate's pending divorce. Since discovering what Enid had done, he had not spoken to or seen her. He'd even returned the gold Rolex, once belonging to her husband, that she had given him. She was here now, he believed, only because it presented a chance to see him.

"But if I could just talk to her," insisted Tate, holding on like a stray dog with a bone.

"Both her attorney and I agree that wouldn't be in Dani's best interest," said Allen. "Permission was granted on the condition that you did not enter her room or approach her unless she wished to speak to you. I believe her actions were quite clear."

Tate's shoulders sagged.

"In time she may be more accepting of her situation."

"In time she won't be my wife! Not if those bastards have any say." Tate waved a hand in the air.

Dr. Allen continued in that damned soothing tone that grated like glass shards.

"Dani may again realize when and where she is. But the shock of the shooting, seeing you fall, witnessing what she believed to be your death—"

Tate interrupted. "Nearly was."

He rubbed his healing jaw.

Dr. Allen continued. "These things, the accident, the home invasion, the intruder, and the attack, all frighten her. Seeing you shot by Enid's husband was too much."

"She thought it was someone else. A murder suspect," said Enid.

"So I understand from Dani. A man somehow connected with a Jane Doe."

Tate pressed his mouth tight, drawing air through his flaring nostrils, trying to hold the fraying thread of control he had left.

The reason Dani had believed the murder victim she'd seen on the television was Willow's mother was because he'd lied to her again, told her Willow was born to a prostitute with a dangerous pimp. Why hadn't he admitted the truth? Had some part of him really believed he could pull this deception off?

Keep both Dani and Enid? Manage the campaign, delude the voters?

He had. Much to his shame, he really had.

But Dani had figured it out and she'd been right. Enid was Willow's mother and he'd been lying again.

How had he ever convinced himself that Enid would sit by and let him keep Dani or that Dani wouldn't see through his lies?

Madness, the reckless acts of a desperate man. He didn't deserve her. Never had.

"Dani needed to feel safe," said Dr. Allen. "So she created this version of reality to defend herself against the real one."

"What's wrong with the real one?" he said and instantly regretted his words.

Allen did not pull her punches.

"Well, in the real one, her husband betrayed her with a colleague in an affair stretching over years. Moved to a house across the street from his mistress, impregnated her and convinced her to give up custody of her baby." Allen cast Enid a withering look that was wasted as Enid kept her eyes down. "In this version, you've lost your appointment to the bench, your home is in foreclosure, and I understand you face bankruptcy. In this reality, you deceived your mentally fragile wife."

"But I didn't set her aside. I did everything to keep her."

That appeared to be the final straw for Enid. "You used me, took my child, and gave it to that," said Enid, her dark eyes blazing as she pointed to Dani, rocking a plastic baby doll behind the observation glass.

The adoption had been rescinded when Dani was committed. He and Enid's attorneys were working out a joint custody agreement for Willow, who now lived with Enid.

"May I ask you a personal question, Mr. Sutton?" asked Dr. Allen.

And it *was* Mr. Sutton again, not Judge Sutton. Tate added that to his many losses.

"Go on," he said and braced.

"Why agree to the divorce if you wish to maintain guardianship of Dani?"

"Because the trustees threatened to sue me for damages. Agreement was the only way to avoid litigation."

"I see. I read there might be criminal charges," Dr. Allen said.

"No. At least, not for me," said Tate.

Another glance at Enid showed her meeting his gaze with something like a look of triumph. They both had avoided arrest, but her husband, Paul, had not. Tate thought this pleased Paul's soon-to-be ex-wife. He didn't understand her. How could she think she'd won? That any of them had won?

The criminal trial for Enid's ex-husband had yet to begin. To date, only Paul Langford had been charged with a crime, and this, Tate believed, was also Enid's fault.

She'd ruined her marriage to have him. It had taken a while, but Paul had eventually figured out his wife was sleeping around with someone and that had upended the Langfords' marriage. When Tate refused to divorce Dani, then at Windwood, Enid and Paul had reconciled, but the affair had continued. When Paul had discovered his wife was pregnant, it all fell apart again.

Unable to father a child, Paul had filed for a separation, leaving Enid penniless.

But how had Paul finally discovered his best friend was the father?

Tate had his suspicions.

Appeasing Enid while handling Dani had been like trying to keep the lid on a trashcan full of M-8os. Once the fuse was lit, the outcome was inevitable.

Enid had once been safe, supportive, and stable. After

Dani's accident, Enid was a welcome harbor from the tumult that marriage to Dani had become.

Now she was a woman scorned.

Their affair had started just after Enid began to work at their practice. Tate was engaged and she married. Their relationship had granted her entrance into the world she craved, one of privilege, elegance, abundance, and real wealth. Her husband, Paul, made a good salary, but that was a far cry from the fortune Dani inherited. Their affair made her greedy. Greedier, if possible.

He turned to go.

"Tate!" Enid grasped his arm with her free hand. "I need to speak to you."

He made her wait, then turned to Dr. Allen. "Could you give us a minute?"

Dr. Allen nodded. "Please don't disturb Dani."

"I understand."

Willow began to fuss and then cry. He glanced from the baby to Dr. Allen. "Would you take Willow for a few moments while we talk?"

Dr. Allen hesitated and then extended her arms toward the baby.

Enid passed over her daughter with barely a glance. Tate added the diaper bag and Dr. Allen hiked the cloth tote to her shoulder before retreating down the corridor.

"I'll be at the end of the hall."

Enid watched the doctor move to the foyer before the elevators, where she paused to watch them.

"Why did you have to tell Paul?" he asked.

"I didn't." A smile curled her lips, the satisfaction uncontainable.

He didn't believe a word.

"Then how did he find out?"

She glanced away, relenting. "She took my child and the life I wanted for us."

"Were things really so bad?" he asked.

She glared. "You promised you'd leave her. How many times? Even I can't remember. But you'd never let her go. So, I had to get *her* to let *you* go."

"How?" He already dreaded the answer.

"I made sure she saw us together. We were in your chambers. You never saw her, but she certainly saw us. Got a real eyeful."

He could not keep the horror from sending a cold shiver of dread over his skin.

"When?"

"I think you know."

He did know. It was just before Christmas, just before the accident. She'd made sure Dani saw them together. That afternoon, his wife had called him from the car screaming about Enid and the affair.

"That's how she found out."

Enid nodded.

He could picture it all now. Dani showing up at Enid's invitation. Seeing them in his chambers, Enid perched on the windowsill, legs spread and his back to the door.

"And now she's divorcing you. Not that she even realizes." She waved a dismissive hand in Dani's direction. "She thought you were cheating already. I just gave her the face."

Tate muttered, "A face that she can no longer recognize."

Enid's smile was cruel. "That's right. She crashed into that overpass. Killed Shelby and ended up in the nuthouse. I'd have been happy with a simple divorce. But you never can anticipate how people will react to bad news, can you?"

"But without Dani, we lose it all. Can't you see that?"

"You mean *you* lose it all."

"You had Paul."

She snorted. "No ambition, that one."

"After he left, I paid for everything. You never had to work a day in your life. All you had to do was—"

She cut him off. "You mean Dani paid. It was never your money, Tate." She glanced up at him. "But after the accident, she was too shattered to divorce you and you still wouldn't. I got tired of waiting."

"So you got pregnant."

"Yes. I knew you'd have to acknowledge your child. But you still held on. Trying to be the fixer, cleaning up her mess and ours."

"Why didn't you stop then?"

"I don't know what you mean."

"Yes, you do. That woman on the lanai and the one in the garage? That was you, wasn't it?"

Enid's smile was triumphant.

"You knew where the cameras were. Came into the lanai from the hedgerow. You pounded on that glass slider. Shouted at her, knowing the cameras were off. Later, you used the garage side entrance to avoid them." Tate swiped a hand over his mouth. "We all thought she was hallucinating. Made her unfit, didn't it?"

"But you protected her from the police. Had your friend Detective Forde keep it out of the papers."

"It was you."

"Prove it."

"I thought she was getting worse," he said.

"The coffee shop rattled her more than the attack."

"You're a monster. If Dani is mad, you're the reason."

"*We're* the reason. You and me."

He glanced at Dani smiling as she adjusted the yellow orchid on the accent table inside her room.

"She knew. Even told me it was you. I didn't believe her."

"Dani was always bright."

"It could have worked out for us. All of us."

"I gave her *my child* because you asked me to. But she was never going to keep Willow or you." She stepped forward, aiming an index finger at him like a gun. "Willow is mine and *you* are mine. If I can't have you, neither will she."

"So you burned it all to the ground. My reputation, career. The campaign. My wife. Our future."

"We can start again. We don't need her money. You can start a private practice."

Tate's life was in ruins and without Dani's money, he was poised to lose everything. Maybe he deserved that.

His shattered jaw would heal. The plastic surgery would help with the Frankenstein appearance of the lower half of his face.

But he'd never be what he might have been. Instead, he was a headline, a disgraced judge, his reputation in tatters and his story a cautionary tale.

Now, if his struggling practice didn't improve, he might just be forced to accept the offer of a ghostwriter to collaborate on a tell-all book. That was, if the dogs running Dani's family trust didn't shut him down again. And he'd have to be very lucky to stay out of prison.

Tate glanced to the observation glass where Dani glided from side to side, rocking the baby doll.

"You told Paul it was me, didn't you? Told him that I was the father. His best friend. How did you think that would help?"

Enid inclined her head toward the closed orange door of room #7 and Dani, clear through the transparent glass as she talked to the invisible sister beside her.

"Put her back in here, didn't it?"

"And Paul in prison."

She shrugged.

Tate pushed. "You sent him after me?"

"Yes. He knew I was sleeping with someone. Thought it was over until he found out I was pregnant and left me again. But I finally told him the truth. I said *you* were the father. How we'd laughed about it. Got him all riled up. Told him you betrayed him. That everyone at the firm knew about us. Everyone but him. It was my gun, you know? Told the police he stole it when I put it in his hand. Asked him to be a man for once in his miserable life. Might as well have cocked it for him."

Behind Enid, three men made a fast approach. The one in the center nodded to Tate, giving the signal they'd gotten it all.

Before him, Enid, unaware of their company, rocked a thumb in Dani's direction.

"You cannot prefer *that* to me."

"Oh, but I do." Tate stepped back as Enid noticed the men.

"Enid Langford," said the detective. "You are under arrest for assault, breaking and entering, and accessory to attempted murder."

Enid's pretty mouth gaped and she turned to Tate.

"Tate, what's happening?"

He lifted his yellow shirt showing her the microphone taped to his chest. The wire had recorded her admission of guilt.

Tate tapped on the door to number seven. Dani stepped from her room and met Enid's gaze.

"Goodbye, Enid," she said.

Tate and Dani stood together as the officers handcuffed Enid and took her away.

The detective remained behind as the patrolmen escorted their struggling suspect down the hallway. He turned to Dani and Tate. "Thank you for your help. Without her confession we didn't have enough to make the arrest."

Tate rubbed his neck. "Yes, well, you're welcome."

Dani knew Tate's cooperation came with a deal to avoid charges related to the attacks by Enid. He'd known who had been terrorizing Dani and had lied to the police. In her mind, he still bore the stain of guilt.

The week Dani had come home from Windwood, Enid had gone into labor. There had been no Thursday-night call for Tate to handle the arrest of his partner's client. That had been Enid calling, screaming, because she was having his baby.

He'd been with her in the hospital during her labor, then stayed for the delivery in the early morning and had never been in court at an arraignment, as he'd told her. This came to Dani by her attorney, Mr. Hewitt, who had spoken at length with Enid Langford. According to Hewitt, Tate had gone to her the next night, too, when Enid had called screaming from the hospital, demanding he pick her up. Tate's story about a fight between Enid and Paul had been another lie, and again, he had been gone all night. By Sunday, he'd somehow convinced Enid to give up her parental rights and come up with the story and paperwork so Dani could adopt.

None of her harvested eggs had miraculously survived the freezer failure. There had been no surrogate. No dangerous, blackmailing prostitute. The woman from the news story that had rocked Dani had been a coincidence. But lack of sleep and failure to faithfully take her medication had caused her latest break with reality.

Tate's lies were not an act of love, not a means to deliver to her what she desired most and could never have. They were all acts of desperation, intended to hide his mistakes and keep the status quo. Under the circumstances, it was hard to blame Enid for lashing out.

Dr. Allen stepped forward to squeeze Dani's arm.

"That was very well done, Dani. You nearly had me convinced."

Her doctor passed Willow to her father and then turned over the diaper bag.

Dani took a long look at the baby she'd once thought was hers.

Since her second break with reality, Dani had fought her way back again. It had been painful, learning of Tate's deception and Enid's betrayal.

Internalizing that Shelby had never been making a recovery in Jacksonville had been the most difficult part.

Now she grieved for her marriage and for her sister.

"If you'll come with me, Mr. Sutton," said the detective.

Tate hesitated, turning to Dani, defying her attorney's injunction to snatch the opportunity to speak with her.

"Dani," said Tate, stepping toward her.

She retreated a step. Until today, she had refused to see or speak to her husband and had signed the papers to begin separation proceedings.

"I don't want to see you yet, Tate," she said.

"But Enid is gone. We can go back. Start again."

She widened the gap between them.

"You can't go back, Tate. Only forward."

"Please forgive me. Give me another chance."

She shook her head. "I'm working on forgiving you and myself. But I won't be your wife. That's over." She turned to Dr. Allen. "Can you see Tate out?"

"Dani? What about the baby?"

Dani stared at the little girl in his arms, who still clutched the blue stuffed dog. She loved Willow, but she couldn't be her mother. It wasn't safe for either of them.

"She's not mine."

It broke her heart to say it, to give Willow back, but she had always striven to do what was best for the girl. This, she was certain, was best.

She ignored his pleas and returned to the room, grateful for the solid door separating her from Tate.

At the knock, Dani glanced through the peephole to spy her doctor waiting.

She ushered her in.

"I came to pick up the toys and the bouncer," she said. "You were magnificent. The detectives told me it was vital Enid see you in a confused state. It helped Tate get her confession. They said Enid implicated herself. She's facing multiple charges."

"It's hard to feel happy about that."

"You deserve justice. She stalked and harassed you. The detective indicated Enid even admitted she provoked her husband, stirring him up, so he'd attack Tate and admitted the handgun belonged to her, not her husband."

That was news Dani had not heard.

"So," said her doctor, "is everything all right with you today?"

"Except Shelby called me again."

"Well, you've now internalized that she's gone."

"It's still nice to hear her voice, even though it's just in my head."

"But perhaps not healthy. We can work on that. She's only on the phone. You aren't seeing her again?"

When she'd first returned to the psychiatric facility, she'd thought she and Shelby had moved into a house together. Over time, Dr. Allen had dismantled that core belief.

"Not often," she said, glancing to the doorway where Shelby stood, casually leaning on the doorjamb.

"Well, one step at a time. I'll check in tomorrow. Call if you need me before then."

Dani walked her out, holding the door as her doctor carried

away the baby bouncer, swaddled baby doll, toys, and infant accoutrements. When she'd cleared the frame, Dani closed the door and blew away a deep breath.

It was over.

The divorce would move through the system. Enid and Paul were both headed for criminal trials. Tate would raise Willow. And she was finally free and safe. In time, she might even leave Windwood and buy a little house close to the café and bookstore.

"How's the coffee?" asked Shelby.

Dani lifted the mug from the table beneath the mirror and took another sip.

"Perfect. Everything is just perfect."

A LETTER FROM JENNA

Dear Reader,

A great big thank-you for choosing to read *The Adoption*. I appreciate you joining Dani as she returns home from Windwood Psychiatric Facility! To be the first to know about all my latest releases, sign up at the following link. Your email address will never be shared and you can unsubscribe at any time.

www.bookouture.com/jenna-kernan

After two, going on three, difficult years facing this global pandemic, my world got smaller. Like many of you, I avoided large gatherings, skipped going to favorite venues, and ate meals at home. I think my own claustrophobia helped me identify with Dani Sutton, trapped in her gilded cage, and helped me bring her to life in this story.

This book presented me with some difficult challenges and, for those readers who choose to scan this letter, first, I have provided you no spoilers. But I will admit that I pondered long and hard about what clues to provide and how much was too much. Walking the line between making the twists come as a surprise, while not making my readers feel cheated, was difficult. I hope you'll let me know how I did.

In this story, I am so pleased to present to you a bit of Florida's Gulf Coast, where I currently live. The beaches are lovely, the golf courses inviting, and outdoor living is at its best. It was a delight to create such hell in this little slice of heaven. Just a quick note on location. Jordan Island, where Dani and Tate Sutton live in a gated community in Tampa, Florida, is not a real place, so if you are looking to relocate, you might have to pick from one of the many actual gated communities!

If you enjoyed *The Adoption*, I would be so grateful if you would write a review. Your review helps new readers discover a story you enjoyed. Even a line or two can make an enormous difference in the success of this book.

Please look for my next domestic thriller, *The Ex-Wives*, where you will meet Elana Bellauru, a wife who is stunned at her husband's miraculous survival after a near drowning because she was sure he was dead when he slipped overboard.

I'd love to know what you thought about Dani's unsettling return to her perfect marriage. Please get in touch on social media, Goodreads, in a review, or on my website.

Be safe. Stay well.

Happy Reading!

Jenna Kernan

www.jennakernan.com

 facebook.com/authorjennakernan

 twitter.com/jennakernan

instagram.com/jenna_kernan

ACKNOWLEDGMENTS

How is it possible that I am already finishing book three and working on book four with my talented Bookouture editor, Ellen Gleeson? Unfortunately, I'm not the only one who noticed her talent. But despite a promotion (I hate it when my editors get promoted), she has stuck with me, and I am so grateful. With her help, I think I've created something special with this book.

I know there are many folks at Bookouture who deserve my thanks as they work on amazing covers, promotion campaigns, packaging, and marketing for this story. From editorial manager, audio production department, the art team, to contracts, book production and the publicists, social media, advertising and marketing teams, everyone across the pond work to ensure this story reaches you. Thank you all for everything you do to make my books shine. I'm so grateful that you have my back.

Many thanks to my agent, Ann Leslie Tuttle, of Dystel, Goderich & Bourret, who encouraged me to try writing domestic thrillers. I appreciate her confidence and know she is always there to offer support and insight.

Finally, I offer my thanks to the writing organizations providing education to mystery, suspense, thriller, and police procedural writers. Thank you to Sisters in Crime, Gulf Coast Sisters in Crime, Mystery Writers of America, Mystery Writers of Florida, Thrill Writers International, Writers Police Academy, Authors Guild, and Novelist, Inc.

Special thanks to my siblings, Amy, Nan, and James, for all

their praise, encouragement, and support! With our mother now gone, I rely on them even more to utter those precious words, "I'm so proud of you!"

And to my husband, Jim, who continues to recommend my books to friends and strangers alike at author events, book festivals, bookstores, pool decks, and area beaches. Thank you, Jim, for the love and for supporting my dreams.

Finally, I am grateful to my readers because a story doesn't live until it is in your hands!

CPSIA information can be obtained
at www.ICGtesting.com
Printed in the USA
LVHW110456130522
718633LV00006B/199